DATE DUE

RUMPOLE AND T...

Adventure calls, and Horace Rumpole lugs his wig, gown and battered suitcase to the Independent State of Neranga to defend the country's Minister of State in the title story of this collection featuring England's best known barrister, in which Rumpole continues to untie the knots of English law and the contradictions of the human heart in his death-defying performances on behalf of justice.

5/97

Rumpole and The Golden Thread

John Mortimer

CHIVERS PRESS

Library of Congress Cataloging-in-Publication Data

Mortimer, John Clifford, 1923–
   Rumpole and the golden thread / by John Mortimer.
      p.   cm.—(Eagle large print)
   ISBN 0–7927–1371–0 (lg. print).—
   ISBN 0–7927–1370–2 (softcover: lg. print)
   1. Rumpole, Horace (Fictitious character)—Fiction.   2. Detective
and mystery stories, English.   3. Lawyers—Fiction.   4. Large type
books.   I. Title.   II. Series.
[PR6025.O7552R78   1992]
823'.914—dc20

92–18447
CIP

British Library Cataloguing in Publication Data available

This Large Print edition is published by Chivers Press, England, and Curley
Publishing, Inc, U.S.A. 1993.

Published in the U.S.A and territories; Canada by arrangement with Penguin
U.S.A. and in the British Commonwealth with Penguin Books Ltd.

U.K. Softback ISBN 0 7451 3426 2
U.S.A. Softback ISBN 0 7927 1370 2

Photoset, printed and bound in Great Britain by
REDWOOD PRESS LIMITED, Melksham, Wiltshire

For Jacqueline Davis

CONTENTS

CONTENTS

RUMPOLE AND
THE GOLDEN THREAD

RUMPOLE AND THE GENUINE ARTICLE

I would like to dedicate this small volume of reminiscences to a much-abused and under-appreciated body of men. They practise many of the virtues most in fashion today. They rely strictly on free enterprise and individual effort. They adhere to strong monetarist principles. They do not join trade unions. Far from being in favour of closed shops, they do their best to see that most shops remain open, particularly during the hours of darkness. They are against state interference of any kind, being rugged individualists to a man. No. I'm not referring to lawyers. Will you please charge your glasses, ladies and gentlemen, and drink to absent friends, to the criminals of England. Without these invaluable citizens there would be no lawyers, no judges, no policemen, no writers of detective stories and absolutely nothing to put in the *News of the World*.

It is better, I suppose, that I raise a solitary glass. I once proposed such a toast at a Chambers party, and my speech was greeted by a studied silence. Claude Erskine-Brown examined his fingernails, our clerk, Henry, buried his nose in his Cinzano Bianco. Uncle Tom, our oldest inhabitant, looked as though he was about to enter a terminal condition. Dianne, who does what passes for typing in our little establishment at Equity Court in the Temple, giggled, it is true, but then Dianne will giggle at almost anything and only becomes serious, I have noticed, whenever I make a joke. A devout barrister known to me as Sam Bollard (of whom

1

more, unfortunately, in the following pages) took me aside afterwards and told me that he considered my remarks to be in excessively bad taste, calculated to cause a breach of the peace and bring our Chambers into disrepute.

Well, where would he be, I asked him, should the carrying of house-breaking implements by night vanish from the face of the earth? He told me that he could manage very well with his civil practice and happily didn't have to rely on the sordid grubbing for a living round the Old Bailey which I appeared to enjoy. I left him, having regretted the fact that men with civil practices are often so remarkably un-civil when addressing their elders.

So, as the night wears on, and as my wife Hilda (whom I must be careful not to refer to as 'She Who Must Be Obeyed'—not, at any rate, when she is in earshot) sleeps in her hairnet, dreaming of those far-off happy days when she cantered down the playing fields of Cheltenham Ladies' College cradling her lacrosse net and aiming a sneaky pass at her old friend Dodo Perkins; as I sit at the kitchen table filling a barrister's notebook with reminiscences (I see the bare bones of a nasty little manslaughter on the opposite page), I pour a glass of Château Thames Embankment (on special offer this week at Pommeroy's Wine Bar—how else would Jack Pommeroy get anyone to buy it?) and drink, alone and in silence, to those industrious lawbreakers who seem to be participating in the one growth industry in our present period of recession. I can safely write that here. Whoever may eventually read these pages, you can bet your life that it won't be Sam Bollard.

I have been back in harness a good three years

since my abortive retirement. I had, as you may remember, upped sticks to join my son Nick and his wife Erica in Florida, the Sunshine State [See *Rumpole's Return*, Penguin Books, 1980].

She Who Must Be Obeyed apparently enjoyed life in that curious part of the world and was starting, somewhat painfully at first, to learn the language. I, as others have done before me, found that Miami had very little to offer unless you happened to be a piece of citrus fruit, and I began to feel an unendurable nostalgia for rain, secretaries rubbing their noses pink with crumpled paper handkerchieves on the platform at Temple Station and the congealed steak and mushroom pie for luncheon in the pub opposite the Old Bailey. I got bored with cross-examining the nut-brown octogenarians we met on the beach, and longed for a good up-and-downer with the Detective Inspector in charge of the case, or even a dramatic dust up with his Honour Judge Bullingham (otherwise known as the Mad Bull). I was a matador with nothing left to do but tease the cat. I needed a foeman worthy of my steel.

It was a nice problem of bloodstains which brought me home to real life at the Old Bailey, and a good deal of diplomatic skill and dogged endurance which eased me back into the peeling leather chair behind the desk in my old room in Equity Court. When I returned, our Head of Chambers, Guthrie Featherstone, Q.C., M.P. (S.D.P.), didn't actually unroll the red carpet for me. In fact, and in the nicest possible way, of course, he informed me that there was no room at the Inn, and would have left me to carry on what was left of my practice from a barrow in Shepherd's

3

Bush Market, if I hadn't seen a way back into my old tenancy.

Well, that's all water under the bridge by now, and the last three years have gone much as the last what is it, almost half a century? That is to say they have passed with a few triumphant moments when the jury came back and said in clear and ringing tones, 'Not Guilty', and a few nasty ones when you have to bid goodbye to a client in the cells (what do you say: 'Win a few, lose a few', or 'See you again in about eight years'?). I have spent some enjoyable evenings in Pommeroy's Wine Bar, and my health has been no worse than usual, my only medical problem being a feeling of pronounced somnolence when listening to my learned friends making speeches, and a distinct nausea when hearing his Honour Judge Bullingham sum up.

So life was going on much as usual, and I was pursuing the even tenor of my way in Equity Court, when I was faced with a somewhat unusual case which caused a good deal of a stir in artistic circles at the time, it being concerned, as so many artistic and, indeed, legal problems are, with the question so easily put yet answered with such confusion, 'What is real and what is the most diabolical fake?'

I first had the unnerving feeling that I was drifting away from reality, and that many of my assumptions were being challenged, when Guthrie Featherstone, Q.C., M.P., knocked briefly on my door and almost immediately inserted his face, which wore an expression of profound, not to say haunted anxiety, into my room.

'Rumpole!' he said, gliding in and closing the door softly behind him, no doubt to block out eavesdroppers. 'I say, Horace, are you working?'

4

'Oh no, Featherstone,' I said, 'I'm standing on my head playing the bagpipes.' The sarcasm was intentional. In fact I was wrestling with a nasty set of accounts, carefully doctored by a delinquent bank clerk. As, like the great apes, my mathematical abilities stop somewhere short at 'one, two, three, many', I have a rooted aversion to fraud cases. Studying accounts leads me to a good deal of blood, tears and the consumption of boxloads of small cigars.

Quite undeterred by the sharpness of my reply, the recently committed Social Democrat moved soundlessly towards my desk and ran a critical eye over my blurred and inaccurate calculations.

'Well,' said Featherstone, 'fraud's a nice clean crime really. Not like most of your practice. No blood. No sex.'

'Do you think so, Featherstone?' I asked casually, the Q.C., M.P., having failed to grip my full attention. 'A bank cashier seems to have lost about half a million pounds. Probably his adding up was no better than mine.'

'Still, it's almost a respectable crime. Your practice has become quite decent lately. We may even see you prosecuting.'

'No thank you,' I said with the determined air of a man who has to draw the line somewhere.

'Why ever not?'

'I'm not going to use my skills, such as they are, to force some poor devil into a condemned Victorian slum where he can be banged up with a couple of psychopaths and his own chamber pot.' I gave my learned Head of Chambers Article One of the Rumpole Creed.

'All the same, you being comparatively quiet of

5

late, Horace, has led the Lord Chancellor's office, I know, to look on these Chambers with a certain amount of, shall we say, "good will"?'

I looked at Featherstone. He was wearing an expression which I can only describe as 'coy'. 'Shall we? Then I'd better get up to something noisy.' I was joking, of course, but Featherstone became distinctly agitated.

'Please, Horace. No. I beg you. Please. You heard about the awful thing that happened to old Moreton Colefax?'

'Featherstone! I'm trying to add up.' I tried to be firm with the fellow, but he sat himself down in my client's chair and started to unburden himself as though he were revealing a dire plot he'd recently stumbled on involving the assassination of the Archbishop of Canterbury and the theft of the Crown Jewels.

'The Lord Chancellor told Moreton that he was going to make him a judge. But the rule is, you mustn't tell anyone till the appointment's official. Well, Moreton told Sam Arbuckle, and Arbuckle told Grantley Simpson and Grantley told Ian and Jasper Rugeley over in Paper Buildings, and Ian and Jasper told Walter Gains whom he happened to meet in Pommeroy's Wine Bar, and...'

'What is this, Featherstone? Some sort of round game?' My attention was not exactly held by this complicated account.

'Not for Moreton Colefax, it wasn't,' Guthrie Featherstone chuckled, and then went serious again. 'The thing became the talk of the Temple and the upshot was, poor old Moreton never got appointed. So if the Lord Chancellor sends for a fellow to make him a judge, Horace, that fellow's

6

lips are sealed. He just mustn't tell a soul!'

'Why are you telling me then?' I only asked for information, I wasn't following the fellow's drift. But the effect was extraordinary. Guthrie sprang to his feet, paling beneath his non-existent tan. 'I'm not telling you anything, Horace. Good heavens, my dear man! What ever gave you the idea I was telling you anything?'

'I'm sorry,' I said, returning to the calculations. 'I should have realized you were just babbling away meaninglessly. What are you, Featherstone, a sort of background noise, like Muzak?'

'Horace, it is vital that you should understand that I have said nothing to you whatsoever.' Featherstone's voice sank to a horrified whisper. 'Just as it is essential to preserve the quiet, *respectable* image of our Chambers. There was that difficult period we went through when the Erskine-Browns were *expecting*, rather too early on in their married lives' [See 'Rumpole and the Course of True Love' in *The Trials of Rumpole*, Penguin Books, 1979].

'They weren't married.' I recalled the happy event.

'Well, exactly! And of course that all passed over quite satisfactorily. We had a marquee in the Temple Gardens, if you remember, for the wedding. I believe I said a few words.'

'A *few* words, Guthrie? That's hardly like you.'

The above somewhat enigmatic conversation was interrupted by the telephone on my desk ringing and, after a few deft passes by Dianne on the intercom in our clerk's room, my wife Hilda's voice came over the line, loud, clear, and unusually displeased.

7

'There's a young girl here, Rumpole,' She Who Must Be Obeyed was reading out the indictment over the phone. 'She is sitting in the kitchen, asking for you. Well, she's making her own cigarettes, and they smell of burnt carpets.'

'But any sort of breath of scandal now. At this historic moment in the life of our Chambers.' Looking, if possible, more ashen than ever, Guthrie was still burbling in the background. And he didn't look particularly cheered up when he heard me address the instrument in my hand along the following lines:

'Something sort of arty-tarty, is she, do you say, Hilda? A young girl who says she's in trouble. What kind of trouble? Well, perhaps I haven't got your vivid imagination, but I quite honestly can't... Well, of course I'm coming home. Don't I always come home in the end?' I put down the telephone. Featherstone was looking at me, appalled, and started to say, in a voice of deep concern, 'I couldn't help overhearing.'

'Couldn't you?' Well I thought he might, if he were a man of tact, have filtered out of the room.

'Horace, is your home life completely satisfactory?' he asked.

'Of course it isn't.' I don't know what the man was thinking about. 'It's exactly as usual. Some girl seems to have aroused the wrath of She Who Must Be Obeyed.'

'Did you say ... some *girl*?'

'Friend of yours, Guthrie?'

'What?'

'I thought it might be someone you had your eye on, from the typing pool, perhaps. I mean, I remember when...' But before I could call the

8

Featherstone mind to remembrance of things past, he went on firmly, 'This is not a time for looking backwards, Horace. Let us look forward! To the fine reputation of this set of Chambers.'

He went to the door and opened it, but before he left the Rumpole presence he said, as though it were a full explanation, 'And do please remember, I haven't told you anything!'

I suppose that was true, in a manner of speaking.

*   *   *

As, from the sound of She Who Must Be Obeyed's voice, there appeared to be a bit of a cold wind blowing in Casa Rumpole (our so-called 'mansion' flat in the Gloucester Road, which bears about as much relation to a mansion as Pommeroy's plonk does to Château Pichon Longueville), I delayed my return home and wandered into my usual retreat, where I saw our clerk Henry there before me. He was leaning nonchalantly against the bar, toying with his usual Cinzano Bianco, taken with ice and a twist of lemon. I began to press him for information which might throw some faint light on the great Featherstone mystery.

'As a barrister's clerk, Henry,' I said, 'you might be said to be at the very heart of the legal profession. You have your finger on the Lord Chancellor's pulse, to coin a phrase. Tell me honestly, has the old fellow lost his marbles?'

'Which old fellow, sir?' Henry seemed mystified. It was an evening for mystification.

'The Lord Chancellor, Henry! Has he gone off his rocker?'

'That's not for me to say, is it?' Our clerk Henry

9

was ever the diplomat, but I pressed on. 'Is his Lordship seriously thinking of making Guthrie Featherstone, Q.C., M.P., a Red Judge? I mean, I know our learned Head of Chambers has given up politics...'

'He's joined the S.D.P.'

'That's exactly what I mean. But a *judge!*'

'Speaking entirely for myself, Mr Rumpole, and I have no inside information...' Henry had decided to play it cautiously.

'Oh, come on. Don't be so pompous and legal, Henry.'

'I would say that Mr Featherstone would cut a fine figure on the Bench.' Our clerk had the sort of voice which could express nothing whatsoever, a genuinely neutral tone.

'Oh, he'd *look* all right,' I agreed. 'He'd fit the costume. But *is* he, Henry? That's what I want to know. *Is* he?'

'Is he *what*, Mr Rumpole?'

'He may *look* like a judge, but is he really the *genuine article*?'

So I left Henry, having hit, almost by chance I suppose, on one of the questions which troubled old Plato, led Bishop Berkeley to some of his more eccentric opinions, and brought a few laughs to Bertrand Russell and a whole trainload of ideas to A. J. Ayer. It was that little matter of the difference between appearance and reality which lay at the heart of the strange case which was about to engage my attention.

★   ★   ★

As I say, I didn't expect much of a welcome from

10

She Who Must Be Obeyed when I put into port at 25B Froxbury Court, and I wasn't disappointed. I had brought a peace offering in the shape of the last bunch of tulips I had found gasping for air in the shop at the Temple tube station.

'Where did you find those, Rumpole?' my wife Hilda asked tersely. 'Been raiding the cemetery?'

'Is she still here?' I hoped to see the cause of Hilda's discontent, and entered the kitchen. The place was empty. The bird, whoever she might have been, had flown.

'By *she* I suppose you mean your girl?' Hilda followed me into the kitchen and tried to bring back life to the tulips with the help of a cut-glass vase.

'She's not "my girl".'

'She came to see you. Then she burst into tears suddenly and left.'

'People who come to see me often burst into tears. It's in the nature of the legal profession.' I tried to sound reassuring. But I was distracted by a strange sound, a metallic clatter, as though someone were throwing beer cans up at our kitchen window.

'Hilda,' I put the question directly. 'What on earth's that?' She took a look out and reported—as it turned out, quite accurately—what she saw. 'There's a small man in a loud suit throwing beer cans up at our window, Rumpole. Probably another of your friends!' At which my wife made off in the direction of our living room with the vase of tulips, and I proceeded to the window to verify the information. What I saw was a small, cunning-looking old cove in a loud check suit, with a yellow stock round his neck. Beside him was a girl in ethnic attire, carrying a large, worn holdall, no doubt of Indian manufacture. The distant view I

11

had of her only told me that she had red hair and looked a great deal too beautiful to have any business with the elderly lunatic who was shying beer cans up at our window. As I stuck my head out to protest, I was greeted by the old party with a loud hail of 'Horace Rumpole! There you are at last!'

'Who are you?' I had no idea why this ancient person, who had the appearance of a superannuated racing tipster, should know my name.

'Don't you remember Blanco Basnet? Fellow you got off at Cambridge Assizes? Marvellous, you were. Just bloody marvellous! Hang on a jiff. Coming up!' At which our visitors made off for the entrance of the building.

The name 'Blanco Basnet' rang only the faintest of bells. I had a vague recollection of some hanger-on round Newmarket, but what had he been charged with? Embezzlement? Common assault? Overfamiliarity with a horse? My reverie was interrupted by a prolonged peal on the front door bell, and I opened up.

'Are you Basnet?' I asked the fellow as Hilda joined us, looking distinctly displeased.

'Course not. I'm Brittling.' He introduced himself. 'Harold Brittling. I was a close chum of old Blanco's, though. And when you got him off without a stain on his bloody character, we drank the night away, if you will recall the occasion, at the Old Plough at Stratford Parva. Time never called while the landlord had a customer. We swapped addresses, don't you remember? I say, is this your girl?' This last remark clearly and inappropriately referred to She Who Must Be Obeyed.

'This is my wife Hilda,' I said with as much

12

dignity as I could muster.

'This is my girl Pauline.' Brittling introduced the beauty dressed in a rug at his side.

'I've met her,' Hilda said coldly. 'Is she your daughter?'

'No, she's my girl.' Brittling enlarged on the subject. 'Don't talk much, but strips down like an early Augustus John. Thighs that simply call out for an HB pencil. I say, Rumpole, your girl Hilda looks distinctly familiar to me. Met before, haven't we?'

'I think it's hardly likely.' Hilda did her best to freeze the little man with a glance. It was ineffective.

'Round the Old Monmouth pub in Greek Street?' Brittling suggested. 'Didn't you hang a bit round the Old Monmouth? Didn't I have the pleasure of escorting you home once, Hilda, when the Guinness stout had been flowing rather too freely?'

At which Brittling, with the girl in tow, moved off towards the sitting room, and I was left with the thought that either the little gnome was completely off his chump or there were hidden depths to She Who Must Be Obeyed.

When we followed him into our room, Brittling furnished some further information.

'You two girls have chummed up already,' he said. 'I sent Pauline to find you, Horace, as I was temporarily detained in the cooler.'

It was with some relief that I began to realize that Brittling had not paid a merely social call. He brought business. He was a customer, a member of the criminal fraternity, and probably quite a respectable little dud-cheque merchant. However, legal etiquette demanded that I spoke to him

13

sharply. 'Look, Brittling,' I said, 'if you've come here for legal advice, you'll have to approach me in the proper manner.'

'I shall approach you in the proper manner, bearing bubbly! Perhaps your girl will go and fetch a few beakers from the kitchen. Then we can start to celebrate!'

At which he started to yank bottles of champagne out of Pauline's holdall, with all the éclat of a conjurer producing rabbits from a hat.

'Celebrate what?' I was puzzled. Nothing good seemed to have happened.

'The case in which I'm going to twist the tail of the con-o-sewers,' Brittling almost shouted. 'And you, my dear Horace, are going to twist the tail of the legal profession. Game for a bit of fun, aren't you?'

At this moment he released the wine, which began to bubble out over the elderly Persian-type floor covering. This, of course, didn't add a lot to Hilda's approval of the proceedings. 'Do be careful,' she said tartly, 'that stuff is going all over the carpet.'

'Then get the glasses, Hilda.' Brittling was giving the orders. 'It's not like you, is it, to hold up a party?'

'Rumpole!' Hilda appealed to me with a look of desperation, but for the moment I couldn't see the point of allowing all the champagne to be drunk up by the carpet. 'No harm in taking a glass of champagne, Hilda,' I said reasonably.

'Or two.' Brittling winked at her. To my amazement, she then went off to fetch the beakers. When Hilda was gone I pressed on with the interrogation of Brittling.

14

'Who are you, exactly?' I asked, as a starter. The question seemed to provoke considerable hilarity in the old buffer.

'He asks who I am, Pauline!' He turned to his companion incredulously. 'Slade Gold Medal. Exhibited in the Salon in Paris. Hung in the Royal Academy. Executed in the Bond Street Galleries. And once, when I was *very* hungry, decorated the pavement outside the National Portrait Gallery. And the secret is—I can *do* it, Horace. So can you. We're pros. Give me a box of Conté crayons and I can run you up a Degas ballet dancer that old Degas would have given his eye teeth to have drawn.'

'His name's Harold Brittling.' The girl, Pauline, spoke at last, and as though that settled the matter. Brittling set off on a survey of the room as Hilda came back with four glasses.

'Who is he?' she asked anxiously as she handed me a glass.

'An artist. Apparently. Hung in the Royal Academy.' That was about all I was able to tell her.

'Not over-pictured, are you? What's this objet d'art?' Brittling had fetched up in front of a particularly watery watercolour presented to Hilda by her bosom chum Dodo, an artwork which I wouldn't give house room to were the choice mine, which of course it wasn't.

'Oh, that's a study of Lamorna Cove, done by my old school friend, Dorothy Mackintosh. Dodo Perkins, as was. She lives in the West Country now.'

'"Dodo" keeps a tea-shop in St Ives.' I filled in the gaps in Hilda's narrative.

'She has sent in to the Royal Academy. On several occasions. Do you like it, Mr...?' She

15

actually seemed to be waiting anxiously for the Brittling verdict.

'Harold,' he corrected her. And, looking at her with particularly clear blue eyes, he added, in a way I can only describe as gallant, 'Do *you* like it, Hilda?'

'Oh, I think it's rather fine.' It was She, the connoisseur, speaking. 'Beautiful in fact. The way Dodo's caught the shadow on the rocks, you know.'

Brittling was sloshing the champagne around, smiling at Hilda, and actually winking at Pauline as he said, 'Then if you think it's fine and beautiful, Hilda, that's what it is to you. To you it's worth a fortune. The mere fact that to me it looks like a rather colourless blob of budgerigar's vomit is totally irrelevant. You pay for what you think is beautiful. That's what our case is all about, isn't it, Horace? What's the difference between a Dodo and a Degas? Nothing but bloody talent which I can supply!'

'Look here, Brittling...' Although grateful for the glass full of nourishing bubbles, I thought the chap was putting the case against Dodo's masterpiece a little strongly.

'Harold,' he suggested.

'Brittling.' I was sticking to the full formality. 'My wife and I are grateful for this glass of...'

'The Widow Cliquot. Non vintage, I'm afraid. But paid for with ready money.'

'But I certainly can't do any case unless you go and consult a solicitor and he cares to instruct me.'

'Oh I see.' Brittling was recharging all our glasses. 'Play it by the rules, eh?'

'Exactly.' I intended to get this prospective client under control.

16

'Then it's much more fun breaking them when the time comes,' said the irresponsible Brittling.

'I must make it quite clear that I don't intend to break any rules for you, Brittling,' I said. 'Come and see me in Chambers with a solicitor.'

'Oh, I walk along the Bois du Boulogne ... With an independent air ...' Brittling began to sing in a way which apparently had nothing whatever to do with matters in question.

'Oh come along, Harold.' The girl Pauline took the old boy's arm and seemed to be urging him towards the door. 'He's not going to take your case on.'

'Why ever not?' Brittling seemed puzzled.

'*She* doesn't like you. And I don't think *he* likes you much either.'

'You can hear them all *declare*, I must be a *millionaire*,' Brittling sang and then looked at me intently. 'Horace Rumpole may not like me,' he said at last, 'but he envies me.'

'Why should he do that?'

'Because of what he has to live with.' Brittling's magnificent gestures seemed to embrace the entire room. 'Pissy watercolours!'

And then they left us, as unexpectedly as they had come, abandoning the rest of the Veuve Cliquot, which we had with our poached eggs for supper. It wasn't until much later, when we were lying at a discreet distance in the matrimonial bed, that I happened to say to Hilda, by way of encouragement, 'I don't suppose we'll see either of them again.'

'Oh yes you will,' she announced, as I thought, tartly. 'You'll do the case. You won't be able to resist it!'

17

'I can resist Mr Harold Brittling extremely easily,' I assured her.

'But *her*. Can you resist *her*, Rumpole?' And she went on in some disgust, 'Those thighs that simply seem to be *asking* for an HB pencil. I don't know when I've heard anything quite so revolting!'

'All the same, old Brittling seems to enjoy life.' I said it quietly, under my breath, but She almost heard me.

'*What* did you say?'

'I said I don't suppose he's got a wife.'

'That's what I thought you said,' And Hilda, somewhat mortified, snapped off the light, having decided it was high time we lost consciousness together.

★   ★   ★

To understand the extraordinary case of the Queen against Harold Brittling, it is necessary to ask if you have a nodding acquaintance with the work of the late Septimus Cragg, R.A. Before he turned up his toes, which I imagine must have been shortly before the last war, Septimus Cragg appeared to the public gaze as just what they expected of the most considerable British painter of his time. His beard, once a flaming red, later a nicotine-stained white, his long procession of English and European mistresses, his farmhouse in Sussex, his huge collection of good-looking children who suffered greatly from never being able to paint as well as their father, his public denunciations of most other living artists, and his frequently pronounced belief that Brighton Pavilion was a far finer manifestation of the human spirit than Chartres Cathedral—all these things brought him constantly to the attention of the gossip columnists, and perhaps made his work undervalued in his final years.

Now, of course, as I discovered when I started to do a little preparation for the defence of Harold Brittling, there has been a considerable boom in Craggs. The generally held view is that he was by far the finest of the British Post-Impressionists, and had he had the luck to be born in Dieppe, a port where a good deal of his life and a great many of his love affairs were celebrated, he might be mentioned in the same breath as such noted Frog artists as Degas and Bonnard. By now the art world will pay a great deal of hard cash for a Cragg in mint condition, particularly if it's a good nude. There's nothing that has the art world reaching for its cheque book, so it seems, as quickly as a good nude.

The rise in expert esteem of the paintings of Septimus Cragg was shown dramatically in the prices fetched in a recent sale at which Harold Brittling was seen to be behaving in a somewhat curious manner. The particular Cragg to come under the hammer was entitled 'Nancy at the Hôtel du Vieux Port, Dieppe', and it appeared to have an impeccable pedigree, having been put up for auction by a Miss Price, an elderly spinster lady who lived in Worthing and was none other than Septimus Cragg's niece. As the bidding rose steadily from fifty to fifty-six thousand pounds, and as the picture was finally knocked down to a Mrs De Moyne of New Haven, Connecticut, for a cool sixty thousand, Harold Brittling, sitting beside a silent and undemonstrative Pauline in the audience, could be seen giggling helplessly. On his way out of the auction, the beaming Brittling was fingered by two officers of the Fine Art and Antiques Department at Scotland Yard and taken into custody. Pauline was sent to enlist the immediate help of Horace Rumpole, and so earned the suspicious disapproval of She Who Must Be Obeyed.

Nancy, whoever she may have been, was clearly a generously built, cheerful young lady, who brought out the best in Septimus Cragg. He had painted her naked, with a mane of copper-coloured hair, standing against the light of a hotel bedroom window, through which the masts and funnels of the old port were hazily visible. In the foreground there was a strip of purplish carpet, a china basin and jug on a wash stand, and the end of a brass bed, over which a man's trousers, fitted with a pair of braces, were dangling negligently. I was looking at a reproduction of the work in question in my Chambers. I hadn't yet seen the glowing original; but even in a flat, coloured photograph, the picture gave off the feeling of a moment of happiness, caught for ever. I felt, looking at it, I must confess, a bit of a pang. There hadn't, I had to face it, been many such mornings in hotel bedrooms in Dieppe in the long life and career of Horace Rumpole, barrister-at-law.

'It's only a reproduction,' Brittling said. 'Doesn't do it a bit of justice.'

And Mr Myers, old Myersy, the solicitor's managing clerk, who has seen me through more tough spots down the Bailey than I've had hot dinners, who sat there with his overcoat pockets bulging with writs and summonses, puffed at his nauseating, bubbling old pipe and said, as though

20

we were looking at a bit of bloodstained sweatshirt or a mortuary photograph, 'That's it, Mr Rumpole. Exhibit J. L. T. (One). That's the evidence.'

Brittling, it seemed, had at least partially come to his senses. He had decided to consult a solicitor and approach me in a more formal manner than the mere lobbing of beer cans at my kitchen window. He looked at the exhibit in question and smiled appreciatively.

'It's a corker, though, as a composition, isn't it?'

'How is it as a forgery? That's what you're charged with, you know,' I reminded him, to bring the conversation down from the high aesthetic plane.

'A smashing composition,' Brittling went on as though he hadn't heard. 'And if you saw the texture of paint, and the way the curtains are moving in the wind from the harbour! There's only one man who could ever paint the air behind a curtain like that.'

'So it's the genuine article!' Myers assured me. 'That's what we're saying, Mr Rumpole.'

'Of course it's genuine!' Brittling called on the support of Keats: '"A thing of beauty . . . is a joy for ever:"'

I helped him with the quotation,

'Its loveliness increases; it will never
Pass into nothingness; but still will keep
A bower quiet for us, and a sleep
Full of sweet dreams, and health, and quiet
    breathing . . .

Quiet breathing in the Nick,' I reminded him somewhat brutally, 'if we don't keep our wits about us. Did you ever know Cragg?'

21

'Septimus...?'

'Did you know him?' I asked, and Brittling embarked on a fragment of autobiography.

'I was the rising star of the Slade School,' he said. 'Cragg was the old lion, the king of the pack. He was always kind to me. Had me down to the farmhouse at Rottingdean. Full of his children by various mothers, and society beauties, waiting to have their portraits painted. There was such a lot of laughter in that house, and so many young people...'

'"Nancy at Dieppe".' I picked up the reproduction. The features were blurred against the light, but didn't there seem to be something vaguely familiar about the girl in the hotel bedroom? 'Do you recognize the model at all?'

'Cragg had so many.' Brittling shrugged.

'Models or girlfriends?'

'It was usually the same thing.'

'Was it really? And *this* one?'

'Seems vaguely familiar.' Brittling echoed my thoughts. I gave him my searching look, reserved for difficult clients. 'The sort of thighs,' I asked him, 'which simply call out for an HB pencil, would you say?'

Brittling didn't seem to resent my suggestion. In fact he turned to me and gave a small but deliberate wink. I didn't like that. Clients who wink at you when you as good as tell them that you think they're guilty can be most unsettling.

*　　*　　*

I was still unsettled as I undressed in the matrimonial bedroom in Froxbury Court. Hilda, in

22

hairnet and bed jacket, was propped up on the pillows doing the *Daily Telegraph* crossword puzzle. As I hung up the striped trousers I thought that it was a scene which would never have been painted by Septimus Cragg. I was reflecting on the difference between my life and that of the rip-roaring old R.A. and I said, thoughtfully, 'It all depends, I suppose, on where your talents lie.'

'What does?' Hilda asked in a disinterested sort of way.

'I mean, if my talents hadn't been for bloodstains, and cross-examining coppers on their notebooks, and addressing juries on the burden of proof... If I'd had an unusual aptitude for jotting down a pair of thighs in a hotel bedroom...'

'You've seen *her* again, haven't you?' Hilda was no longer sounding disinterested.

'I might have been living in a farmhouse in Sussex with eight pool-eyed children with eight different mothers, all devoted to me, and duchesses knocking on my door to have their portraits painted. My work might have meant trips to Venice and Aix-en-Provence instead of London Sessions and the Uxbridge Magistrates Court! No, I didn't see her. She didn't come to the conference.'

'You want to concentrate on what you *can* do, Rumpole. Fine chance *I* ever have of getting invited to the Palace.'

'No need for the black jacket and pin stripes. Throw away the collar like a blunt execution. All you need is an old tweed suit and a young woman who's kind enough to wear nothing but a soulful expression. What's all that about the Palace?'

'They're making Guthrie Featherstone a judge, you know,' Hilda said, as though it were all, in

23

some obscure way, my fault.

'Whoever told you that?'

I felt suddenly sorry for the old Q.C., M.P., and worried that the chump's chance might be blown by a lot of careless talk. For Hilda told me that she had met Marigold Featherstone somewhere near Harrods, and that whilst she had been looking for bargains, the future Lady Marigold had told her that she had acquired a suitable outfit with the 'Princess Di' look for a visit to the Palace on the occasion of our not very learned Head of Chambers being awarded a handle to his name. When Hilda, not a little mystified, had asked her what sort of handle they had in mind, Marigold had rushed off in the direction of Sloane Street, urging Hilda to forget every word she had said, forgetting, of course, that She Who Must Be Obeyed never forgets.

'You didn't tell anyone else this, did you?' I asked.

'Well, no one except Phillida Erskine-Brown. I happened to run into her going into Sainsbury's.'

'You did *what*?'

'And Phillida explained it all to me. If you get made a judge you're knighted as a matter of course, and have to go to Buck House and all that sort of thing. So that was why Marigold was buying a new outfit.'

I was appalled, quite frankly. Phillida Erskine-Brown is a formidable lady advocate, the Portia of our Chambers. As for her husband, as I explained to Hilda, 'Claude Erskine-Brown gossips about the judiciary in the way teenagers gossip about film actors. Star-struck is our Claude. Practically goes down on his knees to anything in

24

ermine! And he pops into Pommeroy's whenever he gets a legal aid cheque. Let's just hope he doesn't get paid until poor old Featherstone's got his bottom safely on the Bench.'

'One thing is quite certain, Rumpole,' said Hilda, filling in a clue. 'There's no earthly chance of your ever getting a handle.'

★   ★   ★

A few weeks later I had slipped in to Pommeroy's Wine Bar for a glass of luncheon when Guthrie Featherstone came up to me and, having looked nervously over his shoulder like a man who expects to be joined at any moment by the Hound of Heaven, said, 'Horace! I came in here to buy a small sherry...'

'No harm in that, Guthrie.' I tried to sound reassuring.

'And Jack Pommeroy, you know what Jack Pommeroy called me?' His voice sank to a horrified whisper. 'He called me "*Judge*"!'

'Well, you'll have to get used to it.' I couldn't be bothered to whisper.

Featherstone looked round, appalled. 'Horace, for God's sake! Don't you see what this means? It means someone's been talking.'

And then his glance fell on a table where Claude Erskine-Brown was knocking back the Beaujolais Villages with assorted barristers. Featherstone's cup of unhappiness was full when Erskine-Brown raised his glass, as though in congratulation.

'Look! Claude Erskine-Brown, raising his glass at me!' Featherstone pointed it out, rather unnecessarily, I thought.

25

'Just a friendly gesture,' I assured him.

'You remember poor old Moreton Colefax, not made a judge because he couldn't keep his mouth shut.' The Q.C., M.P., looked near to tears. 'It's all round the Temple.'

'Of course it's not. Don't worry.'

'Then why is Erskine-Brown drinking to me?'

'He thinks you *look* like a judge. Beauty, after all, Guthrie my old darling, is entirely in the eye of the beholder.' Curiously enough, when I said that, Guthrie Featherstone didn't look particularly cheered up.

*   *   *

In the course of time, however, Guthrie Featherstone, Q.C., M.P., did cheer up, considerably. He fulfilled his destiny, and took on that role which led him to be appointed head boy of his prep school and a prefect at Marlborough, because, quite simply, he never got up anyone's nose and there were no other likely candidates available.

At long last Guthrie's cheerfulness round the Sheridan Club and his dedication to losing golf matches against senior judges earned him his just reward. A man who had spent most of his life in an agony of indecision, who spent months debating such questions as whether we should have a coffee machine in the clerk's room, or did the downstairs loo need redecorating; a fellow who found it so hard to choose between left and right that he became a Social Democrat; a barrister who agonized for hours about whether it would be acceptable to wear a light grey tie in Chambers in April, or whether such

26

jollifications should be confined to the summer months, was appointed one of Her Majesty's judges, and charged to decide great issues of life and liberty.

Arise, Sir Guthrie! From now on barristers, men far older than you, will bow before you. Men and women will be taken off to prison at your decree. You will have made a Lady out of Marigold, and your old mother is no doubt extremely proud of you. There is only one reason, one very good reason, for that smile of amiable bewilderment to fade from the Featherstone features. You may make the most awful pig's breakfast of the case you're trying, and they'll pour scorn on you from a great height in the Court of Appeal.

So Guthrie Featherstone, in the full panoply of a Red Judge at the Old Bailey, was sitting paying polite and somewhat anxious attention to a piece of high comedy entitled R. *v.* Brittling, starring Claude Erskine-Brown for the prosecution, and Horace Rumpole for the defence. As the curtain rose on the second day of the hearing the limelight fell on a Mr Edward Gandolphini, an extremely expensive-looking art expert and connoisseur, with a suit from Savile Row, iron–grey hair and a tan fresh from a short break in the Bahamas. In the audience Pauline was sitting with her embroidered holdall, listening with fierce concentration, and in the dock, the prisoner at the Bar was unconcernedly drawing a devastating portrait of the learned Judge.

'Mr Gandolphini.' Erskine-Brown was examining the witness with all the humble care of a gynaecologist approaching a duchess who had graciously consented to lie down on his couch. 'You are the author of *Cragg and the British Impressionists* and the leading expert on this particular painter?'

'It has been said, my Lord.' The witness flashed his teeth at the learned Judge, who flashed his back.

'I'm sure it has, Mr Gandolphini,' said Featherstone, J.

'And are you also,' Erskine-Brown asked most respectfully, 'the author of many works on twentieth-century painting and adviser to private collectors and galleries throughout the world?'

'I am.' Gandolphini admitted it.

'And have you examined this alleged "Septimus Cragg"?' Erskine-Brown gestured towards the picture which, propped on a chair in front of the jury, revealed a world of secret delight miles away from the Central Criminal Court.

'I have, my Lord.' Mr Gandolphini again addressed himself to the learned Judge. 'I may say it isn't included in any existing catalogue of the artist's works. Of course, at one time, I believe, it was thought it came from a genuine source, the artist's niece in Worthing.'

'Now we know that to be untrue,' said Erskine-Brown with a meaningful look at the jury, and thereby caused me to stagger, filled with extremely righteous indignation, to my feet.

'My Lord!' I trumpeted. 'We know nothing of the sort—until that has been found as a fact by the twelve sensible people who sit in that jury-box and *no one else*!'

'Very well,' said his Lordship, trying to placate everybody. 'Very well, Mr Rumpole. Perhaps he suspected it to be untrue. Is that the situation, Mr Gandolphini?'

Guthrie turned to the witness, smiling, but I wasn't letting him off quite so easily. 'My Lord,

28

how can what this witness suspected possibly be evidence?'

'Mr Rumpole. I know you don't want to be difficult.' As usual Featherstone exhibited his limited understanding of the case. I considered it my duty to be as difficult as possible.

'May I assist, my Lord?' said Erskine-Brown.

'I would be grateful if you would, Mr Erskine-Brown. Mr Rumpole, perhaps we can allow Mr Erskine-Brown to assist us?'

I subsided. I had no desire to take part in this vicarage tea-party, with everyone assisting each other to cucumber sandwiches. I thought that after one day on the Bench Guthrie had learnt the habit of getting cosy with the prosecution.

'Mr Gandolphini,' Erskine-Brown positively purred at the witness, 'if you *had* known that this picture did not in fact come from Miss Price's collection, would you have had some doubts about its authenticity?'

'That question is entirely speculative.' I was on my feet again.

'Mr Rumpole.' Featherstone was being extremely patient. 'Do you want me to rule on the propriety of Mr Erskine-Brown's question?'

'I think the time may have come to make up the judicial mind, yes.'

'Then I rule that Mr Erskine-Brown may ask his question.' Guthrie then smiled at me in the nicest possible way and said, 'Sorry, Mr Rumpole.' The old darling looked broken-hearted.

'Well, Mr Gandolphini?' Erskine-Brown was still waiting for his answer.

'I had a certain doubt about the picture from the start,' Gandolphini said carefully.

29

'From the start ... you had a doubt ...' Featherstone didn't seem to be able to stop talking while he wrote a note.

'Take it slowly now. Just follow his Lordship's pencil,' Erskine-Brown advised the witness and, in the ensuing pause, I happened to whisper to Myersy, 'And you may be sure his pencil's not drawing thighs in Dieppe.'

'Did you say something, Mr Rumpole?' his Lordship asked, worried.

'Nothing, my Lord, of the slightest consequence,' I rose to explain.

'I say that because I have extremely acute hearing.' Featherstone smiled at the jury, and I could think of nothing better to say than, 'Congratulations.'

'I thought the painting very fine.' Gandolphini returned to the matter in hand. 'And certainly in the manner of Septimus Cragg. It is a beautiful piece of work, but I don't think I ever saw a Cragg where the shadows had so much colour in them.'

'Colour? In the shadows? Could I have a look?' The Judge tapped his pencil on the Bench and called, 'Usher.' Obediently the usher carried the artwork up to his Lordship on the bench, and his Lordship got out his magnifying glass and submitted Nancy's warm flesh tints and flowing curves to a careful, legal examination.

'There's a good deal of green, and even purple in the shadows on the naked body, my Lord,' Gandolphini explained.

'Yes, I do see that,' said the Judge. 'Have you seen that, Mr Rumpole? Most interesting! Usher, let Mr Rumpole have a look at that. Do you wish to borrow my glass, Mr Rumpole?'

'No, my Lord. I think I can manage with the naked eye.' I was brought the picture by the Usher and sat staring at it, as though waiting for some sudden revelation.

'Tell us,' Erskine-Brown asked the witness. 'Is "Nancy" a model who appears in any of Cragg's works known to you?'

'In none, my Lord.' Gandolphini shook his head, almost sadly.

'Did Cragg paint most of his models many times?'

'Many, many times, my Lord.'

'Thank you, Mr Gandolphini.'

Erskine-Brown sat, apparently satisfied and I rose up slowly, and slowly turned the picture so the witness could see it. 'You said, did you not, Mr Gandolphini, that this is a beautiful painting.' I began in a way that I was pleased to see the witness didn't expect.

'It's very fine. Yes.'

'Has it not at least sixty thousand pounds' worth of beauty?' I asked and then gave the jury a look.

'I can't say.'

'Can you not? Isn't part of your trade reducing beauty to mere cash!'

'I value pictures, yes.' I could see that Gandolphini was consciously keeping his temper.

'And would you not agree that this is a valuable picture, no matter who painted it?'

'I have said . . .' I knew that he was going to try and avoid answering the question, and I interrupted him. 'You have said it's beautiful. Were you not telling this jury the truth, Mr Gandolphini?'

'Yes, but . . .'

31

'"Beauty is truth, truth beauty,"—that is all
Ye know on earth, and all ye need to know.'

I turned and gave the jury their two bobs' worth of Keats.

'Is that really all we need to know, Mr Rumpole?' said a voice from on high.

'In this case, yes, my Lord.'

'I think I'll want to hear legal argument about that, Mr Rumpole.' Featherstone appeared to be making some form of minor joke, but I answered him seriously. 'Oh, you shall. I promise you, your Lordship.' I turned to the witness. 'Mr Gandolphini, by "beauty" I suppose you mean that this picture brings joy and delight to whoever stands before it?'

'I suppose that would be a definition.'

'You suppose it would. And let us suppose it turned out to have been painted by an even more famous artist than Septimus Cragg. Let us suppose it had been done by Degas or Manet.'

'Who, Mr Rumpole?' I seemed to have gone rather too fast for his Lordship's pencil.

'Manet, my Lord. Edouard Manet.' I explained carefully. 'If it were painted by a more famous artist it wouldn't become more of a thing of beauty and a joy to behold, would it?'

'No ... but ...'

'And if it were painted by a less famous artist—Joe Bloggs, say, or my Lord the learned Judge, one wet Sunday afternoon ...'

'Really, Mr Rumpole!' Featherstone, J., smiled modestly, but I was busy with the con-o-sewer. 'It wouldn't become *less* beautiful, would it, Mr Gandolphini? It would have the same colourful

32

shadows, the same feeling of light and air and breeze from the harbour. The same warmth of the human body?'

'Exactly the same, of course, but...'

'I don't want to interrupt...' Erskine-Brown rose to his feet, wanting to interrupt.

'Then don't, Mr Erskine-Brown!' I suggested. The suggestion had no effect. Erskine-Brown made a humble submission to his Lordship. 'My Lord, in my humble submission we are not investigating the beauty of this work, but the value, and the value of this picture depends on its being a genuine Septimus Cragg. Therefore my learned friend's questions seem quite irrelevant.'

At which Erskine-Brown subsided in satisfaction, and his Lordship called on Rumpole to reply.

'My learned friend regards this as a perfectly ordinary criminal case,' I said. 'Of course it isn't. We are discussing the value of a work of art, a thing of beauty and a joy forever. We are not debating the price of fish!'

There was a sound of incipient applause from the dock, so I whispered to Myersy, and instructed him to remind Brittling that he was not in the pit at the Old Holborn Empire but in the dock at the Old Bailey. I was interrupted by the Judge saying that perhaps I had better pursue another line with the witness.

'My Lord,' I said. 'I think we have heard enough—from Mr Gandolphini.' So I sat and looked triumphantly at the jury, as though I had, in a way they might not have entirely understood, won a point. Then I noticed, to my displeasure, that the learned Judge was engaged in some sort of intimate tête-à-tête with the man Gandolphini, who had not

33

yet left the witness-box.

'Mr Gandolphini, just one point,' said the Judge.

'Yes, my Lord.'

'I happen myself to be extremely fond of Claude Lorrain,' said Featherstone, pronouncing the first name 'Clode' in an exaggerated Frog manner of speaking.

'Oh, my Lord, I do *so* agree.' Gandolphini waxed effusive.

'Absolutely *super* painter, isn't he? Now, I suppose, if you saw a good, a beautiful picture which you were assured came from a reputable source, you might accept that as a "Clode" Lorrain, mightn't you?'

'Certainly, my Lord.'

'But if you were later to learn that the picture had been painted in the seventeenth century and not the eighteenth! Well, you might change your opinion, mightn't you?'

Featherstone looked pleased with himself, but the turn of the conversation seemed to be causing Gandolphini intense embarrassment. 'Well, not really, my Lord,' he murmured.

'Oh, I'm sorry. Will you tell us why not?' The learned Judge looked nettled and prepared to take a note.

Gandolphini hated to do it, but as a reputable art expert he had to say, 'Well. You see. Claude Lorrain *did* paint in the seventeenth century, my Lord.'

It was almost the collapse of the Judge's morale. However, he started to talk rather quickly to cover his embarrassment. 'Oh, yes. Yes, that's right. Of course he did. Perhaps some of the jury will know that . . . or not, as the case may be.' He smiled at

34

the jury, who looked distinctly puzzled, and then at the witness. 'We haven't all got *your* expertise, Mr Gandolphini.'

All I could think of to say was a warning to Mr Justice Featherstone to avoid setting himself up as any sort of con-o-sewer. Wiser counsels prevailed and I didn't say it.

★ ★ ★

For our especial delight we then had an appearance in the witness-box by Mrs De Moyne, a well-manicured lady in a dark, businesslike suit, with horn-rimmed glasses and a voice like the side of a nail file. Mrs De Moyne spoke with the assurance of an art lover who weighs up a Post-Impressionist to the nearest dollar, and gives you the tax advantage of a gift to the Museum of Modern Art without drawing breath. She gave a brief account of her visit to the auction room to preview the Cragg in question, of her being assured that the picture had a perfect pedigree, having come straight from the artist's niece with no dealers involved, and described her successful bidding against stiff competition from a couple of Bond Street galleries and the Italian agent of a collector in Kuwait.

Erskine-Brown asked the witness if she believed she had been buying a genuine Septimus Cragg. 'Of course I did,' rasped Mrs De Moyne. 'I was terribly deceived.' So Erskine-Brown sat down, I'm sure, with a feeling of duty done.

'Mrs De Moyne. Wouldn't you agree,' I asked as I rose to cross-examine, 'that you bought a very beautiful picture?'

35

'Yes,' Mrs De Moyne admitted.

'So beautiful you were prepared to pay sixty thousand pounds for it?'

'Yes, I was.'

'And it is still the same beautiful picture? The picture hasn't changed since you bought it, has it, Mrs De Moyne? Not by one drop of paint! Is the truth of the matter that you're not interested in art but merely in collecting autographs!'

Of course this made the jury titter and brought Erskine-Brown furiously to his hind legs. I apologized for any pain and suffering I might have caused, and went on. 'When did you first doubt that this was a Cragg?' I asked.

'Someone rang me up.'

'*Someone?* What did they say?'

'Do you want to let this evidence in, Mr Rumpole?' The learned Judge was heard to be warning me for my own good.

'Yes, my Lord. I'm curious to know,' I reassured him. So Mrs De Moyne answered the question. 'That was what made me get in touch with the police,' she said. 'The man who called me said the picture wasn't a genuine Cragg, and it never had belonged to Cragg's niece. He also said that I'd got a bargain.'

'A bargain. Why?'

'Because it was better than a Cragg.'

'Did he give you his name?' It was a risky question, dangerous to ask because I didn't know the answer.

'He did, yes. But I was so upset I didn't pay too much attention to it. I don't think I can remember it.'

'Try,' I encouraged her.

36

'White. I think it had "white" in it.'

'Whiting? Whitehead?' I tried a few names on her.

'No.' Mrs De Moyne shook her head defeated. 'I can't remember.'

'Thank you, Mrs De Moyne.' When I sat down I heard a gentle voice in my ear whisper, 'You were wonderful! Harold said you would be.' It was the girl, Pauline, who had left her seat to murmur comforting words to Rumpole.

'Oh nonsense,' I whispered back, but then had to add, for the sake of truthfulness, 'Well, just a bit wonderful, perhaps. How do you think it's going, Myersy?'

The knowing old legal executive in front of me admitted that we were doing better than he expected, which was high praise from such a source, but then he looked towards the witness-box and whispered, 'That's the one I'm afraid of.'

The fearful object in Mr Myers's eyes was a small, grey-haired lady with wind-brightened cheeks and small glittering eyes, wearing a tweed suit and sensible shoes, who took the oath in a clear voice and gave her name as Miss Marjorie Evangeline Price, of 31 Majuba Road, Worthing, and admitted that the late Cragg, R.A., had been her Uncle Septimus.

'Do you know the defendant Brittling?' Erskine-Brown began his examination-in-chief, and I growled, 'Mister Brittling,' insisting on a proper respect for the prisoner at the Bar. I don't think the jury heard me. They were all listening eagerly to Miss Marjorie Evangeline Price, who talked to them as though she were having a cup of afternoon tea with a few friends she'd known for years.

'He came to see me in Worthing. He said he had one of Uncle Septimus's paintings to sell and he wanted me to put it into the auction for him. The real seller didn't want his name brought into it.'

'Did Mr Brittling tell you why?'

'He said it was a businessman who didn't want it to be known that he was selling his pictures. People might have thought he was in financial trouble, apparently.'

'So did you agree to the picture being sold in your name?'

'I'm afraid it was very wrong of me, but he was going to give me a little bit of a percentage. An ex-schoolmistress does get a very small pension.' Miss Price smiled at the jury and they smiled back, as though of course they understood completely. She was, unhappily for old Brittling, the sort of witness that the jury love, a sweet old lady who's not afraid to admit she's wrong.

'Did you have any idea that the picture wasn't genuine?'

'Oh no, of course not. I had no idea of that. Mr Brittling was very charming and persuasive.'

At which Miss Price looked at my client in the dock and smiled. The jury also looked at him, but they didn't smile.

'And how much of the money did Mr Brittling allow you to keep?'

'I think, I'm not sure, I *think* it was ten per cent.'

'How very generous. Thank you, Miss Price.'

Erskine-Brown had shot his bolt and sat down. I rose and put on the sweetest, gentlest voice in the Rumpole repertoire. Cross-examining Miss Price was going to be like walking on eggs. I had to move towards any sort of favourable answer on tiptoe.

38

'Miss Price, do you remember your uncle, Septimus Cragg?' I started to move her gently down Memory Lane.

'I remember him coming to our house when I was a little girl. He had a red beard and a very hairy tweed suit. I remember sitting on his lap.'

His Lordship smiled at her—he was clearly pro-Price.

'Is that all you can remember about him?' I was still probing gently.

'I remember Uncle Septimus telling me that there were two sorts of people in the world—nurses and patients. He seemed to think I'd grow up to be a nurse.'

'Oh, really? And which was he?'

'My Lord, can this possibly be relevant?' Erskine-Brown seemed to think the question was fraught with danger, when I was really only making conversation with the witness.

'I can't see it at the moment, Mr Erskine-Brown,' the Judge admitted.

'Which did he say he was?' I went on, ignoring the unmannerly interruption.

'Oh, he said he could always find someone to look after him. I think he was a bit of a spoiled baby really.'

The jury raised a polite titter, and Erskine-Brown sat down. I looked as though I'd got an answer of great importance.

'Did he? Did he say that? Tell me, Miss Price, do you know who Nancy was?'

'Nancy?' Miss Price looked puzzled.

'This picture is of Nancy, apparently. In an hotel bedroom in Dieppe. Who was Nancy?'

'I'm afraid I have no idea. I suppose she must

have been a'—she gave a small, meaningful pause—'a friend of Uncle Septimus.'

'Yes. I suppose she must have been.' I pointed to the picture which had brought us all to the Old Bailey. 'You've never seen this picture before?'

'Oh no. I didn't ask to see it. Mr Brittling told me about it and, well, of course I trusted him, you see.' Miss Price smiled sweetly at the jury and I sat down. There's no doubt about it. There's nothing more like banging your head against a brick wall than cross-examining a witness who's telling nothing but the truth.

*   *   *

Later that afternoon the Usher came to counsel engaged on the case with a message. The learned Judge would be glad to see us for a cup of tea in his room. So we were received amongst the red leather armchairs, the Law Reports, the silver-framed photographs of Marigold and the Featherstone twins, Simon and Sarah.

The Judge was hovering over the bone china, dispensing the Earl Grey and petit beurres, and the Clerk of the Court was lurking in the background to make sure there was no hanky-panky, I suppose, or an attempt to drop folding money into the Judge's wig.

'Come along, Horace. Sit you down, Claude. Sit you down. You'll take a dish of tea, won't you? What I wanted to ask you fellows is . . . How long is this case going to last?'

'Well, Judge . . . Guthrie . . .' said Erskine-Brown, stirring his tea. 'That rather depends on Rumpole here. He has to put the defence. If there *is*

40

a defence.'

'I don't want to hurry you, Horace. The point is, I may not be able to sit next Monday afternoon.' The Judge gave a secret sort of a smile and said modestly, 'Appointment at the Palace, you know what these things are . . .'

'Marigold got a new outfit for it, has she?' I couldn't resist asking.

'Well, the girls like all that sort of nonsense, don't they?' he said, as though the whole matter were almost too trivial to mention. 'It's not so much an invitation as a Royal command. You know the type of thing.'

'I *don't* know,' I assured him. 'My only Royal command was to join the R.A.F. Ground Staff, as I remember it.'

'Yes, Horace, of course. You old war-horse!' There was a pause while we all had a gulp of tea and a nibble of biscuit. 'How much longer are you going to be?' the Judge asked.

'Well, not long, I suppose. It's rather an absurd little case, isn't it? Bit of a practical joke, really. Isn't that what it is? Just a prank, more or less.' I was working my way towards a small fine should the old idiot Brittling go down; but to my dismay Mr Justice Featherstone looked extremely serious.

'I can't pretend that I find it a joke, exactly,' he said, in his new-found judicial manner.

'Well, I don't suppose that the shades of the prison house begin to fall around the wretched Brittling, do they? I mean, all he did was to pull the legs of a few so-called con-o-sewers.'

'And made himself a considerable sum of money in the process,' said Erskine-Brown, who was clearly anxious to be no sort of help.

41

'It's deceit, Horace. And forgery for personal profit. If your client's convicted I'm afraid I couldn't rule out a custodial sentence.' The Judge bit firmly into the last petit beurre.

'You couldn't?' I sounded incredulous.

'How could I?'

'Not send him to prison for a little bit of "let's pretend"? For a bit of a joke on a pompous profession?' I put down my cup and stood. My outrage was perfectly genuine. 'No. I don't suppose you could.'

Tea with the Judge was over, and I was about to follow Erskine-Brown and the learned Clerk out of his presence, when Mr Justice Featherstone called me back. 'Oh, Horace,' he said, 'a word in your ear.'

'Yes.'

'I've noticed you've fallen into rather a bad habit.'

'Bad habit?' What on earth, I wondered, was he about to accuse me of—being drunk in charge of a forgery case?

'Hands in pockets when you're addressing the Court. It looks so bad, Horace. Such a poor example to the younger men. Keep them out of the pockets, will you? I'm sure you don't mind me pulling you up about it?'

It was the old school prefect speaking. I left him without comment.

*　　*　　*

The hardest part of any case, I have always maintained, comes when your client enters the witness-box. Up until that moment you have been

42

able to protect him by attacking those who give evidence against him, and by concealing from the jury the most irritating aspects of his personality. Once he starts to give evidence, however, the client is on his own. He is like a child who has left its family on the beach and is swimming, in a solitary fashion, out to sea, where no cries of warning can be heard.

I knew Harold Brittling was going to be a bad witness by the enormously confident way that he marched into the box, held the Bible up aloft and promised to tell the truth, the whole truth and nothing but the truth. He was that dreadful sort of witness, the one who can't wait to give evidence, and who has been longing, with unconcealed impatience, for his day in Court. He leant against the top of the box and surveyed us all with an expression of tolerant disdain, as though we had made a bit of a pig's breakfast of his case up to that moment, and it was now up to him to put it right.

I dug my hands as deeply as possible into my pockets, and asked what might prove to be the only really simple question.

'Is your name Harold Reynolds Gainsborough Brittling?'

'Yes, it is. You've got *that* perfectly right, Mr Rumpole.'

I didn't laugh; neither, I noticed, did the jury.

'You came of an artistic family, Mr Brittling?' It seemed a legitimate deduction.

'Oh yes,' said Brittling, and went on modestly, 'I showed an extraordinary aptitude, my Lord, right from the start. At the Slade School, which I entered at the ripe old age of sixteen, I was twice a gold medallist and by far the most brilliant student of my

43

year.'

The jury appeared to be moderately nauseated by this glowing account of himself. I changed the subject. 'Mr Brittling, did you know the late Septimus Cragg?'

'I knew and loved him. There is a comradeship among artists, my Lord, and he was undoubtedly the finest painter of *his* generation. He came to a student exhibition and I think he recognized ... well ...'

I was hoping he wouldn't say 'a fellow genius'; he did.

'After that did you meet Cragg on a number of occasions?'

'You could say that. I became one of the charmed circle at Rottingdean.'

'Mr Brittling. Will you take in your hands Exhibit One.'

The Usher lifted Nancy and carried her to the witness-box. Harold Brittling gave me a look of withering scorn.

'This is a beautiful picture!' he said. 'Please don't call it "Exhibit One", Mr Rumpole. "Exhibit One" might be a blunt instrument or something.'

The witness chuckled at this; no one else in Court smiled. I prayed to God that he'd leave the funnies to his learned Counsel.

'Where did that picture come from, Mr Brittling?'

'I really don't remember very clearly.' He looked airily round the Court as though it were a matter of supreme unimportance.

'You don't remember?' The Judge didn't seem able to believe what he was writing down.

'No, my Lord. When one is leading the life of an

44

artist, small details escape the memory. I suppose Septimus must have given it to me on one of my visits to him. Artists pay these little tributes to each other.'

'Why did you take it to Miss Price and ask her to sell it?' I asked as patiently as possible.

'I suppose I thought that the dealers would have more faith in it if it came from that sort of source. And I rather wanted the old puss to get her little bit of commission.'

One thing emerged clearly from that bit of evidence: the jury didn't approve of Miss Price being called an 'old puss'. In fact, Brittling was going down with them like a cup of cold cod liver oil.

'Mr Brittling. What is your opinion of that picture?' Of course I wanted him to say that it was a genuine Cragg. Instead he closed his eyes and breathed in deeply. 'I think it is the work of the highest genius...'

'Slowly please...' The Judge was writing this art criticism down.

'Just watch his Lordship's pencil,' I advised the witness.

'I think it is a work of great beauty, my Lord... The painting of the curtains, and of the *air* in the room... Quite miraculous!'

'Did Septimus Cragg paint it?' I tried to bring Brittling's attention back to the case.

'It's a lovely thing.' And then the little man actually shrugged his shoulders. 'What does it matter who painted it?'

'For the purpose of this case, you can take it from me—it matters,' I instructed him. 'Now, have you any doubts that it is a genuine Cragg?'

'Only one thing gives me the slightest doubt.' Like all bad witnesses Brittling was incapable of a simple answer.

'What's that?'

'It really seems to be too good for him. It exists beautifully on a height the old boy never reached before.'

'Did you paint that picture, Mr Brittling?' I tried to direct his attention to the charge he was facing.

'Me? Is someone suggesting I did it?' Brittling seemed flattered and delighted.

'Yes, Mr Brittling. Someone is.'

'Well, in all modesty, it really takes my breath away. You are suggesting that I could produce a masterpiece like that!' And Mr Brittling smiled triumphantly round the Court.

'I take it, Mr Rumpole, that the answer means "no".' The Judge was looking understandably confused.

'Yes, of course. If your Lordship pleases.'

Featherstone, J. had interpreted Brittling's answer as a denial of forgery. I thought that no further questions could possibly improve the matter, and I sat down. Erskine-Brown rose to cross-examine with the confident air of a hunter who sees his prey snoozing gently at a range of about two feet.

'Mr Brittling,' he began quietly. 'Did you say you "laundered" the picture through Miss Price?'

'He did *what*, Mr Erskine-Brown?' The Judge was not quite with him.

'*Sold* the picture through Miss Price, my Lord, because it seemed such an unimpeachable source.'

'Yes.' The witness didn't bother to deny it.

'Does that mean that the picture isn't entirely

46

innocent?'

'Mr Erskine-Brown, all great art is innocent.' Brittling was outraged. It seemed that all we had left was the John Keats defence:

'Beauty is truth, truth beauty,'—that is all
Ye know on earth, and all ye need to know.

'Then why this elaborate performance of selling the picture through Miss Price?' Erskine-Brown raised his voice a little.

'Just to tease them a bit. Pull their legs...' The worst was happening. Brittling was chuckling again.

'Pull *whose* legs, Mr Brittling?'

'The art experts! The con-o-sewers. People like Teddy Gandolphini. I just wanted to twist their tails a little.'

'So we have all been brought here, to this Court, for a sort of a joke?' Erskine-Brown acted extreme amazement.

'Oh no. Not just a joke. Something very serious is at stake.' I didn't know what else Brittling was going to say, but I suspected it would be nothing helpful.

'What?' Erskine-Brown asked.

'My reputation.'

'Your reputation as an honest man, Mr Brittling?'

'Oh no. Far more important than that. My reputation as an artist! You see, if I did paint that picture, I must be a genius, mustn't I?'

Brittling beamed round the Court, but once again no one else was smiling. At the end of the day the Judge withdrew the defendant's bail, a bad sign in

47

any case. Harold Brittling, however, seemed to feel he had had a triumph in the witness-box, and departed, with only a moderate show of irritation, for the Nick.

When I left Court—a little late, as we had the argument about bail after the jury had departed—I saw a lonely figure on a bench in the marble hall outside Number 1 Court. It was Pauline, shivering slightly, wrapped in her ethnic clothing, clutching her holdall, and her undoubtedly beautiful face was, I saw when she turned it in my direction, wet with tears. Checking a desire to suggest that the temporary absence of the appalling Brittling might come as something of a relief to his nearest and dearest, I tried to put a cheerful interpretation on recent events.

'Don't worry.' I sat down beside her and groped for a small cigar. 'Bail's quite often stopped, once a defendant's given his evidence. The jury won't know about it. Personally, I think the Judge was just showing off. Well, he's young, and a bit wet round the judicial ears.' There was a silence. Young Pauline didn't seem to be at all cheered up. Then she said, very quietly, 'They'll find Harold guilty, won't they?' She was too bright to be deceived and I exploded in irritation. 'What the hell's the matter with old Harold? He's making his evidence as weak as possible. Does he want to lose his case?'

And then she said something I hadn't expected: 'You know he does, don't you?' She put her hand on my arm in a way I found distinctly appealing.

'Please,' she said, 'will you take me for a drink? I really need one. I'd love it if you would.'

In all the circumstances it seemed a most reasonable request. 'All right,' I said. 'We'll go to

48

Pommeroy's Wine Bar. It's only just over the road.'

'No we won't,' Pauline decided. 'We'll go to the Old Monmouth in Greek Street. I want you to meet somebody.'

*   *   *

The Old Monmouth, to which we travelled by taxi at Pauline's suggestion, turned out to be a large, rather gloomy pub with a past which was considerably more interesting than its present. Behind the bar there were signed photographs, and even sketches by a number of notable artists who drank there before the war and in the forties and fifties. There were also photographs of boxers, dancers and music hall performers, and many caricatures of 'Old Harry', the former proprietor, with a huge handlebar moustache, whose son, 'Young Harry', with a smaller moustache, still appeared occasionally behind the bar.

The habits of artists have changed. Perhaps they now spend their evenings sitting at home in Islington or Kew, drinking rare Burgundy and listening to Vivaldi on the music centre. The days when a painter started the evening with a couple of pints of Guinness and ended stumbling out into Soho with a bottle of whisky in his pocket and an art school model, wearing scarlet lipstick and a beret, on his arm have no doubt gone for ever. At the Old Monmouth pale young men with orange quiffs were engaged in computerized battles on various machines. There were some eager executives in three-piece suits buying drinks for their secretaries, and half a dozen large men loudly discussing the virtues of their motor cars. No one

49

looked in the least like an artist.

★   ★   ★

'They all used to come here,' Pauline said, nostalgic for a past she never knew. 'Augustus John, Sickert, Septimus Cragg. And their women. All their women...'

'Wonder they found room for them all.' I handed her the rum she had requested, and took a gulp of a glass of red wine which made the taste of Pommeroy's plonk seem like Château-Lafite. I couldn't quite imagine what I was doing, drinking in a Soho pub with an extraordinarily personable young woman, and I was thankful for the thought that the least likely person to come through the door was She Who Must Be Obeyed.

So I tossed back the rest of the appalling Spanish-style *vin ordinaire* with the sort of gesture which I imagine Septimus Cragg might have used on a similar occasion.

'It's changed a bit now,' Pauline said, looking round the bar regretfully. 'Space Invaders!' She gave a small smile, and then her smile faded. 'Horace... Can I call you Horace?'

'Please.'

She put a hand on my arm. I didn't avoid it.

'You've been very kind to me. You and Hilda. But it's time you knew the truth.'

I moved a little away from her, somewhat nervously, I must confess. When someone offers to tell you the truth in the middle of a difficult criminal trial it's rarely good news.

'No,' I said firmly.

'What?' She looked up at me, puzzled.

50

'The time for me to know the truth is when this case is over. Too much of the truth now and I'd have to give up defending that offbeat little individual you go around with. Anyway,' I pulled out my watch, 'I've got to get back to Gloucester Road.'

'Please! Please don't leave me!' Her hand was on my arm again, and her words came pouring out, as though she were afraid I'd go before she'd finished. 'Harold said he loved Septimus Cragg. He didn't. He hated him. You see, Septimus had everything Harold wanted—fame, money, women, and a style of his own. Harold can paint brilliantly, but always like other people. So he wanted to get his own back on Septimus, to get his revenge.'

'Look. If you're trying to prove to me my client's guilty...' I was doing my best to break off this dangerous dialogue, but she held my arm now and wouldn't stop talking.

'Don't go. If you'll wait here, just a little while, I'll show you how to prove Harold's completely innocent.'

'Do you really think I care that much?' I asked her.

'Of course you do!'

'Why?'

'Patients and nurses. Septimus said that's how the world is divided. We're the nurses, aren't we, you and I? We've *got* to care, that's our business. Please!'

I looked at her. Her eyes were full of tears again. I cursed her for having said something true, about both of us.

'All right,' I said. 'But this time I'll join you in a rum. No more Château Castanets. Oh, and I'd

51

better make a telephone call.'

I rang Hilda from a phone on the wall near the Space Invader machine. Although there was a good deal of noise in the vicinity, the voice of She Who Must Be Obeyed came over loud and clear.

'Well, Rumpole,' she said, 'I suppose you're going to tell me you were kept late working in Chambers.'

'No,' I said, 'I'm not going to tell you that.'

'Well, what *are* you going to tell me?'

'Guthrie Featherstone put Brittling back in the cooler and I'm with the girlfriend Pauline. Remember her? We're drinking rum together in a bar in Soho and I really have no idea when I'll be back, so don't wait up for me.'

'Don't talk rubbish, Rumpole! You know I don't believe a word of it!' and my wife slammed down the receiver. If such were the price of establishing my client's innocence, I supposed it would have to be paid. I returned to the bar, where Pauline had already lined up a couple of large rums and was in the act of paying for them.

'What did you tell your wife?' she asked, having some feminine instinct, apparently, which told her the nature of my call.

'The truth.'

'I don't suppose she believed it.'

'No. Here, let me do that.' I felt for my wallet.

'It's the least I can do.' She was scooping up the change. 'You were splendid in Court. You were, honestly. The way you handled that awful Gandolphini, and the Judge. You've got what Harold always wanted.'

'What's that?'

'A voice of your own.' We both drank and she

swivelled round on her bar stool to survey the scene in the Old Monmouth pub, and smiled. 'Look,' she said. 'It's here.'

'What?'

'All you need to prove Harold's innocent.'

I looked to a corner of the bar, to where she was looking. An old woman, a shapeless bundle of clothes with a few bright cheap beads, had come in and was sitting at a table in the corner. She started to search in a chaotic handbag with the air of someone who has no real confidence that anything will be found. Pauline had slid off her stool and I followed her across to the new arrival. She didn't seem to notice our existence until Pauline said, quite gently, 'Hullo, Nancy.' Then the woman looked up at me. She seemed enormously old, her face was as covered with lines as a map of the railways. Her grey hair was tousled and untidy, her hands, searching in her handbag, were not clean. But there was still a sort of brightness in her eye as she smiled at me and said, in a voice pickled during long years in the Old Monmouth pub, 'Hullo, young man. I'll have a large port and lemon.'

*   *   *

It is, of course, quite improper for a barrister to talk to a potential witness, so I will draw a veil over the rest of the evening. It's not so difficult to draw the aforesaid veil, as my recollection of events is somewhat hazy. I know that I paid for a good many rums and ports with lemon, and that I learnt more than I can now remember about the lives and loves of many British painters. I can remember walking with two ladies, one old and fragile, one young and

53

beautiful, in the uncertain direction of Leicester Square tube station, and it may be that we linked arms and sang a chorus of the 'Roses of Picardy' together. I can't swear that we didn't.

I had certainly left my companions when I got back to Gloucester Road, and then discovered that the bedroom door was obstructed by some sort of device, probably a lock.

'Is that you, Rumpole?' I heard a voice from within. 'If you find her so fascinating, I wonder you bothered to come home at all.'

'Hilda!' I called, rattling at the handle. 'Where on earth am I expected to sleep?'

'I put your pyjamas on the sofa, Rumpole. Why don't you join them?'

Before I fell asleep in our sitting room, however, I made a telephone call to his home number and woke up our learned prosecutor, Claude Erskine-Brown, and chattered to him, remarkably brightly, along the following lines: 'Oh, Erskine-Brown. Hope I haven't woken you up. I have? Well, isn't it time to feed the baby anyway? Oh, the baby's four now. How time flies. Look. Check something for me, will you? That Mrs De Moyne. Yes. The purchaser. I don't want to drag her back to Court but could your officer ask if the man who rang her was called Blanco Basnet? Yes. 'Blanco'. It means white, you see. Sweet dreams, Erskine-Brown.'

After which, I stretched out, dressed as I was, on the sofa and dreamed a vivid dream in which I was appearing before Mr Justice Featherstone wearing pyjamas, waving a paintbrush, and singing the 'Roses of Picardy' until he sent me to cool off in the cells.

‘You look tired, Rumpole,’ Erskine-Brown and I were sitting side by side in Court awaiting the arrival of Blind Justice in the shape of Featherstone, J. The sledgehammer inside my head was quietening a little, but I still had a remarkably dry mouth and a good deal of stiffness in the limbs after having slept rough in Froxbury Court.

‘Damn hard work, La Vie de Bohème,’ I told him. ‘By the way, Erskine-Brown, what's the news from Mrs De Moyne?’

‘Oh, she remembered the name as soon as the Inspector put it to her. Blanco Basnet. Odd sort of name, isn't it?’

‘Distinctly odd,’ I agreed. But before he could ask for any further explanation the Usher called, ‘Be upstanding’, and upstanding we all were, as the learned Judge manifested himself upon the Bench, was put in position by his learned Clerk, supplied with a notebook and sharpened pencils, and then leant forward to ask me, with a brief wince at the sight of the hands in the Rumpole pockets, ‘Is there another witness for the defence?’

‘Yes, my Lord,’ I said, as casually as possible. ‘I will now call Mrs Nancy Brittling.’

As the Usher left the Court to fetch the witness in question I heard sounds, as of a ginger beer bottle exploding on a hot day, from the dock, to which Harold Brittling had summoned the obedient Myers.

Then the courtroom door opened and the extremely old lady with whom I had sung around Goodge Street made her appearance, not much

55

smartened up for the occasion, although she did wear, as a tribute to the learned Judge, a small straw hat perched inappropriately upon her tousled grey curls. As she took the oath, Myers was whispering to me. 'The client doesn't want this witness called, Mr Rumpole.'

'Tell the client to belt up and draw a picture, Myersy. Leave me to do my work in peace.' Then I turned to the witness-box. 'Are you Mrs Nancy Brittling?'

'Yes, dear. You know that.' The old lady smiled at me and I went on in a voice of formal severity, to discourage any possible revelation about the night before.

'Please address yourself to the learned Judge. Were you married to my client, Harold Reynolds Gainsborough Brittling?'

'It seems a long time ago now, my Lordship.' Nancy confided to Featherstone, J.

'Did Mr Brittling introduce you to the painter Septimus Cragg at Rottingdean?'

'I remember *that*'. Nancy smiled happily. 'It was my nineteenth birthday. I had red hair then, and lots of it. I remember he said I was a stunner.'

'Who said you were a "stunner",' I asked for clarification, 'your husband or . . . ?'

'Oh, Septimus said that, of course.'

'Of course.'

'And Septimus asked me to pop across to Dieppe with him the next weekend,' Nancy said proudly.

'What did you feel about that?' The old lady turned to the jury and I could see them respond to a smile that still had in it, after more than half a century, some relic of the warmth of a nineteen-year-old girl.

56

'Oh,' she said, 'I was thrilled to bits.'

'And what was Harold Brittling's reaction to the course of events?'

'He was sick as a dog, my Lordship.' It was an answer which found considerable favour with the jury, so naturally Erskine-Brown rose to protest.

'My Lord, I don't know what the relevance of this is. We seem to be wandering into some rather sordid divorce matter.'

'Mr Erskine-Brown!' I gave it to him between the eyebrows. 'My client has already heard the cell door bang behind him as a result of this charge, of which he is wholly innocent. And when I am proving his innocence, I will *not* be interrupted!'

'My Lord, it's quite intolerable that Mr Rumpole should talk to the jury about cell doors banging!'

'Is it really? I thought that was what this case is all about.'

At which point the learned Judge came in to pour a little oil.

'I think we must let Mr Rumpole take his own course, Mr Erskine-Brown,' he said. 'It may be quicker in the end.'

'I am much obliged to your Lordship.' I gave a servile little bow, and even took my hands out of my pockets. Then I turned to the witness. 'Mrs Brittling, did you go to Dieppe with Septimus Cragg, and while you were there together, did he paint you in the bedroom of the Hôtel du Vieux Port?'

'He painted me in the nude, my Lordship. I tell you, I was a bit of something worth painting in those days.'

Laughter from the jury, and a discreet smile from the learned Judge, were accompanied by a pained sigh from Erskine-Brown. I asked the Usher to take Exhibit One to the witness, and Nancy looked at the picture and smiled, happily lost, for a moment, in the remembrance of things past.

'Will you look at Exhibit One, Mrs Brittling?'

'Yes. That's the picture. I saw Septimus paint that. In the bedroom at Dieppe.'

And the signature...?' Erskine-Brown had told the jury that all forged pictures carried large signatures, as this one did. But Nancy Brittling was there to prove him wrong.

'I saw Septimus paint his signature. And, we were so happy together, just for a bit of fun, he let me paint my name too.

'Let his Lordship see.'

So the Usher trundled up to the learned Judge with the picture, and once again Guthrie raised his magnifying glass respectfully to it.

'It's a bit dark. I did it in sort of purple, at the edge of the carpet. I just wrote "Nancy", that's all.'

'Mr Rumpole,' Featherstone, J., said, and I blessed him for it. 'I think she's right about that.'

'Yes, my Lord. I have looked and I think she is. Mrs Brittling, do you know how your husband got hold of that picture?'

Once again, the evidence was accompanied by popping and fizzing noises from the dock as the prisoner's wife explained, with some gentle amusement, 'Oh yes. Septimus gave it to *me*, but when I brought it home to Harold he fussed so much that in the end I let him have the picture. Well, after a time Harold and I separated and I suppose he kept hold of it until he wanted to pretend he'd painted it himself.'

'Thank you, Mrs Brittling.' I sat down, happy in

58

my work. The sledgehammer had quietened and I stretched out my legs, preparing to watch Erskine-Brown beat his head against the brick wall of a truthful witness.

'Mrs Brittling,' he began. 'Why have you come here to give this evidence? It must be painful for you, to remember those rather sordid events.'

'Painful? Oh, no!' Nancy looked at him and smiled. 'It's a pure pleasure, my dear, to see that picture again and to remember what I looked like, when I was nineteen and happy.'

*　　*　　*

The next morning I addressed the jury, and I was able to offer them the solution to the mystery of Harold Brittling and the disputed Septimus Cragg. I started by reminding them of one of Nancy's answers: '". . . he kept hold of it until he wanted to pretend he'd painted it himself." Harold Brittling, you may think, ladies and gentlemen of the jury,' I said, 'had one driving passion in his life—his almost insane jealousy of Septimus Cragg. Cragg became his young wife's lover. But worse than that in Brittling's eyes, Cragg was a great painter and Brittling was second rate, with no style of his own. So now, years after Cragg's death, Brittling planned his revenge. He was going to prove that he could paint a better Cragg than Cragg ever painted. He would prove that this fine picture was his work and not Cragg's. That was his revenge for a weekend in Dieppe, and a lifetime's humiliation. To achieve that revenge Brittling was prepared to sell his Cragg in a devious way that would be bound to attract suspicion. He was prepared to get a friend of his

59

named Blanco Basnet to telephone Mrs De Moyne and claim that the picture was not a genuine Cragg, but something a great deal better. He was prepared to face a charge of forgery. He was prepared to go to prison. He was prepared to give his evidence to you in such a way as to lead you to believe that he was the true painter of a work of genius. Don't be deceived, members of the jury, Brittling is no forger. He is a fake criminal and not a real one. He is not guilty of the crime he is charged with. He is guilty only of the bitterness felt for men of genius by the merely talented. You may think, members of the jury, as you bring in your verdict of "Not Guilty", that that is an understandable emotion. You may even feel pity for a poor painter who could not even produce a forgery of his own.'

As I sat down, the ginger beer bottle in the dock finally exploded and Brittling shouted, in an unmannerly way, at his defending counsel, 'You bastard, Rumpole!' he yelled, 'you've joined the con-o-sewers!'

★   ★   ★

'Good win, Horace. Of course, I always thought your client was innocent.'

'Did you now?'

The Judge had invited me in for a glass of very reasonable Amontillado after the jury brought in their verdict and, as the case was now over, we were alone in his room.

'Oh yes. One gets a nose for these things. One can soon assess a witness and know if he's telling the truth. Have to do that all the time in this job. Oh, and Horace . . .'

60

'Yes, Judge?'

His Lordship continued in some embarrassment. 'That bit of a tizz I was in, about the great secret getting out. No need to mention that to anyone, eh?'

'Oh, I rang the Lord Chancellor's office about that. The day after we met in Pommeroy's,' I told him, and casually slipped my hands into my pockets.

'You *what*?' Featherstone looked at me in a wild surmise.

'I assured them you hadn't said a word to anyone and it was just a sort of silly joke put about by Claude Erskine-Brown. I mean, no one in the Temple ever dreamed that they'd make *you* a Judge.'

'Horace! Did you say that?'

'Of course I did.' He took time to consider the matter and then pronounced judgement. 'Then you got me out of a nasty spot! I was afraid Marigold had been a bit indiscreet. Horace, I owe you an immense debt of gratitude.'

'Yes. You do,' I agreed. His Lordship looked closely at me, and some doubt seemed to have crept into his voice as he said, 'Horace. *Did* you ring the Lord Chancellor's office? Are you telling me the truth?'

I looked at him with the clear eyes of a reliable witness. 'Can't you tell, Judge? I thought you had such an infallible judicial eye for discovering if a witness is lying or not. Not slipping a bit, are you?'

★   ★   ★

'What is it, Rumpole. Not flowers again?'

61

'Bubbly! Non vintage. Pommeroy's sparkling—on special offer. And I paid for it myself!' I had brought Hilda a peace offering which I set about opening on the kitchen table as soon as I returned to the matrimonial home.

'Where's the girl now?' she asked suspiciously.

'God knows. Gone off into the sunset with the old chump. He'll never forgive me for getting him acquitted, so I don't suppose we'll be seeing either of them again.'

The cork came out with a satisfying pop, and I began to fill a couple of glasses with the health-giving bubbles.

'I should have thought you'd had quite enough to drink with her last night!' Hilda was only a little mortified.

'Oh, forget her. She was a girl with soft eyes, and red hair, who passed through the Old Bailey and then was heard no more.'

I handed Hilda a glass, and raised mine in a toast.

'"Beauty is truth, truth beauty,"—that is all
Ye know on earth, and all ye need to know.'

I looked at She Who Must Be Obeyed and then I said, 'It isn't, is it, though? We need to know a damn sight more than that!'

RUMPOLE AND THE GOLDEN THREAD

There is no doubt about it, life at the Bar can have stretches of the hum and the drum. A long succession of petty thefts, minor frauds and unsensational indecencies, prolonged by the tedious speeches of learned friends and the leisurely summings up of judges who seemed to have nothing much to say and all the time in the world in which to say it, produced, after a month or six, a feeling of pronounced discontent. There was no summer that year, and precious little spring. The rain fell regularly on the Inner London Sessions, and on Acton, and on the Uxbridge Magistrates Court. Most members of the jury seemed to have bad colds, their noses were pink and they sucked Zubes in their box. The courtrooms smelled of lozenges and resounded to hacking coughs. The pound was falling and my spirits with it. I began to dream of sandy deserts, the cool shade of a sparkling oasis, almond eyes behind latticed windows, the call of the *muezzin* in the dusty pink of the evening, things which I had never seen and were unlikely to be found between Snaresbrook and Reading Crown Court. I took to remembering a neglected piece of James Elroy Flecker which had enraptured me during my schooldays, describing, as it did, the journey of a number of persons of the Middle Eastern persuasion to a place romantically called 'Samarkand'.

These verses were running through my head as I joined She Who Must Be Obeyed at the sink after supper one night (lamb chops, frozen peas and a

63

bottle of Pommeroy's worst).

> 'Have we not Indian carpets, dark as wine,
>   Turbans and sashes, gowns and bows and
>   veils,
> And broideries of intricate design,
>   And printed hangings in enormous bales?'

As a matter of fact we hadn't. We were in the kitchen at 25B Froxbury Court (our alleged mansion flat in the Gloucester Road), my good self and She Who Must Be Obeyed, and far from being clad in turbans and sashes, sipping sherbet and sniffing oriental perfumes, we were dressed in a pair of aprons and doing the washing up; that is to say, I was up to my elbows in the Fairy Liquid and Hilda was wielding a doughty dishcloth. The words kept going round in my head, and I gave Hilda a snatch or two of the magical East.

'"We are the Pilgrims, master;"' I told her,

> 'We shall go
> Always a little further: it may be
> Beyond that last blue mountain barred with
>   snow,
> Across that angry or that glimmering sea,
>
> White on a throne or guarded in a cave
>   There lives a prophet who can understand
> Why men were born ...'

'What are you talking about, Rumpole?' Hilda asked. I gave her the best answer possible ...

> 'but surely we are brave,

Who make the Golden Journey to
Samarkand.'

'Rumpole! This plate's not washed up properly at
all.' Hilda had been staring critically at it, now she
dropped it back into the suds for me to do again.
'"Away, for we are ready to a man!"' I told her,

'Our camels sniff the evening and are glad.
Lead on, O Master of the Caravan:
Lead on the Merchant-Princes of Bagdad.'

'I don't know why you always choose the
washing. Why can't you dry?' said Hilda, who
didn't seem keen on crossing the desert.
'Washing's more fun.' So it was, comparatively
speaking.
'It's not much fun when you leave bits of gravy
untouched by the mop, Rumpole!'
'What's it matter—a bit of yesterday's gravy
never did anyone any harm. "Is not Baghdad, the
beautiful? O stay!"'
'If a thing's worth doing it's worth doing
properly,' said Hilda.
'Not much chance of adventure round here in
Gloucester Road, is there, Hilda? Unless you count
the choice between drying up the dishes or sloshing
them about in a mess of bottled soap suds.'
'You're getting a little too old for adventure,
Rumpole.' She was drying up a fork very
thoroughly indeed.
'Oh yes. You know what I spent the last three
weeks doing? A serious case of unpaid V.A.T. on
plastic egg timers—in Sydenham!' Travels
Rumpole East Away? Of course the answer was
65

'no', I realized, as I pulled out a coffee cup which seemed to have lost its handle in the stormy sink.

'You'd better get a tea towel and help with the rest of the drying. You've done quite enough damage already.'

At which point, and it is strange how things often happen in answer to some unspoken wish or silent prayer, the telephone on our kitchen wall gave urgent tongue. As Hilda answered it, I had no idea what sort of wish the genie of the telephone had come to answer, or how near to disaster its unseen voice would eventually bring me.

'Hello, 4052, Hilda Rumpole.' Hilda listened, then lowered the receiver with her hand over it and hissed at me in a voice pregnant with suspicion.

'Justitia, Rumpole. Who's *she*?'

'*She's* a sort of blind goddess, Hilda, who goes around lumbered with a sword and a blooming great pair of scales.' I took the instrument from her, and Hilda heard me say, 'Rumpole speaking... Yes, Justitia International. I know your organization. Yes... Who...? Oh yes. He remembers *me*? I taught him at the crammers. Criminal practice.'

'Who is it, Rumpole?' But I was still in close conversation with the unseen caller. 'Well, yes. Just before the war, as a matter of fact. Down a sort of cellar in Fetter lane... Oh... Well, I've read in *The Times* occasionally... Got into some sort of trouble over there, has he? Lunch with you tomorrow? La Venezia in Fleet Street? I don't really see why not.'

I put down the telephone, and when I turned to Hilda I was smiling as though I could smell, on the wind blowing up from Gloucester Road tube

66

station, the spice-laden breezes of Africa.

'What's the matter with you, Rumpole? You look remarkably pleased with yourself!' As she put away the plates Hilda was frowning suspiciously. I found an open bottle and poured out a couple of glasses of Pommeroy's ordinary.

'Dodo's coming to stay next week, remember?' As I showed no immediate reaction she repeated the information. 'My old school friend, Dodo Mackintosh, will be here for a couple of days next week. You won't forget that, will you, Rumpole?'

I handed her a glass of wine. Life seemed to have improved for the better all round. 'Dodo descending on us, eh? That makes it even better.'

'Makes what better?' Hilda asked. I raised my glass and turned towards the East as I said, '"We take the Golden Road to Samarkand!"'

★   ★   ★

Justitia International, as you may know, is an organization which attempts to see that trials are fair and justice done in even further away places with stranger-sounding names than the Uxbridge Magistrates Court. It exists on hope, an overdraft, and donations from such public-spirited citizens as still care if a foreign politician is hanged, or a Third World writer imprisoned after some trial which has been about as predictable as a poker game with a card sharper. To lands which will still receive them (a small and ever-shrinking number), Justitia will send English barristers to defend the oppressed; to other parts of the world observers are sent, who write reports about the proceedings. Such reports are filed away. Protests are sent. Sometimes letters are written to *The Times* and occasionally a prisoner is released or an injustice remedied. As I say, Justitia has no vast sums of money, so I thought it very decent of Amanda Pinkerton, the International Secretary, to take me out to lunch at a small trattoria in Fleet Street, where we sat over the remains of our spaghetti bolognaise and Chianti, studying an illustrated folder entitled 'Neranga Today'. I found Miss Pinkerton to be a large, energetic lady in her forties, given to wearing an assortment of coloured scarves and heavyweight costume jewellery, so she looked as if she had just returned from the bazaar.

'"Neranga,"' she read out to me, as though she were giving an elementary geography lesson to a class of backward and dyslexic ten-year-olds. '"A lump of land carved out by the British, who called it New Somerset. Capital, Nova Lombaro. Deeply divided into two tribes, the Apu and the Matatu, who hate each other so much that if an Apu man marries a Matatu girl, both their families throw them out and they're cursed forever."'

'Same sort of thing that goes on in Surrey,' I suggested.

'Yes. Well...' Miss Pinkerton turned a page and we were met with the face of an African with horn-rimmed glasses, a cotton cap and robe, standing in front of a microphone, apparently addressing a meeting of UNESCO. 'The Prime Minister,' Miss Pinkerton explained. 'Dr Christopher Mabile, a member of the Matatu tribe, warriors and head hunters not so long ago. He's a Marxist. Educated by the Jesuit Fathers, who sent him to Balliol. Got his medical degree in Moscow and postgrad in Cuba. When the country got independence, he had to have a token Apu in his Cabinet. So he made David Mazenze Minister of Home Affairs.' She turned the page and showed me another photograph.

'Looks older than I remember,' I told her. 'Well, I suppose it's only to be expected.'

'David's one of the more peaceful Apus. The British locked him up for about ten years, but he never bore a grudge. Moderate socialist. Good friend to Justitia. Sound on land reform and contraception. Excellent Chairman of the Famine Programme. And ...' her eyes became somewhat misty, 'he's got an absolutely *marvellous* voice.'

'But did he *do* it, do you think?' I asked. It seemed important.

Miss Pinkerton's mind, however, was clearly on other matters. 'It's a sort of thrilling voice! Of course, the Apu people absolutely *worship* David.'

The photograph was of an African with a noble head, short, grizzled hair, a strong neck and amused eyes. He was wearing an open-necked shirt and smoking a pipe. I thought back to a stuffy cellar off Fetter lane, the offices of Pinchbeck and Swattling, legal crammers who could guarantee to force you through the Bar exams in about six months. It was there I had taught young David Mazenze the elements of our Criminal Law, which, together with Wordsworth, Shakespeare and Oxford marmalade, must be one of our most valuable exports.

It was a shortage of briefs, in the years after my return to civilian life from a somewhat inglorious career in the R.A.F. Ground Staff, which led me to take on part-time work at the crammers. I may not have taught much law, in the strict sense of the

69

word, but I gave young David Mazenze and his fellow students from India, Fiji, Singapore and Godalming the basic speech to the jury, which should always refer to the 'Golden Thread' which runs through our justice—the immutable principle that everyone is innocent unless twelve good men and women and true are certain that the only possible answer is that they must be guilty. I also gave my class a lecture on my pre-war triumph in the Penge Bungalow Murders, a case which careful readers of these reminiscences will remember I won after a two-week hearing alone and without a leader. David Mazenze may not have emerged from my lessons the greatest academic lawyer in the world, but he knew something about bloodstains and how to cross-examine a policeman on his notebook, and he knew almost all there is to be known about the burden of proof.

When he went back to his native Neranga, David practised law, took up politics, and had that essential training for all successful African politicians—a fairly long term of imprisonment by the British. Then he was released, Neranga got its independence, and David Mazenze became the Apu representative in Dr Mabile's predominantly Matatu government. Each year he sent us a Christmas card, much decorated with snow and robins and holly, and best wishes to 'My old Mentor, Horace Rumpole and his Good Lady'. For a number of years, I am ashamed to say, I had forgotten to send one back.

I learned the basic facts of David Mazenze's case from Miss Pinkerton at that luncheon. The road to the capital of Neranga, Nova Lombaro, leads through many miles of scrubland and bush. One rainy night the fat and self-important Bishop Kareele, himself a remarkably devious politician, was being driven by a clergyman in a Mercedes along this road. They were stopped by an unknown African who waved the car down. As soon as they stopped the Bishop was shot, the clergyman ran into the bush and would live to give evidence.

Later the police raided David Mazenze's bungalow and found him calmly smoking his pipe and listening to the Fauré *Requiem*. He was arrested and refused bail by Chief Justice Sir Worthington Banzana, who was, quite coincidentally, a member of the Matatu tribe. As he was dragged from his house by the brutal officers of the law, David shouted a short sentence to his distracted wife, Grace. It consisted of the simple words, 'Horace Rumpole, Equity Court in the Temple.'

'But what I want to know is,' I told Miss Pinkerton, 'did he do in the dear old Bish?'

'We've had reports from reliable sources that Mabile's got David locked up in the most ghastly conditions! There may have been torture.'

Disturbing, no doubt, but hardly an answer to my question, which I repeated. 'But did our David *do* it?'

'I don't know whether we've actually *asked* him that.' Miss Pinkerton flipped vaguely through her file. 'Oh, here's Pam.' A secretary, a younger but equally eager version of Miss Pinkerton, who seemed to have bought her clothing at an army surplus store instead of an oriental bazaar, came into the restaurant at that moment in a state of high excitement.

'We've had a cable from Jonathan Mazenze,' Pam announced.

71

'David's younger brother,' Miss Pinkerton explained. 'He's been a tower of strength. What's it say, Pam?'

At which Pam pulled the cable from the pocket of her fatigues and read, '"Barrister Rumpole will be allowed to represent David at trial. Visa being arranged. Greetings, Jonathan Mazenze."'

'We're in luck!' said Miss Pinkerton. 'Is there anything else you want to know?'

'Only one thing,' I said. 'What do they give a chap for murder, in those particular parts?'

'It's death, isn't it, Mandy?' Pam asked casually. I closed my eyes. I was back in the shadow of the gallows which fell, every day, over my conduct of the Penge Bungalow Murders and I didn't know whether I was still strong enough to face it.

'Oh yes.' Miss Pinkerton sounded almost cheerful. 'The Prime Minister can't wait to hang David. You've got to save his life.'

So that was all I had to do. It was enough worry to be going on with, so I didn't think of the fact that should have concerned me most. If I had done so I might have wondered why Horace Rumpole, an elderly junior barrister, and not even an artificial silk, had been admitted so easily to the Nerangan Bar.

★　　　★　　　★

I was in the clerk's room next morning, sorting through the circulars, advertisements for life insurance and filing systems, together with *billets-doux* from Her Majesty's Customs and Excise and the Inland Revenue, which seem to constitute the bulk of my mail, and I happened to ask Henry, our clerk, in a casual sort of way, if he had any exciting work in store for me.

'Not according to my diary, Mr Rumpole.' Henry flipped through his book of engagements. 'There's a little murder down the Bailey. But that won't be for a few weeks.'

'Mysterious crime done with a broken Guinness bottle in a crowded pub in Kilburn. Routine stuff. Legal Spam!' I spoke of the 'little murder' with some contempt. 'It's a pity with all your talents as a clerk, Henry, that you can't find me something more exotic.'

'Perhaps you'd care to find your own exotica, if you're not satisfied with my clerking, Mr Rumpole!' Henry sounded distinctly nettled.

'I have done. A brief will be arriving, Henry, from Justitia International. I am defending the Minister of Home Affairs in the High Court of Neranga.' It sounded, as I said it, fairly impressive.

'You'll be away from Chambers?' I was afraid I detected a note of relief in Henry's voice, the clear inference being that it was not altogether a picnic clerking for Rumpole. 'Certainly I shall be away, Henry,' I reassured him. 'They will look round Inner London Sessions and they will find me gone. They will whisper, " Travels Rumpole East Away?"'

'You seem very cheerful about it, Mr Rumpole.' Dianne paused in her non-stop rattling of her typewriter.

'My camels sniff the evening, Dianne, and are glad,' I told her, and then turned, more confidently, to Henry. 'She Who Must Be Obeyed's old school friend, Dodo Mackintosh, will be coming for a short stay next week and I will have to miss the jollifications. Adventure calls, Henry, and how can Rumpole be deaf to it?' I moved to the door, anxious to be on my way. 'Send a cable if there's anything urgent.'

'A cable?' Henry sounded as though he'd never heard of the device.

'Or at least a pigeon.' As I finally left the clerk's room, a grey and unremarkable barrister called Hoskins came in and nearly knocked me over. 'Look out, Rumpole,' he said. 'Where are you going?'

I passed on, declaiming,

'For what land
Leave I the dim-moon city of delight?
I make the Golden Journey to Samarkand.'

'It's too bad, Rumpole. You'll miss Dodo,' Hilda said a few evenings later.

'Hilda! Africa is waiting. The smoke-signals are drifting up from the hills and in the jungle, the tom-toms are beating. The message is, "Rumpole is coming, the Great Man of Law." What message am I to send back? "Sorry, visit cancelled owing to the arrival of Dodo Mackintosh in Gloucester Road"?'

'But why *you*, Rumpole?'

'There was something to be said for the old days of the Empire. Almost all African politicians were students in the Temple. Gandhi started it.'

'Was Gandhi *African*?' Hilda quibbled.

'Maybe not. But they returned to their native bush with an intimate knowledge of the ABC tea-rooms, Pommeroy's Wine Bar and the Penge Bungalow Murders.'

'You'll have to have shots.'

74

'Why, Hilda? I'm not going to a war.'

'Against tropical diseases. I'll send you round to Dr MacClintock [this was our Scottish quack who had once tried to psychoanalyse my alleged libidinous tendencies] [See *Rumpole's Return*, Penguin Books, 1980] and I'll go to D. H. Evans in the morning and get three yards of butter muslin.'

'What on earth for?'

'Mosquitoes,' Hilda said darkly. 'We don't want to lose you to the malaria, Rumpole. And for heaven's sake don't eat lettuce.'

★   ★   ★

I had forgotten—one forgets pain so quickly—about the delights of long-distance air travel, which I have described, when I suffered it between London and Miami, as offering all the joys of the rush hour on the Bakerloo Line plus the element of fear. There I was now, packed into an airless cigar-shaped tube which hurtled through space playing selections from *The Sound of Music* or showing an unwatchable film about little green men from outer space. Now and again food, which after some careful processing had been robbed of all taste, was pushed in front of me by ladies in some type of paramilitary uniform, who had clearly been trained by a period of supervising a recalcitrant pack of Brownies. Eventually, with the aid of about four half-bottles of claret (Château Heathrow), I fell into a sort of coma, shot through with lurid and fearful considerations of the penalty for failure in the David Mazenze case. I mean, how do you do a case of capital murder? Death, if you ask a wrong question. Death, if you don't object to the right bit of evidence. Death, round every legal corner. How *can* you do it? Answer: do it like every other case. Win it if you can. Win it, or else. As I began to doze, I spoke to myself severely, 'Pull yourself together, Rumpole! There was a death sentence when you did the Penge Bungalow Murders. Your finest hour.' Penge... Death... We take the Golden Road... to the Death Penalty.

Claret-induced sleep began to overtake me when I was woken by the trumpet call of the Brownie supervisor.

'Wakey, wakey, sir! Don't we want our meal?'

The Customs Hall at Nova Lombaro's 'Mabile Airport', named, of course, after the Prime Minister, was a large echoing shed. Even at night it was breathlessly hot without air conditioning. I was crumpled, sweating, exhausted and still trembling in time to the engines and *The Sound of Music*. My mouth was dry, and as I lugged my red bag in which my wig and gown travelled, my battered suitcase and my briefcase towards a customs officer apparently wearing the uniform of a Major-General in the Neranga Army, I smelled the dry, sweet smell of Africa and felt, weakened as I was by lack of sleep, sudden and irrational fear.

'Object of visit?' The customs officer looked at me with considerable contempt.

'Justice,' I murmured sleepily and he pointed at my suitcase. 'Open!'

I struggled with the battered and rusty fastenings and then the case flew open, disgorging what seemed to be about a mile of white muslin, bought for me by Hilda at D. H. Evans.

'Your dress?' the customs officer appeared to be giggling.

76

'No. My mosquito net. My wife got it for me.' After the muslin, a whole chemist's shop of pill bottles was revealed.

'Drugs? *Stupefiants.*' The official was understandably suspicious, particularly when he discovered a hypodermic syringe which Dr MacClintock had supplied for me to give myself some 'shots in case of tropical disease'.

'Certainly not! Just my wife's going-away present.'

I might have been in serious trouble, but an extremely elegant African, whom I judged to be about forty, came up; he was wearing a grey suit with a silkish sheen to it, carrying a crocodile-skin briefcase, and smoking a cigarette through an ivory holder. He was followed by a porter with a couple of matching suitcases and surrounded by the aura of an enormously elegant aftershave. He had clearly jetted in from some Third World jamboree, and after he had exchanged a few words with the customs man in their native tongue, not only was his luggage passed, but my own traps were chalkmarked as fit for importation into Neranga. My deliverer looked at me in some amusement and said, 'Horace Rumpole?'

'A piece of him,' I admitted.

'I'm agin you in the Mazenze case. Looking forward to seeing how you Old Bailey fellows handle a homicide.' At which he flipped out a wallet and gave me a card on which was engraved, with many flourishes, 'The Honourable Rupert Taboro. Attorney-General of the Independent State of Neranga.' 'Anything you need,' Taboro said, 'just ask for the Attorney-General.'

'Thank you very much.'

'Don't mention it, old fellow. After all, we learned friends have got to stick together.'

The law officer swanned off and I humped my bags out of customs and was immediately greeted by a young man in a white shirt and dark trousers who had a huge glittering smile of welcome ready for me.

'Mr Rumpole?'

I admitted it again.

'I am Freddy Ruingo, sir, instructing solicitor. You got through all the formalities?'

'Surprisingly.'

'Come on, I'll take you to the car. Then we go to the prison. Then we have a reception David's wife and brother give for you. You'll meet the leaders of our Apu People's Party.'

'It sounds,' I said, 'an evening packed with excitement.'

* * *

So we walked out into the hot African night, and heard the deafening racket set up by insects, howling dogs, the starting of reluctant cars and the scream of brakes at unseen accidents. Freddy Ruingo piled my luggage into the boot of a rusty old Jaguar, whose rear window was a hole surrounded by splintered glass. I sat beside Freddy, still feeling that I was in a sort of dream, as he drove, very fast, out of the town and down a long pot-holed road surrounded by darkness, along which, regardless of the danger to their lives from my instructing solicitor's driving, a stream of people—women with loads on their heads or carrying babies, men laughing and pushing bicycles—were walking in an

78

endless procession.

'I can't understand why your Mr Mazenze hasn't got some smart British Q.C. to defend him,' I shouted over the rattling and roaring of the Jaguar.

'Oh, David believes in the very common man, Mr Rumpole,' Freddy Ruingo assured me. 'He just wanted some ordinary little lawyer like yourself. A perfectly lowly fellow.'

'Thank you very much!' I gasped as we ricocheted across a pot-hole.

'But someone typical of British justice. Quite incorruptible. Not draughty in this car, are you?'

'No!' In fact I was sweating and mopping my brow with the old red spotted handkerchief.

'Some clever Matatu chucked an assegai through the back window of my Jag. They fell out of the trees, those fellows,' Freddy said contemptuously.

None too soon we arrived at a long, low building in the middle of a collection of huts. It was, apparently, some District Police Headquarters, which was considered more secure than the prison in Nova Lombaro. After a considerable wait we entered the Superintendent's office and met another youngish African, wearing knife-edged grey flannel trousers, suede shoes and a blazer with brass buttons. He also sported what might well have been a rowing club tie. After he and Freddy had exchanged a few Nerangan greetings, this officer nodded in my direction and said, 'You've come to see David?'

'Let me introduce Mr Horace Rumpole. Barrister-at-law. Inner Temple.' Freddy did the honours. 'Superintendent Akimbu. Special Branch.'

'You see, we've got David at District Police

79

Headquarters,' Superintendent Akimbu explained. 'We don't want him mixed up with the plebs in Lombaro jail. You want to visit our dungeons, Mr Rumpole?'

He was smiling, but I looked back at him with strong disfavour. I had been warned of this by Miss Amanda Pinkerton in the Fleet Street trattoria. Human rights, I had already begun to suspect, might count for very little in Neranga.

'I want to see my client, yes.'

The Superintendent rose to his feet. He was taller than I had expected, and very thin. 'It's an honour to meet you, Mr Rumpole. You know Croydon well?'

'Not too well, actually.' I was a little taken aback by the question.

'I did six months with your Special Branch in London. The Old Baptist's Head in Croydon. Wonderful draught Bass! Remember me to it. This way please.'

He led me out of a side door and down a passage to another door guarded by a policeman in khaki shorts, who was carrying an automatic rifle.

'We've got your client chained to the wall in here.' The Superintendent was still smiling. 'Better watch out for the rats, you know, and the water dripping from the ceiling!' He nodded to the policeman, who unlocked the door. We were greeted by the sound of some celestial music, which David Mazenze later told me was his favourite Fauré *Requiem*. 'Justitia International,' the Superintendent said as he left Freddy Ruingo and me with our client. 'Poor dears. They have such vivid imaginations.'

The room we had been shown into was large and

80

airy. There were table lamps and a big electric fan, some of David Mazenze's own pictures hung on the walls and on a table were bottles of wine, a bowl of fruit and a gramophone, which was playing as we came in. There was a photograph of David's wife, Grace, and their children beside a pile of records. The man in the chair, smoking a pipe and listening to the music, hadn't moved as we came in, but now he stood up slowly, switched off the music and came towards us.

When I had known him he had been a young, rather over-eager African student. Now he was a grey-haired man who looked as if he had great reserves of physical energy and was a natural leader. His voice was low, melodious but compelling, and his manner was very gentle, as though he were used to getting his own way without being violently assertive.

'Dear old Horace Rumpole! What's your tipple? Bordeaux, if my memory serves me right?'

'I won't say no.'

'You too, Freddy?' I was looking round the room as David Mazenze set about opening what seemed to be a very reasonable bit of the château-bottled.

'Wait until they hear about this in Wormwood Scrubs!' I said.

'I have a few friends in the French Embassy,' David Mazenze handed me a glass.

'Your friends at Justitia however...' I drank, and decided it was probably the best glass of Margaux to be had in Central Africa.

'Such good chaps. If not all that experienced politically.' David Mazenze smiled.

'They said I'd find you in the Château d'If. With rising damp and the bread and water just out of

81

reach.'

'Even Dr Death wouldn't dare to do that to me.'

'Dr?'

'Le bon docteur Christopher Mabile. The Prime Minister whose culture is firmly founded on the Inquisition *and* the K.G.B.'

'Stirred up with some of the basic cannibalism of the Matatu tribe.' Freddy Ruingo had found a chair in a corner and was grinning at us over his claret glass.

'Forgive Freddy. He makes such primitive remarks! Tribalism is our curse, however. Just as the British class system is yours. Horace, do find yourself a pew, why don't you?' David Mazenze went back to his armchair, but I was wandering round the room looking at the titles of his books.

'P. G. Wodehouse.' I picked up a paperback.

'I think of England so often.' David Mazenze was puffing on his pipe. 'I long for your Cotswolds. If Dr Death ever lets me see them again. If I'm hanged, think of this, Horace. There is some corner of a Nerangan jail house that is forever Moreton-in-Marsh.' He took out his pipe and laughed. I thought that I had never seen a man facing a death sentence looking so confoundedly cheerful. I wondered if it was courage, or the certainty of innocence, or had he, perhaps, spent a day with the wine? It was time to get down to business, so I sat and started to undo the tape on my brief. David Mazenze waited politely for me to begin.

'The dead man. Bishop Kareele...' I thought that was as good a starting-point as any.

'A trouble-maker!' David Mazenze frowned slightly. 'As only an African bishop can be. He

82

wanted the Prime Minister's job. He wanted my job. He was always causing trouble between my Apus and the Matatu people. I told you, Horace. Tribal hatred is the curse of our politics!'

'The evidence is that you threatened him,' I was turning over the statements. 'You quarrelled outside the Parliament building and you said to the Bishop, "I'll kill you."'

'All right, I quarrelled with the man.' David Mazenze shrugged. 'He quarrelled with everyone.'

'Death is fixed at around 9.30 p.m. on the 13th. That's when the shots were heard. Where were you then, exactly?'

He knocked out his pipe, got up and walked over to the window, where he stood looking out into the noisy darkness.

'Does it matter?'

'Of course it matters.' I hoped he remembered my basic training on alibis.

'I had a speech to make the next day. An important statement of policy at our Apu People's Party Congress. I went out in my car to drive around and think about it.'

'What time did you go out?' I lit a small cigar and began to make some notes.

'I've said in my statement. About 8.30.'

'What time did you get home?'

'After eleven. My wife Grace made some coffee and we listened to music. I always listen to music for half an hour before turning in.'

'What was the speech?'

'What?' He turned round to look at me, apparently surprised by the question.

'What were you going to say?'

'It was a plea for friendship between the Apu and

83

the Matatu people. That we should all work together, for the good of Neranga.'

'Did you ever make it?'

'How could I? I was arrested.' He came and sat beside me. We were silent for a moment. Then he said, 'Well. How does it look to you?'

'Identification cases are always tricky. And I've known healthier alibis.' I suddenly felt very tired. The only thing I wanted to do was to clean my teeth, go to bed, pull the pillow round my ears and forget all about charges of capital murder.

'You won't win this on alibis,' David Mazenze said. 'You know what you'll have to rely on?'

'I would welcome suggestions.'

'On the Common Law of England! The Presumption of Innocence, you know what you taught me: the Golden Thread which goes through the history of the law. I like that phrase so very much.'

'You have a remarkable memory for what I told you at the crammers all those years ago.' I was flattered.

'A man is innocent until he's proved guilty. Better that ten guilty men should go free than one who is not guilty should be convicted, for to convict the innocent is . . .' The words sounded particularly convincing in his dark velvet voice, and I joined in the chorus, 'To spit in the face of justice.'

'Do you still use that one, Horace'—the Apu leader was smiling nostalgically—'in your speeches to the jury at the old London Sessions?'

'I must confess I do. From time to time. A jury in Neranga can't be much different.'

'Mr Rumpole.' Freddy Ruingo was about to say something, but the words of my favourite speech had banished exhaustion and started the adrenalin coursing through my veins. I stood and addressed the others as though they were the jury. 'The evidence calls for guesswork in this case, members of the jury,' I said and went on, warming to the occasion. 'Now you may pick the winner of the Derby by guesswork, but it is no way to bring in a verdict on a charge of *capital* murder against a fellow human being.'

'Steady on, Mr Rumpole.' Freddy Ruingo managed to get his word in. 'We have no jury.'

'No jury?' I was incredulous, appalled.

'You British abolished juries in murder cases when Neranga was still "New Somerset".' David Mazenze appeared to think it was something of a joke.

'*We* did that?' I was more appalled than ever.

'I must say, Dr Death followed your example quite enthusiastically,' Freddy admitted.

'No jury. And the Judge?'

'Worthington Banzana,' David Mazenze told me. '*Sir* Worthington. You remember that old judge, Horace? What did you say he always ordered for tea after death sentences?'

'Muffins. You mean Twyburne?'

'Exactly. Well, our Chief Justice is like your Mr Justice Twyburne.' He laughed. 'Only black!'

'And he is Dr Death's chicken. He will run for him, wherever he wants him to go.' Freddy Ruingo wasn't, I must admit, being particularly encouraging.

★ ★ ★

About half of my heavy task was done, and the day

85

seemed to have already lasted several years, when we left the Police House and bumped off, along what appeared to be Neranga's single road, to the Mazenze residence. There the leading lights of the Apu People's Party, or A.P.P., were, Freddy assured me, assembled to do honour to the great white barrister who had dropped out of the skies by courtesy of Justitia International.

When we got to the bungalow the sound of old pop records was mixed with the noises of the night. It didn't seem that the Mazenze family, or the Apu leaders, were sitting wrapped in gloom, stricken by the danger that hung over their hero's head. Freddy and I squeezed our way past a crowd of young men and girls in the open doorway and went down a passage towards a big comfortable room with doors which opened on to a verandah. The room seemed full of people, women in brightly printed cotton frocks, men in shirts and trousers, dancing, or drinking, or arguing, with children running among their feet. As I entered, the gramophone was immediately switched off and the assembled company burst into a verse of 'For He's a Jolly Good Fellow'. I stood propped against the doorway, smoking a small cigar, and praying that I shouldn't fall asleep standing there, like a horse.

'Beer? Seven-Up? Scotch on the rocks?' said Freddy Ruingo, who was minding me.

I chose beer, which Freddy brought back in the form of a cold tin of Tuborg. He also brought a placid, middle-aged woman, whose hair was just starting to turn grey, and introduced her as David Mazenze's wife, Grace.

'Mrs Mazenze.' I shook her hand. She looked at me trustingly.

'It is kind you came to us.'

'Nice of you to ask me.'

'You came to save David, I mean.'

'I can't promise that, you know.'

I began to feel the awful burden on the defending lawyer, the need to work miracles.

'David remembers you so well. He has often talked about you. He has so much faith in you.'

'I'll do everything I can. But in the end a barrister's not much better than his case.' Mrs Mazenze was looking at me, hurt by my lack of complete confidence. 'You can't make bricks without straw,' I told her.

'I don't understand.' She shook her head and there were tears in her eyes.

'What we could do with is a bit of evidence.'

Before I could tell her what I thought were the gaps in the case, however, we were interrupted by a tall, thinnish young African, brightly dressed in his native costume. His features were sharper than David's, his eyes narrower and his nose thinner, and when he spoke, his voice was higher and less melodious.

'Don't you worry, Grace,' he said to her, 'no one can hurt David. David is one of the immortals.' He turned and held out a hand to me; it had a pale palm and curiously long fingers. 'Welcome to Neranga, Mr Rumpole. Welcome to the home of the Apu people. I am Jonathan Mazenze, David's little brother.'

'Little John?' I found myself looking up at him.

'Oh yes. And was my big brother delighted to see you, his old hero from his student days! He said you used to tease the judges. He said you used to pull their legs unmercifully.'

'Well, I did pull a few judicial legs, I suppose.' I was yawning modestly.

'And that you always dropped cigar ash down your stomach.'

'Did he remember that?' I brushed a deposit about the size of the eruption of Vesuvius off my shirt front. At which point a woman who had been handing round plates of food came up to speak to Grace, who excused herself and left us. Jonathan looked after her and then turned to me.

'What did you tell Grace we needed to win the case for David?'

'A witness or two would be a help,' I muttered.

'What sort of witness do you want, exactly?'

'Someone who saw David Mazenze at the time of the murder. He says he was just driving round aimlessly, composing his speech.'

Jonathan laughed, apparently at the simplicity of my requirements. 'You want some fellows who saw him? I can arrange it. How many fellows do you want, half a dozen?'

I was too tired not to let my anger show. 'No, you can't arrange it! I want a witness who'll stand up in Court and tell the truth.'

'How very British you are, Mr Horace Rumpole!' Jonathan smiled down on me now.

'That's why I'm here, you know. As a representative of British justice.'

Jonathan suddenly stopped smiling. He spoke quietly, but with great intensity. 'David doesn't need all that humbug,' he said. 'He needs the anger of the Apu people. If David is found guilty there are three thousand Apus with their guns hidden in the bush who will rescue him in one hour! That's how we win this case, don't you worry, old barrister!'

'Really? I prefer to rely on the way we do it down the Old Bailey,' I said, somewhat coldly.

'Dr Death's gone too far this time. The Apu people are on the move!'

'And I must be on the move too,' I told him. 'Which way is the gents?'

Going to the lavatory in foreign parts is, in my limited experience, to take your life in your hands, but the Mazenze facilities were clean and efficient. There was a pile of old numbers of the *New Statesman* and *New Society*, caricatures of David on the walls, and all the basic comforts. It may be that I dropped asleep for a moment or two, and when I emerged the music had stopped. I was in the long passage which led to what must have been a back door open to the night. I caught a glimpse of a very beautiful young girl in African dress looking in, asking what seemed to be an urgent question. Grace Mazenze, who was standing with her back to me, said something and then closed the door, shutting out the girl. I stood watching, and Grace went back to the living room. I followed her to find the room was empty. The doors on to the verandah were open and all the guests, together with Grace, seemed to have moved out into the darkness, from which came a sound of rhythmic shouting.

When I moved on to the verandah, I saw that the night was filled with people, and there were rows of white eyes, white teeth, white shirts, glimmering. Jonathan Mazenze was standing above the crowd with his fist raised, chanting, 'AH . . . PU . . . AH . . . PU . . . AH . . . PU,' and the chorus of voices took up the chant.

'What's all this?' I asked Freddy Ruingo, who

89

had manifested himself beside me. 'A party political broadcast on behalf of the Apu People's Party?'

*　　　*　　　*

By the time I got to the old Majestic Hotel in Nova Lombaro, which was to be my home during the trial in Neranga, I felt to a great degree disorientated in time and space. I found it hard to remember where I was, or when I got there, or what time it might be. So I stood, swaying gently, in a hotel lounge which cannot have changed much since it was used by the white businessmen, farmers and district officers of 'New Somerset'. Only now there was a large, and no doubt obligatory photograph of the Prime Minister behind the reception desk, where there once must have been one of the Queen.

I was giving instructions for my morning call to the somewhat confused African porter behind the desk, when I was vaguely conscious of a tall, grey-haired Englishman in an old tropical suit who was moving towards me with a couple of middle-aged orientals in tow.

'Six o'clock call, please,' I said to the porter. 'Room 51. Mr Rumpole. R . . . U . . . M . . . P . . . O . . . L . . . E.'

'Mr Rumbold, I presume,' said the Englishman, who must have heard me.

'Rumpole.'

'All hail! I was dining with Mr and Mrs Singapore here. We all call each other after our countries, as diplomats, don't we, Mrs Singapore? I'm Mr Old England. Arthur Remnant, British High Commissioner. This is our notable British barrister. Remind me of your name again.'

'Rumpole.' I wondered how long I could keep this up. Mr and Mrs Singapore were smiling at me as though I had said something funny.

'I must invite you to the High Commission,' said the man Remnant. 'Our problem is, the cook's so terribly anglophile that everything tastes of Bisto. I say, it must be exciting for you, doing a murder trial, out *here*.' His voice sank to an eerie whisper. 'Topping!'

'Ripping!' I said. I supposed it was expected of me.

'No, I mean "topping".' Remnant explained with a smile. 'Swinging. We're so Victorian in Neranga. Full of Baptist chapels, and plum jam and the death penalty. The Black Cap does add a bit of zest to a murder trial, doesn't it?'

'I don't suppose my client thinks so.' The High Commissioner was beginning to sicken me a little.

'Well, I suppose not. You know, I was amazed when they gave permission for you to come here.' He started to move away from me with the Singapores. 'Christopher Mabile's got something up his sleeve. Such a brilliant politician. We could do with *him* in Commonwealth Relations. Anyway, welcome, Rumbelow. We'll throw a little cocktail for you!'

'How very topping!' I said to his back. It was my last word of the evening.

At last I went upstairs and pulled off my tie, which seemed to have become, during that endless evening, unreasonably tight. I heard the sound of driving rain and turned to the window. The curtain was blowing back, heavy rain was splashing the sill and the carpet. I closed the window, and looked for

91

a moment at the wet glass and out into the darkness. A few minutes later I was asleep.

*   *   *

It rained for the next three days. I sat in the hotel and ate large, indigestible meals that looked back to the days of New Somerset. Features of the menu were castle puddings doused in custard, and a large, trembling, pink blancmange. I studied weather reports, maps, and the characters of Nerangan politicians. I had a couple more inconclusive conferences with my client, who seemed anxious to discuss P. G. Wodehouse, my old cases, the shortcomings of UNESCO, the role of barristers in the Third World and the lasting benefits of British rule in the New Neranga; anything, in fact, except the small question of his defence. When I mentioned the trial he would smile, spend a good deal of time lighting his pipe and, as soon as possible, turn on the Fauré *Requiem*.

Freddy Ruingo took me to see the scene of the crime. It looked exactly like any other part of that endless, overcrowded road to Nova Lombaro. We didn't get out of the car, but a crowd of wet, black, shining children milled round us, demanding cigarettes. The rain came through the back window of the Jaguar, which Freddy hadn't yet been able to get mended.

The fourth day of my stay in Neranga started with blinding sunshine. I got out of a taxi, sweating in a black jacket and striped trousers, and carried my briefcase and red robe bag up the steps of the white-pillared portico of the British-built High Court of Justice. The steps were crowded with people, some faces I remembered from the night of the party, many more strange to me. At the top of the steps, resplendent in his bright cottons, stood Jonathan Mazenze. He was smiling and seemed to be leading the low chanting of the people around him. The syllables emerging were not 'AH . . . PU . . .' this time. Listening hard I could have sworn they were 'RUM . . . POLE!' I lifted a hand in salutation and went into the building.

The robing room in the Nova Lombaro High Court was a good deal more comfortable than that at the Old Bailey. It was a high room, with cedarwood lockers and long mirrors. An attendant in a white uniform made me a cup of Nescafé as I changed my shirt and prepared to put on the blunt execution of a winged collar. It was then that I realized that my packing, for all the medicines and mosquito nets I had bought, was lacking in one vital commodity.

'Damn,' I said aloud. 'Where do you get a front collar stud in Africa?'

'Right here, my learned friend.' Mr Rupert Taboro, Attorney-General and prosecuting Counsel, had stolen up beside me and was holding out a leather stud-box. 'I had a gross of these little chaps flown in from Harrods,' he said. 'Be my guest.'

'That's remarkably civil of you.' I took a stud and fixed the collar.

'Merely in accordance with the best traditions of the Bar. I see young Jonathan Mazenze had his friends from Rent-an-Apu out there to greet you.'

'Yes. I found it rather encouraging,' I told him. 'The people cheering on my victory.'

'*Your* victory?' Taboro smiled tolerantly at me.

93

'Do you really think that's what they want?'

And, before I could ask him what the hell he meant, he had glided away about his business.

*   *   *

Apart from the fact that all the faces under the white wigs, except for mine, were black, the Court was set out exactly as it is in the Old Bailey. Only the big, slowly revolving wooden fans on the ceiling, and the Court attendants in white uniforms and small red fezes, were different from the buzzing air conditioning and black-gowned ushers in England. The public gallery, instead of containing one old man in a mackintosh and a party of schoolgirls, was crammed with loyal members of the Apu tribe, prepared, if anyone gave them half a chance, to cheer for the prisoner.

The only other white faces in the Court belonged to half a dozen reporters from European papers who had come to report on the trial of a well-known African politician; and were hoping, no doubt, to be able to describe a further collapse of justice in a Third World state.

I had sat, during the Attorney-General's opening, staring up at our learned Judge. Sir Worthington Banzana was a small, broad-shouldered, stocky man, whom I judged to be about seventy years old. He had been more or less silent during the early stages of the trial, and had noticeably refrained from welcoming a visitor from across the sea to the Nerangan Bar. In fact he had hardly glanced in my direction. So I took a few notes and tried to calm a bubbling and over-eager Freddy Ruingo, who kept moving from his seat in front of me to whisper to

94

the prisoner in the dock. David Mazenze seemed strangely uninterested in the proceedings.

I glanced round the Court. I could see Mrs Grace Mazenze looking down at me with trusting anxiety from the public gallery. I turned away from her to look at the first prosecution witness, a plump young African in a crumpled suit, who was glistening with sweat as he answered the calm, reassuring questions of my learned friend, Mr Rupert Taboro.

'Are you Magnus Nagoma?'

'I am.'

'You are in government service?'

'I am Permanent Private Secretary to the Minister for Home Affairs.'

'The defendant is your boss?' Taboro glanced at the dock.

'He is, yes.'

'My boss...' The Chief Justice repeated in a deep and gravelly voice as he made a note.

'Do you remember a day last July when you went to meet your boss outside the Parliament building?' Taboro asked, smiling gently.

'I do, yes. He was there with Bishop Tareele. They were having an argument.'

'A heated argument?'

'Please don't lead!' I growled a warning from my seat.

'I hear my learned friend's objection.' Taboro smiled at the Judge, who looked at me for the first time. It was by no means a smile of friendliness. '*I* don't, I must confess.' He was tapping his pencil on his desk with suppressed irritation. 'Mr Rumpole! Is it no longer customary in England to stand on your hind legs if you wish to make an objection?'

I thought it right and proper to climb to my feet

95

at this juncture. 'Then I wish to object, my Lord, to a leading question.'

'It was very heated this argument, yes.' The witness burst in on our argument uninvited, and the Chief Justice smiled at me for the first time. 'Too late, I think, Mr Rumpole,' he said, and I subsided. What we had was undoubtedly a black version of Judge Bullingham, the terror of the Old Bailey, but somewhat quicker off the mark than his English equivalent.

'Did the defendant say anything to the Bishop?' Taboro was pursuing the even tenor of his way.

'Yes. He said "I'll kill you."'

There was a stir in Court, the usual reaction to a piece of important and damaging evidence, and the Judge was careful to repeat the words as he wrote them down. '"I'll kill you,"' he said.

'That's an old judicial trick,' I whispered to Freddy Ruingo, and then I suggested a little practical demonstration we might indulge in when I rose to cross-examine. The judicial pencil tapped again, and I was addressed from on high.

'Mr Rumpole,' said Sir Worthington menacingly. 'Please do not hesitate to rise if you have something to say.'

'I have nothing whatever to say, my Lord.' I rose to about halfway and then sank back in to my seat.

'Then it is customary to remain silent when seated. Did not your old pupil master teach you that? Was he not C. H. Wystan of the Inner Temple?'

I hadn't bargained for a Nerangan Chief Justice with an encyclopaedic knowledge of English barristers. He had even remembered the name of my sainted father-in-law, Daddy to She Who Must

Be Obeyed, who had guided my first faltering steps in his own inexpert sort of way when I first went into Chambers.

'What happened then, Mr Nagoma?' Taboro went on when the judicial rebuke was over.

'We got into the Minister's car,' the witness answered.

'Just you and Mazenze?'

'Yes.'

'What did the defendant say?'

'He said, "Who will rid me of this turbulent priest?"'

'And by "turbulent priest", who did you take him to mean?' Taboro was taking no chances.

'He meant the Bishop.'

'Yes. Thank you, Mr Nagoma.' Taboro sat down smiling. I took off my wig, applied the red spotted handkerchief to the brow, replaced the wig and rose to cross-examine.

'Mr Nagoma . . .' I started, and then, as arranged, Freddy tugged at my gown and whispered, 'This man is a Matatu. Naturally he is hostile to David.'

So I whispered angrily back, loudly enough for everyone in the Court to hear. 'Look, if you interrupt my cross-examination, I'll kill you!'

My Apu supporters in the public gallery took the point and laughed. The Chief Justice's pencil got to work again, and rapped the desk in an angry manner.

'Mr Rumpole. There is no jury here!' he reminded me.

'My Lord, I'm sorry we abolished that great institution.' I took the opportunity of denouncing a retrograde step.

'That was a jury trick you pulled quite

97

shamelessly, Mr Rumpole. It was not worthy of a former pupil of Mr C. H. Wystan.'

Not worthy of Wystan, a man who knew nothing whatever about bloodstains! I controlled myself with difficulty. 'It was not a trick. It was a demonstration.' I told the Judge. 'I am about to put the question to the witness.'

'Put it then, Mr Rumpole. Without play-acting please!'

It was too early in the case to quarrel with the Judge, and there was—oh the pity of it!—no jury. I addressed myself to the witness. 'Were not the words used to the Bishop just as I've used them to my learned instructing solicitor, as a bit of meaningless abuse?' I asked Nagoma.

'I don't know that, sir.'

'Do you not? And do you not know what they were quarrelling about? "The freedom of religious instruction in the Schools Enabling Bill". Apparently the Bishop was putting up what is known as a filibuster and talking for hours to delay matters.'

Taboro half rose, and made a funny. 'I'm sure that is a process well known to my learned friend,' he said.

The Chief Justice and the police officers and about half of the public, who were, no doubt, of the Matatu tribe, had an excellent laugh at this gem. When the hilarity had died down, I asked another question.

'It was a moment of irritation at some unparliamentary behaviour, isn't that so?'

'Mr Rumpole.' The Judge was serious again. 'The witness was *outside* the parliament building. How can he answer?'

98

'He can answer this. Was it meant seriously?'

Mr Nagoma, bless his heart, hesitated for a long time before he said, 'I don't know. Quite honestly.'

'Yes. Thank you, Mr Nagoma.' I was grateful. 'And when he said, "Who can rid me of this turbulent priest?" you recognized the quotation, I imagine?'

'Quotation? No.' Mr Nagoma looked blank and the Chief Justice's disapproval was turned on him for a change.

'Oh really!' The pencil was thrown down on to the desk on this occasion. 'It beats me how some of you fellows get into the Civil Service, let alone become Ministers' secretaries. Henry the Second said that of Thomas à Becket in the year—what year was it, Mr Rumpole?' For the first time he asked me a question which was not an attack.

'I don't immediately recollect.'

'Oh, I do. I recollect.' The wily old Judge had clearly known the answer all the time. 'It was 1170, I'm sure.'

But he had delivered himself into my hands. I looked hard at the foreign reporters, my only jury, and said loudly, 'And I'm sure Henry the Second was never charged with murder!'

I shouldn't have under-estimated Sir Worthington Banzana. He came back fighting with a smile and said, 'Although St Thomas à Becket, just like the unfortunate Bishop Kareele, found himself dead as mutton. Yes, Mr Rumpole?'

'No more questions, my Lord.'

I sat down and looked gloomily round the Court as Mr Nagoma left the witness-box with obvious relief, and a young clergyman, whose head seemed to emerge reluctantly from a dog collar several sizes

99

too large for his neck, replaced him. The darling old Chief Justice, I thought, was beginning to make me feel almost nostalgic for Judge Bullingham, and the fog descending comfortably on Ludgate Circus, and Henry sending me out to do a little V.A.T. fraud with absolutely no danger of anyone being condemned to death. I had never thought that the Golden Road to Samarkand would prove such hard going.

★   ★   ★

It was at about this time that, on the other side of the world, Mr Myers, my favourite solicitor's clerk, or 'legal executive', as they are called today, stepped into our clerk's room in Chambers with a brief concerning the unfortunate killing in the Kilburn pub.

'Mr Rumpole in, is he?' Mr Myers asked Henry.

'I think he just slipped out for a moment to Central Africa. You wanted to see him, Mr Myers?'

'Fixed this little murder of his—down the Bailey for the 21st of the month. 10.30 start.' Myers put the brief on Henry's desk. 'He will be there, won't he, Henry?'

'I'll get him back for you by then. Leave it with me, Myersy,' Henry assured him.

'Central Africa! What's Mr Rumpole gone there for?'

'I rather gather his wife's got a visitor at home.'

'Oh, well then. That explains it.' Mr Myers went on his busy way and Henry turned to Dianne and said, 'We've got to get Mr Rumpole back for the 21st, Dianne. We can't have him out there forever, not sunning himself in the tropics. What did he say, send him a cable?'

Dianne sighed, got out her pencil and notebook, and prepared to take dictation.

* * *

Across that angry or that glimmering sea I was cross-examining the Reverend Kenneth Cuazango, the young clergyman who had been driving Bishop Kareele on the night of the murder. In spite of the huge fans, the courtroom was growing more stifling as the day wore on, and the Chief Justice had fallen into a temporary silence.

'You say that when you first heard shots you jumped out of the car and ran with your head *down?*'

'Yes.'

'So you didn't see the attacker at that time?'

'No. I told you, sir. I saw him through the windscreen.'

'When you reached your house—after a run of how long?'

'About three miles. That's all.'

'Did you telephone the police immediately?'

'Almost immediately, sir.'

'Almost immediately,' the Judge muttered as he wrote.

'What did you do first, when you got home?'

'I changed my clothes first. I was soaked to the skin.'

'Exactly!' I picked up a sheet of paper supplied by Freddy. 'I have a metereological report here. There was heavy rain that night, was there not, between the hours of nine and eleven o'clock?'

'Didn't I say that?'

'No. I'm sorry, you didn't. And when it rains in Neranga it's not a gentle April shower, is it? It's a cataract!'

'Call it Noah's Flood?' The reverend young gentleman smiled.

'Why not? The windscreen was streaming with water, wasn't it? You couldn't possibly have identified my client!'

The Chief Justice, of course, couldn't resist an interruption. '*Could* you identify him?' He asked the witness, in a way that made the answer he wanted perfectly clear.

'I'm sure I could.' But the Bishop's chaplain didn't sound entirely convinced.

'I'm sure I could...' The Judge wrote down the words, but not the doubt, and looked at me. 'You see, Mr Rumpole?'

'I see, my Lord. But *he* couldn't.'

'Isn't that the fact which *I* shall have to decide?' The Chief Justice gave me a wide, and I thought dangerous, smile.

*　　*　　*

It had been a long, hot and hard day, and I sat in the big, empty lounge of the Majestic Hotel drinking cold beer. (Wine seemed to be served only in the confines of the prison, and a glass of whisky would have absorbed almost my entire fee from Justitia International.) I was trying to remember a bit of old Wordsworth, partly because it would stop me thinking of the trial, but mainly because it gave me an obscure feeling of comfort.

In the soothing thoughts that spring

102

Out of human suffering;
In the faith that looks through death,
In years that bring the philosophic mind.

But before the mind could become too philosophical, I was brought back to the matter in hand by the sight of Mrs Grace Mazenze being directed by the porter across the waste land of the lounge towards my table. She sat down, refused my offer of refreshment and seemed reluctant to start talking. At last she said, 'That Judge, sir! He wants to hang David.' I took a swig of beer, having no particular comfort for her. 'You said you needed evidence,' she went on.

'Yes.'

'A witness?'

'Your brother-in-law offered me any amount of useless ones.'

'Jonathan! He wants to make an Apu martyr of David.' She spoke with a sudden vehemence. 'I want my David alive, though.'

'Are you sure you wouldn't like a drink?'

'Nothing, thank you.' There was another silence, and then she said, 'I have a witness for you. One who tells the truth.'

'The best sort,' I assured her.

'Only one thing is wrong. David wouldn't allow this one witness to come for him. Not if he knew. He would forbid it.'

'Why ever . . . ?' I was puzzled.

'This is a person of the Matatu people. David would never agree to such a witness.'

'It's the evidence that matters, for God's sake. Not the family background.'

'You may know very much law, Mr Rumpole,

but you don't understand our country. Also, I'm afraid, David would not want this witness,' her voice sank almost to a whisper, 'for my sake.'

'For *your* sake?'

'This is something David try to keep a secret from me! Too late now for secrets. I think so.'

She opened a smart handbag she was carrying, a contrast to her bright African costume, and brought out a sheet of paper, covered with handwriting. I took it and looked at her. Then I read what had been written in primitive, badly spelled English and realized that bedtime would have to be indefinitely postponed.

*   *   *

An hour later I was sitting in David Mazenze's comfortably appointed cell in the District Police Headquarters. I was drinking wine, and thought he had probably drunk more than a bottle. He was playing music—not Fauré this time, but a Mozart piano concerto. I didn't show him the document I had read in the hotel, and some instinct stopped me telling him about it at once. So I sat for a minute in silence, staring into my glass.

'Don't look do down in the dumps, old fellow.' David Mazenze smiled at me.

'You may not have noticed, but the Chief Justice is against us.'

At which my client looked entirely unconcerned. 'A member of the Matatu tribe, and the Prime Minister's little chicken?' he said. 'Why shouldn't he be against an Apu leader? Everything is going as expected.'

'We've got to win this case.' I got up restlessly

and went for a walk round the cell.

'Don't worry, old fellow. You're doing exactly what is needed.' My client, I thought, was trying to cheer me up.

'What's that?' I asked.

'Upholding the best traditions of British justice for the foreign papers. When we lose, everyone will know this Dr Death has no respect for the law. So our revolution will be perfectly justified.'

I switched off Mozart. What he was saying had suddenly become too important for even the most enticing distraction.

'Your *revolution?*'

David Mazenze refilled his glass and drank deeply. 'Our boys in the bush, Horace, yes. They will attack on the day I am convicted. No sentence will ever be carried out against David Mazenze. Now then, has that taken a bit of a weight off your mind?'

'Not really.'

I felt entirely lost, aimless and deceived. I asked the question that had been nagging at me since our last inconclusive conference.

'Tell me the truth,' I said. 'Are you saying that I was brought out here to lose this case?'

'Calm down,' David Mazenze said soothingly. 'You were brought out here to make your speech about the Golden Thread, Horace.'

'And then to *lose?*' I stood in front of him, no longer able to control my temper, exhausted by the long, apparently pointless day.

'It will be Dr Death who loses in the end, Horace. And the Judge. Some of our boys in the bush are likely to pass a motion of censure on that old Chief Justice Banzana.'

'I was brought out here to *lose!*' I shouted at him in my certainty. 'No wonder you didn't want an important Q.C.! Old Horace Rumpole is good enough to utter a few legal platitudes, and accept defeat gracefully. Is that it? Look, I was going to tell you ...'

'Tell me what, Horace?' He went to the gramophone and turned the music on again. He sat and closed his eyes, apparently bored by our conversation. It was then that I decided on a course which was, I must reluctantly admit, entirely unprofessional.

'No. I see it wouldn't do any good,' I said. 'Do you know what the Golden Thread that runs through British justice is?'

'Yes, Horace. I know that,' David Mazenze murmured through the Mozart.

'Rumpole presumes every case to be winnable until it's lost. I don't know any other way of doing them. And you can tell that to your "Boys in the Bush".'

'Thank you for coming to see me, Horace. I appreciate your efforts.'

But I had knocked on the door and the guard was letting me out. From then on I would have to do the Mazenze case alone and without a client.

*   *   *

The next morning I found my opponent adjusting his wig in front of the robing-room mirror. He was smoking a black Balkan Sobranie cigarette in his white ivory holder. I waved the scrap of paper I had been given by Mrs Grace Mazenze in his general direction.

'My learned friend!' said Taboro, in a pitying sort of way. 'His Lordship is giving you a bit of a bully ragging, I'm afraid.'

'Look, I should have served you with an alibi notice. Under British law.' I started, ignoring the commiserations.

'Under our law too.'

'If I show you a statement, would you object to my calling the witness?'

Rupert Taboro took my precious document and glanced at it. The only sign of his surprise was the lift of about half an inch in the angle of his cigarette holder. He handed the statement back to me with a smile of absolute friendliness.

'I shall raise no objection at all to this witness being called, at short notice. See you in Court, old fellow.' So he left me, as I was wishing to goodness that my Judge was as sympathetic as my prosecutor.

Freddy Ruingo came up to me in the crowded passage outside the Court and said he'd been talking to David Mazenze, and that our client had decided that, as the charge was beneath his contempt, he was not going to give evidence. 'So it's up to you now, sir. The great final speech on the presumption of innocence. Isn't that it?'

'Not quite yet.'

'Not?'

'We may have to go through certain legal formalities first.'

As I pushed my way on through the crowd, I met Grace standing by the door of the Court. She told me that my witness was there, and ready to give evidence.

          ★   ★   ★

'I will now call Mrs *Mabel* Mazenze.' The Chief Justice made a note, the reporters looked interested, Freddy turned to me with a look of almost comic dismay, Jonathan rose in his seat in the public gallery and my client shouted, 'No!' furiously from the dock. The Court attendant called for silence, but David was struggling with the warder in the dock and insisting that he would not have the witness called. In a moment's silence I heard the tap of the Judge's pencil.

'The defendant will be silent or I will have him taken down below and the trial will take place in his absence. Yes. Continue, Mr Rumpole.'

'Mrs Mabel Mazenze!' I heard the call outside the Court.

And then the young African girl came in and the Court was hushed; everyone was staring at her remarkable beauty. I remembered the glimpse I had had of her face, through an open door at the end of a passage, on that first night I had arrived in Neranga. She was in the witness-box now, holding up the Bible in a slim, brown hand.

'Are you Mabel Mazenze?' I asked her, when she had been sworn.

'Yes.'

'Mrs Mabel Mazenze. Are you a lady of the Matatu tribe?'

'Is she Matatu woman? Is that what you mean, Mr Rumpole?' the Chief Justice rumbled in the background.

'I was trying to put it a little more elegantly, my Lord.'

The Judge turned to the witness. 'Don't mind

108

the elegance. You Matatu woman?'

'Yes, sir.' She gave him a glittering smile.

'And are you married to David Mazenze, the defendant in this case?'

I heard the Court buzz. The reporters were writing, Apu supporters in the public benches were looking shocked and puzzled. Rupert Taboro looked at the ceiling. Grace looked severely at the witness.

'The officer in charge has told us that your client's wife is called *Grace* Mazenze, Mr Rumpole.' The Chief Justice registered elaborate surprise. I obliged him by asking the witness, 'Did he also go through a ceremony of marriage with you, according to the tribal customs of the Matatu people, on the 8th of March, 1979?'

A door banged somewhere behind me. It was Jonathan Mazenze leaving Court.

'Yes, he did,' the witness agreed. 'David and I did. We kept it secret. Both our people would make us great mischief if they knew of it. And David having a wife of his own people also...' Her voice trailed away as she looked round the Court, to meet hostile Apu eyes.

'The 8th of March this year was the anniversary of that ceremony. Where did David spend that evening?' I asked her.

'With me,' she answered clearly.

'Where was he between nine and eleven that rainy evening?'

'In my ... in our house, here in Nova Lombaro. He was with me from before nine o'clock.'

'When did he leave?'

'About quarter past eleven. He went to sleep in his bed at home with Grace as he had a big speech to make the next day. He thought with me he would not do so much sleeping.'

Mabel looked round the Court, smiling. There was some laughter, but not from the Apu spectators. Grace looked at her with a sort of solemn curiosity, as I asked, 'Has it been difficult for you to come here and give evidence?'

'I think my family never see me again when they know what I did with an Apu man,' Mabel answered seriously.

'*Why* have you come here to give evidence?'

'Only because I know David cannot have killed the old man. Only because of that.' She looked at the prisoner in the dock. He avoided her eye. 'And to save his life...'

'Thank you, Mrs Mabel Mazenze.' I sat down and the Chief Justice asked the Attorney-General if he wished to cross-examine the witness. To my extreme surprise Rupert Taboro said that he had no questions to ask. I rose to my feet, determined to make the most of the situation.

'Perhaps my learned friend would help me. Does that mean that the prosecution accepts this witness's evidence?'

'It simply means, my Lord,' Taboro said in his most treacly voice, 'that we have no questions we wish to put.'

'I must insist...'

But the Chief Justice looked down on me and smiled mirthlessly. 'No good insisting, Mr Rumpole. In the end it will be a matter entirely for me!'

★   ★   ★

I wasn't able to deal with the Judge's remark until after the prosecutor's final speech, which was a fair and reasonable summary of the facts. After he had finished I made my own oration, and I must say it was one of my best, along familiar lines perhaps, but given a feeling of freshness by being made in unfamiliar surroundings. The Court was very quiet. My client was sitting in the dock with his head in his hands. Perhaps, I thought, he had given up hope, but I hadn't. I reached my peroration and I said:

'It is *not* a matter entirely for your Lordship.' And I said it fearlessly. 'It is a matter for our Common Law! And when London is but a memory and the Old Bailey has sunk back into the primeval mud, my country will be remembered for three things: the British Breakfast, *The Oxford Book of English Verse* and the Presumption of Innocence! That presumption is the Golden Thread which runs through the whole history of our Criminal Law—so, whether a murder has been committed in the Old Kent Road or on the way to Nova Lombaro, no man shall be convicted if there is a reasonable doubt as to his guilt. And at the end of the day, how can any Court be certain sure that that fearless young woman Mabel Mazenze has not come to tell us the plain and simple truth?'

When I had finished I sat down exhausted. My shirt was sticking to my back. I felt I had made a long journey, and I was now tired out, with nowhere further to go. Had I, I wondered for a low, despairing moment, made the great 'Golden Thread' speech for the last time? Was it some irony of fate, some obscure joke, that I should make it finally before a Court full of strange faces in the middle of Africa? I told myself that I had done all I could, that I had said every possible word in David Mazenze's defence, that the decision to call Mabel was inevitable.

But then I thought of the consequences of any mistake I might have made, and I found myself shivering in the stifling Court. Through all this the Chief Justice had been summing up, going through the facts of the case, and his voice seemed to be coming from a long way off. I forced myself to pay attention and, at first, I wished I hadn't.

'Neranga ranks high on the list of civilized countries,' the deep judicial voice was saying. 'We observe the rule of law. This is demonstrated by the fact that we have allowed a barrister in from England. He is a "junior" barrister. In England they have quite elderly "juniors", barristers as "long in the tooth", he will not mind my saying this, as Mr Horace Rumpole.'

There was some sycophantic laughter from parts of the Court, in which, I was sorry to see, my learned friend Mr Taboro joined.

'Mr Horace Rumpole has come to plead here,' the Judge went on, 'as a guest at our Bar. But he has told us nothing we didn't already know. We know that a man is innocent until he's proved guilty. That is the Golden Thread which runs through the law of Neranga. This law is also followed in Britain, I believe. The Court has the evidence of identification given by the Reverend Kenneth Cuazango. On the other hand, we have the positive evidence of Mabel Mazenze, the Matatu woman whom the defendant, a well-known member of the Apu tribe, has married as a second wife—a backward form of indulgence which is not in the

112

best tradition of the New Neranga of Prime Minister Christopher Mabile. In these circumstances the Court is unable to feel that the prosecution has proved this case beyond reasonable doubt. Acting entirely on the principles of ancient Common Law, we pronounce on David Mazenze, whatever we may think of his morality, a verdict of "Not Guilty". Let the defendant be discharged.'

'Be upstanding in Court!' the attendant shouted.

We all stood and, as he left us, I bowed low, and with astonished gratitude, to the Chief Justice, Sir Worthington Banzana. I seemed to be bowing in the middle of an enormous silence. Then the Court began to empty quickly. I saw David Mazenze leaving the dock and, planning to meet him when he had received his congratulations, I turned to Freddy Ruingo.

'We did it, Freddy!' I smiled at him. 'We notched up a triumph, I'm sure you'll agree. We brought the Golden Thread to Samarkand!' But Mr Ruingo had made off and was dodging away among the crowd as though in some maze. The kindest word was spoken to me by my opponent, who came up smiling. 'Good win, my learned friend,' he said. 'Heartfelt congratulations.'

'Thank you. You were a great help.' I meant it. 'I'd better go and see my client.'

I moved away, but Taboro put a hand on my arm. 'I should warn you, old fellow. You may not find him particularly grateful.'

'I *did* save his life.' I looked at him, puzzled. But Taboro shook his head sadly. 'You also broadcast the fact that the leader of the Apu People's Party had got himself hitched to a Matatu woman. Not too good that, politically speaking. But then, I

113

don't suppose you're tremendously interested in local politics. Oh, before you go,'—he held out a well-manicured hand—'could I have my stud back, please?'

I took off my collar then and there and gave it to him. It seemed that I owed quite enough to Rupert Taboro.

I went up to the robing room to change, and met no one except the attendant in charge of wigs and gowns, who also seemed aloof, as though anxious to get me out of his domain as soon as possible. When I came downstairs the passage outside the Court was empty and silent.

I came out on to the steps of the Law Courts, and was hit in the face by the heat and blinding sunshine. And as I stood there blinking, two Nerangan policemen in khaki shorts with revolvers bumping against their hips, came running towards me. They grabbed my arms and hustled me, too astonished to protest, into a waiting police car. The engine roared, the tyres screeched on the burning road, and we were off, scattering chickens and children and the remnants of a crowd. It had happened at long, long last. After an endless career in crime, I was under arrest.

Of course I always knew I'd end up in the Nick. It was my nightmare, a recurring dream from the days when I was a nipper. I could hardly close my eyes without hearing a voice somewhere saying, 'And the least sentence I can possibly pass on you is about a hundred years in the chokey.' Extraordinary thing, perhaps that's what made me take up the law. These thoughts were racing, in a confused fashion, through my head as I was hustled into the presence of Mr Akimbu, the blazered

114

Superintendent of Police. He was holding a cable and looking at me with extreme hostility. 'Mr Rumpole. Will you please explain this cablegram which we have intercepted. Addressed to you, I think, at the Hotel Majestic.'

I took the document in question, looked at the signature and felt a flood of relief. Of course, I realized that the thing could have been phrased more happily.

'Please take your time—we have the whole night before us.'

The Superintendent's words were not particularly encouraging. I read him the message on the cable: '"Murder fixed for 21st of this month at 10.30 a.m. Signed Henry."'

'What murder, Mr Rumpole? And who is your associate, "Henry"?'

Akimbu stood up and moved towards me. I felt a sense of pleasurable anticipation from the policemen by the door. The interrogation was about to begin.

'Good heavens. This is really very funny!' I smiled round the room, and got no reaction.

'Funny? You find murder "funny", Mr Rumpole?'

'No. No, of course. It *is* a real murder. A very real murder.' I heard myself babbling. I clearly had no talent for being interrogated.

'The 21st. That will be...' The Superintendent examined a calendar on the wall. 'Ten days from now.' He turned on me triumphant.

'Ten days from now I shall be back in England. No need for you to worry.'

'Leaving the dirty side of the business, I suppose,' the Superintendent almost sneered, 'to

115

this Henry.'

At which moment an intercom buzzed on his desk. The Superintendent answered with a Nerangan word, and a moment later a police officer opened the door to admit Arthur Remnant, Her Majesty's High Commissioner to the State of Neranga.

'There you are, Rumbold!' He came in smiling. 'You know what, my dear fellow, you need a good lawyer!'

★   ★   ★

I was booked back on the midnight plane. Earlier in the evening I was invited for cocktails at the High Commission. There was a fair sprinkling of guests—politicians, the Head of Nerangan Radio and his good lady, and some leading members of the Nerangan Bar, who smiled at me in a knowing sort of way but otherwise avoided my company. I stood under a portrait of the Queen and drank a reviving whisky and soda. Remnant looked at me as though it would take him a long time to get over the joke and said, 'It was a splendid result. Just what our brilliant Prime Minister always had in mind!'

'The Prime Minister wanted me to *win*?' I confess I wasn't following his drift.

'Just the way to please the International Monetary Fund, old fellow, and reassure Barclays Bank, and put Christopher Mabile in line for a "K" at the next Commonwealth Prime Ministers' Conference. You've probably earned him a bally knighthood, apart from the fact that you've seen off David Mazenze.'

'Seen him off? I was under the impression that

116

I'd got him acquitted.' Never had a remarkable victory, I thought, been met with such a singular lack of acclaim.

'The Apus would never have let him hang,' Remnant explained patiently, as to a child. 'They'd have risen in their thousands—plenty of guns available in the bush, didn't they tell you? But they're a lazy people. Nothing in today's verdict to get them going. And they won't move a finger for a leader who married a Matatu woman.'

'Just a minute. I want to know...' But Remnant was moving away from me.

'What do you want to know, old fellow?'

'Who shot the Bishop?'

'The poor old Bishop! A politician who had outstayed his welcome. Of course, we'd know exactly what to do with him in England. Too bad there's no House of Lords in Neranga.'

'There you are, Mr Horace Rumpole.' I heard a deep and familiar voice behind me and turned to see a small, smiling Chief Justice. Beside him stood a man in bright African costume. The lights of the room reflected in his thick horn-rimmed glasses and made it impossible to see his eyes. I needed no introduction to tell me that I was in the presence of the Prime Minister, Dr Christopher Mabile, my former client's 'Dr Death'.

'Congratulations, Mr Rumpole.' The Prime Minister's voice was dry, academically precise. 'I hear you put up a first-rate show. You know the Chief Justice, of course. Your old sparring partner!'

They both looked at me as though I were a rare specimen who might soon become extinct.

'It has been a pleasure to have a British barrister among us,' the Prime Minister said. 'When are you leaving us?'

'Tonight.'

'Such a short visit! You should have stayed longer. Gone up country. We could have shown you some of our old tribal customs.'

'Thank you, Prime Minister,' I told him. 'I think I've seen them.'

*   *   *

It was only a week later, at breakfast in Froxbury Court, when I saw in *The Times* newspaper a photograph of a small part of the road to Nova Lombaro. The picture showed a battered car, riddled with bullets. The door was swinging open, and in the passenger seat was the crumpled, murdered body of David Mazenze, the former leader of the Apu People's Party, an organization which had now been taken over, so the story under the photograph informed the *Times* readers, 'by the deceased's younger brother, Mr Jonathan Mazenze'. The story ended, 'No arrest has yet taken place, according to the Attorney-General, Mr Rupert Taboro.' Neranga, quite clearly, was still a country which believed in the death penalty.

When I read the story out to Hilda all she said was, 'Mazenze ... Apu ... Rupert Taboro ... what extraordinary names.'

'Yes,' I said, 'almost as odd as Rumpole and Dodo Mackintosh.'

The world news was bad that day. Hilda's old school friend was still with us, sitting on the other side of the kitchen table, regarding me with pursed lips and an expression of disapproval.

'Wasn't it good of Dodo to stay on another week,'

Hilda said, 'so you could see something of her?'

I gulped my coffee, got up and struggled into my jacket. 'Well, off to work!' I said as brightly as possible.

'You will be home early, won't you, dear? Dodo does like her game of three-handed whist, you know.'

I was on my way to the door, planning a leisurely aperitif at Pommeroy's Wine Bar.

'Anyway, where are you going today?' said She Who Must Be Obeyed.

'I'm going to the Old Bailey,' I answered her. 'Samarkand is definitely off.'

RUMPOLE AND THE OLD BOY NET

To call the public school where I spent some of the worst years of my life 'minor' would be to flatter it. It was a small, poorly run penal colony on the Norfolk coast where the water habitually froze in the bogs and, on one remarkable occasion, we all believed, turned the glass of Milton, which contained the Headmaster's teeth, into a solid block of ice. Such education as was on offer had to be wrung out of reluctant masters whose own ambition was to rush from the classroom and huddle round the common room fire. It's true that Jimmie Jameson, a somewhat primitive type of Scottish Circuit Judge, had been to Linklaters, as, for a short spell when his parents were abroad, had old Keith from the Lord Chancellor's office. Apart from having once been asked to organize the Old Linklaters at the Bar [See 'Rumpole and the Fascist Beast' in *The Trials of Rumpole*, Penguin Books, 1979], I have never had much to do with my old school acquaintances, and having possessed the Old Linklater tie (I used it to secure a bulky set of books I was taking by train to a case in Chester about thirty years ago and haven't seen it since) has never helped me in the slightest degree on my way through life. Say 'I'm an Old Linklater' to most men of power and influence in this world, and their answer is most likely to be 'Mine's a Scotch.'

It is not so, of course, with the great public schools such as Eton, Harrow, Winchester and Lawnhurst. Having 'swung, swung together, with their bodies between their knees' at school, the

121

ex-pupils of such places are liable to stick to each other for the rest of their natural lives. No sooner have they left school, but they meet up again in the Cabinet, or the House of Lords, or on the Board of the United Metropolitan Bank, or perhaps at an address in Barnardine Square which, as you may or may not know, is not a million miles from Victoria Station.

But I am going too fast. I should watch his Lordship's pencil, or my rapidly fading biro. All I wished to bring to your attention at the moment is the remarkable loyalty, as some would say, or the unspeakable clannishness, as others would hold, of the English public school system. Now I would ask you to turn, as my wife Hilda did on that gusty March morning at breakfast time in our mansion flat at 25B Froxbury Court, to the news pages of the *Daily Telegraph*. Hilda takes the *Telegraph*, although I prefer the Obituaries and the crossword in *The Times*. The *Telegraph* gives Hilda much that she needs, including detailed coverage of many scandalous events. On that particular morning the stories on offer in Hilda's favourite journal included one entitled, 'London Vice House Catered for Top People', and described the committal at the Central Criminal Court of a couple named Lee, on charges of blackmail and keeping a disorderly house.

'Can you understand it, Rumpole?'

'Understand what, Hilda?' I was spreading butter on my toast and couldn't see that the news item presented any form of intellectual challenge.

'These members of the aristocracy, top civil servants, and a vicar! Well really, haven't they got wives?' No doubt she was referring to the patrons of the Lee house in Barnardine Square.

122

'Life at the top isn't all roses, Hilda. Is that the marmalade gone to ground under your *Daily Telegraph*?'

'Well! Surely a wife's enough for anyone.'

'Quite enough,' I said, munching toast and Oxford marmalade.

'So why—run after other women?' Hilda seemed genuinely puzzled.

'I must confess, I'm baffled.' It was, I supposed, decidedly rum. I stood up, finishing my toast. Hilda looked at me critically, apparently finding that I might come last in any contest for the best-dressed barrister.

'Rumpole,' she said, 'come here. You've got marmalade on your waistcoat!' She fetched a damp teacloth from the kitchen sink and started to dab at me in a violent manner.

'I quite like marmalade on it,' I protested.

'You've got to be careful of your appearance now Guthrie Featherstone's been made a judge.'

'Out of respect to the dead?' I wasn't following her drift.

'Because you're going to take your rightful place, now Guthrie's gone, as Head of Chambers! Well, they said they'd come to a final decision, didn't they, when you got back from the jungle?'

'It wasn't the jungle, Hilda. It was the High Court of Neranga. Chief Justice Sir Worthington Banzana presiding.'

Hilda, however, pursued her own train of thought and disregarded the connection. 'There isn't another Q.C. to take Guthrie's place. You're the only candidate! I shall ask my friend Dodo Mackintosh to take on the catering at your first Chambers party. Marigold Featherstone will never

123

have put on a do like it.'

I sighed. 'Those occasions are quite grim enough without Dodo's rock cakes.'

'Nonsense. Dodo's pastry's as light as a feather.' She stood back, apparently noticing some sartorial improvement in my good self. 'There now. You look more like a Head of Chambers! Someone fit to take the place Daddy once occupied!'

I beat it hastily to the door. Hilda hadn't noticed that, for the sake of greater comfort after my return from Africa, I had taken to wearing a delightful old pair of brown suede shoes with the dark blue suit I wore when I wasn't actually engaged in any of Her Majesty's Courts of Justice. Whilst I was working in Chambers I hoped that the Sovereign wouldn't notice my feet.

∗   ∗   ∗

About an hour later I put my head round the door of the clerk's room in Equity Court and saw Henry checking the diary and Dianne busily decorating her fingernails with some preparation that smelled of model aeroplanes.

'This be the verse you grave for me:
"Here he lies where he longed to be;
Home is the sailor, home from the sea,
    And the hunter home from the hill!"'

I announced.

'You're back then, Mr Rumpole.' Henry scarcely lifted his eyes from the diary.

'And not much thanks to you, Henry,' I said. 'That idiotic cable you sent me to Africa! I was

124

almost dragged off to execution.'

'It was my duty to keep you informed, sir, about your position at the Old Bailey.'

'They thought I was going to *do* a murder. Not appear in one.'

'Oh really!' Dianne gave one of her silvery laughs. 'How dreadful!'

'Anyway,' said Henry, who didn't seem to appreciate the dire effects of his message. 'That murder's gone off. It won't be this term.'

'I came back ready for anything. Are you trying to tell me there's no work, Henry?' I started to open the various bills and circulars which had been awaiting my return.

'Oh, it's not as bad as that, sir. Mr Staines rang. He wanted a con. today, in the bawdy house case, R. *v.* Lee.'

My heart leapt up at the sight of what might be said to be a bit of a *cause célèbre*.

'Keep thy foot out of brothels, Henry! Such places are no doubt more entertaining to litigate about than to visit. Tell Stainey that I'm ready for him.' I did a quick sorting job on my correspondence. 'On Her Majesty's Service! Hasn't our gracious Queen anything better to do than to keep writing me letters?' I shed a pile of expendable mail and opened another envelope. 'What's this? A communication from L.A.C.! "Lawyers As Churchgoers—Moral Purpose in the Law—A Call to Witness for all Believing Barristers"!' I let that one follow the circulars. 'Brothel case, eh? Not much danger of finding a moral purpose in that, I suppose.'

At this point Claude Erskine-Brown came into our clerk's room, started to collect his letters, and

125

looked up to see the traveller returned.

'Rumpole! We thought you'd gone native. We pictured you ruling some primitive tribe under a bong tree!'

'Most amusing, Erskine-Brown!' I gave him a rapidly disappearing smile. 'Well, now I suppose I've got to take over the extremely primitive tribe in these Chambers?'

I realized that She Who Must Be Obeyed would never let me hear the last of it if I didn't claim my rightful place as Head, now that Guthrie Featherstone had been translated.

'We're deciding the Head of Chambers problem at the end of the month. When we have our meeting.' Erskine-Brown was always a stickler for formality.

'And after that I'll have to shoulder the cares of office. No one in Mr Justice Featherstone's old room, is there, Henry?'

'I don't think so, but...'

I had left him and was going up to take possession of the Captain's Quarters before he could finish his sentence. However, as I was mounting the stairs, Erskine-Brown came panting after me; apparently he had something to communicate in the deepest confidence.

'Horace. I think I should let you know. I've done it!'

'Then your only course is to plead guilty.' I gave him sound legal advice, but the fellow looked distinctly miffed.

'I have applied for silk, Rumpole,' he said with dignity. 'I think I've got a reasonable chance. Philly's right behind me.'

'I can't see her.' I looked behind him in vain.

126

'I mean,' he said, with some impatience, 'my wife is right behind me in my application for silk. "Claude Erskine-Brown, Q.C." How do you think it sounds?'

'Pretty encouraging, if you happen to be on the other side.' He looked displeased at that, so I went on brightly, 'Tell me, Claude. When is this Q.C. business likely to happen?'

'In about six weeks' time.'

'*After* the decision as to Head of Chambers?'

'Yes. I suppose so. After that.'

'Well, that's all right then. Best of British luck.'

I gave the man a reassuring slap on the shoulder. Of course, if he were to acquire a silk gown before the Chambers meeting, Claude would be entitled to that position which Hilda had set her heart on for me. As it was, I could see no way of stopping the 'Rumpole for Head of Chambers' bandwagon. I entered into my inheritance, Guthrie Featherstone's old room, and heard the sound of a woman in tears.

The woman in question was, in fact, no more than a mere slip of a girl. She was wearing dark clothes, had longish dark hair and, from what I could see of her face, she was extremely personable. At that moment she was in clear distress; her eyes were pinkish, she was dabbing at them with a small handkerchief which she had wound into a ball, and an occasional sob escaped her.

'I'm sorry.' I didn't quite know why I was apologizing; perhaps it was because I had intruded on private grief. 'Can I help at all?'

She looked up at me guiltily, as though I had caught her doing something wrong. 'I thought it was all right to come in here,' she excused herself. 'Doesn't this room belong to a judge who doesn't

127

come here any more?'

'Bare ruin'd choirs, where late old Guthrie sang. Yes, that's right.' I was overcome by curiosity. 'What's the trouble? Shoplifting? You look too young for a divorce.'

'I'm a b . . . b . . . barrister.' She sobbed again.

'Oh, bad luck!' I was sorry it seemed to be causing her such distress, and I offered her a large red-and-white spotted handkerchief as a back-up to the sodden ball of lace she was clutching.

'I'm Mrs Erskine-Brown's pupil. Thanks.' She dabbed her eyes again.

'Mrs Erskine-Brown, Phillida Trant that was, the Portia of our Chambers? Miss Trant now has a pupil? How time flies!' Much had happened, it seemed, during my absence in the tropics.

'She left me in a case after lunch at Tower Bridge. Well, there was a terrible argument about the evidence and I said I couldn't do it without my learned leader, Miss Trant, who was in a difficulty.'

'You should have plunged in—taken your chance,' I told her.

'And the Magistrate said, "What sort of difficulty?" and I said, "I think she's still at the hairdresser."'

I could understand our Portia's irritation with her tactless and inexperienced pupil. 'You forgot the most important lesson at the Bar,' I told her. 'Protect the private life of your learned pupil master—*or* mistress.'

'Now Mrs Erskine-Brown says I'm wet behind the ears and I'd better get a nice job in the Glove Department at Harrods. She says that they probably won't want another woman in Chambers anyway.' She gave one final sniff, and handed me

128

back my handkerchief.

'Got a name, I suppose?' I asked her.

'Fiona Allways.'

'Well, it's not your fault,' I comforted her.

'It's all I've ever wanted to *be*,' Fiona Allways explained. 'When the girls at school wanted to ride show-jumpers, I just stood in front of the mirror and made speeches in murder cases!'

I looked at her, made a decision and went to sit behind Featherstone's old desk.

'I've got a conference later. You could take a note of it, if you'd like to. Make yourself useful. No particular objection to prostitution, have you?' To my dismay she seemed to be about to cry again. 'Well, what on earth's the matter now?'

Miss Allways looked at me, fighting back her tears, and said, 'I suppose that's all you think I'm fit for!'

*   *   *

The police had been keeping observation on the Lees' large Victorian house in Barnardine Square for weeks. They had chronicled, in boring detail, the visits of a large number of middle-aged men of respectable appearance to that address and had seen girls arrive in the morning and leave at night.

On the day of the arrest, a particularly respectable middle-aged man arrived on the doorstep, rang the bell, and was heard to say in to the door speaker, 'I'm a caller. Come to visit a friendly house.' He was a man who would subsequently become unknown to the world as 'Mr X'. As the door was opened, police officers invaded the house and flushed out a large number of distinguished citizens in positions of unusual friendliness with certain youngish ladies. Mr X was asked for his name and address and subsequently gave a lengthy statement to the police. Both Mr Napier Lee, the owner of the premises, and his wife, Mrs Lorraine Lee, were present when the police raided. Mr Lee protested and said that an Englishman's home was, after all, his castle. Mrs Lee asked if the matter couldn't be dealt with in a civilized manner, and invited the officers to take a nice cup of Earl Grey tea. Now Mr and Mrs Lee were in conference with my learned self; also present were Mr Staines, our solicitor, and Miss Fiona Allways, who had so far recovered her spirits as to be able to take a note.

'Apart from the little matter of keeping a disorderly house,' I reminded the assembled company, 'there's an extremely unpleasant charge of blackmail.'

'Demanding money with menaces. I have explained that to the clients,' said Mr Staines.

'Neither Napier nor I can understand anyone saying that about us, can we, Nappy?' Mrs Lee sounded deeply hurt. 'All our clients are such awfully decent people. Public school, of course, and I do think that makes *such* a difference.'

This Madame, I thought, would appear to be the most appalling old snob. I looked at my visitors. Mr and Mrs Lee were the sort of genteel, greying couple you might meet any day at the Chelsea Flower Show. He was wearing an elderly tweed suit, meticulously polished shoes, and what I later assumed to be an Old Lawnhurst tie. Mrs Lee was in twinset and pearls, with a tweed skirt and brogues. Only Mr Staines, the solicitor, who

130

affected striped suits and a number of rings, looked anything like a ponce.

'All our visitors are thoroughly good sorts, Mr Rumpole,' Mr Lee assured me. 'All out of the absolutely top drawer, not a four-letter man among them! And I'll tell you something else my lady and I have noticed, haven't we, Lorraine?'

'What's that, Nappy?' His wife smiled vaguely.

'Absolutely no side. I mean, they come into our home and behave just like one of us.'

'I'm sure they do,' I murmured.

'Napier was at Lawnhurst,' Mrs Lee told me proudly. 'Down for it from birth, weren't you, Nappy?'

'Oh yes. The guv'nor put me down for Lawnhurst at birth.'

We had had enough, I thought, of childhood reminiscences, and I spoke a little sharply. 'Mrs Lorraine Lee, Mr Napier Lee, it may be all very pleasant to sit here, over a cup of tea, and discuss the merits of the public school system, but you are charged with obtaining money by threats from a certain...'

'Please, Mr Rumpole!' Mrs Lee held up her hand in a call for discretion.

'There's no need to name names, is there?' Mr Napier Lee asked anxiously.

'Not when it comes to a man in his position.' Mrs Lee was referring, deferentially, to the future 'Mr X'.

'Lawnhurst, New College Oxford, the Brigade of Guards and then the Ministry.' Mr Lee gave the man's curriculum vitae.

'Napier was destined for the Foreign Office if his guv'nor hadn't had a bit of bad luck in the City,

131

weren't you Nappy?' Mrs Lee was now positively glowing with pride.

'Well, dear. I never had the "parlez-vous" for the Foreign Office.' Mr Lee smiled at his wife modestly. I was anxious to return to the case and picked up a couple of accounts from the brief.

'This gentleman in question seems, from time to time, to have paid your gas bills,' I reminded them.

'When business was slack, I'm not denying it, he helped us out, Mr Rumpole.' Mrs Lee smiled with extreme candour.

'And did you threaten to publish his little secret?' It was the sixty-four-thousand-dollar question, but the Lees rejected the suggestion with disdain.

'Oh no. He knew we'd never have done that. Didn't he, Nappy?' Mrs Lee appealed to her husband.

'Of course he knew. That would have been against the code, wouldn't it?'

'Sneaking! One does not sneak, does one?' Mrs Lee gathered up her handbag, as though to bring the proceedings to an end. 'Well Nappy,' she said, 'I really think that's all we can tell Mr Rumpole.'

'No, it's not,' I said firmly. 'You can tell me something else. How did you get into this business?' I asked Mrs Lee. 'Looking at you, a small cardigan shop in Cheltenham Spa might have seemed more appropriate.'

'Napier had a bit of bad luck in the City. Also his health wasn't quite up to it after the war.'

'Ticker a bit dicky. You know the sort of thing.'

'It was Nappy's war service.'

'Four years playing a long innings against Brother Boche.'

'And Napier had a dicky ticker.'

132

'Then I happened to run into a friend. Quite by chance,' Mr Lee told me. 'Well, we discussed the possibilities of a business along the lines of the one we're running now.'

'A friendly house!' Mrs Lee smiled. 'For the nicer sort of customer. People Nappy got to know on the "Old Boy Net".'

'And this fellow very decently came up with a spot of capital.'

'And was this helpful friend someone you'd known for a long time?'

'Oh yes. An old "mate", you understand. From way back. Of course, we'd drifted apart a bit, over the years.'

'An old school friend, perhaps?' I suggested.

'Oh, Napier couldn't possibly tell you that.' Mrs Lee pursed her lips.

'No. I couldn't tell you that,' Napier agreed.

'Against the code?' I wondered.

'The unwritten law,' Napier said. 'The sort of thing that just isn't done. It would be as unthinkable as . . .' He searched for some suitable enormity. 'Well, as wearing brown suede shoes with a blue suit, for instance.' Then he looked down at my feet.

'Don't worry,' I said. 'I wasn't at Lawnhurst, you know.'

When the conference was over, I went into the clerk's room to say goodnight to the workers. There Henry told me, somewhat puzzled, that he had just had a telephone call from She Who Must Be Obeyed.

'Did she want me?' I wondered what I had done amiss.

'She seemed to want to speak to *me*, sir. On the

subject of snacks.'

'*Snacks*, Henry?'

'Sausage rolls. Rolled-up asparagus. She said her friend, Mrs Mackintosh would provide us with little cheesy things, sir. I told her we weren't having the Chambers party until after the meeting, and then we'd be able to welcome our new Head of Chambers.'

'Head of Chambers! She Who Must Be Obeyed has set her heart on it. She won't take no for an answer. You follow me?' I looked hard and long at Henry. I wanted to be sure that the man was on my side in my bid for the leadership.

★ ★ ★

It was a sunny morning on the day the Lees' trial started, and I decided to take a slightly longer walk along the Embankment down to the Bailey. As the wind sent small white clouds chasing each other across the sky, and the seagulls came swooping in over Temple Gardens, I was put in mind of certain lines by the old sheep of the Lake District:

> Earth has not anything to show more fair:
> Dull would he be of soul who could pass by
> A sight so touching in its majesty...

A sight not quite so touching in its majesty was likely to be his Honour Judge Bullingham. The Mad Bull had been picked by some practical joker on the Bailey staff to try the case of the frightfully nice bawdy house keepers. Did the Bull go to a public school? I wondered. I couldn't remember. Probably he went to some establishment where they played soccer with a cannon ball and learning to read was an optional extra.

I passed Ludgate Circus and turned up towards the dome of the Old Bailey. I was just about to cross the road and dive in through the swing doors, when I heard a panting sound at my elbow, and Hoskins, a fairly unmemorable barrister in our Chambers, was at my side.

'Rumpole,' said Hoskins, 'You've got back from Africa!'

'No, Hoskins. I'm still there, dispensing tribal justice in a loin cloth and a top hat. What're you talking about?'

'Just to let you know that I'm against you in the brothel case. Sam Ballard's leading me.'

'Who?' The name was unknown to me.

'Sam Ballard. The Q.C. from the North–East Circuit. You know, the one who's coming to practise in London. Haven't you been told?'

'Yes. You've just told me.' I was glad Hoskins was on the other side in our case and not helping me. His mind seemed to be wandering.

'But you haven't been told anything else about him?' Hoskins looked surprisingly embarrassed.

'No. What is there to tell?'

'You'll get on with him like a house on fire,' Hoskins assured me. 'He's Chairman of L.A.C., you know'—"Lawyers As Churchgoers".'

Having climbed laboriously into the wig and gown (did I detect, still hanging in the horsehair, the dry scented smell of Africa?), I made my way to Judge Bullingham's Court attended by my small retinue consisting of Miss Fiona Allways and Mr Staines.

When I got to the courtroom door, I found a tall,

135

somewhat stooping figure waiting for me. He was, I supposed, younger than he looked. He seemed the sort of man who had felt the weight of heavy responsibilities in the nursery: his brow was furrowed by a look of anxiety and his mouth was drawn down in an expression of almost permanent disapproval. He wore his black Court coat and striped trousers like a suit of mourning and, in all the circumstances, his silk Q.C.'s gown seemed something of a frivolity. His face was pale, and when he spoke his tone was slow and sepulchral. I suppose you could sum the matter up by saying that he was a character who might have been quite nice looking, when he was alive.

'Are you Horace Rumpole?' The question seemed to contain a lurking accusation.

'I suppose I must be.'

'Sam Ballard.' He introduced himself. 'I'm leading for the Crown. In "Lee". By the way, I passed Chambers this morning. In fact I dropped something in your tray.'

'Did you, Bollard?' I said airily. 'Can't say I noticed.'

'It was about a meeting of LAC.' He pronounced it as one word, like the place Sir Lancelot came from. 'I do hope you can find time to join us. We *should* value your contribution.'

'"Lawyers As Churchgoers"? I may have to give that a miss, Bollard. My doctor has advised me to avoid all excitement.'

'Ballard.'

'Yes, of course. I imagine your little get-together might put considerable strain on the ticker. Where do you meet? Pentonville Women's Institute? The whole orgy topped up by barn dancing and silent

136

prayer?'

'Henry warned me about you, Rumpole.' The man was unsmiling.

'Henry?' I wondered why Henry had discussed my character with this lay reader.

'Henry the clerk. He said you had a sense of humour.'

'Only a mild one, Bollard. Nothing fatal. You've managed to keep free of it? What do you do? Jog a lot, I imagine.' He looked at me in silence for a long time and then said, more in sorrow than in anger, 'Some of our keenest members scoffed at the outset.'

'I dare say they did.' Fascinating as this conversation was, duty called. I had to tear myself away, and moved towards the door of the Court. As I did so, I uttered a pious thought. 'Well, all I hope is that this little prosecution will be conducted in a thoroughly Christian spirit.'

'You can rely on me for that.'

I was almost through the door as I said, 'Perhaps you'll show a certain reluctance about casting the first stone.'

*   *   *

Far from showing any reluctance in the stone-throwing department, the lugubrious Ballard fired off a volley of moderately lethal rocks in the course of his opening speech to the jury.

There I sat facing Judge Bullingham, who glowered like a larger white (or rather purplish) Sir Worthington Banzana, and I looked round the Court to which I had come home from my travels. I saw the Lees, sitting calmly in the dock as though

137

they had just been asked to drop in for a cup of tea. I glanced at the Press box which was more than usually full, R. *v.* Lee being, it seemed, a bit of a draw and likely to fill the Sunday papers for the next couple of weeks. Prominent among the journalists I saw a youngish girl in a boiler suit and glasses, who wore a button bearing the legend HOME COUNTIES TELEVISION. I thought that she was smiling at me and I smiled back, somewhat flattered, until I saw that the message was being beamed at Fiona Allways, who was sitting beside me, industriously writing down Ballard's rubbish. Then I closed my eyes, hoping to indicate to the jury that nothing the prosecution said could possibly be of the slightest interest. Steadily, remorselessly, the voice of the Ballard droned on.

'Decent men, family men, men who had earned the respect of the community and were placed in positions of trust, found themselves tempted by this house, 66 Barnardine Square, Victoria. Some of you may know Victoria, members of the jury, you may know its brightly lit streets and British Railway Terminal. I'm sure none of you know the darker streets, where the market is in human flesh. Men left that particular house, members of the jury, with their consciences burdened with guilt and their wallets lightened. In the case of one of the witnesses I am about to call, the financial gain to those who exercised this appalling trade was considerably more. This is the subject of Count Two of the indictment, my Lord.'

I opened my eyes as the Judge weighed in with, 'Yes, Mr Ballard. I am sure the jury understand. The *blackmail!*' The Bull looked at the jury to remind them that this was a very grave charge

138

indeed and then glowered at me as though it were all my fault.

I smiled back at Bullingham in a friendly fashion.

'Among the many respectable figures who fell to the temptations of 66 Barnardine Square...' Ballard went on, and I began to speculate, in a random sort of way, as to who the many respectable figures might be. Doctors? Politicians? Police officers? Lawyers? *Lawyers? Judges!* I looked at his Honour Judge Roger Bullingham with a wild surmise. I thought I must ask my clients. Of course, they'd never tell me. But a Bull in a knocking shop! The idea was almost too good to be true. I couldn't suppress a momentary gasp of merriment.

'Did you say something, Mr Rumpole?' The Bull cast a scowl in my direction.

'Nothing at all, my Lord!' I rose slightly and then sank into silence.

'I should remind everyone in Court that this is a most serious case.' The Judge made a pronouncement. 'The charges are extremely grave, and if the evidence as outlined by Mr Ballard is true... Of course, I haven't begun to make up my mind about it yet.'

'Haven't you, Bull?' I muttered to myself in the most *sotto* of possible *voces* as his Lordship continued.

'Then all I can say is that the activities at this property in Victoria were very wicked indeed. So we will have no laughter from anywhere in the Court.' After a meaningful look at counsel for the defence, the Judge smiled on the prosecution. 'Yes, Mr Ballard.'

'If your Lordship pleases.' My opponent bobbed

139

a small bow to the learned Bull and then carried on with his work. 'Members of the jury,' he said. 'A suitable motto to be written up over the door of 66 Barnardine Square is that which Dante chose for his Inferno...' I didn't think much of that for a legal reference. His Lordship probably thought that Dante was someone who did conjuring tricks on television, but Ballard soldiered on with: '"Abandon hope all ye who enter here." Because, of course, once he was in the door, and once the spiders got to know who he was, a fact which they took great pains to find out, the fly was trapped. He couldn't get away, and if he was a man who enjoyed a high and responsible position, he would pay anything, you may think, to buy the silence of this brazen woman and her procuring husband...'

The jury looked at the couple in the dock. Napier Lee had his hand cupped over his ear and a gently pained expression as a result of what he was able to hear. At which point Ballard announced that he would call his first witness. I noticed that this announcement was not accompanied by any name, and then the Usher went out of Court and returned, after a longer lapse of time than usual, with a tall, distinguished-looking, grey-haired man wearing a dark suit, a striped shirt with a stiff white collar, and a Guards tie. He walked across the Court with the stiff-upper-lipped expression of an officer and gentleman marching out to face a firing squad. Once in the box he lifted the Bible, raised his eyes to heaven and repeated the oath as though it were his last will and testament. When he had finished he put the Good Book down carefully on the ledge in front of him, and turned to face the fusillade of Ballard's questions. Before he did so, I gave vent to

140

a loud mutter of 'Name please.'

Triggered off by this perfectly normal request, Ballard made an application to the learned Judge.

'My Lord,' he started confidently, 'I would like to make the usual application in a blackmail case. I ask that this witness should be known simply as Mr X and that your Lordship directs that the ladies and gentlemen of the Press should not repeat his name under any circumstances.'

I glanced at the Press box and saw the young lady television reporter look up from her notebook and stare hard at the man in the witness-box. Meanwhile, the Judge was nodding his agreement. 'That seems to be a very proper order to make, in view of this gentleman's position,' he said. 'I imagine you have no objection, Mr Rumpole?'

I rose slowly to my feet, glowing with helpfulness.

'I would have no objection, my Lord, provided a similar concession is made for the benefit of my clients.'

'My Lord.' My words had clearly alarmed my learned friend. 'Perhaps we should continue with this in the absence of the jury, if there is to be an argument.' Well, he could bet his old hair shirt there was going to be an argument.

'Very well. Members of the jury.' Bullingham smiled in an ingratiating manner at the twelve good men and women and true. 'Unfortunately, legal matters arise from time to time which have to be resolved. Would you go to your room? We shouldn't have to detain you long.'

The jury filed out, grateful for a smoke and a cup of Old Bailey coffee. The boiler-suited girl in the Press box was writing furiously in her notebook. As

141

the door closed on the last jury member the Bull fixed me with a malevolent eye.

'Now, Mr Rumpole,' he said. 'Did I hear a somewhat unusual argument with regard to the defendants in this case?'

'That they should be known as Mr and Mrs Y? Why not, my Lord?' I asked innocently. 'My learned friend talks about embarrassment. Mr and Mrs Napier Lee have been spattered over the front pages of every newspaper in England. "Alleged Vice Queen Arrested"; "The Darby and Joan Who Owned the House of Shame"; "Charged with Being the Top People's Madame" ... and so on. They have had to submit to a barrage of prejudicial publicity whilst this client of theirs can creep into Court under cover of a letter of the alphabet and preserve his precious respectability intact!'

'Mr Rumpole. There is no charge against this gentleman. He is innocent of any crime!' His Lordship seemed to be turning a darker shade of purple.

'So are my clients innocent!' I did my bit to match the Judge's outrage. 'Until they're proven guilty. Or doesn't that rule still apply in your Lordship's Court?' I was regarded with a look of admiration from Miss Fiona Allways and the boiler-suited television lady, and a trumpet of indignation from the Bench.

'Mr Rumpole! This Court is entitled to some respect.'

'I am so full of respect to this Court, my Lord, that I give it credit for still applying the law of England—or has that been changed while I was out of the country? I merely ask for information.' I tried a charming smile, which was about as calming

142

as a red rag to the Bull. He came charging to judgement. 'Your application that your clients' names should not be published is refused, Mr Rumpole,' he said. 'This case can be reported in full so far as they are concerned.'

'And they will no doubt be delighted to contribute to the pleasures of the great British Breakfast.' I bowed with great courtesy and sat. 'If your Lordship pleases.'

'Now, Mr Ballard.' The Judge turned to the more congenial matter of dealing with the prosecution. 'Your application for this witness to remain anonymous is made on good authority?'

'Certainly, my Lord. The Contempt of Court Act gives your Lordship power to order that the witness's name should never be published.'

'In perpetuity?' I grumbled from a seated position.

'My learned friend says, "In perpetuity?" and the answer would be "yes",' Ballard answered without hesitation.

'I suppose your argument would be,' the Judge suggested helpfully, 'that if this witness's secrets are exposed to the public, then in effect the blackmail threat would have been successful. Is that your argument, Mr Ballard?' Of course it was, once the Judge had told him.

'Yes, it is, my Lord. And your Lordship puts it so much better than I can.' At least Ballard's religious integrity didn't prevent a little grovelling on occasions.

'What's your answer to *that*, Mr Rumpole?' His Lordship turned to the defence.

'What blackmail?' I rose with apparent reluctance. 'What blackmail is your Lordship referring to? I merely ask for information.'

'We all know what this case is about,' Bullingham rumbled.

I responded with another burst of carefully simulated outrage. 'There hasn't yet been a word of evidence about blackmail,' I said. 'Nothing has been proved. Nothing! In my submission your Lordship cannot make a decision based on unproven allegations. And one more thing...'

'Yes, Mr Rumpole.' The Judge looked pointedly at the clock and sighed.

'One more principle of which this Court should be reminded. British justice is meant to take place in public. Justice is not to be seen cowering behind an initial.'

'Is that all, Mr Rumpole?' His Lordship sighed again.

It was all that was fit for mixed company, so I bowed with elaborate courtesy. 'If your Lordship pleases. With the greatest respect.' I bowed again. 'I think your Lordship has my argument.' I did a final gesture of mock subservience and sat down.

'Yes, Mr Rumpole. I think I have. I see it's nearly one o'clock, but I'll give judgement on this point now, so that the witness may have his lunch with some degree of peace of mind.' The Judge smiled at the silent figure in the witness-box, and continued. 'The defendants, through their counsel, seem particularly anxious that this gentleman's patronage of their alleged house of ill repute should become widely known to the public.'

Turning round I saw Mrs Lee, deeply wounded, shake her head. Bullingham continued with grim determination. 'If that were allowed it would be a blackmailer's charter. No victim would ever dare to

144

go to the police. I am determined that this witness's
high reputation shall be protected. He will give his
evidence to the jury as "Mr X" *after* luncheon.
Thank you, Mr Ballard.'

The usher called us to our feet and the Judge left
us. I told Stainey to inform the Lee family that I
would visit them in the cells shortly and gathered
up my papers. When I got outside the Court I saw
Fiona Allways, my learned note-taker, in close
conversation with the lady from the Press box.
When she saw me, Fiona said to her, 'See you,
Izzy. See you here after lunch,' and joined me on
my journey to the lifts.

'Who was that?' I asked by way of idle chatter.

'Isobel Vincent. She was a prefect when I was at
Benenden. I hero-worshipped her rather,' Miss
Allways admitted.

'Do girls have an "Old Boy Net" too?'

'Izzy works for Home Counties News,' Fiona
Allways sounded deeply impressed. 'She's
tremendously into Women's Liberation.'

'So am I!' I said as we waited for the lift.

'You?'

'All for Women's Liberation. Particularly the
liberation of Mrs Lorraine Lee.'

The lift arrived and we stepped into it and sank
towards the cells. As we did so Miss Allways was
looking at me with the sort of admiration she had
previously reserved for Izzy, the fearless television
reporter.

'I say, Rumpole. You *were* splendid. Really
fighting.'

'Let's say—going through the motions towards a
graceful defeat.'

'Well, I think it's *jolly* unfair. Keeping his name a

145

secret.'

'Do you, Fiona?'

She spoke with a passion which I found unexpected. 'I mean, those sort of places wouldn't exist at all, would they, if it weren't for the Mr Xs?' She looked at the papers I was clutching. 'The name's in your brief, isn't it? I suppose *you* know what his name is?'

'He signed his deposition. I know it, yes,' I admitted.

'So you could tell anybody...?'

'Contempt of Court, Fiona,' I told her, 'should be a silent exercise, like meditation.'

The lift stopped and we got out in the basement. We passed the carefully preserved door of Old Newgate prison, rang for a screw and were finally admitted to the dungeon department of the Central Criminal Court.

'We don't want his name splashed around the papers, Mr Rumpole. We wouldn't want that.' I don't know what it was about Mrs Lorraine Lee, but she could make the dreary little interview room, with its plastic table and old tin which did for an ashtray, seem somehow cosy and refined. Both of the Lees were looking at me, more in sorrow than in anger. I was taking exercise, walking up and down the confined space as I smoked a small cigar, and Fiona was sitting at the table nonchalantly turning the pages of my brief.

'Damned painful for him to be asked to give his name, in *his* position,' Napier Lee agreed with his good lady.

'We abide by the code, you see,' Mrs Lee said. 'The unwritten law. All the chaps who come to our house know they can trust us.'

146

'The "Old Boy Net"!' I said with some asperity. 'Look, he's "sneaked" on you. Why not return the compliment?'

'That's not how it works, I'm afraid.' Mr Lee shook his head. 'Whatever he's done, we've got to do the decent thing.'

'We think the Judge is a perfect gentleman, don't we, Nappy?' Mrs Lee amazed me by saying.

'He understands the code, you see,' her husband agreed.

'He didn't want the poor fellow's name mentioned. That would've been terribly embarrassing.'

'And it would be terribly embarrassing, Mrs Lorraine Lee, if you and your husband got five years for blackmail!' I suggested. 'I mean, you might be as snug as bugs in the Nick, but what's going to happen to me? I just can't afford to lose cases, not at this particular point in my career. I'm just about to be elected to high office in my Chambers.' Then I turned on her and asked, 'Why just the gas bill?'

'What?' Lorraine seemed confused.

'Use a lot of gas, did you, at Barnardine Square?' I pressed my inquiries.

'Not particularly,' Napier Lee said. 'The bills used to lie out on the hall table and, well, he offered to pay one or two—out of kindness, really.'

'Just a tremendously decent gesture,' his wife agreed. 'It was over and above the call of duty.'

'*How* did he pay them, exactly?'

'Oh, he used to give us a cheque,' Mrs Lee told me.

'A cheque!' I was astonished. 'In a house of ill repute? Mr X is either very naïve or...'

'Or what?' Napier Lee was puzzled, as though the point had never occurred to him before.

'I don't know. And we may never have a chance to find out.' I stubbed out the cigar end and was preparing to leave them, when Mr Lee uttered a mild rebuke. 'We don't like it called a house of ill repute, Mr Rumpole. We call it a friendly house.'

*   *   *

My usual luncheon, when engaged on a case down the Bailey, consisted of a quickly snatched sandwich and a glass of stout in the pub opposite if I was in a hurry, or a steak pie washed down with *vin* extremely *ordinaire* in the same resort. Our visit to the cells had left us so little time, however, that Fiona Allways and I took the lift up to the Bar Mess, the eatery on the top floor. This is a place I habitually avoid. It is always full of barristers telling each other of the brilliant way they dealt with discovery of documents, or the coup they brought off in some hire-purchase claim in Luton. The large room was resonant with the sort of buzz and clatter that usually accompanies school dinners, and there was a marked absence of cheerful atmosphere.

My reluctance to mingle freely with the learned friends at the trough was justified by the fact that, when Fiona and I put down our ham salads at the long table, we found ourselves sitting opposite the lugubrious Ballard, who was peeling himself a chocolate biscuit.

'Hello, Ballard,' I said, making the best of things. 'Enjoyed the sermon.'

'Did you, Rumpole?' A shadow of a smile flitted across his face, and was promptly dismissed.

148

'Haven't had such a good time since our old school parson gave us three quarters of an hour on hell fire,' I assured him. 'Always eat here, do you?'

'Don't you use the Bar Mess?' Ballard seemed puzzled.

'As a matter of fact, no. I prefer the pub—you get the chance of rubbing shoulders with a few decent criminals.'

To my surprise, the Ballard smile returned, and his tone was unexpectedly friendly. 'Perhaps you'll take me to your pub sometime. I mean, we should get rather better acquainted,' he said.

'Should we?' I could see no pressing reason for this bizarre suggestion.

'Well, we're going to have to spend a good deal of time together.'

'Why? This case isn't going to go on for ever, is it? Talking of which...'

'Yes?'

'Sam. I might come along to one of those churchgoers' meetings of yours...' I, too, was having a go at the friendly approach.

'Really?' The man seemed gratified.

'I mean, there is a great deal to be said for introducing a little more Christian spirit into the law...'

'I'm so glad you think so.' Those who had seen St Paul on the road to Damascus no doubt looked a little like Ballard, Q.C., peering at Rumpole.

'Oh, I do,' I assured him. 'There is more joy in heaven, as I understand it, old darling, over one sinner that repenteth, and all that sort of thing.'

'That sort of thing, yes,' Ballard agreed.

'And if two sinners repenteth,' I was getting nearer to the nub, the heart of this unusual conversation. 'I mean, repent to the tune of pleading guilty to keeping a disorderly house, wilt though not drop the blackmail charges, old cock?'

'No.' All smiles were discontinued. Ballard closed his teeth firmly on his chocolate biscuit.

'Did I hear you aright?' I said, with a good deal of sorrow.

'I said, "No." It's quite impossible.'

'Look here.' I wrestled patiently for the man's soul. 'Is that an entirely Christian attitude? Forgive them their trespasses, unto seventy times seven! Well, there's only one little count of blackmail.'

'No doubt they may be forgiven eventually. After a suitable period of confinement.' Ballard masticated unmercifully.

'The Mad Bull is quite capable of giving them five years for blackmail.' I pointed out the brutal facts of the matter.

'is *that* what you call the learned Judge?' Ballard looked at me severely. 'I had thought in terms of seven, for blackmail. And the top sentence for keeping a disorderly house is six months. Is that the reasoning behind your appeal to Christian principles, Rumpole?'

'You show a remarkably cynical attitude, for a churchgoer.' It pained me to find the man so worldly.

'As a churchgoer, I have a duty to protect public decency. I don't know what your particular morality is.'

'It mainly consists of getting unfortunate sinners out of trouble. You don't learn about that, apparently, in your scripture lessons.'

'Blessed are the blackmailers, for they shall walk out without a stain on their characters.' A hint of

150

the smile returned. 'Is that your version of the Sermon on the Mount, Rumpole?'

'"Prisons are built with stones of law, brothels with bricks of religion." That's William Blake, not me. And I'll give you another quotation: "I come not to call the righteous, but the sinners to repentance." Matthew 8, verse 13.'

'How do *you* know that?' Ballard was clearly surprised.

'My old father was a cleric. And I'll tell you something. He hated Bible classes.'

A silence fell between us. Ballard was rolling the silver-paper wrapping of his chocolate biscuit between his fingers. 'It's a pretty odd sort of story, isn't it, for blackmail?' I said.

'It seems a painfully usual one to me.'

'Does it? If you were in a brothel, would you write out a couple of cheques on the NatWest, and sign them with your real name? Particularly if you're such a shy, retiring violet as your precious witness Mr X.'

Ballard looked at his watch. 'The Judge'll be coming back,' he said firmly.

The theological debate was over. Ballard left us and Fiona Allways looked at me in evident distress. 'Five years!' she said. 'They'd really get five years?'

I finished my Bar Mess light ale and gave her my learned opinion. 'You know what we need in this case? A witness who knows something about Mr X. No one's going to come rushing to our aid while his name's kept a deadly secret. There, Fiona old girl, is the rub.'

★   ★   ★

151

The gentleman in the Guards tie gave his damning evidence of blackmail to an attentive jury and an appreciative Bull, and it wasn't until later in the afternoon that I rose to cross-examine.

'You won't mind me calling you Mr X?' I started politely.

'No.'

'I thought you wouldn't. For how long were you a habitué of this house of ill repute?'

'Really, Mr Rumpole,' the Judge protested. 'Does that make the slightest difference?'

'Please answer the question.' I kept my eye on the witness. 'Unless my Lord rules against it, on a point of law.' My Lord didn't.

'I had been visiting there for about five years.'

'On your way home from directing the nation's affairs?' The question had the desired effect on his Lordship, who uttered a loud rebuke. 'Mr Rumpole!'

'Very well,' I said in my usual conciliatory fashion. 'On your way home from work. Before you got lost in the bosom of your family, it was your practice to visit 66 Barnardine Square?'

'Yes,' Mr X answered reluctantly.

'How did you first hear of this place of resort?'

'Hear of it?' The witness seemed puzzled by the question.

'Yes. Bit of gossip at the Club, was it? Or an advertisement in the *Times* personal column?'

There was a welcome little patter of laughter in Court. The Judge didn't join in. It took some time for Mr X to answer.

'I heard about it from a friend.'

'An *old* friend? I don't mean in years, but a friend of long standing?'

'Yes.'

'I really can't imagine what the relevance of these questions is.' Ballard rose to protest, and the Judge came to his assistance.

'Mr Rumpole. What *has* this got to do with it?' he asked wearily.

'My Lord.' I decided to go into a bit of an aria. 'I'm fighting this case in the dark, with my hands tied behind my back, against a prosecution witness who has chosen to shelter behind anonymity. I must be allowed to cross-examine him as I think fit. After all, it would greatly add to the costs of this case if it had to be reconsidered ... elsewhere.'

His Honour Judge Bullingham was no fool. He got the clear reference to the Court of Appeal, where his interventions might not look so attractive on the transcript of evidence as they sounded in the flesh. He thought briefly and then came out, in judicial tones, with 'I think we may allow Mr Rumpole to pursue his line, Mr Ballard.' Then he turned to me and said, 'It remains to be seen, of course, Mr Rumpole, if these questions will do your clients any good, in the eyes of the jury.'

So, having registered a sort of minor and equivocal success, I turned back to the witness. 'Was it a friend you had known from your schooldays, by any chance?' For that I got a reluctant agreement.

'You had kept up with him?' I went on.

'No. We met again after an interval of a good many years.'

'Where did you meet?'

'In a public house.'

'In the Victoria area?' I took a gamble and asked.

'Somewhere near there. Yes.'

153

'Meet a nice type of girl in that public house, do you?'

'Mr Rumpole!' The Bull was growing restive again and had to be dealt with.

'My Lord. I withdraw the question. What did your friend tell you?' I asked the witness.

'He told me that he'd been ill. And that he'd had a bit of bad luck in business. He said he had a house near Victoria Station and his wife and he were starting a business there.'

'A business . . . in agreeable ladies?'

We were then treated to a long pause before Mr X said, 'Yes.'

So, with a good deal of the preparatory work done, I decided to be daring and ask a question to which I didn't know the answer—always a considerable risk in cross-examination.

'Did you offer to put a little much-needed capital into this business? I mean, the Court has kept your name a secret because you are so respectable, Mr X. Were you in fact an investor in a bawdy house?'

The jury looked so interested in the answer that Ballard rose to make an objection. 'My Lord,' he said. 'The witness should be warned.'

'I *do* know my job, Mr Ballard.' For the first time, Bullingham sounded a little testy with the prosecution. Then he turned to the witness and said, 'I should warn you that you are not bound to answer any question that might incriminate you. Now, do you wish to answer Mr Rumpole's question or would you prefer not to?'

There was a long pause during which perhaps Mr X's whole life flashed before his eyes, in slow motion. At long last he said, in the nicest possible way, 'I would prefer not to, my Lord.'

154

I looked hard at the jury, raised an eyebrow or two, and repeated, 'You would prefer not to?' As no answer came from the witness-box I tried another question. 'Can you answer this. How long ago was the meeting in the public house in Victoria?'

'About five years ago.' Mr X appeared to be back in answering mood.

'And was the public house the Barnardine Arms?'

'Yes.'

'And was the old school friend in question by any chance Mr Napier Lee, the male defendant in this case?' He had only to say, 'No,' politely, and I would have had to sit down with egg all over my silly face. However, my luck stayed in, and Mr X gave us a very quiet, 'Yes.'

'Speak up, Mr X,' I said.

'Yes, my Lord, it was. Mr Napier Lee.'

For some obscure reason, best known to Himself, God seemed to be on my side that day.

'So you met Mr Lee some five years ago,' I continued the cross-examination. 'And his wife, Mrs Lorraine Lee?'

'I met her shortly afterwards.'

'When you started to patronize their business?'

'Yes.'

'So ever since he was an inky school boy in the fourth form at Lawnhurst, Mr Napier Lee has known exactly who you were.'

'We met in Lower Five actually.'

'In Lower Five. Oh yes. I stand corrected. So he has had at least five years to blackmail you, if he wanted to.'

Mr X gave a puzzled look at the jury, but they looked as if they saw the point perfectly well. Then he answered, 'Yes.'

155

'And neither he nor his wife made any suggestion of this sort until six months ago?'

'That is right,' Mr X admitted.

'When you were asked to pay a couple of trivial little gas and electricity bills.' I opened my brief then, not a thing I find I have to do too often, and fished out copies of the documents in question. 'Bills for £45 and £37.53.' Mr X agreed. He seemed to have something of a head for figures.

'And you paid these bills for the Lees by cheque?'

'Yes.'

'Why on earth . . . ?' My eyebrows went up again, and I turned to the jury.

'Because, as I have told you, Mr Rumpole, they threatened to tell my employers about my visits to their . . . house unless I did so.'

'I don't mean *that*.' I showed a little well-calculated impatience. 'I mean why pay by *cheque*?'

'I . . . I don't know exactly . . .' Mr X faltered. The point seemed not to have occurred to him.

'Did you ever pay by cheque when you visited this house on any other occasion?'

'No.'

'Always in cash?'

'Of course.'

'Yes. Of course,' I agreed. 'Because you didn't want to leave a record of your name in connection with the Lees' "business".' I paused as meaningfully as I could, and then asked, 'But on the occasion of this alleged blackmail you *did* want to leave a record?'

'I told you . . . I don't know why I paid them by cheque.' Mr X was looking to Ballard for help.

None was immediately forthcoming.

'Was it because you wanted evidence on which to base this unfounded allegation of blackmail against my clients?' I suggested.

'No!' Mr X protested vehemently, and then added, weakly, 'I suppose I just didn't think about it.'

'Thank you, Mr X!' I gave the jury a last meaningful look and then sat down with the feeling of a job well done. His Lordship leant forward and, in a quiet and reassuring tone of voice, did his best to repair the damage.

'Mr X. I suppose you paid the ... "girls" at this establishment in cash?' Bullingham's smile said, 'We're all men of the world here, now aren't we?'

'Yes, my Lord. I did,' Mr X answered, encouraged.

'Did it strike you as a different matter when you were paying the Gas Board and the Electricity Board?'

'Yes, my Lord.' The witness took the hint gratefully.

'You saw no particular harm in paying those two great authorities by cheque?' Bullingham suggested gently.

'No harm at all, my Lord.' Mr X was clearly feeling better.

'Very well, we'll rise now.' The Judge smiled at the jury, conscious of a job pretty well done. 'Shall we say, 10.30 tomorrow morning?'

*   *   *

That night Hilda and I were sitting at leisure in the living room of our 'mansion' flat at 25B Froxbury

157

Court in the Gloucester Road. She Who Must Be Obeyed was knitting some garment. I have no idea what it was, except that it was long and pink and was no doubt destined for her old school friend Dodo Mackintosh, and I was smoking a small cigar, watching the tide go down in a glass of Pommeroy's very ordinary, when She asked me, not with the air of anyone who intended to listen too closely to the answer, 'Went the day well?' or words to that effect.

'You could describe it as a nightmare,' I confided in her, blowing out smoke.

'You mean it's not going well?'

'Well.' I gave one of my mirthless laughs. 'We've got a prosecutor who wears a hair shirt and seems to have done his pupillage with the Inquisition. The Mad Bull is madder than ever. The chief witness has this in common with the late Lohengrin—no one must ever ask him his name. And my clients think it's in the best public school tradition to get convicted of blackmail. There we are, all together at the Old Bailey,

Rolled round in earth's diurnal course,
With rocks, and stones, and trees . . .

It's making my head ache.'

My glass seemed to have drained itself during this monologue. I rose to refresh it from the bottle.

'I mean in Chambers. The *Headship*, Rumpole! Is it going to be ours?' Hilda asked with some impatience.

'You have great legal ambitions, Hilda. I'm sorry, I can't bring you back the Lord Chief Justice's chain of office with a bottle of Pommeroy's

Château Plonkenheim.' I raised my glass to her, in recognition of her fighting spirit, and drank.

'I'm not looking for Lord Chancellor, Rumpole,' Hilda told me patiently. 'Just Head of Daddy's old Chambers. Of course, I was brought up in the law.' There was a pause. She looked at me with some suspicion, her knitting needles clicked, and then she asked, 'There's no one more senior than you, is there? No one else they might appoint?'

'No one who has been longer in the bottle as an Old Bailey hack, no,' I reassured her.

'And no silks?' For a moment, Hilda stopped knitting, as though her fingers were frozen in suspense. I gave her encouraging news. 'Not as yet. Erskine-Brown's application doesn't come up till after the meeting.'

'Then it's in the bag, isn't it?' Hilda breathed a sigh of relief, and her knitting needles clicked again.

'Fear not, Hilda. So far as I can see, your election is assured.' I poured another glass to drink to her success. I must say, She Who Must Be Obeyed smiled with some satisfaction.

'Dodo's agreed to help me out at the party,' she told me. 'She does all sorts of dips.'

'Damned versatile, old Dodo,' I agreed, and then with a mind to see what, if anything, was going on in the world outside Froxbury Court, I switched on the small and misty television set we hire from Mr Mehta who keeps a shop full of electrical appliances on our corner of the Gloucester Road. Thanks to the wonders of science, I was immediately rewarded by the sight of Fiona Allways's friend Isobel Vincent, who was clutching a microphone, wearing her boiler suit, standing under the dome of the Old

159

Bailey, and giving a waiting world much too much news of the events that had occurred in Court during that eventful day.

'The Top People's Disorderly House Case,' said Izzy. 'Home Counties News can reveal the fact that Mr X is in fact the very senior civil servant at the Foreign Office, Sir Cuthbert Pericles. He is just one of the men, highly placed in public life, who are believed to have visited the house in Barnardine Square. This is Isobel Vincent, Home Counties News, at the Old Bailey.'

I switched off the set, Isobel Vincent shrank to a small point of light and vanished, unhappily not off the face of the earth. I looked at Hilda, appalled. 'My God,' I said. 'What a disaster!'

'Whatever is it, Rumpole?' Hilda sighed. Again she was not over-interested.

'You were nearest the window, Hilda. Didn't you hear a loud noise,' I asked her, 'coming from Kensington?'

'What sort of noise?'

'His Honour Judge Bullingham,' I suggested, 'blowing up?'

★   ★   ★

The next day, his Honour was still in one piece, although sitting on the Bench breathing heavily and a darker purple than ever. I began to fear that we were about to witness one of the few recorded cases of spontaneous combustion. He was delivering a pretty decided judgement on Miss Isobel Vincent, who stood, still defiantly boiler-suited, in the well of the Court in front of him, about as apologetic as St Joan when called on to answer a nasty heresy

160

charge before the Inquisition.

'In almost half a century's experience at the Bar and on the Bench, I have never known such a flagrant, wicked and inexcusable Contempt of Court!' Bullingham boomed. I must say I wasn't giving him my full attention. I was turning to the door hoping that at any minute Mr Staines, my instructing solicitor, might come into Court with the news I was hoping and praying for.

Meanwhile Isobel was still looking noble, Fiona Allways was trying to look at no one in particular, and the Judge was still carrying on. 'I have heard that your employers, Home Counties Television, had no idea that you were disobeying a Court Order. That will be investigated. If anyone who has been in this Court, anyone at all, had anything to do with this matter...' At this point his Lordship could be seen glaring at Horace Rumpole. 'They will be sought out and punished.'

And then the miracle happened. Old Stainey filtered back into Court and whispered the news that the man I was waiting for was without, and he wanted to know if I would call him first.

'Of course I'll call him first,' I whispered back. 'It shouldn't be long now. The Bull's running out of steam.'

'I will send the papers to the proper quarter in order that it may be decided what action shall be taken against this most foolish and wicked young woman...' The Judge dismissed Isobel then, and she left the Court with her head held high and a look at Fiona which caused that young lady to blush slightly. Shortly thereafter the show was on the road again, and I was on my hind legs opening our defence to the jury.

161

'Members of the jury. It is my duty to outline to you the evidence the defence is going to call. I'm going to call a witness . . .'—well, I hoped to God I was going to call a witness—'who may be able to penetrate the pall of secrecy which has fallen over this case. Someone, perhaps, may have the bad manners and rotten taste to tell us the truth about the evidence. Someone may be able to cast aside the "Old Boy Net" and let the secret out. Ladies and gentlemen of the jury, I will now call . . .' I paused long enough to stoop and whisper to old Staines, who was sitting in front of me, 'Whom the hell will I now call, Stainey?'

'Mr Stephen Lucas,' Mr Staines whispered back.

'I will now call Mr Simon . . .' I started.

'Stephen!' Another whisper from Stainey.

'Mr Stephen Lucas.' I was confident at last.

'Very well, Mr Rumpole.' The Judge picked up his pencil with an air of resignation, and prepared to make a few jottings. And then a man came into Court, entered the witness-box as though he had a day full of far better things to do, and promised to tell us the truth, the whole truth and nothing but the truth. He was a smaller, fatter, more jovial type of person than Mr X, but when he spoke it was with the impatient confidence of someone who had spent many years in a trusted position in the corridors of power. He gave his name as Stephen Lucas.

'Are you a member of the Foreign Office Legal Department?' I asked him.

'Yes, I am.'

'And do you know the witness we have called "Mr X"? I have asked him to remain in Court so that you may identify him.'

162

The witness looked down at the man who was sitting in front of Ballard with as much detachment as if Mr X were something that had just arrived in his 'In tray'.

'Yes, I do,' he said.

'Are you a friend of his?'

'We meet, of course, in the Foreign Office,' Lucas said cautiously. 'I would say I've known him fairly well, and over a long period.'

'Of course. Do you remember having lunch with him at his Club about a year ago? Was that at his invitation?'

'Yes, it was.'

'What did he discuss, do you remember?'

'Well, we discussed a number of things, the work of my department and so on, and then he asked me some questions about the recent Contempt of Court Act. He seemed to want my opinion about it, as a lawyer. It's not really my subject, but I told him what I knew.'

'What aspect of the Act was our "Mr X" particularly interested in?'

'In the Court's power to order that the name of a witness in a blackmail case should be kept secret, perhaps for ever.' The witness paused. The jury were looking at him with interest and the Bull, I was pleased to see, was writing busily. Then Lucas went on with his story. 'I remember his saying that if you didn't want your name to come out in a particular scandal or something of that sort, all you would have to do would be to accuse someone of blackmail.'

'Mr Lucas, what made you remember this conversation?' I asked, to pre-empt a bit of Ballard's cross-examination.

163

'It was last night, when I heard Mr X's name on the television news. I thought it might have some bearing on this case.'

The Judge frowned, and I went on quickly to prevent any unfriendly comment from the Bench. 'Tell us, Mr Lucas. You say you've known Mr X for a long time. You weren't at school together, by any chance?'

'No. I wasn't at Lawnhurst,' Lucas admitted.

'Or at any public school?'

'No.'

Thank God, I thought, or we'd never have got a word out of him. I sat down and Ballard was up with his long black silk gown flapping with indignation.

'So, Mr Lucas, you would never have come here to give evidence if there hadn't been a flagrant Contempt of Court and Mr X's name had not appeared on the television news.'

'That's right.' Lucas seemed to be not in the least worried by the course of events.

'It's most unfortunate, I agree, Mr Ballard.' The Judge looked sadly at the prosecutor. 'But I don't see what I can do about it. I can't exclude this evidence.'

'Oh no, my Lord. But it *is* most unfortunate.' Ballard seemed to be regretting some huge historical disaster, like the Decline and Fall of the Roman Empire.

'Of course it is.' The Judge cast a meaningful glance at the Rumpole faction. 'But the harm's been done.' Whether it was harm or good, of course, depended on which side you were sitting.

Well, in due course the Lees gave evidence and denied the blackmail in a pained sort of way, and

164

answered Ballard's passionate denunciations with excessively polite murmurs of dissent, as though they were regretfully declining the offer of more bread and butter. Later in the proceedings, my learned opponent gave the jury another two-hour sermon, during the course of which I was delighted to see them getting somewhat restive. And then, almost before I knew it, final speech time was round again.

'Mr X couldn't give up his visits to the friendly house in Barnardine Square, members of the jury,' I told them. 'But he was always terrified that the place might be raided and his name would come out in the ensuing scandal. So he hit on this somewhat over-ingenious device: a couple of cheques, a sure proof that he had paid money to the Lees, could lay the basis for a trumped-up blackmail charge that would keep his name a secret for ever! It was an elaborate plan, complicated, expensive and entirely futile. Just the sort of plan, you may think, that would occur to someone high in the government of our country. Why was it futile? Because Mr X need have had no fear. The Lees would never have betrayed his pathetic little secrets. You see, it was for them, as it never was for him, a question of morality. They had their code.'

At the end of it all the Judge summed up with surprising moderation. The jury stayed out for three hours, and mugs of tea were being served in the cells when we got down to discuss the result with Mr and Mrs Napier Lee.

*   *   *

'A great win on the blackmail, Mr Rumpole.' Mr

Staines, at least, could always be relied on to say the right thing.

'Wasn't it, Stainey! Six months for the disorderly house, I'm afraid,' I said regretfully.

'I just hope "Custard" doesn't think we sneaked on him.' Mr Lee looked extremely worried.

'He knows we'd never do a thing like that!' Mrs Lorraine Lee was consoling him.

'Who the hell's "Custard"?' I felt I was losing my grip.

'Pericles. His name's Cuthbert, so we called him "Custard" at school.'

'I suppose that follows,' I admitted.

'*We* know we didn't break the code, Nappy. We've got that to comfort us,' Lorraine told her husband. And I thought that I'd add my own two pennyworth of consolation for them both.

'They'll probably send you to an open Nick,' I said. 'You might meet some of the chaps from school.'

'I never went to Lawnhurst,' Mrs Lee said regretfully.

'By Jove, that's a point.' Napier seemed suddenly depressed.

'Daddy had set his heart on Roedean for me. But it was a question of the readies,' Mrs Lee explained.

But Napier seemed to realize quite suddenly that he was about to be separated from his wife. 'It's boys only where I'm going, I suppose?' he said.

'I'm afraid so. No co-education.' I had to break it to him.

'Sorry, old girl. We'll be separated.' He held out his hand to his wife, and she took it.

'Not for long, Nappy,' she said. 'And we've had a marvellous offer for the freehold.'

'Not to mention the good will!'

'Then you've just got to bear it for six months,' I said as I moved to the door, the rest of the legal team following behind me.

'When a chap's been to Lawnhurst, Mr Rumpole,' Napier said, 'he can't really feel afraid of prison.'

When we left them, they were still holding hands.

Walking back to Chambers with Miss Fiona Allways, I could feel her deep embarrassment and fear of the subject which I knew perfectly well I would have to mention. There was a fine rain falling over Fleet Street then. The buses were roaring beside us, no one could hear what I had to say and, I hoped to goodness, no one had guessed Miss Allways's secret; otherwise hers might have been one of the shortest careers in the history of the legal profession.

'You'd better learn something quickly, Fiona,' I told her. 'If you want to be a barrister, keep the rules!'

'I don't know what you mean ...' she started unconvincingly, and then blushed beneath her headscarf.

'Don't you?' I looked at her. 'Don't worry. I don't imagine Mzz Isobel Vincent is going to reveal her sources. She's all out for glorious martyrdom, and I bet she doesn't want to share her publicity with anyone.' We were turning into the Temple entrance, and I stopped, faced her, and said with all the power I could command, 'But you have to keep the rules! You can swear at them, argue your way round them, do your damnedest to change them, but if you break the rules yourself, how the hell are

167

you going to help the other idiots out of trouble?'

Miss Allways looked at me for a long time, and I hoped to God I wasn't going to see her in tears ever again. 'I'll never get a place in Chambers now,' she said.

'I don't know. Perhaps you will. Perhaps you won't,' I said briskly and started to walk into our place of work. 'You can help me out on another little cause or matter.'

'Can I?' Miss Allways trotted behind me eagerly. I told her what I had in mind. 'Look up the cases on Contempt of Court, why don't you?' I suggested. 'We may be having to cope with the defence of Mzz Vincent, and we've got to keep the good Mzz out of chokey. Martyrs make me exceedingly nervous.'

*   *   *

When I got into the clerk's room, Henry told me that a Chambers meeting was about to take place—a forum, I instantly realized, for preliminary discussions on the Headship, at which the way would be smoothed for the Rumpole take-over at Number 3 Equity Court. So, in the shortest possible time, the ambitions of She Who Must Be Obeyed might be fulfilled. Before I went upstairs, Henry handed me a letter which, he said, had been delivered by hand as a matter of urgency. I stuffed it into my pocket and went upstairs to what had been Guthrie Featherstone's room, and would now, I thought, be my room in perpetuity.

As I got to the head of the stairs, I heard the buzz of voices and, for a moment, I was puzzled that the meeting should have started without my good self

168

as the natural Chairperson and Master of Ceremonies. Then I supposed that they were merely chattering about the splendours and miseries of their days in various Courts. I advanced a couple of steps, threw open the door, entered the room, and then, it is no exaggeration to say, I was frozen in horror and dismay.

Of all the nasty moments in Macbeth's life, and they certainly came to him thick and fast after his encounter with the witches, I have always thought that by far the worst must have come when he went to take his old place at the dinner party and found that the ghost of Banquo had got there before him, and was glowering at the poor old Thane in a blood-bolter'd and accusing sort of way. So it was for me on the occasion of that Chambers meeting, only the person in the chair behind Guthrie's old desk, the man in the seat of honour directing the proceedings, was not Banquo but Sam Ballard, One of Her Majesty's Counsel and founder member of the Lawyers As Churchgoers Society.

'Come along, Rumpole, you're late.' This spectre spoke. 'And would you mind shutting the door.'

'Bollard.' I looked around the room which contained Claude Erskine-Brown, Hoskins, Uncle Tom (our oldest inhabitant) and five or six other assorted barristers. Mrs Phillida Erskine-Brown, our Portia, was apparently away doing a long firm fraud in York.

'What's this?' I asked Ballard. 'A prayer meeting or something? What on earth are you doing here?'

'Hasn't anyone told you?' The man, Ballard, seemed genuinely puzzled. 'Featherstone, J., said he'd written you a note as soon as he knew you were back from Africa.'

169

I pulled the letter Henry had given me from my pocket, and saw it was embossed with the insignia of the Royal Courts of Justice. I have kept the Featherstone letter in my Black Museum to this day, together with other criminally used instruments of murder and mayhem, so I can now give it to you verbatim. All you will miss is Guthrie's haphazard and occasionally illegible handwriting.

'Dear old Horace, old boy,' the letter ran. 'Just a brief note to introduce Sam Ballard, who was, in fact, my fag master at Marlborough, and is now a silk with an excellent practice in the Midlands.' As I read this I felt a faint hope: perhaps the wretched Bollard would stay in the Midlands. 'But,' the letter went on, 'Sam came to us looking for a London home. All the other fellows agreed and, as you were off in the jungle, we know you'd have no objection. Someone'll have to take over as Head of Chambers as I'm detained "During Her Majesty's Pleasure". And Sam Ballard is clearly a likely candidate. But I don't want to interfere, at this distance, with the democratic process of my old set. Marigold joins me in sending all our best wishes to you and Hilda. May you soldier on for many years yet, old fellow. Guthrie Featherstone.'

'Glad you could make it to the meeting, Rumpole.' Hoskins was smiling at me.

'Are you?' I took a seat by the door.

'We thought Roger Bullingham might have put you in chokey, Horace, on a little matter of Contempt of Court!' Claude was having his little joke.

'Oh, Erskine-Brown, you're so amusing!'

'Well. Now we're all assembled . . .' The Bollard

170

throat was being cleared in an ecclesiastical manner.

'Dearly beloved brethren,' I muttered.

'I suppose we should decide who is going to approach the Inn, as the new Head of this Chambers,' Ballard ploughed on regardless. 'Now I don't suppose it's a matter we should want to discuss in a public meeting.'

'What do you suggest we do, Bollard?' I asked. 'Go into a session of silent prayer, and then send puffs of smoke up from the clerk's room? Let's have it out, for God's sake.'

'Speaking for myself, I have been in these Chambers for a good many years,' Erskine-Brown weighed in.

'Not half as long as Rumpole!' Uncle Tom made the first pro-me remark. I thanked him for it silently.

'Rumpole's been here since the year dot, as far as I can remember,' Uncle Tom added, less helpfully.

'And although I've not yet been able to put on the knee breeches and silk gown, as you have, Ballard,' Erskine-Brown gave a modest grin, 'my application is in to the Lord Chancellor's office and I can't imagine there'll be any difficulty.'

'Don't count your chickens, old darling,' I warned him.

'Why? Have you heard anything?' I was relieved to see a look of anxiety on the Erskine-Brown face.

'There's many a slip,' I improvised, 'between the knee breeches and the hip.' This managed to get a lone chuckle from Uncle Tom.

'Of course, I'm a complete newcomer here,' Ballard started off again, very seriously.

'Yes, you are,' I agreed. 'They just dropped you in with today's *Times*.'

171

'But whoever heads these Chambers will, I hope, be able to take the position seriously.' Ballard gave me an aloof sort of look.

'Here endeth the first lesson,' I said.

'It's also terribly important that whoever heads us should be a barrister entirely *sans reproche*,' Claude suggested.

'Oh, *absolument*, Erskine-Brown,' I said.

'Our Chambers is riding high at the moment. One of our number has just been made up to the High Court Bench,' Claude went on.

'Oh, I agree.' Hoskins always agreed. 'We should remember that this election is caused because Guthrie Featherstone has been made a judge.'

'The age of miracles is not dead.' I did a bit of agreeing myself.

'We must be careful to keep our high reputation,' Erskine-Brown said. 'It would be most unfortunate if we had a Head who could possibly be accused of sharp practice.' He gave a casual glance in my direction, and I asked him, 'What do you mean exactly, Erskine-Brown?'

'I don't think there should be any speculation arising out of the recent case at the Old Bailey,' Ballard was delighted to say. 'It's true a question of Contempt of Court *did* arise, but that issue still has to be decided. There has been no finding as to how the information was "leaked". Of course,' he also gave me a look, 'one hopes that the "leak" didn't come from any member of the legal profession.'

'Does one really hope that?' I asked, but Ballard ignored the question.

'So I would ask you all to put the regrettable matter of a flagrant Contempt out of your minds for the purposes of this decision. Wouldn't you agree that that is the fair approach?'

'Oh, Bollard,' I thought. 'How very clever!'

'Well now. Rumpole, as an old member of this set...'

'Of course he's old. Rumpole can't help being old!' Uncle Tom explained to the meeting.

'Have you anything to say?' Ballard asked.

'Why sentence of death should not be passed against me?' I said, and then addressed them all. 'Only this. Don't forget the claims of someone who has been associated with these Chambers for far, far longer than any of you, who grew up in these fly-blown rooms and on this dusty staircase, who doesn't aspire to silk, or judicial office, or even to appearing before the Uxbridge Magistrates, one whose whole ambition is centred on that meaningless title, "Head of Chambers"!'

'What's Rumpole talking about?' Uncle Tom asked no one in particular.

'He means himself,' said Claude.

'No, Erskine-Brown,' I assured him. 'I don't mean me.'

I was thinking, of course, of She Who Must Be Obeyed, whose ambition to be married to the Head of her father's old Chambers was, thinking again of the old Scottish Tragedy, much like Lady Macbeth's bizarre longing to see her husband tricked out in Duncan's crown. When I got home to our mansion flat, She was ambling round a hot stove, and once again She asked me how it went.

'Half and half,' I told her.

'What?'

'The Lees got off the blackmail. Six months apiece on the disorderly house.'

'I don't mean in Court! I mean in *Chambers*.'

173

'Well, it's in Court that things happen, Hilda. People don't get sent to prison in Chambers. Well, not yet, anyway.'

'Oh, don't be so tiresome, Rumpole. I mean in the Chambers meeting! Has it been decided yet?'

It was time to attack an evening bottle of the ordinary claret with a corkscrew, and I did so without delay. Someone had to celebrate something.

'Well. Not finally,' I told her.

'But in principle, Rumpole. I mean, it's been decided in principle?'

'Yes. Yes, I think so.'

'The Chambers party's on the 29th. That's when they'll announce the decision, isn't it?'

'I shouldn't bother to go to that, Hilda.' I poured her a generous slurp. 'They're pretty grim occasions.'

'This won't be grim!' She assured me. 'It'll be a triumph, Rumpole. And nothing on earth is going to keep me away!'

*   *   *

Until the day of the Chambers party dawned, I avoided discussing the subject further with Hilda, and She remained determined to join in what she felt sure would be the jollifications. Not long before the party, our assorted barristers voted on the question of leadership, but for one reason or another I didn't bring home to Hilda the result of their decision. On the day in question, several large cardboard boxes, filled, so it seemed, with 'cocktail snacks', were brought by Hilda's friend, Dodo Mackintosh, round to the mansion flat, and I had to

174

ferry them down to Chambers by taxi.

So, at the end of the day, we all assembled in the former Featherstone room, where Henry and Dianne had set up a bar on the desk, and had Dodo's delicacies set out on plates ready for handing round. Hilda was there, resplendent in what seemed to be a new rig-out, and there were a few other wives and girlfriends, although Mrs Phillida Erskine-Brown, whose practice seemed to be growing to gigantic proportions, was now away doing an arson in Swansea.

I hovered around, keeping within pouring distance of the bar, and I heard my wife in close conversation with the blasted Ballard. She seemed to be giving him a guided tour of Dodo's cookery, which he was consuming steadily without interrupting her flow of words.

'These are cheese-and-oniony, and those are the little sausage arrangements, if that's what you'd prefer,' I heard Hilda telling him. 'Of course, I'll be looking after these parties now. Marigold Featherstone was a sweet person, wasn't she? But I don't think she took a great interest in the canapés.' The same could not be said of Ballard. He took another couple of items from a plate, and Hilda went on talking. 'That's a little prawny sort of vol-au-vent arrangement. Frightfully light, isn't it? I do want these evenings to be a success for Rumpole!'

There was a scatter of applause then for Henry, who requested silence by bumping a glass on the desk, and Uncle Tom was called on to say a few moderately ill-chosen words.

'It falls to me,' he started, 'as the oldest member of Chambers, in the matter of years, to do honours

175

here tonight.'

'Uncle Tom!' Hilda called out to him in high excitement. He stopped and gave her a look of some surprise. 'Mrs Rumpole?'

'Carry on then, Uncle Tom,' Hilda gave her permission gracefully.

'Thank you. I remember Number 3 Equity Court years ago, when old C. H. Wystan was Head of Chambers.'

'Uncle Tom remembers Daddy!' Hilda announced to the world in general.

'Exactly. And Horace Rumpole and I used to hang about waiting for work. I used to practice approach shots with an old mashie niblick! It seemed my one legal ambition was to get my balls into the waste-paper basket in the clerk's room.'

This last sentence caused Miss Fiona Allways to choke on an asparagus roll, and have to be slapped on the back by Henry. Uncle Tom went on with his past history of Equity Court.

'Then the present Mr Justice Featherstone came to head us. Of course, he was then plain Guthrie Featherstone, Q.C., M.P. And now another chapter opens in our history . . .'

'Hear, hear!' Hilda applauded loudly.

'The man I have to introduce as our new Head, agreed on by a comfortable majority, is well known, not only in legal circles but in the Church . . .' Uncle Tom said, and in this puzzled She Who Must Be Obeyed. She looked at me, startled, and murmured, 'Rumpole religious?'

'He is a man deeply concerned with problems of morality,' Uncle Tom continued, warming to his work. 'I happened to be taking dinner with old Tuppy Timpson, ex-Canon of Southwark

Cathedral, and he said, "Little bird told me about your new Head of Chambers. You've got a sound man there. And one who walketh in the ways of righteousness, even through the Valley of the Central Criminal Court."'

'The ways of righteousness!' Hilda was laughing. 'You ought to see him at breakfast, particularly when he's in a nasty temper!'

'Hilda!' I whispered to her, begging her to stop.

'Not much of the ways of righteousness then, Uncle Tom,' She said, but the oldest inhabitant was into his peroration.

'So let us raise a glass, ladies and gentlemen, to our new Head of Chambers. I give you our dear old Chambers, Number 3 Equity Court, coupled with the name . . .'

'Rumpole!' Hilda said loudly, but Uncle Tom was louder when he announced, 'The name of Sam Ballard, One of Her Majesty's Counsel. Long may he reign over us!'

They were all drinking to the Bollard health and all I could say was, 'Amen.' Then I turned to Hilda, and there were tears in her eyes.

'I'm sorry old girl.' I felt I should comfort her. 'You never told me!'

'I funked it.' It was perfectly true.

'Passed over again!' She dabbed her eyes with her handkerchief, sniffed and looked extremely bleak.

'Cheer up,' I said. 'It's not the end of the world. You know you're still a great advocate. Terrific in an argument. Who cares about being Head of Chambers?'

Henry had found a bottle of Pommeroy's special offer champagne to toast our new leader, and I got my fingers round it. Hilda looked at me coldly, and

177

then pronounced judgement.

'You're a failure, Rumpole!' she said.

'Then take a slurp of champagne, why don't you?' I filled our glasses. 'Let's drink to failure!'

But Hilda was looking across to where Ballard stood masticating.

'He's eating *all* Dodo's little cheesy bits. The *cheek* of it!' she said. She sounded furious and I knew, with considerable relief, that She Who Must Be Obeyed was herself again.

RUMPOLE AND THE FEMALE OF THE SPECIES

It may be said by those who read these memoirs, particularly by those of the female persuasion, that Rumpole is in some ways unsympathetic to the aspirations of women. This may be because, in the privacy of my own thoughts and when writing late at night in the solitary confines of my kitchen, I refer to my wife, Hilda Rumpole, as 'She Who Must Be Obeyed'. It is true that I have given her this title, but Hilda's character, her air of easy command which might, if she had been born in other circumstances, have brought empires under her sway, and her undisputed government of our daily life at Froxbury Court, entitles her to no less an acclamation. Those who feel that I am not firmly on the female side in the Battle of the Sexes may care to consider my long struggle to get Miss Fiona Allways accepted as a member of our Chambers at Equity Court, and those who might think that I only engaged myself in this struggle to annoy the egregious Bollard and irritate Claude Erskine-Brown are guilty of a quite unworthy cynicism.

The dispute over the entry of Miss Allways into our close-knit group of learned friends arose during the time that our Chambers had a brief in the Pond Hill bank job. We were charged with the defence of Tony Timson.

I have written repeatedly elsewhere of the Timsons, the large family of South London villains who, many years ago, appointed me their Attorney-General and whose unending efforts have brought a considerable amount of work to Equity Court. Tony Timson belonged to the younger generation of the clan. He occupied a pleasant, semi-detached house on a South London estate with his wife, April, and their child, Vincent. His house was lavishly furnished with a large variety of video-recording machines, television sets, hi-fi equipment, spindriers, eye-line grills, ultraviolet-ray cookers, deep freezes and suchlike aids to gracious living. Many of these articles were said to be the fruit of Tony Timson's tireless night work.

When Inspector Broome called at the Timson house shortly after the Pond Hill bank job, he found the young master alone and playing 'Home Sweet Home' on a newly acquired electric organ. He also found five thousand pounds in crisp, new, neatly packaged twenty-pound notes in the gleaming Super Snow White Extra Deluxe model washing machine. Tony Timson was ripped from the bosom of his wife April and young Vincent, and placed within the confines of Brixton Prison, and I wondered if I should ultimately get the brief.

The appointment of Rumpole for the defence should, of course, have been a foregone conclusion. But the Timson Solicitor-General was Mr Bernard, and between that gentleman and Rumpole there was a bit of a cold wind blowing, owing to a tiff which had taken place one day at the Uxbridge Magistrates Court. I had arrived at this particular Palais de Justice a little late one day, owing to a tailback on the Piccadilly Line, only to discover that the gutless Bernard had allowed our client of the day to plead guilty to a charge of handling. He had thrown in the towel!

I hadn't actually been rude to Mr Bernard. I had

merely improved his education by quoting Shakespeare's *Richard II*. 'O, villain, viper, damned without redemption!' I said to my instructing solicitor, 'Would you make peace? Terrible hell make war upon your spotted soul for this.' Mr Bernard, it seemed, hadn't appreciated the quality of the lines and there was, as I say, an east wind blowing between us. So I wasn't greatly surprised when Henry gave me an account of what happened when Bernard came into our clerk's room and gave Henry the brief in R. *v.* Timson. Henry said that he supposed that would be for Mr Rumpole.

'You suppose wrong, young man,' Mr Bernard said firmly.

'Do I?' Henry raised his eyebrows.

'The brief is clearly marked for the attention of Mrs Phillida Erskine-Brown,' Bernard pointed out, and Henry saw that it was so. 'I can put up with a good deal, Henry, from members of the so-called senior branch of our great profession,' Mr Bernard told him, 'but I will not be called a villainous viper in the clear hearing of the Clerk to the Uxbridge Magistrates Court.'

At which point Mrs Phillida Erskine-Brown, now an extremely successful lady barrister, entered the clerk's room and Henry handed her the papers.

'A wonderfully prepared brief, I don't doubt, like all Mr Bernard's work.' Phillida smiled with great charm at the glowing solicitor, and then asked tactfully, 'How's your daughter, Mr Bernard? Polytechnic going well still, is it?' Mrs Erskine-Brown, since the days when she was plain Miss Phillida Trant, hadn't got where she was by legal ability alone; she was expert at public relations.

'Three A's,' Mr Bernard was delighted to say. 'Thank you for asking.'

'And *still* keeping up her figure skating, I bet. Chip off the old block, wouldn't you say so, Henry? See you in Brixton, Mr Bernard.'

She flashed another smile and went on her way, whereupon Bernard told Henry that he always thought that Mrs Erskine-Brown had a real feeling for the law.

★ ★ ★

I had decided to improve the facilities in our mansion flat at Froxbury Court by erecting a shelf on our living-room wall to accommodate such necessities as *The Oxford Book of English Verse* (the Quiller-Couch edition), Professor Andrew Ackerman on *The Importance of Bloodstains in the Detection of Crime*, Archbold's *Criminal Pleading and Practice*—a little out of date, and a spare bottle or two of Château Thames Embankment of a fairly recent year. I celebrated my entry into the construction industry by buying what I think is known as a 'kit' of Easy-Do Convenience Shelving and a few basic tools, and in no time at all, such was my natural feeling for woodwork, I had the shelf up and triumphantly bearing its load.

When I showed the results of my labours to Hilda, she didn't immediately congratulate me, but asked, unnecessarily I thought, if I had 'plugged' the wall in accordance with the instructions that came in the 'Easy-Do' box.

'I never read the instructions to counsel before doing a murder, Hilda,' I told her firmly. 'Rely on the facts, and the instinct of the advocate. It's never let me down yet in Court.'

'Well, I do notice you haven't been in Court very much lately.' Hilda took an unfair advantage.

'A temporary lull in business. Nothing serious,' I assured her.

'It's because you're rude to solicitors.' Hilda, of course, knew best. I didn't want to argue the matter further, so I told her that my new shelf was firm as a rock, and added an air of distinction to our living room.

'Are you sure it's straight?' Hilda asked. 'I think it's definitely at an angle.'

'Oh really, Hilda! It's because *you're* at an angle,' I said, I'm afraid a little impatiently. 'One small gin and tonic at lunchtime and you do your well-known imitation of the Leaning Tower of Pisa.'

'Well, if that's how you talk to solicitors,' Hilda was starting to tidy away my carpenter's tools and sweep up the sawdust, 'no wonder I've got you at home all day.' As I have remarked earlier, there is a good deal to be said in favour of She Who Must Be Obeyed, but she's hardly a fair opponent in an argument.

★   ★   ★

I left our improved home and went down to Chambers and, there being not much else to engage my attention before a five o'clock Chambers meeting, I took a little time off to instruct Miss Fiona Allways, who had proudly acquired a case entirely of her own, in the art of making a final speech for the defence. Picture us then, alone in my room, the teacher Rumpole standing as though to address the Court and the pupil Allways sitting obediently to learn.

'Soon this case will be over, members of the jury.' I gave her my usual peroration. 'In a little while you will go back to your jobs and your families, and you will forget all about it. At most it is only a small part of your lives. But for my client it is the *whole* of his life! And it is that life I leave with confidence in your hands, certain that there can be only one verdict in this case—"Not Guilty"!... Sink down exhausted then, Fiona,' I told her, 'mopping the brow.' I sat and plied a large red spotted handkerchief. 'Good end to a final speech, don't you think?'

'Will it work just as well for me?' she asked doubtfully. 'I mean, my man's only accused of nicking six frozen chicken pieces from Safeways.'

'Goes just as well on any occasion!' I assured her.

And then Claude Erskine-Brown put his head round the door and told me that Bernard was upstairs and just about to start the Chambers meeting. Erskine-Brown then retired and Fiona looked at me in a despondent sort of manner.

'Is this when they decide,' she sounded desperately anxious, 'if they're going to let me stay on here?'

'Don't worry. I shall tell them...' I promised her.

'What?'

'Well, let me think. Something like, "The female of the species is more deadly than the male." Look on the bright side, Miss Allways. Perk up, Fiona. I've cracked far tougher Courts than that lot up there!'

I went to the door without any real idea of how to

184

handle the case of Allways and then, as so often happens, thank God, inspiration struck. I turned back towards her.

'Oh, by the way,' I said. 'Just one question. You know old Claude, who just popped his head in here?'

'Mr Erskine-Brown?'

'He doesn't tickle your fancy, does he, by any chance? You don't find him devastatingly attractive?'

'Of course not!' Fiona managed her first smile of the day. 'He's hardly Paul Newman, is he?'

'No, I suppose he isn't.' I must confess the news came to me as something of a relief. 'Well, that's all right then. I'll see what I can do.'

Ballard had made a few changes, none of them very much for the better, in Featherstone's old room. Guthrie's comfortable chairs had gone, and his silver cigarette-box, his picture of Marigold and the children, his comforting sherry decanter and bone china tea service and his perfectly harmless watercolours. Ballard had few luxuries except a number of etchings of English cathedrals in plain, light oak frames, the corners of which protruded in a Gothic and ecclesiastical manner, and an old tin of ginger biscuits which stood on his desk, and which he never offered about.

'Sorry. Am I late for Evensong?' I asked cheerfully as I sat beside Uncle Tom. Ballard, without a glance in my direction, continued with the business in hand.

'We have to consider an application by Fiona Allways for a permanent seat in Chambers,' he said. 'Mrs Erskine-Brown, you were her pupil master.'

'Mistress,' I corrected him, but nobody noticed.

185

'It's an extremely tough life at the Bar for a woman,' Phillida spoke from the depths of her experience. 'I'm by no means sure that Allways has got what it takes. Just as a for instance, she burst into tears when left alone at Thames Magistrates Court.'

'I know exactly how she felt,' I said. 'That was never my favourite tribunal.'

'Of course. Rumpole's done a case with her.' Ballard looked at me in a vaguely accusing manner.

'She took a note for me once. Something about her I liked,' I had to admit. And when Hoskins asked me what it was, I said that she felt strongly about winning cases.

'Who is this fellow Allways?' Uncle Tom asked with an expression of mild bewilderment.

'This fellow's a girl, Uncle Tom,' I told him.

'Oh, good heavens. Are we getting another one of them?' Our oldest inhabitant grumbled, and Mrs Erskine-Brown brought the discussion up to date by saying, 'I really don't think that the mere fact that this girl is a girl should guarantee her a place at 3 Equity Court.'

'Philly's perfectly right.' Claude came in as a dutiful husband should. 'We shouldn't take in a token woman, like a token black.'

'Are we taking in a black woman, then?' Uncle Tom merely asked for clarity.

'Why not?' I said. 'I could've brought one back from Africa.'

'This is obviously a problem that has to be taken seriously.' Ballard spoke disapprovingly from the chair.

'Well, I think we should go for a well-established man. Someone who's got to know a few solicitors,

186

who can bring work to Chambers,' Mrs
Erskine-Brown suggested politically.

'Steady on, Portia old fellow,' I cautioned her.
'Whatever happened to the quality of mercy?'

'I honestly don't see what mercy has to do with
it.'

'Dear God,' I was moved to say. 'It seems but
yesterday that Miss Phillida Trant, white in the wig
and a newcomer to the ladies' robing room, was
accusing Henry of hiding the key to the lavatory, as
a sexist gesture! Can it be that now you've stormed
the citadel you want to slam the door behind you?'

'Really, Rumpole!' Ballard called me to order.
'You're not addressing a jury now. I don't think
anyone could possibly accuse this Chambers of
having the slightest prejudice against female
barristers.'

'Of course not. Provided they settle somewhere
else, no doubt we find them quite delightful,' I
agreed.

'I believe I've told you all that I've applied for a
silk gown.' Erskine-Brown was never tired of telling
us this.

'And I'm sure you'll look extremely pretty in it,'
I assured him.

'And from what I hear, quite informally of
course...'

'In the bag, is it, Erskine-Brown?'

'That's not for me to say, but Philly is, of course,
right behind me in this.'

'Absolutely,' his wife assured him. The
Erskine-Browns were in a conjugal mood that day.
And he rambled on, saying, 'So with two Q.C.s at
the top, it would be a great pity if these Chambers
became weak in the tail.'

'What would be a pity?' Uncle Tom asked me.

'If our tail got weak, Uncle Tom.'

'Of course it would.' It was a puzzling meeting for the old boy. Erskine-Brown didn't further enlighten him by saying, 'I'm not interested in the sex side, of course.' I noticed then that his wife was looking into the middle distance in a detached sort of way. 'But I just don't feel that Allways is the right person to carry on the best traditions of these Chambers.'

'I agree,' Hoskins agreed.

'So Fiona Allways can swell the ranks of the unemployed?' I asked with some asperity.

'Oh, come on, Rumpole. She's got a rich daddy. She's not going to starve.'

'Only miss the one thing she's ever wanted to do,' I grumbled, but Ballard was collecting the final views of the meeting. He asked Uncle Tom for his considered opinion.

'I remember a Fiona. Used to work in the List Office.' Uncle Tom wasn't particularly helpful. 'She wasn't black, of course. No, I'm against it.'

'Well, I think I've got the sense of the meeting. I shall tell Miss Allways that she'll have to look elsewhere.'

It was time for quick thinking, and I thought extremely quickly. The best way to confuse lawyers is to tell them about a law which they think they've forgotten.

'Just a moment.' I hauled a diary out of my waistcoat pocket.

'What is it, Rumpole?' Ballard sounded impatient.

'This isn't the third Thursday of the Hilary Term!' I said severely.

188

'Of course it isn't.' Erskine-Brown had not got my point, but I had, just in time. 'Well!' I said positively. 'We always decide questions of Chambers entry on the third Thursday of the Hilary Term. It was the rule of my sainted father-in-law's day. Guthrie Featherstone, Q.C., observed it religiously. Of course, if the new broom wants to make any *radical* changes . . . ?' I looked at Ballard in a strict sort of way, and I must say he flinched.

'Well. No,' he said. 'I suppose not. Are you sure it's the rule?' He looked at Erskine-Brown, who couldn't say he remembered it.

'You were in rompers, Erskine-Brown, when this thing was first decided,' I told him impatiently. 'Our old clerk, Albert, said it was impossible otherwise, from a book-keeping point of view. I do think we should keep to the rules, don't you, Ballard? I mean, we can't have anarchy at Equity Court!'

'That's in four weeks' time.' Ballard was consulting his diary now.

'Exactly!'

Ballard put away his diary and came to a decision. 'We'll deal with it then. It shouldn't take long, as we've reached a conclusion.'

'Oh no. A mere formality,' I agreed.

'What are you playing at, Rumpole?' Mrs Erskine-Brown was looking at me with some suspicion.

'Nothing much, Portia,' I assured her. 'Merely keeping up the best traditions of these Chambers.'

★　　★　　★

The Pond Hill branch of the United Metropolitan Bank was held up by a number of men in stocking masks, who carried holdalls from which emerged a sawn-off shotgun or two and a sledgehammer for shattering the glass in front of the cashier. When the robbery was complete the four masked men ran to the getaway car, a stolen Ford Cortina, which was waiting for them outside the bank, and it was this vehicle, the prosecution alleged, that Tony Timson had been driving. On the way to the car one of the men stumbled and fell. He was seized upon by an officer on traffic duty, and later found to be a Mr Gerry Molloy—a remarkable fact when you consider the deep hostility which has always existed between the Timson family and the clan Molloy. Indeed, these two tribes have hated each other for as long as I can remember and I have already chronicled an instance of their feud [See 'Rumpole and the Younger Generation' in *Rumpole of the Bailey*, Penguin Books, 1978].

It seems that all the other men engaged on the Pond Hill enterprise were Molloys. They got away, so it was hardly to be wondered at that Mr Gerald Molloy decided to become a grass and involve a Timson when he told his story to the police.

In the course of time Mrs Erskine-Brown and her instructing solicitor went to Brixton to see their client but, as I later heard from him and from Mr Bernard, Tony Timson seemed to have only one thing on his mind as he walked into the interview room and said, 'Where's Mr Rumpole?'

Phillida Erskine-Brown, in her jolliest, 'we're all lads together' voice, merely said, 'Care for a fag, Tony?' Tony didn't mind if he did, and when Phillida had lit it for him, Bernard broke the bad

190

news.

'This is Mrs Erskine-Brown, Tony,' he said. 'She's going to be your brief.'

'I see they've charged you with taking part in the robbery, not merely the receiving. Of course, they've done that on Gerry Molloy's evidence.' Phillida started off in a businesslike way, but Tony Timson was looking at his solicitor in a kind of panic and paying no attention to her at all.

'Mr Rumpole's always the Timson's brief,' he said. 'You know that, Mr Bernard. Mr Rumpole defended my dad, and my Uncle Cyril and saw me through my Juvenile Court and my Borstal training . . .'

'Mr Rumpole can't have done all that well for you if you got Borstal training,' Bernard said reasonably.

'Well . . .' Tony looked at Phillida for support. 'Win a few, lose a few, you know that, missus?'

'Any reason why Gerry Molloy should grass on you, Tony?' Phillida tried to return to the matter in hand.

'Look. It's good of you to come here but . . .'

At which Phillida, no doubt in an attempt to reassure the client, lapsed into robbers' argot. 'You ever had a meet with him where any sort of bank job was ever mentioned?' she asked. 'Molloy says in the deps that he was the sledge, two others had sawn-offs in their holdalls, and you were the driver. He says you're pretty good on wheels, Tony.'

'This is highly embarrassing, this is.' Tony looked suitably pained at Phillida's personal knowledge of crime.

'What is, Tony?' She did her best to sound deeply sympathetic.

191

'You being a woman and all. It don't feel right, not with a woman.'

'Don't think of me as a woman, Tony,' she tried to reassure him. 'Think of me entirely as a brief.'

'It's no good.' Tony shook his head. 'I keep thinking of my wife, April.'

'Well, of course she's worried about you. That's only natural, seeing you got nicked, Tony.'

'I don't mean that. I mean I wouldn't want a woman like my April to take on my job, would I? Briefs, and us what gets ourselves into a bit of trouble down the Bailey and that. It's all man's work, innit?'

Well, that may come as a shrewd shock to all readers of those women's pages which I have occasionally glanced at in Fiona Allways's *Guardian*, but I'm told that it is exactly what Tony Timson said. As a consequence it was a rueful Phillida Erskine-Brown who walked away from the interview room, across the yard where the screws exercised the alsatians and the trusties weeded the flower beds, towards the gate.

'The Timsons are such *old-fashioned* villains.' Mr Bernard apologized for them. 'They're always about half a century behind the times.'

'It's not your fault, Mr Bernard,' said Phillida miserably.

'You wait till my wife gets to hear about this! They're pretty hot on women's rights in the Hammersmith S.D.P.' Bernard was clearly deeply affronted.

'It's the client's right to choose.' Phillida was taking it on the chin.

'It's decent of you to be like that about it, Mrs Erskine-Brown. It's absolutely no reflection on you,

192

of course. But...' Bernard looked deeply embarrassed. 'I'm afraid I'll have to take in a chap to lead you.'

They had arrived at the gatehouse and were about to be sprung, when Phillida Erskine-Brown looked at Mr Bernard and said she wondered who the chap would be exactly.

'It goes against the grain,' said Bernard, 'but we've really got no choice, have we?'

*　　*　　*

A good deal later that evening I was on my way home when I happened to pass Pommeroy's Wine Bar and, in the hope that they might be offloading cooking claret at a reasonable rate, I went in and saw, alone and palely loitering at the bar with an oldish sandwich and a glass of hock, none other than Claude Erskine-Brown. I saw the chance of playing another card in the long game of 'Getting Fiona into Chambers', and I engaged the woebegone figure in conversation, the burden of which was that Phillida was so enormously busy at the Bar that the sandwich might well have to do for the Erskine-Brown supper.

'Of course,' I said sympathetically. 'Your wife must be pretty hard pressed now she's taken the Timsons off me.'

'She doesn't get home in the evenings until Tristan's gone to bed,' Erskine-Brown told me, and I looked at him and said, 'Just as well.'

'Do you think so?' The man sounded slightly offended.

'Just as well young Fiona Allways isn't coming into Chambers,' I explained.

'You agree that we shouldn't take her?'

'In all the circumstances, well, perhaps I'd better not say anything.'

'*What* do you mean, Rumpole?' Erskine-Brown was puzzled.

'It might have raised all sorts of problems. I mean, it might have got too much for you to handle.'

'*What* might have got too much for me to handle?'

'It would create all sorts of difficulties, in the spring, and all that sort of thing. We don't want the delicate perfume of young Fiona floating round Chambers, do we?' I said, as casually as possible.

'Well, I don't suppose I'd've seen much of her.'

'Oh, but you would, you know.'

'Not as a silk.'

'You'd've been thrown together. Chambers meetings. Brushing past each other in the clerk's room. Before you knew where you were you'd be popping out for tea and a couple of chocky biscuits in the ABC.' I looked as gravely concerned as I knew how. 'Terribly dangerous!'

'Why on earth?' He still hadn't quite caught my drift.

'Well, you know exactly what these young lady barristers are, impressionable, passionate even, and enormously impressed with the older legal hack, especially one teetering on the verge of knee breeches and a silk gown.'

'You don't mean . . . ?' I could see that now he had perked up considerably.

'And she seems to find you extremely personable, Claude!' I laid it on thick. 'You put her in distinct mind, so she has told me, of a film

194

actor—"Newman", could that be the name?' I
asked innocently, and drained my glass. At which
moment, Claude Erskine-Brown took off his
spectacles and admired himself in one of the
mirrors, decorated with fronds of frosty vegetation,
that cover Pommeroy's walls. 'Ridiculous!' he said,
but I could see that the old fish was well and truly
hooked.

'Of course it's ridiculous,' I agreed. 'But on
second thoughts, far better she doesn't get into
Chambers. Wouldn't you agree?' I left him then,
but as I went out of Pommeroy's, Erskine-Brown
was still looking at himself shortsightedly in the
mirror.

The next day Henry gave me the glad news that I
was to be *leading* the extraordinarily busy Mrs
Phillida Erskine-Brown in the Timson defence. It
seemed that Mr Bernard had seen sense on the
subject of our little disagreement at Uxbridge, but
Henry told me, extremely severely, that he couldn't
go on clerking for me if I called my instructing
solicitor a 'viper' again. I asked him if he'd pass
'snake', assured him I wasn't serious, and then
went up to seek out our new Head of Chambers in
his lair.

I was going to play the next card in the Fiona
Allways game. I knocked at the door, heard a cry of
'Who is it?' and found Ballard with a cup of tea and
a ginger biscuit working on some massive
prosecution involving a large number of villains
who were all represented by different-coloured
pencils.

'Oh. It's you.' Our leader didn't sound
particularly welcoming. All the same I came in,
pushed Ballard's papers aside and sat on the edge of

his desk.

'Just thought I ought to give you a friendly warning,' I started confidentially.

'Isn't it you that needs warning? Henry tells me that you've taken to being offensive to Mr Bernard.'

I lit up a small cigar and blew out smoke. Ballard coughed pointedly.

'It doesn't do Chambers any good, you know, insulting a solicitor,' he told me. By way of an answer I closed my eyes and tried a vivid description.

'Fascinating character!' I began. 'Marvellous hair, burnished like autumn leaves. Tender white neck, sticking out of the starched white collar . . .'

'Mr Bernard?' Ballard was puzzled.

'Of course not!' I put him right. 'I was speaking of Miss Phillida Trant, now Mrs Erskine-Brown.' I brought out the packet of small cigars and offered it. 'You don't smoke, I suppose?'

'You know I don't.'

'What *do* you do, I wonder?' There was a short diversion as Ballard blew my ash off his depositions and then I said thoughtfully, 'Gorgeous creature in many ways, our Portia.'

'With a most enviable practice, I understand,' Ballard agreed. 'Perhaps she's polite to solicitors.'

'Determined to rise to the absolute top.'

'I have the highest respect for Phillida, of course, but . . .'

'Devious.' I supplied the word. 'A brilliant mind, of course, but devious!'

'Rumpole. What are you trying to tell me?' Ballard seemed anxious to bring our dialogue to a swift conclusion.

'The way she got you to show your sexual

196

prejudices at that Chambers meeting!' I said with admiration.

'My *what*...?'

'Your blind and Victorian opposition to women in the legal profession. I believe she's writing a report on that to the Bar Council. Plus ten articles for the *Observer*, in depth.'

'But Rumpole, she spoke *against* Allways.' Ballard was already arguing weakly.

'What a tactician!' For the sake of emphasis, I gave Ballard a brisk slap on the shoulder.

'She seemed totally opposed to the girl.'

I slipped off his desk and took a turn round the room. 'Just to lead you on, don't you see? To get *you* to show your hand. You walked right into it, Bollard. I can see the headlines now! "Christian barrister presides over sexist redoubt!" "Bollard, Q.C., puts the clock back fifty years."'

'Ballard.' He corrected me without too much conviction and said, 'I didn't take that attitude, surely.'

'You will have done!' I assured him, 'by the time our Phillida's finished with you. Don't cross her, Bollard, I warn you. She has the ear of the Lord Chancellor. I don't know if you were ever hoping for some sort of minor judgeship...' I went to the door and then turned back to Ballard. 'Of course, you have one thing in your favour.'

'What's that?' He seemed prepared to clutch at a straw. It was then that I played the ace. 'Our Portia seems to have taken something of a shine to you,' I told him. '"Craggily handsome" I think was the way she put it. I suppose there's just a chance you might get round her. Try using your irresistible charm.'

I left him then. The poor old darling was looking like a person who has to choose between a public execution and a heady draught of hemlock.

*　　*　　*

Whatever may be said about the equality of the sexes, there is still something about the nature of women which parts the average man almost entirely from his marbles. Faced with most problems, both Erskine-Brown and Ballard might have proved reasonably resolute. When the question concerned a moderately personable young woman, they became as clay in the potter's hands. These thoughts passed through my mind as I lay in bed that night staring at the ceiling, while Hilda sat at the dressing table in night attire, brushing her hair before coming to bed.

'What are you thinking, Rumpole?' she asked. 'I know you, Rumpole. You're lying there *thinking* about something!'

'I was thinking,' I confessed, 'about man's attitude to the female of the species.'

'Oh, were you indeed?' Hilda sounded deeply suspicious.

'On the one hand the presence of a woman strikes him with terror!'

'Really, Rumpole, don't be absurd,' Hilda said severely.

'And fierce resentment.'

'Is *that* what you were thinking?'

'And yet he finds her not only indispensable, but quite irresistible. Faced with a whiff of perfume, for instance, he is reduced to a state bordering on imbecility.'

'Rumpole. Are you really?' Hilda's voice had softened considerably. The room became redolent with the smell of lavender water. Hilda was spraying on perfume.

'She is a woman, therefore may be woo'd;
She is a woman, therefore may be won;'

I repeated sleepily.

I saw Hilda emerge from her dressing gown and make towards the bed. She said, 'Oh, Rumpole ...' quite tenderly. But then sleep claimed me, and I heard no more.

*   *   *

One afternoon I turned up at the gates of Brixton Prison with my learned junior, Mrs Phillida Erskine-Brown, and there was Mr Bernard waiting for us and replying to my hearty greeting in a somewhat guarded manner.

'Hail to thee blythe Bernard!' I said, and he replied, 'we're taking you in on the express wishes of the client, Mr Rumpole. Just for this case.'

I then became aware of a pleasant-looking young woman with blonde hair and a small, rather plump child who was sitting slumped in a pushchair, regarding me with a wary eye.

'Mr Rumpole.' The lady introduced herself. 'I'm April Timson. Tony's that glad that you're going to be his brief.'

My companion looked less than flattered, but I greeted our client's family warmly.

'Mrs Timson, good of you to say so. And who's this young hopeful?'

199

'That's our young Vince. Been in to see his dad,' said the child's proud mother.

'Delighted to meet you, Vincent,' I said, and managed to leave a thought with April which might pay off in the course of time. 'Let me know,' I said, 'the moment he gets into trouble.'

★   ★   ★

'Straight up, it's a sodding plant,' said Tony Timson, and then turned apologetically to my junior. 'Pardon my French.'

'Don't be so silly, Tony.' Phillida didn't like not being taken for one of the boys. We were sitting in a small glass-walled room in the interview block at Brixton, and I felt I had to question Tony further as to his suggested defence.

'What sort of a plant are you suggesting,' I asked. 'A floribunda of the Serious Crimes Squad or an exotic bloom cultivated by the Molloys?'

'That D.I. Broome. He's got no love for the Timsons,' Tony grumbled.

'Neither have the Molloys.'

'That's true, Mr Rumpole. That's very true.'

'A plant by the supergrass's family? I suppose it's possible.' I considered the suggestion.

'I'd say it's typical.'

'So some person unknown brought in the cash and popped it into your Super Snow White Extra DeLuxe Easy-Wash?' I framed the charge.

'The jury may now wonder how Tony can afford all these luxuries out of window-cleaning,' Phillida suggested.

'It's not a luxury. My April says it's just something you got to have,' said Tony, the proud householder.

'You know how he affords these things, Portia?' I explained our case to one not expert in the Timson branch of the law. 'Tony's a minor villain. Small stuff. Let's have a look at his form.' I plucked a sheet of paper from my brief. 'Warehouse-breaking, shop-breaking, criminal damage to a set of traffic lights...'

'I misjudged a turning, Mr Rumpole,' Tony admitted. It was the item of which he seemed slightly ashamed. But there was more to come.

'Careless driving, dangerous driving, failing to report an accident,' I read out. 'Look here, old sweetheart. If I get you out of this, do promise not to give me a lift home.'

★   ★   ★

That same evening, Claude Erskine-Brown put his head round the door of my room, where Miss Fiona Allways was looking up a bit of law, and invited her to join him in a bottle of Pommeroy's bubbly. Naturally anxious to be on friendly terms with those who held her legal future in their hands, she accepted the invitation, and I am indebted to her for an account of what then took place.

Once ensconced at a corner table in the shadowy regions of the wine bar, Erskine-Brown took off his spectacles and sighed as though worn out by the cares of office.

'It can be lonely at the top, Fiona,' he said. 'I mean, you may wonder what it feels like to be on the verge of becoming a Q.C.' Perhaps he was waiting for her to say something, but as she didn't he repeated with a sigh, 'I'll tell you. Lonely.'

'But you've got Mrs Erskine-Brown.' Fiona was puzzled.

Claude gave her a sad little smile. 'Mrs Erskine-Brown! I seem to see so little of Phillida nowadays. Pressure of work, of course. No,' he went on seriously, 'there comes a time in this job when a person feels terribly alone.'

'I suppose so.' Fiona felt the topic was becoming exhausted.

'I envy you those happy, carefree days when you hop from Magistrates Court to Magistrates Court, picking up little crumbs of indecent exposure.'

'Frozen chicken,' Fiona corrected him.

'What?' Erskine-Brown looked puzzled.

'I was doing a case about frozen chicken pieces. It seemed quite a responsibility to me.'

As the subject had moved from himself Claude's attention wandered. He looked across to the bar and said, 'Is that old Rumpole over there?'

'Why?' Fiona asked, in all innocence. 'Can't you see without your glasses?'

In fact, and this Erskine-Brown didn't notice, perhaps because she was hidden in the mêlée at the bar, I had come into the joint with Phillida in order that we might refresh ourselves after a hard conference at Brixton. I said I hoped she had no hard feelings about me being taken in to lead her in the Timson affair. She confessed to just a few hard feelings, but was then sporting enough to buy us a perfectly reasonable bottle.

'Criminals and barristers, Portia,' I told her as Jack Pommeroy was uncorking the claret. 'Both extremely conservative professions...'

But before she had time to absorb this thought, Phillida was off like a hound on the scent towards a

202

corner of the room. Again I have to rely on Miss Allways's account for what was going on at the distant table.

'And if ever you have the slightest problem,' Erskine-Brown was saying gently, 'of a legal nature, or anything else come to that, don't hesitate, Fiona. A silk's door is always open to a member of Chambers, however junior.'

'A member of Chambers?' Fiona repeated hopefully.

'I'm sure. I mean, some old squares are tremendously prejudiced against women, of course. But speaking for myself...' He put a hand on one of Fiona's which she had left lying about on the table. 'I have absolutely no objection to a pretty face around Number 3 Equity Court.'

'Haven't you, Claude?' Mrs Erskine-Brown had fetched up beside the table and spoke with considerable asperity.

'Oh, Philly.' Erskine-Brown hastily withdrew his hand. 'Are you going to join us for a drink? You know Fiona, of course...'

'Yes. I know Allways.' Phillida looked suspiciously at the gold-topped bottle. 'What is it? Somebody's birthday? No, I'm not joining you two. I'm going to go straight back to Chambers and write a letter.'

At which Phillida Erskine-Brown banged out of Pommeroy's, leaving her husband with a somewhat foolish expression on his face, and me with an entire bottle of claret.

Phillida, always as good as her word, did go back to her room in Chambers and started to write a lengthy and important letter to an official quarter. It was whilst she was doing this that there came a tap at her door, which she ignored, and then the devout Ballard entered uninvited. This time I have to rely on our Portia for a full account of what transpired, and when she told me, over a rather hilarious celebratory bottle about a month later, her recollection may have grown somewhat dim; but she swears that it was a Ballard transformed who came gliding up to her desk. He was wearing a somewhat garish spotted tie (in pink and blue, as she remembered it), a matching silk handkerchief lolled from his top pocket, and surrounding the man was a fairly overpowering odour of some aftershave which the manufacturers advertise as 'Trouble-starter'. He was also smiling.

'I saw your light on,' Ballard murmured. Apparently Phillida didn't find this a statement of earth-shaking interest and went on writing.

'Mrs Erskine-Brown,' Ballard tried again. 'You won't mind me calling you Phyllis?'

'If you want to, but it doesn't happen to be my name.' Phillida didn't look up from her writing.

'Burning the midnight oil?'

'It's only half past six.'

Although she had given him little encouragement, Ballard came and perched, no doubt as he thought, jauntily, on the corner of her desk and made what seemed to Phillida to be an entirely unnecessary disclosure. 'I've never married of course,' he said.

'Lucky you!' Phillida said with meaning as she went on with her work.

'I lead what I imagine you'd call a bit of a bachelor life in Dulwich. Decent-sized flat, though, all that sort of thing.'

'Oh, good,' Phillida said in as neutral a manner as

possible.

'But I don't want you to run away with the idea that I don't like *women*, because I do like women ... very much indeed. I am a perfectly normal sort of chap in that regard,' Ballard assured her.

'Oh, jolly good.' Phillida was still busy.

'In fact, I have to confess this to you. I find the sight of a woman wigged and wearing a winged collar surprisingly, well, let's be honest about this, alluring.' There was a considerable pause and then he blurted out, 'I saw you the other day, going up the stairs in the Law Courts. Robed up!'

'Did you? I was on my way to do a divorce.' Phillida was folding her letter with grim determination.

'Well, I just didn't want you to be under any illusions.' Ballard stood and gave Phillida what was no doubt meant to be a challenging look. 'I'm thoroughly in favour of women, from every point of view.'

'I'm sure the news will come as an enormous relief to the women of the world!' She licked the envelope and stuck it down. What she said seemed to have a strange effect on Ballard and he became extremely nervous.

'Oh, I don't want it published in the papers!' he said anxiously. 'I thought I'd make it perfectly clear to you, in the course of private conversation.'

'Well, you've made it clear, Ballard.' Phillida looked him in the eye for the first time, and didn't particularly like what she saw.

'Please, "Sam",' he corrected her skittishly.

'All right, "Sam". You've made it terribly clear,' she repeated.

'Look. Some day when you're not in Court,' he

205

was smiling at her again, 'why don't you let me take you out to a spot of lunch? They do a very decent set meal at the Ludgate Hotel.'

Phillida looked at him with amazement and contempt. She then got up and walked past him to the door, taking her letter. 'I've got to put this out to post,' was all she had to say to that.

I had gone back to our clerk's room to pick up some forgotten papers and was alone there, Henry and Dianne having left for some unknown destination, when Phillida came to put her letter in the 'Post' tray on Dianne's desk.

'What on earth happened, Portia?' I asked her. 'You left me to finish the bottle.'

'Has everyone in this Chambers gone completely out of their heads?' she replied with another question.

'Everyone?'

'Ballard just made the most disgusting suggestion to me.' She did seem extremely angry.

'Bollard did? Whatever was it?' I asked, delighted.

'He invited me to have the set lunch at the Ludgate Hotel. And as for my so-called husband...' Words failing her, she went to the door. 'Goodnight, Rumpole!'

'Goodnight, Portia.'

It was then that I looked down at the letter she'd just written. The envelope was addressed to 'The Lord Chancellor, The Lord Chancellor's Office, The House of Lords, London, s.w.i.'

A good deal, I thought, was going on under the calm surface of life in our Chambers at Equity Court. I was speculating on the precise nature of such movements with considerable pleasure as I started to walk to the Temple station. On my way I found Miss Fiona Allways waiting for a bus.

'I say,' she hailed me. 'Any more news about my getting into Chambers?'

'There is a tide in the affairs of women barristers, Fiona,' I told her, 'which, taken at the flood, leads God knows where.'

'What's that mean, exactly?'

'It means that they'll either let you in, or they'll throw *me* out.' I moved on towards Hilda and home. 'Best of luck,' I said, 'to both of us.'

★ ★ ★

His Honour Judge Leonard Dover was a fairly recent appointment to the collection of Old Bailey judges. He was a youngish man, in his mid forties perhaps, certainly young enough to be my son, had fate chosen to inflict such a blow. He wore rimless glasses and was a fairly rimless character. He was the sort of judge who has about as many laughs in him as a digital computer, and seemed to have been programmed by the Civil Service. Press all the right buttons—you know the type—and he gives you seven years in the Nick. I have often thought that if he were plugged into the mains, Judge Dover could go on passing stiff sentences for ever.

On my way into Dover's Court I had passed Mrs April Timson, made up to the nines and wearing a sky-blue trouser suit, come to celebrate her husband's day of fame. She accosted me anxiously.

'Tony says you've never let the Timsons down, Mr Rumpole.'

'Mrs Timson!' I greeted her. 'Where's young Vincent today? Otherwise engaged?'

'He's with my friend, Chrissie. She's my neighbour and she's minding him. What are our chances, Mr Rumpole?'

'Talk to you later,' I said, not caring to commit myself.

After the jury had been sworn in, Judge Dover leant towards them and said, in his usual unremarkable monotone, 'Nothing that I am going to say now must be taken against the defendant in any way...'

I stirred in my seat. Whatever was going on, I didn't like the sound of it.

'This is a case in which it seems there is a particular danger of your being approached ... by someone,' Dover went on, sounding grave. 'That often happens in trials of alleged armed robbery by what is known as a "gang" of serious professional criminals.'

It was time to throw a spanner in his programming. 'My Lord,' I said firmly, and rose to the hind legs, but Dover was locked in conversation with the jury.

'You will be particularly on your guard, and purely for your assistance, of course, you will be kept under police observation.' He seemed to notice me at long last. 'What is it, Mr Rumpole? Don't you want this jury to be protected from interference?'

'I don't want the jury to be told this is a case concerning a serious crime before they've heard one word of evidence,' I said with all possible vehemence. 'I don't want hints that my client belongs to a gang of serious professionals when the truth may be that he's nothing but a snapper-up of unconsidered trifles. I don't want the jury nobbled, but nobbled they have already been, in my respectful submission, by your Lordship's warning.'

'Mr Rumpole! That's an extraordinary suggestion, coming from you.'

'It was made to answer an extraordinary statement coming from your Lordship.'

'What is your application, Mr Rumpole?' Judge Dover asked in a voice several degrees below zero.

'My Lord, I ask that a fresh jury be empanelled, who will have heard no prejudicial suggestions against my client.'

'Your application is refused.' I had pressed the wrong button and got the automatic print-out. There was nothing for it but to sit down looking extremely hard done by.

'Members of the jury.' The Judge turned back to them. 'I have already made it perfectly clear to you that nothing I have said contains any suggestion whatever against Mr Timson. Does that satisfy you, Mr Rumpole?'

'About as much as a glass of cold carrot juice, old darling,' I muttered to Phillida.

'I'm sorry, I didn't hear you, Mr Rumpole.'

'I said, I suppose it will have to, My Lord.' I rose in a perfunctory manner.

'Yes, Mr Rumpole,' the Judge said. 'I suppose it will.'

★　　　★　　　★

Back in the alleged mansion flat things weren't going too well either. Hilda, in the course of tidying up, found my old *Oxford Book of English Verse* on a chair (I had been seeking solace in the 'Intimations of Immortality' the night before), and she put it on my excellent shelf. No doubt she thumped it down a fair bit, for my elegant carpentry creaked and then collapsed, casting a good many books and a certain amount of wine to the ground. I have spoken already of the strength of my wife's character. Apparently she went out, purchased a number of rawlplugs and an electric drill and started a career as a handyman, the full effects of which weren't noticed by me for some time.

*   *   *

In Court, the prosecution was in the hands of Mr Hilary Onslow, a languid-looking young man whose fair curly hair came sprouting out from under his wig. In spite of his air of well-born indifference, he could be, at times, a formidable opponent. One of the earliest witnesses was the supergrass, Gerry Molloy, an overweight character with a red face and glossy black hair, who sweated a good deal and seemed about to burst out of his buttons.

'Mr Molloy. I want to come now to the facts of the Pond Hill bank raid.'

'The Pond Hill job. Yes, sir.' Gerry sounded only too eager to help.

'How many of you were engaged on that particular enterprise?'

'There was two with sawn-offs. One collector . . .'

'And you with the sledgehammer?' Onslow asked.

'I was the sledge man, yes. There was five of us altogether.'

'Five of you counting the driver?'

'Yes, sir.'

'Did you *see* the driver?'

'Course I did.' The witness sounded very sure of himself. 'The driver picked me up at the meet.'

'Had you seen him before?'

'Seen him before?' Molloy thought carefully, and then answered, 'No, sir . . .'

'Some weeks later did you attend an identification parade?' Onslow turned to me and asked languidly 'Is there any dispute as to whom he picked out at the I.D.?'

'No dispute as to that. No,' I granted him.

'Thank you, Mr Rumpole.' The Judge gave me a faint look of approval.

'Delighted to be of assistance, my Lord,' I rose to say, and sank back into my seat as quickly as possible.

'Did you pick out the defendant, Mr Timson?' Onslow asked.

Tony Timson was staring at the witness from the dock. Gerry Molloy looked away to avoid his accusing eyes and met a glare from April Timson in the public gallery.

'Yes.' The answer was a little muted. 'I pointed to him. I got no hesitation.'

'Thank you, Mr Molloy.'

Hilary Onslow sat and crossed his long legs elegantly. I rose, full of righteous indignation, and looked at the jury in a pained manner as I cast my questions in the general direction of the witness-box.

'Mr Molloy. You have turned Queen's Evidence in this case?'

'Come again?' The answer was impertinent, so I put my voice up several decibels. 'Translated into everyday language, Mr Molloy, you are a grass. Not

211

even a "supergrass". A common or garden ordinary bit of a grass.'

There was a welcome stir of laughter from the jury, immediately silenced by the computer on the Bench.

'Members of the jury,' Judge Dover reminded them, if they needed reminding, 'this is not a place of public entertainment. This witness is giving evidence for the prosecution,' he added, as though that covered the matter.

'You're giving evidence for the prosecution because you were caught.' I turned to the witness-box then. 'Not being a particularly efficient sledge, you tripped over your holdall in the street and missed the getaway car. You were apprehended, Mr Molloy, in the gutter!'

'They nicked me, yes,' Molloy admitted.

'And you have already been sentenced to two years for your part in the robbery?'

'I got a two, yes.'

'A considerable reduction because you agreed with the police to grass on your colleagues,' I suggested.

'I got under the odds, yes,' he agreed, less readily.

'Considerably under the odds, Mr Molloy, and for that you were prepared to betray your own family?'

'Come again?'

'Three of your colleagues were members of the clan Molloy.'

'They were Molloys, yes.'

'And only one Timson?'

'Yes.'

'And as the Montagues to the Capulets, I put it to
212

you, so are the Timsons to the Molloys.'

'Did you say the "Montagues", Mr Rumpole?' The Judge seemed puzzled by a name he hadn't heard in the case before, so my literary reference was lost on the computer.

'I simply meant that the Molloys hate and despise the Timsons. Isn't that so, Mr Gerry Molloy?' I asked the witness.

'We never got on, no. It's traditional. Although...'

'Although what?'

'I believe my cousin Shawn's wife what he's separated from lives quite close to Tony Timson and his wife and...'

I interrupted a speech which I thought might somewhat blur the picture I had just painted. 'Apart from that, it's true, isn't it, that the Molloys are in a different league from the Timsons?'

'What league is that, Mr Rumpole?' Judge Dover looked puzzled.

'The big league, my Lord.' I helped him understand. 'You and your relations, according to your evidence, did the Barclays Bank in Penge, the Midland, Croydon, and the NatWest in Barking...' I was back with the witness.

'That's what I've said.' He was sweating more now, and two of his lower shirt buttons had gone off about their own affairs.

'Spreading your favours evenly round the money market. Have you ever known a Timson to be present at a bank robbery before, Mr Molloy?'

'Not as I can remember. But my brother Charlie was off sick and we was short of a driver.'

'Perhaps you were. Unhappily all your Molloy colleagues seem to have vanished.'

213

At which point my learned friend, Mr Hilary Onslow, felt it right to unwind his legs and draw himself to his great height. 'My Lord,' he said, 'I explained to the jury that determined efforts to trace the other participants in this robbery are still being made by the police...'

'If my learned friend wishes to give evidence, perhaps your Lordship would like him to go into the witness-box,' I said, and got the automatic judicial rebuke: 'Mr Rumpole. That comment was quite uncalled-for.'

'Steady on, Rumpole. Don't tease him.' Phillida whispered a bit of sound advice, so I said, with deep humility, 'So it was, my Lord. I entirely agree.' I turned back, with no humility at all, to Gerry Molloy. 'With your relations all gone to ground you had to have a victim, didn't you, to justify your privileged treatment as a grass?' The jury, who looked extremely interested, clearly saw the point. The witness pretended that he didn't.

'A victim?' He was playing for time, I gave him none.

'So you decided to pick one out of the despised Timsons and put him in the frame.'

'Put him in the *what*, Mr Rumpole?' The Judge affected not to understand. I hadn't time to teach him plain English.

'Put him in the driver's seat, where he certainly never was,' I suggested to the supergrass.

'He was there. I told you.' Gerry Molloy was growing indignant.

'Where did you meet?'

'One of the Molloy houses,' he said, after a pause.

'Which one?'

214

'I think it was Michael's ... Or Vic's. I can't be sure.'

'Can't you ... ?'

'It was Shawn's,' he decided.

'And having decided to frame Tony,' I went on quickly, 'was it some member of the Molloy family who planted a packet of stolen banknotes in the Timson home?'

'It couldn't have been him, could it, Mr Rumpole?' The Judge was looking back in his notes. 'This witness has been in custody ever since...'

'Since the robbery, yes, my Lord,' I agreed, and then asked Molloy, 'Did you receive visits in prison, before you made your statement?'

'A few visits, yes.'

'From your wife?'

'One or two.'

'And was it through her that the word was sent out to plant the money on Tony Timson?'

I made the suggestion for the benefit of the jury, but it deeply shocked Gerald Supergrass Molloy. 'I wouldn't ask my wife to do them sort of messages,' he said, deeply pained.

*   *   *

Back at home Hilda, swathed in an overall, was drilling the wall to receive a new consignment of 'Easy-Do' shelving in a completely professional manner. I was also plugging away in Court, asking a few pertinent questions of Detective Inspector Broome, the officer in charge of the case.

'Gerry Molloy made his statement two days after the robbery, at about 2.30 in the afternoon?' I

215

suggested.

'2.35, to be precise.' The D.I. put me right.

'Oh, please. I'm sure my Lord would like you to be very precise. You went straight round to Tony Timson's house?'

'We did.'

'In a police car, with the siren blaring?'

'I think we had the siren on for some of the time. We were in a hurry.'

'And you were lucky enough to find him at home?'

'Well, he wasn't out doing window-cleaning, sir.'

There was a small titter from the jury. I interrupted it as soon as possible.

'My client opened the door to you at once?'

'Soon as we knocked. Yes.'

'No sort of interval while he tried to move the money to a more sensible hiding place, for instance?'

'Perhaps he was happy with it where it was.'

Before he got another laugh, I came in quickly with 'Or perhaps, Inspector, he had no idea that the money had been put there.'

'I don't know about that.'

'Don't you? One last matter. Was it Gerry Molloy who told you that Tony Timson was a dangerous member of a big-time robbery firm who might try and nobble the jury?'

'Molloy told us that, yes.' Inspector Broome was a little reluctant to answer.

'So a solemn warning was given by the learned Judge on the word of a self-confessed sledgehammer man who has already been convicted of malicious wounding, robbery and grievous bodily harm.'

216

'Yes.' The short answer came even more reluctantly from the Inspector.

'And doesn't that solemn warning give a quite unfair impression of Tony Timson?'

'Unfair, sir?' Broome did his best to look puzzled.

'You'd never put Tony Timson in for the serious crime award, would you? He's a small-time thief, who specializes in relieving householders of their home entertainment, video machines, teasmades and the like...'

'That would seem to be so, yes,' the Inspector admitted.

'So if I said to you that this robbery was quite out of Tony Timson's league, how would you translate that suggestion?'

'I would say it's out of character, sir. Judging by past form.' So I sat down with some heartfelt thanks to Detective Inspector Broome.

At the end of the day I went with Phillida and Bernard to visit our client in the cells. He appeared pleased with our progress, but I hadn't yet an answer to what seemed to me the single important question in the case.

'The money in the washing machine, Tony,' I asked him. 'It must have been put there by someone. Does April go out much?'

'She takes young Vince round her friend's.'

'Her friend Chrissie?' The question seemed important to me, but Tony answered vaguely, 'I think that's her name. I don't know the woman.'

'Money found in the kitchen,' I said thoughtfully. 'I don't suppose you do much cooking, do you, Tony?'

'Oh, leave it out, Mr Rumpole!' Tony found the

217

suggestion highly diverting.

'Never wash up?'

'Course I don't!' He could hardly suppress his laughter. 'That's April's job, innit?'

'I suppose it's only barristers who spend the evenings up to their wrists in the Fairy Liquid. Yes... And of course you don't run young Vince's smalls through the washing machine?'

'Now would I be expected to do a job like that?' He looked to Mrs Erskine-Brown for support. 'Would I?'

'You mean, it would be a bit like having a woman defend you?' Phillida asked in a pointed sort of way. Tony Timson had the grace to look apologetic.

'I never meant nothing personal,' he said. 'It just doesn't seem natural.'

'Really.' Phillida was unappeased. 'As a matter of fact my husband is quite a good performer on the spindrier.'

'Poor bloke!' Tony was laughing again.

I interrupted the badinage. 'Let's take it that you leave such matters to April. When does she do the washing, Tony? On a Monday?'

'Suppose so.' He didn't sound particularly interested.

'The bank raid was on Monday. Gerry Molloy made his statement on Wednesday afternoon and the police were round at once. Whoever put it there didn't have much time.'

'I don't know,' and he added hopelessly, 'I just never go near the bleeding washing machine.'

I gathered up my brief and prepared to return to the free world.

'See you tomorrow, Tony,' I said. 'Come on, Portia. I think we've got what we wanted.'

When I left the Old Bailey that evening and stepped off the pavement, a small white sports car, driven with great speed and expertise, flashed past me, almost cutting me off somewhere past my prime, and, passing two or three slowly moving taxis on the inside, zipped off and was lost in the traffic. I caught sight of a blonde head behind the wheel and deduced that the driver was none other than that devoted housewife, Mrs April Timson.

*   *   *

I didn't sleep much that night. I was busy putting two and two together to make about five thousand nicker. Around dawn I drifted off and dreamt of washing machines and spindriers, and Ballard was bringing me a bouquet of roses and inviting me to lunch, and Fiona Allways had decided to leave the Bar and take up life as a coalminer, saying the pay was so much better.

So I arrived at the Old Bailey in a somewhat jaded condition. Having robed for the day's work, I went up to the canteen on the third floor and bought myself a black coffee and a slightly flaccid sausage roll. I wasn't enjoying them much when Erskine-Brown came up to me in a state of considerable distress, holding out a copy of *The Times* in a trembling hand. The poor fellow looked decidedly seedy.

'The silk list, Rumpole!' he stammered. 'Have you seen the new Q.C.s?'

'Haven't got beyond the crossword.' I opened the paper and found the relevant page. 'Well, here's your name. What are you worrying about?'

'*My* name?' Erskine-Brown asked bitterly.

219

'Erskine-Brown. *Mrs!*' I read the entry more carefully. 'Oh, I do see.' I felt for the man, my heart bled for him.

'She never warned me, Rumpole! I had no idea she'd applied. Had you?'

'No.' I honestly hadn't. 'Haven't you asked her about it?'

'She left home before the paper came. And now she's gone to ground in the ladies' robing room!' Then he asked with a faint hope, 'Do you think it might be some sort of misprint?'

I might have sat there for some time commiserating with Claude, but I saw a blonde head and a blue trouser suit by the tea-urns. I rose, excused myself to the still suffering, still junior barrister, and arrived alongside Mrs April Timson just in time to pay for her coffee.

'You're very kind, Mr Rumpole,' she said.

'Sometimes,' I agreed. She moved to a table. I went with her. 'Young Vincent well this morning, is he? Chrissie Molloy looking after him properly?'

'Chrissie's all right.' She sat and then looked up at me and spoke very quietly. 'Tony doesn't know she's a Molloy.'

I sat down beside her and took my time in lighting a small cigar. 'No. Mrs Timson,' I said. 'Tony doesn't know very much, does he?'

'We were at school together. Me and Chrissie. Anyway, she and Shawn Molloy's separated.'

'But still friends,' I suggested. 'Close enough for the Molloy firm to meet at Chrissie's house.' I blew out smoke and then asked, 'When did you know they were short of a driver?'

'I may have heard . . . someone mention it.' She looked away from me and stirred her coffee. So I

220

told her the whole story, as though she didn't know. 'Your husband wouldn't have been the slightest use in a getaway car, would he?' I said. 'He'd have had three parking tickets and hit a milk float before they'd got clear of the bank. You, on the other hand, I happen to have noticed, are distinctly nippy, driving through traffic.' A silence fell between us. It lasted until I said, 'What was the matter? Tony not ambitious enough for you?'

'Why ever should you think . . . ?' She looked up at me then. Whatever it was meant to be, the look was not innocent.

'Because of where you put the money,' I told her quietly. 'It was the one place in the house you knew your husband would never look.'

She had the nerve of an accomplished villain, had Mrs April Timson. She took a long swig of coffee and then she asked me what I was going to do.

'The real question is,' I said, 'what are *you* going to do?' And then I gave her my legal advice. 'Leave it out, April,' I said. 'Give it up, Mrs Timson. Keep away from it. It's men's work, you know. Let the men make a mess of it.' I paused to let the advice sink in, then I stood up to go. 'It was the first time, I imagine. Better make it the last.'

★   ★   ★

I got into Court some time before the learned computer took his seat on the Bench. As soon as Phillida arrived I gave her, believing it right to take my junior into my full confidence, my solution to the case, and an account of my conversation with April Timson.

She thought for a moment, and then asked, 'But

why didn't Gerry Molloy identify *her*?'

'He was ashamed, don't you understand? He didn't want to admit that the great Molloys went out with a *woman* driver!'

'What on earth are we going to do?'

'We can't prove it was April. Let's hope they can't prove it was Tony. The jury don't much care for the mini-grass, and the Molloys *might* have planted the money.'

Hilary Onslow came in then, gave us a cheerful 'Good morning', and took his place. I spoke to Phillida in a whisper.

'Only one thing we can do, Portia. I'll just give them the speech about reasonable doubt.'

'No. *I* will ...' she said firmly.

'What?' I wasn't following her drift.

'I'm *your* leader now. Don't you read *The Times*, Rumpole? I have taken silk!'

At which point the Usher shouted, 'Be upstanding,' and Judge Dover was upon us. He looked at the defence team, said, 'Yes, Mr Rumpole?' and then saw that Phillida was on her feet.

'Mrs Erskine-Brown. I believe that certain congratulations are in order?'

'Yes, my Lord. I believe they are,' said our Portia, and announced that she would now call the defendant.

Tony gave evidence. As he denied knowing anything about the money, or the whereabouts of the Pond Hill bank, or even the exact situation of his own washing machine, he was a difficult witness to cross-examine. Onslow did his best, and made a moderately effective final speech, and then I sat quietly and listened to Mrs Phillida Erskine-Brown,

222

now my learned leader. I smiled as I heard her reach a familiar peroration.

'Members of the jury.' She was addressing them with carefully controlled emotion. 'Soon this case will be over. In a little while you will go back to your jobs and your families, and you will forget about it. At most it is only a small part of your lives, but for my client, Tony Timson, it is the *whole* of his life! And it is that life I leave with confidence in your hands, certain that there can be only one verdict in this case, "Not Guilty"!'

And then Phillida sank down in her seat exhausted, just as I had taught her to, as I had taught Fiona Allways, and anyone else who would care to listen.

★   ★   ★

'Good speech.' I congratulated Phillida as we came out of Court when the Timson case was over.

'Yes. It always was.'

'Portia of Belmont... Phillida Erskine-Brown, née Trant... and Fiona Allways ... the great tradition of female advocates should be carried on!' I lit a small cigar.

Phillida looked at me. 'It's not enough for you that we won Timson, is it? Not enough that you got the jury to disbelieve Gerry Molloy and think the money may have been planted. You want to win the Allways case as well.'

'Well,' I said reasonably, 'why shouldn't we take on Fiona?'

'Over my dead body!'

She moved towards the lifts. I followed her.

'But *why*?'

'She was making a play for Claude. I found them all over each other in Pommeroy's. That's when I got so angry I applied for silk.'

'Without telling your husband?' I asked sorrowfully.

'I'm afraid so.'

'I'd better come clean about this.' I took off my wig, and stood looking at her. She looked back at me, deeply suspicious. 'What've you been up to, Rumpole?'

'Well, I just wanted your Claude to look on Miss Allways with a warm and friendly eye. I mean, I thought that'd increase her chances of getting in, so . . .'

'You wanted Claude to *warm* to her . . .' Phillida's voice was rising to a note of outrage.

'I thought it might help. Yes,' I admitted.

'Rumpole! I suppose you told him that she fancied him.'

'Now, Portia. Would I do such a thing?' I protested.

'Very probably. If you wanted to win badly enough. I imagine you told him she thought he looked like Robert Redford.'

'No. I protest!' I was hurt. 'That is utterly and entirely untrue! I told him she thought he looked like a fellow called Newman.'

'And had Allways actually said that?' Phillida was still uncertain of the facts.

'Well, if you want me to be entirely honest . . .'

'It would make a change,' she said, unnecessarily, I thought.

'Well, no. She hadn't.'

And then, quite unexpectedly, our Portia smiled. 'Poor old Claude,' she said. 'You know what you were doing, Rumpole? You can't rely on a girl to get in on her own talents, can you? You have to manipulate and rely on everyone else's vanity. You were simply exploiting the male sex.'

'So now you know,' I asked her, 'will you vote for Fiona?'

'Tell me one good reason.'

'Ballard's against her.'

'I suppose that's one good reason. And because of you I've ended up a silk. What on earth can I tell Claude?' She seemed, for a delightful moment, overcome with guilt, and blushed very prettily, as though she had to admit the existence of a lover.

'Tell him,' I suggested, 'that the Lord Chancellor just thought there weren't enough women silks. So that's why you got it. He'll feel better if he thinks there's no damn merit about this thing.'

'I suppose so.' She looked a little disappointed as she asked me, 'Is that true?'

'Quite possibly,' I told her. After all, I hadn't undertaken to tell her the *whole* truth about anything.

When I got home that night, Hilda asked me if I had noticed anything. Suspecting that she had had a new hair-do or bought a new dress, I said that of course she was looking extremely pretty.

'Not me,' she said. 'Look at the walls.'

The shelf I had put up was not only firmly screwed and looking even better than usual, it seemed to have pupped and there were shelves all over the place, gamely supporting potted plants and glasses, telephone directories and bottles of plonk.

'What did you do, Hilda,' I asked her. 'Did you get a man in?'

'Yes,' she said. 'Me.'

225

It all ended once again with a Chambers party. The excuse for that particular shindig was the swearing-in at the House of Lords of Mrs Phillida Erskine-Brown as One of Her Majesty's Counsel. She made a resplendent figure as she came to split a few bottles of champagne with us in Ballard's room. Her handsome female face peeped out between the long spaniel's ears of her full-bottomed wig. She wore a long silk gown with a black purse on her back. There were lace cuffs on her tailed coat, and lace at her throat. Her black skirt ended with black stockings and diamond-buckled shoes. She carried her white gloves in one hand and a glass of Mercier (on offer at Pommeroy's) in the other. Just when matters were going with a certain amount of swing, Ballard took it upon himself to make a speech.

'In our great profession...' he was saying, and I muttered an, 'Amen.' 'We are sometimes accused of prejudice against the female sex.'

'Shame!' said Erskine-Brown.

'That may be true of some sets of Chambers, but it cannot be said of us at 3 Equity Court,' Ballard continued. 'As in many other things, we take the lead and set the example! Today we celebrate the well-deserved promotion of Mrs Phillida Erskine-Brown to the front row!'

'Philly looks very fine in a silk gown, doesn't she, Rumpole?' the proud husband said to me.

'Gorgeous!' I agreed.

'And we welcome a new member of our set. Young Fiona Allways,' Ballard concluded. All around me barristers were toasting the triumph of women.

'You know, between ourselves, Philly got it because it's the Lord Chancellor's policy to appoint more *women* Q.C.'s,' Erskine-Brown told me confidentially.

'How appalling.' I looked on the man with considerable sympathy. 'You're a victim of sexual discrimination!'

'But Philly's made me a promise. Next year she's going to take some time off.'

'Good. I might get my work back.'

'We're going to have'—his voice sank confidentially—'a little companion for Tristan.'

'Isolde?' I suggested.

'Oh, really, Rumpole!'

I moved away from him as I saw Phillida in all her glory go up to Fiona, who was wearing wide trousers which, coming to just below the knees, had the appearance of a widish split skirt.

'Well done, Allways!' Phillida gave the girl an encouraging smile. 'Welcome to Chambers.'

'Thank you, Mrs Erskine-Brown.' Fiona seemed genuinely pleased. But Phillida had stopped smiling.

'Oh, just one thing, Allways. No culottes!'

'Oh,' said Fiona. 'Really?'

'If you want to get on at the bar, and it is a pretty tough profession,' Phillida told her, 'just don't go in for those sort of baggy trouser arrangements. It's just not on.'

'No. Remember that, Fiona,' I put my oar in. 'A fellow looks so much better in a skirt.'

RUMPOLE AND THE SPORTING LIFE

'Rumpole,' said She Who Must Be Obeyed over breakfast one morning in the mansion flat. 'We're going to the Bar Races on Saturday, aren't we?' It was less a question than a statement of fact, less a statement of fact than a Royal command. It was no use protesting, for instance, that Rumpole has never been a racing man.

Claude Erskine-Brown, somewhat disappointed in his application for silk, had come to the conclusion that a more active part in the social life of the Bar might bring him to the attention of the powers that be. He joined the Bar Golfing Society, he put up for election to the Bar Council, and he decided that it would be just as well to be seen hobnobbing with those sporting judges who patronized the Bar Races. He decided to make up a party for this event, but Ballard, quite naturally, didn't approve of gambling, and Hoskins didn't want to lose his girls' school fees on a piece of fallible horseflesh. Accordingly, it was suggested that a party should be made up of the Erskine-Browns, Henry our clerk (who, being by far the wealthiest of us, undertook to supply three or four bottles of champagne), Uncle Tom, and the Rumpoles.

'We must go, Rumpole,' Hilda said as soon as she heard of the invitation. 'Daddy always went to the Bar Races.'

I had a distant memory of attending this annual point-to-point with C. H. Wystan when he was Head of Chambers. We journeyed down to the

Cotswolds in his large and hearse-like motor, feasted on ham sandwiches and rock cakes, and the warmish hock flowed like cement. Once or twice, as I remember it, Hilda Wystan was in the party, and She would be in charge of the thermos and getting her father perched on his shooting stick in time to see the end of the Barristers' Handicap.

Over the course of the years fewer barristers have been able to find the spare currency to keep horses in livery, being hard pushed to keep their nearest and dearest in regular feed and stabling. The Barristers' Races have therefore shrunk to one event in an afternoon of races for adjacent hunts and military sportsmen, but a few alcoholic juniors with a taste for hunting still put their mounts, like nervous clients, to various jumps and hazards, and a great many judges and barristers and barristers' wives dress up in old caps and trilby hats, tweeds and green padded waistcoats, and consume, with icy fingers, large picnics from the boots of their motor cars and so join happily in the Sport of Kings.

'It'll be like the old days, won't it, Rumpole?' Hilda said as she daubed the ham sandwiches with mustard and wrapped them in greaseproof paper. 'And it'll do you so much good to have a day out in the countryside.' I was already marvelling at the English longing to journey vast distances to some damp and uncomfortable place and then, with none of the normal facilities such as knives and forks and dining-room furniture, eat a packed meal. I was busy storing as many bottles as possible of the Château Fleet Street into my red robe bag in the hope that I might, with their assistance, be able to keep out the cold.

We left London at a ridiculously early hour in the Erskine-Brown Volvo Estate. Phillida Erskine-Brown, Q.C., was wearing a sort of tweed cape and deerstalker, which gave her the curious appearance of a red-headed and personable female Sherlock Holmes. Claude, a great one for uniforms, was wearing the regulation padded waistcoat and green wellies. Uncle Tom sported an old hacking jacket with leather patches, and Henry wore a tweed suit with knife-edge creases, a sheepskin car coat and had, slung about his neck, a huge pair of racing binoculars. You have the complete picture when I tell you that Hilda was in a tweed two-piece with brogues and a Burberry, and I was in the old Sunday jacket, cavalry twill bags and everyday mac. When we had all assembled in the street outside Froxbury Court, I piled my bag of booze and Hilda's sandwiches into the hatchback, as Henry rather quaintly called it, and it was tally ho and we were off to the races. A fine drizzle was falling then, and it went on falling for the rest of the day.

The point-to-point course was a fairly representative slice of the English countryside. There was a damp and distinct prospect of fields and hedgerows and a hillside on which the cars were parked and the bookies had set up their stands. The Mecca of the place, the large tent in which food and drink were supplied, had been pitched next to the saddling enclosure. I would have wished to spend most of the afternoon under canvas, but Hilda, encouraged by Phillida Erskine-Brown, who showed considerable sporting interest, insisted on trekking down to the rails to watch the finish of each race, and then climbing back to the bookies to put money on another loser.

231

My involvement with the sporting life, and the events which led to one of the most interesting murder cases of the Rumpole career (I put it not far below the Penge Bungalow affair in the list of my more engaging cases) started as we were watching the three o'clock race, in which members of the adjacent hunts contested the field with a few barristers. We were positioned near to the last fence as a bunch of riders, helmeted, goggled and pounding through a cloud of flying mud, approached the high brushwood and flung their horses at it.

'Into the last fence now and it's Number 13, Atlantic Hero, owned and ridden by the Honourable Jonathan Postern of the Tester Hunt in the pink and green colours,' the loudspeaker, crackling out a rasping commentary, informed us.

'Come on, Atlantic Hero! Don't hang about, Atlantic Hero!' Hilda was shouting lustily. For the first time in a long day it seemed that one of our party had backed a winner. What with the pounding of hooves and the shouts of the aficionados, I wasn't sure that Hilda's fancied animal could hear her. And then the last horse crashed through the brushwood, landed awkwardly, deposited its rider on the ground and galloped off as though happy to be out of the contest.

'And there's another one down,' the loudspeaker crackled. 'Number 11, Tricycle. Ridden by Maurice Fishbourne of the Tester Hunt.'

Two St John Ambulancemen with a stretcher were pounding out to the fallen rider as the victory of Atlantic Hero was announced, and Hilda sent up a resounding cheer. I looked around and saw a handsome women in her early thirties, dressed in the regulation headscarf and padded waistcoat, running towards the fallen rider. My attention was held, I suppose, because her face seemed vaguely familiar. Her mouth was open as she ran, as though in a silent scream. And then I saw the horseless rider sit up and stretch out his hand for a pair of gold-rimmed glasses. One lens had been shattered in his fall. He seemed a slight, unsportsmanlike character, who smiled a nervous apology at the ambulancemen and then stood, unsteadily, hooking on his glasses. At this the woman in the headscarf stopped running, her mouth closed, and she turned quickly and walked away in the general direction of the refreshment tent.

'First, Number 13, Atlantic Hero. Second, Number 8, Flashpoint. Third, Number 4, Ironside...' the loudspeaker told us.

'Come along, Rumpole, for heaven's sake! We've got to collect my winnings.' Hilda was triumphant.

'What did you have on it? One quid each way?' I asked her. 'We shall be able to retire to Biarritz.'

So our group started to plod up the hill, where the increasing rain was producing yet more mud. As we made our way to the old and reliable firm where Hilda proudly collected the fruits of 50p each way, Uncle Tom and Henry were discussing form for the 3.30, the Barristers' Handicap.

'His clerk tells me that Mr Lorrimer's not all that fit,' Henry was saying. 'He's been overworking on his Revenue cases.'

'Likely to fall at the first fence.' Uncle Tom marked his race card and then asked, 'Harley Waters, Q.C., in good condition, is he? Been taking his oats and all that?'

233

'Rather too liberally, his clerk informs me, sir. The fancy is,' Henry lowered his voice confidentially, 'Mr E. Smith on Decree Absolute.'

'Mr Smith in good form, is he?' Uncle Tom sounded anxious.

'Teetotal, according to his clerk.' Henry had no doubts. 'And he does press-ups in Chambers.'

When bets had been laid on various members of the Bar, we went into the tent where Hilda was determined to fritter away her winnings on loose living and self-indulgence. I was bringing up the rearguard with Erskine-Brown, when I heard a dry and elderly voice calling, 'There you are, Rumpole! Ah, Erskine-Brown . . .' Claude immediately raised his hat and I turned to see the small, wrinkled, parchment-coloured face, inappropriately crowned by a jaunty bowler hat, of Mr Justice Twyburne, one of the old school of spine-chilling judges of the Queen's Bench, a man so old that he had been appointed before the age for retirement was inflicted on the Judiciary, and who stayed on—to the terror of unwary criminals and barristers alike.

'I haven't had you before me lately,' said this antique Judge. 'I suppose you don't get the *serious* crime nowadays.'

'I have been engaged elsewhere,' I said loftily and looked towards the bar as an avenue of escape. 'I must join my wife. She's spending the winnings.'

'Been having a little flutter here, have you? I don't see you as a gambling man, Rumpole?' The tent was full of horsy girls in well-fitting jods, and convivial farmers. It was my fate to be stuck with this daunting old codger.

'I suppose a person can't spend a lifetime in Old Bailey trials without getting a bit of a taste for games of chance,' I told him.

'What's that supposed to mean?' Mr Justice Twyburne clearly didn't like the analogy.

'Don't you ever feel that forecasting the results of cases is rather like sticking a pin in the *Sporting Life* with your eyes shut?' I asked him.

'The aim of an English criminal trial is to do justice,' the Judge said coldly. 'I don't see how you can possibly compare it to a horse race. Good day, Erskine-Brown.' He touched the rim of his bowler with a yellow-gloved hand, and went off to pass an adverse judgement on the animals in the saddling enclosure. When he had gone, Erskine-Brown looked at me as though I had failed to stand up during the National Anthem, or had been caught filling out my football pools while doing a case in the House of Lords.

'Rumpole!' he protested. 'Twyburne's our oldest Judge.'

'I know,' I answered him with some distaste. 'One of the few survivors who's ever passed a death sentence. They say he ordered muffins at his Club after those occasions.'

And then the rider of Atlantic Hero and the author of Hilda's good fortune came into the tent, recognizable to us by his green and pink silks and his white, mud-splattered riding breeches as well as the silver cup he was carrying. He was followed by a considerable retinue, including at least two pretty girls, a tall young man with longish hair and an amused expression and, bringing up the rear, the woman who had run with such distress towards the fallen rider.

As the crackling loudspeaker had told us, the victor of the three o'clock (the Adjacent Hunts

235

Challenge Cup) was Jonathan Postern. I was watching as the Hon. Jonathan slapped his silver trophy down on the bar and shouted to one of the fresh-faced waitresses who had just served drinks to Hilda.

'Come on, sweetheart. Fill this jerry up with champers!'

'A loving cup—Jonno, how excessively brill!' one of the pretty girls chirruped as she held the arm of the winning rider. My attention was momentarily engaged by Hilda handing me a small rum. A bit of a disappointment, I thought. With her luck I expected her at least to fill my gum boots with champagne. As I sank my nose towards the rum, I heard the dulcet tones of Miss Fiona Allways greeting Hilda and the Erskine-Browns. She was dressed like most of the other girls in a padded waistcoat, green cord trousers, a sweater and the sort of man's flat cap which charladies used to wear.

'I see you're in uniform too, Fiona,' I greeted her. 'All you khaki figures, slogging through the mud to the encampment, put me in distinct mind of the retreat from Mons.'

'You were never at the retreat from Mons,' Erskine-Brown told Fiona, unnecessarily, I thought. 'Rumpole was in the R.A.F. Ground Staff. Weren't you, Rumpole?'

'All right. It puts me in mind of the Naafi at R.A.F. Dungeness after a heavy night,' I was saying, when the woman I had seen rushing to the fallen rider came up to greet Fiona. Then I knew why I had thought there was a familiar look to her.

'Hullo, Pimpsey,' the woman said.

'Oh, hi, Sprod,' Fiona answered.

'Disgusting to see you,' said the woman, and I

236

made the somewhat obvious comment, 'You two obviously know each other.'

'My big sister, Jennifer Postern. This is Rumpole, Mrs Rumpole,' Fiona introduced us.

'How riveting!' Jennifer turned to me. 'I've heard so much about you. Pimpsey says you got her into Chambers. By some miracle!'

'Well, it was one of my trickier cases,' I admitted.

'Oh, but Pimpsey says you win them all, because you're the most super barrister in the whole of England. Absolutely brill, thinks Pimpsey.'

'Did you come on your own, Fiona?' Claude had moved away from his wife and was asking Fiona a quiet and hopeful question.

'No. With my boyfriend, Jeremy Jowling. He's rather dull, but he *is* a solicitor. He's the one doing the serious drinking.'

We looked across to the group by Jonathan Postern. Jeremy Jowling appeared to be the longish-haired, amused young man who had just received a dark brown whisky. Hilda recognized her favourite rider's racing colours then and trumpeted loudly, 'Oh look. That's my gorgeous winner!'

'I say, your wife. Is she really the one you call "She Who Must..."' Jennifer whispered to me.

'No. She's the one I call "Mrs Rumpole",' I answered. Hilda was, after all, almost within earshot, but her attention was still on the young man in racing silks.

'Rumpole! That's the chap who won for me. On Atlantic Hero,' she told me once again. I looked at the winner and realized how remarkably handsome he was. He had close-cropped curly hair and a straight nose, putting me in mind of those Greek statues in which the eyelids are somehow heavy with exhaustion at maintaining the heroic pose. If Jonathan Postern looked like some minor antique deity, he was surrounded by his votive priestesses. As he drank from the huge silver cup, a number of girls kissed him, none of whom was his wife.

'Such a nice-looking young man. Do you know him?' Hilda said admiringly to Jennifer, who answered, 'He's my husband.'

'Oh, really? I do feel I should thank him personally.'

'Come on then. Why don't we whizz over?'

So our group moved over towards Jonathan Postern's celebration.

Hilda, flushed with her winnings and a small rum, engaged the hero in conversation at once.

'I just had to say "Well done". It does make a day at the races so much more thrilling when you're on a winner!'

'Were you? I can't say I saw you,' Jonathan answered, and then said, in a loud aside to one of the attendant maidens, 'Who are these amazing old wrinklies?'

'This is Mr and Mrs Rumpole, Jonno. And Mr Claude Erskine-Brown.' Fiona looked at him disapprovingly.

'Mr Rumpole's a *tremendous* legal eagle,' Jennifer Postern explained to her husband.

'My God! You're not one of the galloping barristers?' the Hon. Jonathan asked me.

'Hardly.'

'None of your lot got placed. Terribly bad luck.' He raised the chalice 'Care for a swig?'

'Thank you.'

238

I might have saved my thanks, for I never got a drink. At that moment the rider who fell, the man whose name the loudspeaker had given as Maurice Fishbourne, muddy and with his glasses broken, came into the tent and was peering round with a look of shortsighted amiability. Jonathan raised the cup and had a long refreshing drink, ignoring me.

'Thank you very much,' I muttered.

Jonathan lowered the cup and, still holding it, looked across at Fishbourne and called, 'Fishface!'

'He's cutting us dead!' one of the maidens said.

'He's being frightfully grand,' said another.

'Come on, Fish. Don't be weedy!' a red-haired girl in a hacking jacket shouted.

Fishbourne came towards them smiling in a hopelessly ingratiating way. Hilda, who was in a mood to greet anyone, greeted him. 'Good afternoon.'

'Oh, this is Maurice Fishbourne. He lives next to Jennifer and Jonno.' Fiona was keeping her head admirably in a difficult social situation.

'D ... delighted to meet you.' Fishbourne came towards us grinning weakly. His stammer seemed as much part of his character as his broken spectacles.

'How did you manage to stick on till the last fence, Fishy? Superglue?' Jonathan bayed at him, and the entourage laughed.

'He was hanging on to the mane. I saw him!' It was Jennifer Postern, joining in.

'C ... congratulations, Jonathan.' The man Fishbourne seemed to be perfectly civil.

'Oh, aren't you a lovely loser! If you want to ride something in the next race, why not try a bicycle?'

Once again the claque laughed at Jonathan

Postern's sally, and once again Jennifer joined in.

'I'm not r . . . riding in the next race.' Fishbourne smiled round at the laughing faces.

'Is Mummy taking you home to tea?' Again, to my surprise, it was Jennifer who asked the question. It didn't sound kindly meant.

'I'm driving Mother home, yes, Jennifer.' Fishbourne looked at her through his broken lens.

'Come on, Fishy. Have a slug of champers!' Jonathan Postern invited him.

'Oh . . . Th . . . thanks.' Fishbourne took the chalice.

'It's quite all right, only got all our germs in it,' one of the girls said.

Fishbourne smiled and started to drink. Jonathan knocked the bottom of the cup sending a wave of champagne over Fishbourne's face and down his neck. He emerged wet and still grinning to look round at his tormentors as though delighted to afford them all a little harmless fun.

*　　*　　*

At the next memorable breakfast we shared at Froxbury Court I noticed, in a state of considerable shock, that Hilda was reading *Country Life*. Not only did she read it to herself, she gave me a nugget from this strange periodical.

'"Lodge for sale on gentleman's estate, in wooded country near Tester."'

'Why are you reading that, Hilda?' I asked her. 'Were there no *Daily Telegraphs*?'

'"Three bedrooms, two receps, with access to good, rough shooting",' she went on. 'Doesn't that sound attractive, Rumpole?'

'I honestly think I have enough troubles in my life without you taking up rough shooting.'

'What did you say?'

'I said it might be more peaceful in Tooting. Or in Gloucester Road. Or round the Inner London Sessions, or the Old Bailey. I mean, there you can go out for a walk without being in imminent danger of a charge of buckshot or whatever it is.'

'Nonsense, Rumpole!' Hilda was flicking over glossy pages full of Georgian manor houses and sporting prints. 'That day at the Bar Races made me realize what we're missing.'

'Mud?' I suggested.

'The countryside, Rumpole! Now, if we sold our lease here...'

'We could buy a deer park, and a Palladian mansion. Fancy having your *Country Life* ironed by the butler?'

'Daddy always said that what a barrister needed was a place in the country,' Hilda said with quiet dignity.

'13 Acacia Road, Horsham. Wasn't that your Daddy's stately home?' I asked as I folded up *The Times*, preparing for my journey to the Temple.

'Can't you see us, Rumpole?' Hilda began to look distinctly dreamy. 'Sitting by a log fire, taking a glass of sherry, perhaps, as the sun sets over the home wood...'

'I see us with the boiler out, and all trains to London cancelled, and mud up to your elbows.' I stood up, gulping coffee. 'And out in the home wood there's bound to be someone killing something.'

Not long after that an elderly man called Figgis, who lived in a cottage in the woods on Jonathan

241

Postern's Tester estate heard a shot and a woman's cry. He ran out of his overgrown garden and, just outside his tangled hedge, propped up against a fallen tree, he saw the dead body of the rider and owner of Atlantic Hero. Standing not a dozen yards away from him and holding a shotgun was Fiona's sister, Jennifer. Figgis asked her what had happened and her answer was one that was going to prove a serious problem to her defending counsel. 'I did it,' she said, and added, somewhat lamely, 'It was an accident.'

*　　*　　*

'Sprod wants you to defend her,' Fiona said.

'That's because you've been giving your sister a quite exaggerated view of my abilities in matters of shotgun wounds, murder and sudden death,' I told her.

'Is it really possible to exaggerate your abilities?'

'Perhaps not,' I said modestly.

'Why shouldn't my sister have the best counsel available?'

She sat down in my client's chair. I lit a small cigar and looked at her. She had rushed back from Court to see me when she heard the news. Still in her stiff white collar and bands, she looked absurdly young, like a distressed choirboy.

'Friends,' I said.

'What?' She frowned, puzzled.

'One rule at the Bar, Fiona. Never appear for friends. Your judgement gets blurred. You care too much. You can't see the weaknesses in your own case. And if you lose, of course, they never, ever forgive you.'

'My sister's not your friend. Quite honestly, you hardly know her.'

'But I know you, Fiona.' I hoped I sounded gentle.

'Of course, but...'

'All the trouble I had to get you in here! I did it by some pretty ruthless manoeuvring, if you want to know the truth. And then to have to spend the rest of my life avoiding your eye in the clerk's room, ducking over to the other side of the road when I saw you walking back from the Bailey, and never feeling safe to pop into Pommeroy's for a strengthener in case I found you staring at me more in sorrow than in anger because I lost your sister's case. Life would be intolerable!'

'I do understand that,' she admitted. 'But...'

'But me no buts, Fiona,' I said firmly.

'I was only going to say, "But you're not going to lose it, are you?"'

So, in the course of time, and much against my better judgement, I found myself sitting in the corner of a railway carriage, studying a brief which contained a bundle of not uninteresting mortuary photographs. I was on my way to Tester Crown Court, to play my part in the case of the Queen against Jennifer Postern.

*   *   *

In London you hardly ever see death, I thought, as I looked from the photograph of the wounded body of Jonathan Postern to the fields and woodlands, the streams and bridges, the greystone houses and farm buildings of the Cotswold countryside. Once or twice in a lifetime, you may see an old age

243

pensioner, perhaps, collapsed on a cold night in the tube, or a shape under a blanket and a small crowd as you drive past an accident.

In that peaceful landscape they saw death every day. They watched hounds tearing foxes to pieces or coursing hares. They hung up magpies and jays in the woods as a warning to others. No doubt at the end of the garden I saw from the passing train there was some retired naval man tearfully putting down his dog. Death is a routine event in the country. Well, I asked myself, what's a husband more or less in the shooting season?

And then we were in the outskirts of a grey, stony town. The train gasped to a standstill and I heard a porter calling, 'Tester! Change here for Deepside and Watching Junction.'

When I got outside the station, burdened, as usual on my travels, with my suitcase, briefcase and robe bag, I was hailed by the young man I had seen briefly in Jonathan Postern's entourage, and who had been pointed out as the boyfriend of Miss Fiona Allways.

'Horace Rumpole!' he was calling as he tried to stuff an extremely large and melancholy-looking dog into the back seat of a battered sports car. 'Do hop in. I'm Jeremy Jowling, instructing you. Don't mind Agatha. She's a soppy old date really. Here, let me take your luggage.' As we put my travelling wardrobe into his boot, I fitted myself with some difficulty into the sports car. The front seat was covered with dog hairs and the Hound of the Baskervilles was breathing lugubriously down my neck.

'Where'd you like to go first,' young Jowling said as he forced himself into the driver's seat and

244

switched on the engine. 'The Tester Arms or the prison?'

'Which is the least uncomfortable?' I asked him.

'I'd say the prison. Run you there, shall I? I must say it's all a G.M.B.U...'

'G.M.B.U?' I asked, puzzled, as we roared off through the heart of Tester.

'Grand Military Balls-up,' he explained. 'Years since we had a murder in the Tester Hunt. Well, it'll get those dotty blood sports protesters going. Agatha! For God's sake don't kiss Mr Rumpole!'

I had, in fact, felt the slap of a warm tongue on the back of the neck. I leant forward and lit a small cigar. As he squeaked past a bus and slipped by as the light went red, I wondered how useful Fiona's swain would be in the coming trial.

'You're a partner?' I asked him.

'In Jowling and Leonard. My old man's firm, quite honestly. But he doesn't care for murder. So he handed this case on to me. "Well, my boy," he said. "You may as well start at the bottom..." You knew Jonathan Postern at all?'

'Only momentarily.'

'People round here had a tremendous lot of time for Jonno.'

'I'm sorry.' I meant it.

'What?'

'It's not what you need in a murder case, a well-liked corpse.'

'Well, you'd know about that, wouldn't you? Agatha. Don't kiss! I shan't tell you again. Only one trouble with Jonno Postern. He had a bad case of the M.T.F.s.'

'The *what*?' The young man seemed to need a simultaneous translation.

'Must Touch Flesh! Particularly the flesh of Debbie Pavier. Well, that's what the row was all about, wasn't it? A Grand Military Shout-up. I mean, if it hadn't been for that the constabulary might have taken Sprod's story about an accident, and no questions asked.'

'Debbie Pavier?' I asked. 'Was she the girl who was kissing him in the tent at the races?'

'One of them, yes. All the girls were crazy about Jonno.'

Tester prison was a smallish Victorian castle, not far from the centre of town. Jennifer Postern had been brought up from Holloway and we sat in a small, dark interview room and I rummaged in my brief and asked her questions. She seemed remarkably calm and self-possessed. She had none of the prison pallor I was used to in my clients, but seemed to bring into the stuffy little room a fresh breeze from the countryside.

'It was an accident,' she told me, as she had told the old man Figgis.

'Your housekeeper says you were quarrelling with your husband that afternoon.'

'Bit of a hangover. After some serious drinking the night before.'

'Do you remember saying something about "killing him"?'

'Isn't it the sort of thing one says?' Jennifer asked with a smile.

'Is it?'

'Well, don't you quarrel sometimes, with She Who...?'

'Happily, neither of us owns a shotgun.' I meant it. 'After the quarrel your husband went out?'

'Jonno wanted a walk, I suppose. To cool off.'

246

'And so did you?'

'Yes. I went out after he did.'

'And you took your twenty-bore with you?'

'You know something about guns?' For the first time, I thought, she looked a little worried.

'A little. Why did you take it?'

'I thought it might calm my nerves if I shot something.'

'Not the most tactful way of explaining your feelings to the jury.' I ground out the end of a small cigar on the tin ashtray on the table.

'I meant rough shooting. A rabbit, perhaps, or a pigeon or . . .'

'The gun was loaded when you met your husband in the wood?'

'Of course.'

'And the safety catch?'

'I put up a pheasant and I was about to have a shot, and then I remembered it was after February. Closed season for pheasants.' But not for husbands, I thought, but didn't say, as Jennifer went on, 'I must have forgotten to put the safety catch on again. I walked on a little.'

'Down the track in the wood?' I had another bundle of photographs in my brief, not of the mortuary but of rural scenes.

'Yes.'

'And then?'

She paused, seemed to be in some difficulty, and looked to the young solicitor for help. 'I've told Jeremy,' she said.

'Tell me.'

Her hesitation didn't last long. She took in a deep breath and said, 'I saw Jonno coming towards me.'

'He was still angry?'

'No, I don't think so. He looked perfectly calm, actually.'

'And you?'

'Oh, I was calm enough. I walked towards him. The track was rough, you know. Brambles. It needed clearing. And I must have tripped and . . . Well, that's how it happened.'

I looked at her in silence and then slapped my pockets. 'You don't have a small cigar about you?'

'No.' She was smiling and seemed relieved.

'Stupid of me. I must have left them in the car.' I turned to Jeremy Jowling. 'Your dog's probably guarding them with her fangs bared.'

'I'll whizz out and get them. Back in a jiff.'

Jeremy went obediently. I sat looking at Jennifer. 'He's one of your lot, isn't he?' I asked her when we were alone.

'Jeremy? Well, we knew his father, of course,' Jennifer answered vaguely.

'One of your lot,' I stood and spoke my mind to her. 'But I'm not. I don't wear green welly boots. I don't travel with a firearm and a bloody great mastiff in the back of my car. I'm even unfamiliar with your language—which seems to me to have been designed for the express purpose of saying nothing at all. I have landed in your midst, Mrs Postern, like a creature from outer space. You can speak to me as to a perfect stranger.'

'What do you want me to say?' She was smiling up at me with maddening politeness.

'Anything you think I ought to know.'

There was a pause. She continued to smile and then said, as she had always done, 'It was an accident.'

248

The Postern house was a long, grey Georgian manor in a small park which was bounded by the woods. The rough track I had seen in the photographs started at the edge of the parkland and passed the hedge which surrounded a small, tumbledown cottage. That afternoon I stood on the track near to a fallen tree, holding a shotgun in my hands. The weapon was the property of my instructing solicitor and I held it as though I were about to shoot a startled and unwary pheasant. Then I stumbled on the rough and overgrown ground and brought the gun up to point to Jeremy Jowling's chest, roughly the area in which Jonathan Postern had received the fatal charge of shot.

'I suppose it's possible,' I speculated. 'More likely I'd've shot your feet off, though.'

Jeremy took the gun from me gently.

'Never, never let your gun
Pointed be at anyone.
That it should unloaded be
Matters not the least to me.'

'Come again?'

'You don't know that?' He sounded incredulous.

'No. We must have learnt different nursery rhymes.' Then an uncomfortable thought struck me. 'Jennifer Postern would've known it, though, wouldn't she? She must have learnt gun training on her Nanny's knee.' I was looking moodily at the ground, the trees and the bushes, the track that runs through the wood.

'Her father was a terrific shot. Runs in the

family. What are you looking at?'

'The scene of the crime,' I told him. 'The *locus* in *quo*.'

'What do you do now?' Jeremy was interested to know. 'Crawl about on your hands and knees collecting bits of cigarette ash in an old envelope?'

'Not exactly. The *locus* in *quo* looks just like any old bit of the English countryside to me.'

I moved a little way along the track to a sign on a post, which bore the direction TO BADGER'S WOOD, and a picture of the appropriate animal.

'Where's that lead to?' I asked. 'More Postern country?'

'Fishbourne country, actually.'

'Who?'

'Maurice Fishbourne. Something of a weed with a good deal of money. Gets ragged a lot for trying to ride at point-to-points. Invariably hits the deck.'

'Fishface!' Yes, of course I remembered.

'You know him?'

'Hardly at all. He isn't a friend of the Posterns?'

'They can't stand him. No one can, actually. He's not P.L.U. exactly.'

'People Like Us?' I hazarded a guess.

'Well, he puts up those poncy little signs on his land and gets all his cash from laxatives: "Fishbourne's keep you regular."'

I was looking at the top windows of the cottage which were visible above the tangled hedge. 'I rely on medicinal claret myself,' I told him. And then I was startled by a raucous cry, coming from somewhere quite near us. It was a strangely sad sound, like the lament for some irreparable loss. 'What the hell's that?' I asked Jeremy. 'Someone in pain?'

250

'Not at all. That is a yell of pure randiness. Look, I'll show you.' He led me to a gap in the hedge and a gate into the untended cottage garden. And there, on the grass, was a rough coop in which a plump brown bird with a beady eye was imprisoned and letting people know about it. 'That's a calling bird. A cock pheasant,' Jeremy told me.

'A calling pheasant in a cage,
Puts all Heaven in a rage,'

I suggested, and went on,

'The wanton boy that kills the fly
Shall feel the spider's enmity.'

'Figgis, the old devil who lives here, keeps it to entice all the Postern pheasants into his front garden. Of course, when they get there he knocks them off from his front window with a shotgun. Cunning isn't it?'

'Did Jonathan Postern know he was being robbed?'

'I suppose he just let it go on. He couldn't get Figgis out of the cottage. Old Jonno was a bit of an innocent in spite of everything.'

I was looking at the cottage. A thin line of smoke was coming out of the chimney. 'Did you say "Figgis"?'

'I bet he's in there. Want to talk to him?'

'Talk to a prosecution witness?' I looked at Jeremy with deep disapproval. 'Not sporting, old fellow. Definitely not sporting.'

But as we moved away I saw a shape behind the blurred glass of a downstairs window. The

251

prosecution witness was no doubt watching us with interest.

★   ★   ★

When I got to know the Tester Arms Hotel I realized how right Jeremy Jowling had been to take me straight to the prison. That evening I had what was known as the 'set meal'; Pâté Maison in the form of liver ice-cream, a steak from the rump of some elderly animal lightly singed under the X-ray machine, a cheeseboard aptly named because the Cheddar tasted exactly like wood, and a bottle of chilled claret which made Pommeroy's plonk seem like Château-Lafite.

I didn't sleep well that night. It wasn't just the firewood in the mattress, or the intense cold, or the noise in the water pipes like a giant's indigestion. I had sat up until well after midnight reading the post mortem report of a certain Dr Overton, a local man no doubt and hitherto unknown to me, and looking again and again at the photographs of the wound. Thoughts about shotguns raced through my head all night, and in the dawn I ordered the cooked breakfast which was there in about an hour's time, cold as charity but better than dinner. At exactly nine o'clock I put through a call to the Forensic Department at St Cuthbert's Hospital in London and asked to speak to Professor Andrew Ackerman.

There are two people in England who know most of what there is to know about bloodstains: Horace Rumpole and Professor Andrew Ackerman. I have crossed swords with the good Prof across many a courtroom, one of the most recent occasions being in the case of a strange young man who fell in with

252

an appalling religious sect. It was a case which turned on a nice point of blood, and I think I got one up on Ackerman on that occasion [See *Rumpole's Return*, Penguin Books, 1980]. We are firm friends, however, and once a year Andrew Ackerman invites me to lunch at the Athenaeum, where we discuss various corpses of our acquaintance over a chop. My night thoughts on the Postern case had convinced me that what I now needed was a bit of help from the good Professor. By good fortune I got hold of him before he went down to the morgue, and the conversation we had about shotgun wounds was long and enthralling.

In due course young Jeremy Jowling came up to my room to fetch me for the *corrida* and, as I buttoned myself into the black jacket and waistcoat, I asked him if he'd read Dr Overton's report.

'I've glanced at it,' Jeremy said.

I was tying up my brief. 'Sure of himself, our Dr Overton. Perhaps a little too sure of himself for an *experienced* pathologist. Know anything about him?'

'Never heard of him. Gravely usually does all the stiffs for the Home Office.'

'How interesting!' I was checking the robes, and fitting the thick bundle of papers into my briefcase.

'What're our chances?' Jeremy Jowling asked with a small show of nerves.

'Speaking as a sporting man—you'd like to know the odds?'

'Any better than evens?'

'It's not exactly an easy defence,' I admitted. 'But she's a woman. She was probably badly treated by her husband. All we need is a sympathetic judge.'

And then young Jeremy Jowling dropped his bombshell. 'We've got a fellow called Mr Justice

Twyburne,' he said, as though he were referring to the state of the weather. I must confess that the Rumpole jaw dropped.

'What do you think?' He must have noticed my dismay.

'I think—the odds have lengthened considerably.'

'Why? What's he like then?'

I sat down, recovered my breath, lit a small cigar to steady my nerves and asked young Jowling if he remembered Martin Muschamp.

'No...'

'One of the last death penalty cases. He went out with a gang, and was tried for shooting a copper. Twyburne summed up dead against him. Couple of years later another boy confessed and Marty Muschamp was cleared by a Home Office Inquiry.'

'That was all right then,' Jeremy suggested.

'Oh, lovely for everyone. Except for Martin Muschamp. He'd already been hanged.' I got up and went to the door. 'Don't worry too much. We don't do that sort of thing any more.'

*　　*　　*

Mervyn Harmsway was a pleasant, middle-aged prosecutor, who, so I was told, had a pretty Queen Anne house in Tester, and an impressive collection of Crown Derby. He opened the case perfectly fairly in the chilly atmosphere of Twyburne's Court, and the old Judge, more paper-coloured than ever, listened without expression.

The Court was full. I recognized a few faces, including the pretty girls who had kissed Jonno at the point-to-point. Fiona was in mufti on the bench

254

behind me, and her sister smiled at her, apparently unworried, from the dock. The solid-looking county jury listened to Harmsway as though they were determined not to let anyone know what they were thinking.

'That is all I have to say in opening this sad case, members of the jury,' Harmsway finished. 'And now, with the assistance of my learned friend Mr Gavin Pinker, I hope to fairly put the evidence before you.'

'You are causing me a great deal of pain, Mr Harmsway.' A dry voice came from the Bench.

'I'm sorry, my Lord?' Harmsway looked puzzled.

'Please. Don't split them.' The Judge was looking extremely pained.

'Don't split what, my Lord?'

'Your infinitives!' his Lordship cracked back. 'This is a distressing case, in all conscience. Do we have to add to the disagreeable nature of the proceedings the sound of you tormenting the English language? You hope to put the evidence fairly.'

'Yes, my Lord.' Harmsway looked cowed.

'Then why don't you start to do it?' Twyburne asked testily.

'My learned friend, Mr Pinker, will call the first witness.'

Poor old Harmsway subsided, deflated, to his seat. His junior, Gavin Pinker, who seemed made of sterner stuff, rose and announced that he would now call Mrs Marian Hempe. As the Posterns' dear old housekeeper waddled into the witness-box and took the oath, Harmsway whispered to me bitterly, 'What a charming Judge!'

'Don't worry, old darling,' I comforted him.

255

'Twyburne's quite impartial. He'll be just as ghastly to me.' And then I turned my attention to the dialogue between Mrs Hempe and Mr Gavin Pinker.

'Mrs Hempe. How long have you worked for the Posterns?' Pinker started quietly.

'Ten years now, for Master Jonathan. And his father before him.'

'You don't live in?'

'I comes on my bicycle. They drive me home if it's a late dinner.'

'On the afternoon that Jonathan Postern died . . . did you hear anything going on, between him and his wife?'

'Yes. They was quarrelling, like. In the sitting room. I could hear voices.'

'Whose voices?'

'Both, I reckon.'

'Could you hear any words?'

'I hear two words.'

'What were they?'

'"Kill you"—I heard that said. Loud. By her.'

'By Mrs Postern.' Pinker paused to let the evidence sink in. 'And after that?'

'Then I see Mr Postern go out. He walked towards the woods.'

'What happened then?'

'Mrs Postern stayed indoors. Then *she* went out.'

'How long did she stay out?'

'I don't rightly know. Ten minutes, quarter of an hour perhaps. Then she came back and got it.'

'Got what?'

Mrs Hempe pursed her lips as though about to have to mention some indelicacy, looked at the jury and said, 'Her shotgun.'

256

'Did you see her get it?' Pinker asked.

'No. But I see her go out with it under her arm. She went back towards the woods again.'

'That is the direction Mr Postern had taken?'

'Yes.'

'What happened next? Just tell the jury.'

'I heard a shot from the wood,' Mrs Hempe just told the jury.

'From the way they'd both gone.'

'Yes.'

'Thank you, Mrs Hempe.'

Gavin Pinker consulted Harmsway, who took the view that Mrs Hempe had done all that could be expected of her to scupper the defence, and I rose to cross-examine. I knew I would get nowhere at all by calling Mrs Hempe a liar, so I began to investigate the points that interested me, hoping to get the cooperation of the good Mrs Hempe.

'You heard *one* shot?' I asked her.

'No. I heard others.'

'You heard others. When?'

'I heard some shooting from the wood. That was before Mrs Postern went out.'

'But after *Mr* Postern went out?'

'Yes?'

'After *Mrs* Postern went out, how many shots did you hear?'

'Just one.'

'Are you sure of that?'

'I'll take my Bible oath to it.' Mrs Hempe sounded nettled.

'Just *one* shot and that is all?'

'It was enough, wasn't it?'

The jury nodded in sympathy with the witness. I hurried on to another topic. 'Now, you heard these

257

words, "Kill you". You've sworn that was all you heard her say?'

'That's right.'

I took my courage in my hands and launched an extremely dangerous question. 'You didn't hear her say, "*I'll* kill you", for instance?' I suggested, and held my breath until the witness gave me a hesitant and reluctant, 'No.'

'So she might possibly have been warning him that someone else might kill him?'

'I suppose so,' Mrs Hempe sounded extremely grudging. 'But she was the only one there, wasn't she?'

'Exactly.' Twyburne was no longer able to restrain himself. 'Are you suggesting that someone else might have killed him, Mr Rumpole?'

'My Lord. I was merely exploring the possibilities.' I gave the old darling my most charming smile and sat down.

* * *

Sometime during that morning I glanced up at the public gallery and saw the face of Maurice Fishbourne staring down at me through a new pair of spectacles. Mr Figgis from the cottage in the woods near the Postern house was in the witness-box. He was a grizzled, stooping man in his late sixties, I judged, wearing an old torn tweed jacket. He was imperfectly shaved, and his shirt looked as though it hadn't been washed for some time. He was an old man who lived alone. Harmsway took him through his evidence-in-chief and then I rose to cross-examine.

'When did you first see Mrs Postern on that day?'

258

'When she was holding the shotgun. Standing about ten yards off him.' Figgis was only too anxious to repeat his evidence.

'Eventually you took the gun off her and broke it open?'

'I did, yes.'

'How many cartridges had been fired?'

'Just the one.' Figgis seemed to think the evidence damning, but I blessed him silently for it.

'Just the one,' I repeated for the jury. 'You ejected the spent cartridge?'

'Yes.'

'And did you go with her back to the house where she telephoned the police?'

'I did.' The old man seemed proud of the important part he played in these stirring events.

'And was her gun in your possession until the police arrived?'

'Yes.'

'I'm much obliged.' I gave the jury another look. 'Now, when you first saw Mrs Postern, what did she say, *exactly*?'

'She said, "*I* did it. It was an accident."'

'She said, "*I* did it." Might it not have been, "I *did* it"?'

'Is there a dispute as to what your client said, Mr Rumpole?' Twyburne was irritated at what he clearly thought was a quibble.

'No dispute as to what she said, my Lord. I am only interested to discover where the emphasis was put.'

'*You* may be interested in that, Mr Rumpole. It remains to be seen in the fullness of time whether the point interests the jury.' Twyburne looked at the jury and sighed heavily. The solid citizens

259

continued to give nothing away.

'It may be a question of some importance, my Lord.'

'The words are there.' And then Twyburne delivered himself into my hands. 'How they were said seems to be a matter of unimportant insignificance,' he said weightily.

'May I suggest that it might be better to say, "of insignificance", my Lord.' I was extremely polite.

'What?' The Judge looked as puzzled as Harmsway had been on a similar occasion.

'"Unimportant insignificance" might be a bit of a tautology, might it not? Something of a torment to the English language,' I suggested innocently. The barristers in Court seemed too stunned to laugh. There was a moment's appalled silence when it seemed that the Judge might be prepared to commit me for Contempt of Court. Then he said quietly, 'Ask your question, Mr Rumpole.'

'Thanks awfully.' Harmsway gave me a whisper of gratitude, and I whispered back, 'Don't mention it.' Then I asked Figgis again if he could remember how Jennifer Postern had emphasized the words of her admission.

'She said, "*I* did it,"' he decided, after a good deal of thought.

'Now I wonder why she said that,' I speculated. 'There was no one *else* about who could have done it, was there?'

'Not as I could see.'

'Not that you could see.' I gave the jury time to think about that answer and then attacked another subject.

'Mr Figgis. Do you keep a calling pheasant?'

'I don't know what you mean,' he protested.

'Oh, I think you do. A cock bird in a cage whose cries invite numerous lady pheasants to visit your front garden when you knock them off from your downstairs window. So far as I can gather, you must have pheasant for breakfast, dinner and tea.'

That got a small laugh from the jury. Figgis smiled modestly. 'Maybe I does a bit of that,' he admitted.

'Mr Rumpole. This witness is not on trial for poaching.' Twyburne was getting edgy. 'Has this evidence the slightest relevance to this case?'

'No doubt the jury will tell us that, my Lord. In the fullness of time.' I turned back to the witness before the Judge could get at me again. 'On the day you have been telling us about...'

'The day I see Mr Postern dead?'

'That's it. What had you been doing that afternoon?'

'I was in my cottage.'

'And as usual you were doing a bit of shooting, were you?'

'I may have been...' His answer was extremely reluctant.

'And your cottage is not more than fifteen yards from the scene of this alleged crime?'

'Mr Rumpole!' The Judge came to Figgis's rescue. 'May I remind you that your client admitted shooting her husband with a shotgun and shotgun wounds and pellets were found in her husband's body.'

'Your Lordship may remind me of that, but I can assure you I haven't forgotten it. Thank you, Mr Figgis.' I smiled politely at the Judge, the witness, the jury and anyone else I could think of and sat down. Harmsway announced that he had no further

261

questions for the witness.

'Very well.' Mr Justice Twyburne looked at the clock, and gave a small, wintry smile at the jury. 'Members of the jury. This may be a convenient moment for you to obtain some refreshment. Be back at ten past two, please.'

So the Judge rose. As I was about to leave, Fiona came up to me and asked if I was coming down to see 'Sprod'.

'I don't think so,' I told her. 'Not till she's ready to tell me what happened.'

At which moment the Judge's clerk came up to me and said he had a message from his master.

'Am I under arrest?'

'On the contrary, sir. You're invited to lunch in the lodgings.'

'This case is full of surprises.'

'The car's outside. We travel in robes, sir.'

On my way out to the Judge's Rolls, I saw Maurice Fishbourne. He was standing on the pavement outside the Court, and he seemed about to speak to me, but then he changed his mind and turned away.

*   *   *

The invitation to take lunch in the Judges' 'lodgings', referred to above, may require some explanation for those not deeply versed in legal matters. In the olden days judges, barristers and their respective clerks and hangers-on, used to roll up in large coaches on circuit from one Assize town to the other, emptying the jails and usually despatching their inhabitants to some further proceedings beyond the grave. Each town had to

262

provide fitting accommodation for the judges' regular visits. A house was set aside, provided with silver, decanters, wine and servants, bed linen and firewood and all appropriate comforts by the municipality, and was known as the 'Judges' lodging'.

Although the same enlightened planner (his name now escapes me) who abolished the greater part of the railways also cut out the circuit system—as though it were a rather slow branch line from Ashby de la Zouch—Red Judges, Judges of the Queen's Bench, still go on tour and sit to try criminal cases in provincial centres and once there, become prisoners in their own lodgings. They are waited on by elderly retainers, they have no worries about queueing at Tesco's, and they find it difficult to go to the pictures without a police escort. I have often wondered what would induce anyone to sentence themselves to such long terms of confinement.

The lodgings, of course, are usually large and pleasant old houses, and the one at Tester was no exception. It was of a warm red brick, much decorated by honeysuckle and clematis and surrounded by a carefully manicured lawn. We had travelled there with a couple of policemen on motorbikes as outriders and I resisted a strong temptation to wave in a royal fashion to a little crowd of women at a bus stop. We left our wigs on the hall table, where they lay like dead and dirty white birds while we ate in our robes. Twyburne sat at the head of the table, Rumpole for the defence on his right, and Harmsway and Pinker on his left. The lunch, which was plain but excellent, passed without any particular embarrassment, except that

263

Twyburne ignored me and addressed all his remarks to the prosecution team. As the butler served coffee and put the decanter of port on the table, Twyburne was finishing a well-used anecdote.

'"He sat beside me in the cinema, sir," said the girl in the indecency case, "and put his hand up my skirt." "Very well," said the old Recorder, with his eye on the clock at lunchtime, "I suggest we leave it there until five past two."'

Twyburne's shoulders heaved and he laughed soundlessly at this. Pinker and Harmsway burst into almost uncontrollable mirth, and the Judge pushed the decanter in their direction. I was not laughing, and perhaps it was because he felt some sort of a challenge that the Judge turned to me for the first time.

'Well now. No more arguments about grammar this afternoon, eh, Rumpole?' he said.

'Possibly not.' I was making no promises.

'All the same, you stood up to me pretty well.' Twyburne was smiling in a patronizing sort of way. 'That's what we need in our job. Guts and determination to stick to an argument.'

'Even if it's wrong?' I asked him.

'Mistakes can usually be put right.' He took an apple from a dish in front of him and began to peel it slowly and with great accuracy. Still angry at being ignored over the last half-hour, I said, 'I suppose not in the death penalty days.'

'Oh, you're thinking of the young fellow who went out on the robbery. Case where they shot a policeman?' Twyburne spoke vaguely, as though it were a minor matter that had happened a long time ago.

'Martin Muschamp,' I reminded him firmly.

'Muschamp. Yes. Nothing else I could have done about that. I summed up the evidence—it was pretty damning, of course—and I left the matter to the jury.' He had finished peeling the apple now, and divided it into neat quarters.

'So it was just the luck of the draw, really?' I asked him.

'All this argument about the death penalty. We managed to take it in our stride. Did our duty. We didn't enjoy it, of course. Lot of nonsense talked about judges eating muffins after death sentences. Well, you couldn't get muffins in the Army and Navy Club.' He looked at me and seemed to be waiting for a comment, or an apology. I didn't oblige him. 'All you could do was sum up and leave the matter to the jury.' There was a new note in his voice now. It was no longer the voice of a Judge, but of an advocate, pleading for something. At last he said, 'Nothing else I could do, was there?'

I had a sudden feeling that Mr Justice Twyburne wanted to be forgiven, but who was I to forgive him? The only answer I had was, 'I don't know.'

A long silence followed and ended when Twyburne popped a quarter of the apple in to his mouth, chewed it and asked, 'Are you a gardener, Rumpole?'

'I'm afraid not.' I was no use to him.

'Excuse me, Judge, where . . . ?' Harmsway asked, and when the Judge told him it was on the right just outside the door, he left, followed by his learned junior.

'I'm a rose man myself,' the Judge told me when we were left alone. 'Of course, it's been difficult to get round all the pruning since my wife died. Come and look at this.' Twyburne got up and went to the sideboard. I knew now, without a doubt, that he wanted me to feel pity for him. He took a silver-framed photograph off the long stretch of mahogany. I was looking at two little girls in the garden.

'The Mrs Sam Macreadys are flowering well, don't you think? And that's two of the grandchildren. I've got six now, altogether. This one's the budding show-jumper.'

He put the photograph down slowly and looked at me. He seemed very tired and enormously old. 'I think I summed up Muschamp quite fairly,' he said.

'Didn't you tell the jury they might well not believe a word of his evidence?' I wasn't letting him off.

'That was my personal opinion. They were quite free to come to their own conclusion, wouldn't you agree?'

I said nothing. I didn't want to give him what he wanted from me, not even a crumb of comfort. We stood facing each other in silence for a moment, and then Harmsway came back from the lavatory.

'So kind of you, Judge,' he said. 'Such an agreeable luncheon.'

*   *   *

When we had made our royal progress back to Court I cross-examined Detective Inspector Clover, the comfortable, rubicund local officer in charge of the case. I took hold of Exhibit One, which was Jennifer Postern's shotgun, and held it up for his inspection. I put my questions gently. I was saving all my strength for the coming battle with Dr Overton, the pathologist.

'This was the gun that fired the shot. You're satisfied of that, Inspector?'

'Quite satisfied, sir.'

'It was, of course, immediately submitted to the ballistics expert, Mr Collinson, whose evidence has been read. You know his view is that only one barrel had been fired within the hours before he saw it?'

'Yes.'

'And you found one cartridge case and one only at the scene of the crime?'

'Yes.'

'So your view of this case, after the most thorough inquiries by the police, is that Mrs Postern fired one shot at her husband and one shot only?'

The good Inspector turned to the Judge and gave me what I wanted. 'That is absolutely clear, my Lord,' he said.

'Absolutely clear.' I looked at the jury, willing them to remember what he'd said, and then I let the Inspector go.

Dr Overton was young and extremely pleased with himself. He stood in the witness-box, with his reports and the mortuary photographs spread out in front of him, and lectured us as though we were a collection of housewives taking a course in elementary pathology on the University of the Air. He smiled at the jury after every answer and, when addressed by the Judge, he bowed like an over-eager hall porter working his way up to a generous tip. He wore a neat blue suit, his hair came over the tops of his ears, and he sported a small moustache. As Harmsway took him through his evidence, I stirred in my seat restlessly. I couldn't wait for my turn to cross-examine.

'Dr Overton, have you investigated previous cases of death by shotgun wounds?' I began, when my opportunity came at last.

'I think one.' He smiled modestly at the jury.

'Just one. And have you been called on to give evidence in a murder trial before?'

'Well, no. Not, actually . . .'

'Congratulations on your debut.' I gave him a smile for which he wasn't grateful. 'Why was it that you were called in to perform the post mortem in this most important case? Is not Dr Gravely the most experienced and aptly named Home Office pathologist for the Tester district?'

'Dr Gravely was away at a conference in Scarborough. I was called in at short notice.'

'And saw your big chance?'

'His big chance of *what*, Mr Rumpole?' Twyburne didn't like my tone with the young doctor.

'Perhaps your big chance of ingratiating yourself with the local police by agreeing with their conclusions?' I suggested.

'I did agree with their conclusions, yes.'

'And with their view that Jonathan Postern's body had received the impact of one, and only one, shotgun wound.'

'That was my conclusion.' The doctor gave the Judge another small bow, and Twyburne gave him a shadowy smile of approval.

'From which we may draw the inference that it was the shot from Mrs Postern's gun which caused his death, either deliberately, or by accident?'

'Yes.' Dr Overton felt it was quite safe to agree.

'Shotgun pellets enter the body at one central point surrounded by an area of scatter?'

'That's true.'

'And the area of scatter is larger if the gun has been fired from a greater distance.' Elementary, of course, but I wanted also to give the jury a lesson in first principles.

'I agree.' Dr Overton was clearly feeling that he was emerging from my cross-examination unscathed. I was doing my best to lure him into a false sense of security. 'I'm glad you do. Take Photograph Three, if you will.'

The witness, the Judge and the jury opened the volume of mortuary photographs.

'You have made a pencil circle round the entry hole which you consider fatal. It's the right side of the chest in the jury's photograph.'

'I see that, yes.'

'That is where you consider the fatal shot entered?'

'I'm sure of it.'

'Absolutely positive?'

'I have no doubts whatever on the subject, Mr Rumpole.' For a moment I felt sorry for the young doctor—he was so sure of everything. I hardened my heart and said, 'There is another, smaller wound to the left, and a little above that, is there not? Perhaps you would like to borrow my glass?' I held out a magnifying glass, but the doctor scorned its assistance.

'No. I can see perfectly well, thank you.'

'Is that the darker spot on the photograph? Just show us where you're looking.' Twyburne was following carefully. Dr Overton held up his photograph and pointed and then gave another little bow.

'Yes. At about two o'clock from the pencil circle, members of the jury,' said the Judge. The jury found it and some nodded.

'What did you take *that* to be?' I asked the witness.

'I took that to be part of the scatter,' the doctor said very positively, hoping that would settle the matter. It didn't.

'Could it not be the central wound of a second shot, fired, perhaps, from some yards further away?' I suggested. I was rewarded by a considerable pause and when Dr Overton spoke again it was with rather less confidence. 'I suppose that's a possibility.'

'It wasn't a minute ago, was it, Dr Overton?'

'*Just* a possibility, my Lord,' the witness appealed to the Judge, but got no help.

'So when you told us you were absolutely certain there was only one shot, you were giving this jury an opinion which was not entirely reliable.' I saw the jury looking fairly sternly at the witness.

'I see no reason to suppose that there was more than one shot.' Dr Overton tried a retreat to his previously held position.

'But it's a *possibility*!'

'Yes,' he had to admit.

'What would turn that possibility into a probability, Dr Overton?'

'Well, I suppose if there was some strong additional evidence.' He made a concession which he clearly believed was safe.

'And you say there is *none*?'

'Not so far as I know, my Lord.' Another small

270

bow to the Judge was received in sepulchral silence by Twyburne.

'What this jury has to consider, Dr Overton, is the extent of your knowledge. How many pellets, on an average, are there in a twenty-bore shotgun cartridge?' I had the satisfying feeling that I had fired him a question he wasn't prepared for. The doctor frowned, and answered with extreme care, 'I would say ... about an ounce of shot.'

'Well done. Very promising.' Now I was being the teacher. 'And so how many pellets are there in an ounce of shot?'

'How many pellets?' he frowned.

'Are you hard of hearing, Dr Overton?'

'Not in the least.'

'Then could you force yourself to tell this jury the answer to my question.'

'I think, my Lord,' he said with a small bow of apology now, 'I would have to look that up.'

It was time for a bit of carefully controlled indignation, and I said, 'It didn't occur to you to look it up before you came here to give so-called expert evidence against a lady of unblemished character on a charge of murder?'

'No,' was the only answer possible.

'Then let us see if you remember this. When you carried out your post mortem examination you found a large number of shotgun pellets in the body, did you not?'

'A very large number indeed.' He seemed pleased by the fact; so was I.

'I'm obliged. Did you count them?'

'May I look at my notes?' But Dr Overton was now looking at Inspector Clover, sitting in the well of the Court, for help.

271

'Look at anything you like,' I said, 'except the inspector in charge of the case. He's not going to be able to help, you know.'

'Mr Rumpole!' I heard a dry voice from the Bench and apologized at once, of course. 'Your Lordship objected to that observation? Then I will withdraw it and we can get on with something more interesting. How many pellets did you find in the deceased's body, Dr Overton?'

'About four hundred and eighty, my Lord . . .' he said, and the Judge made a careful note.

'And there may have been others you didn't find?'

'There may well have been.'

'Now let me tell you something, doctor, which may be a help to you if you ever come to give evidence in a murder trial again. Your average cartridge for a twenty-bore shotgun contains two hundred and fifty pellets.'

'Well, I must accept that, of course.' The doctor couldn't very well do anything else. It was all in Ackerman.

'So does not the presence in the deceased's body of almost double that number of pellets indicate to you that there were probably two shots?'

The silence seemed endless. The Judge sat with his pencil poised over his notebook. In the dock Jennifer Postern looked as though the answer concerned her not at all. Then Dr Overton said, 'It might do so . . .'

'Might it not?' I came down on the answer quickly. 'And if Mrs Postern only fired one shot, might not some *other* person have fired the other?'

'Surely that is a conclusion for the jury, Mr Rumpole,' Twyburne suggested, but this time it

272

was not a rebuke.

'My Lord, it will be my submission that it is the *only* conclusion. Thank you, Dr Overton.' I started to sit down, then changed my mind. 'Oh, doctor, before you go...' Dr Overton was leaving the witness-box with considerable relief. He paused disconcertedly as I held up the small volume which had been my inspiration for the day. 'If you intend to continue in your present line of work, I would recommend a study by Professor Andrew Ackerman on *Gunshot Wounds in Forensic Medicine.* Such a useful little volume, and quite easy reading for the beginner.'

* * *

'Of course, that cross-examination was wonderful entertainment, Rumpole.' Miss Allways had come up to me after the Judge had left Court, and I was packing up my brief for another evening of quiet contemplation.

'One of my best, Fiona,' I said with becoming modesty. 'Perhaps my very best of a medical witness. Luckily I couldn't warm to Dr Overton.'

'But where does it get my sister?' Fiona asked.

'Just possibly, off.'

She frowned, as though she couldn't see it personally. 'Sprod says it was an accident. Are you suggesting that there were two accidents?'

'No, Fiona. Only one accident.'

'What are you getting at?'

'Your sister's not too keen on the truth coming out in this case, is she, Fiona? Tell her I'll be down to the cells to see her first thing tomorrow morning.'

273

'Why not tonight?'

'Not tonight. No. I'm going back to the Tester Arms. I've got to see somebody else first.'

★   ★   ★

I had seen Fishbourne hanging about in the back of the Court when I was talking to Fiona, which is why I had announced my evening's plans in as loud a voice as possible. But when I turned away from her he had gone and I couldn't find him in the corridor or waiting for me outside the building. So I went back to the hotel, had a bath to wash away the courtroom atmosphere and changed into an old pair of grey flannels and a tweed jacket that had seen better days. No one rang to say that I had a visitor and, as I struggled through the appalling grapefruit segments, battery hen and frozen veg, no one came up to my table.

Only as I sat in the residents' lounge, with a bottle of less than average claret and a small cigar, was my patience rewarded. He was coming towards me through a maze of deserted coffee tables.

'Thank you for coming, Mr Fishbourne,' I said. 'Do please sit down.'

He sat, refused a drink, and looked at me as though desperate for good news. 'Y . . . y . . . you can't get her off, can you?' he said.

'Suppose you tell me the answer to that, Mr Fishbourne.'

'I mean, I d . . . don't see how you can. She said she did it.'

'What she said was, "*I* did it,"' I reminded him. 'Who else did she think might have done it, do you suppose?'

He looked at me then, I was glad to see, with considerable surprise. My suggestion, it seemed was one that hadn't occurred to him before.

'It couldn't possibly've been me.' He spoke quite calmly, without indignation or protest.

'*Couldn't?*'

"I d ... didn't see him. I'd gone up to London. Quite unexpectedly. I had a call from our solicitors and I went up just after lunch. All sorts of people saw me.'

I had no doubt they had, and felt a surge of relief. 'That's what we call an alibi in the trade,' I told him. 'Our first bit of luck in this case. But you know why Postern came to see you, don't you? I mean, it wasn't to criticize your riding abilities.'

'N ... n ... no. It wasn't for that.' He was looking at me, deciding to trust me. Then he accepted a glass of wine and started to tell me the whole story.

*   *   *

'How did you guess?' Jennifer Postern asked me when we met, early the next morning, in the cells under Tester Court. We had been given thick mugs of tea by the lady dock officer, and I felt easier in my mind than I had since the trial began.

'I saw you when Fishface fell at the last fence,' I told her. 'I thought you were his wife. Then you laughed at him with the others, so I knew you were hiding something. I suppose Jonathan found out about you and Maurice Fishbourne.'

'It's such a mess.' For the first time, she lost her extraordinary composure. She bowed her head, her hands were over her face and her shoulders

275

shaking. Then she made a great effort, looked up, and said, 'What do you want me to do?'

'Why not try telling the truth? Sometimes people win cases like that. What do you say—shall we give it a try?'

So, when the Court assembled, I called Jennifer Postern into the witness-box, and she swore to tell the truth, the whole truth and nothing but the truth.

'Mrs Postern,' I went straight to the heart of the case, 'the afternoon your husband died you had a quarrel. What was that quarrel about?'

'About Maurice Fishbourne.'

Twyburne looked up at a new name; the jury were puzzled. I explained with a question, 'He is your next-door neighbour?'

'Yes.'

'What did you tell your husband?'

'I told Jonno that I loved Maurice and if he would divorce me we hoped to marry. I had been unhappy with my husband for a long time.' Now she had made up her mind to tell her story, Jennifer spoke simply and convincingly.

'Had Jonathan Postern been violent to you?'

'Yes. Quite often.'

'And so, on the afternoon you quarrelled . . . ?'

'Jonno said he'd go over and see Maurice and tell him never to see me again. He threatened to beat Maurice up. I knew Maurice could have a violent temper and that he hated Jonno. I think I shouted at my husband that if he went, Maurice might kill him.'

'Was Mrs Hempe in the house when you shouted that?'

'She was, yes.'

'And might have heard part of it?'

'Yes. Easily.'

'Had Maurice told you he might kill your husband?'

'When he heard how Jonno had treated me. Yes.'

'Did you take these threats seriously?'

'I knew that Maurice was a very determined man. He has a very strong will.'

'Let's come to the time when your husband left the house.'

'Jonno said he was going out to cool off, but after a while I thought he'd gone to Maurice's, so I decided to follow him. I got as far as the track by Figgis's cottage and I saw Jonathan. There was blood . . .' She paused, seemed unable to go on, and then controlled herself. 'I saw that he was dead.'

'What did you think?'

'Of course I thought that Maurice had done it.' She looked at the jury. 'It was just by Maurice's wood. I thought he'd met Jonathan there and they quarrelled and . . .' For a moment her voice faded.

'And?'

'I knew Maurice wouldn't be able to get away with it.' She was summoning up reserves of strength. 'I thought he'd be convicted of murdering Jonathan. Oh, I was in a sort of panic, I suppose.'

'So what did you decide to do?' I asked her very quietly.

The Court and the jury were totally silent, almost breathless with attention as Jennifer answered, 'I decided to pretend I'd shot Jonathan. By mistake. In an accident. I went back to the house and got my shotgun. When I got to the wood again Jonathan was still there. I put in one cartridge and I fired.' Now she'd said it, the witness looked enormously

277

relieved.

'One shot only?'

'Yes, only one.'

'Into his dead body?'

Jennifer's answer was hardly above a whisper.
'Yes.'

*   *   *

In the course of time my task was done, and I sat
listening to Mr Justice Twyburne summing up to
the jury. He spoke quietly: at times we had to strain
our ears to hear him. With his lined face and thin
neck emerging from a stiff collar that seemed too
big for him, he looked like an aged tortoise. He was
a lonely old Judge who refused to retire and who
had come to me, of all people, for reassurance. And
then he looked at me, and I gave his words my full
attention.

'Members of the jury,' the Judge was saying,
'contrary to the views of *some people*, a British
criminal trial cannot be compared in any way to a
horse race.' He turned back to the jury. 'You do not
get the result by closing your eyes and sticking a pin
into the list of runners. If you are sure that, for
whatever reason, Mrs Postern deliberately shot at
her husband with the intention of killing him or
doing him serious harm, why then you must convict
her. But if you think that the account she gave you
might be true, I say *might* be true, then she is
entitled to be acquitted. There is some support for
Mrs Postern's story, is there not, in the medical
evidence?' Twyburne paused, searching for a place
in his notebook. I was filled with amazement, as I
slowly realized we were getting a fair, even a

278

favourable summing up. I wondered for a moment if we had Martin Muschamp to thank for it. Then Twyburne went on to the jury, 'You have to consider the possibility that, in an accident caused by the man Figgis shooting from the window of his cottage, Mr Postern met his death on that woodland track. That Mrs Postern, coming on the body, assumed her lover to have been responsible, and took extraordinary steps to cover up what she thought had been a crime. This is not a Court of morals, members of the jury, and it is not a racetrack. What we are concerned with is certainty, and the truth.'

* * *

Hilda had the television on as I let myself into Casa Rumpole at Froxbury Court. It was booming news from Tester Assizes, and telling a waiting world that Jennifer Postern had been acquitted.

'Well, Rumpole,' said Hilda. 'I suppose you think you've done something frightfully clever.'

She was standing by the mantelpiece, on which she had put the photograph of a gentleman's lodge near Tester, cut carefully out of *Country Life*. Hilda was still hankering, quite clearly, for rural living and membership of the County set.

'No.' I told her, 'I think I've done something absolutely "brill".'

I went into the kitchen, opened a well-earned bottle of Pommeroy's plonk, and brought my wife a brimming glassful. Then I raised my own beaker in a toast. 'To Jennifer Postern,' I said. 'A wonderful woman in some ways. She took the most extraordinary risks to protect the man she loved.'

'Fiona's sister?' Hilda was frowning.

'Yes. Doesn't look all that much like Fiona.' I was staring at the cutting on the mantelpiece. 'Far more beautiful, don't you think? Fine-looking woman. We'll be able to see a good deal of her if we take that gentleman's lodge arrangement near Tester you're always talking about. Jennifer promises to give me shooting lessons.'

'Shooting lessons? *You*, Rumpole?' She was clearly worried.

'Oh yes. We plan to spend a good deal of time together. You'll be kept busy, I suppose, bottling fruit.'

Hilda went to the mantelpiece. She looked thoughtful.

'Rumpole. I've been thinking. It's really very convenient for us, this flat in the Gloucester Road.'

'Yes, but . . .'

'We can always have days out in the country.'

'I suppose that's true, but . . .'

'I think I've decided against Tester.'

She Who Must Be Obeyed took the advertisement, crumpled it up and threw it into the waste-paper basket.

'Well, Hilda,' I said. 'It's entirely your decision, but perhaps it'll be better for our health, living quietly in London.'

RUMPOLE AND THE LAST RESORT

I have almost caught up with myself. Decent crime
has not been too thick on the ground recently, and
time has been hanging a little heavily on the
Rumpole hands. I have had a good deal of leisure to
spend on these chronicles of the splendours and
miseries of an Old Bailey hack and, although I have
enjoyed writing them, describing and remembering
is something of a second-hand occupation. I am
happiest, I must confess, with the whiff of battle in
my nostrils, with the Judge and the prosecuting
counsel stacked against me, with the jury
unconvinced, and everything to play for as I rear to
my hind legs and start to cross-examine the
principal witness for the Crown. There has been a
notable decrease in the number of briefs in my tray
in Chambers of late, and I have often set out for
Number 3 Equity Court with nothing but the *Times*
crossword and the notebook in which I have spent
otherwise undemanding days recalling old murders
and other offences. A barrister's triumphs are
short-lived: a notable victory may provide gossip
round the Temple for a week or two; a row with the
Judge may be remembered a little longer; but those
you have got off don't wish to be reminded of the
cells where they met you, and those whose cases
you have lost aren't often keen to share memories.
By and large, trials are over and done with when
you pack up your robes and leave Court after the
verdict. For that reason it has been some
satisfaction to me to write these accounts, although
the truth of the matter is, as I have already hinted,

that I haven't had very much else to do.

So up to date have I become that I can recount no more cases of sufficient interest and importance which have engaged my talents since my unexpected return from retirement. All I have left to do is something new to me—that is, to write about a case as I am doing it, in the hope that it will turn out to be sufficiently unusual to be included among these papers which will form some sort of memorial to the transient life of Horace Rumpole, barrister-at-law. I am soon to go into Court with one of my dwindling number of briefs, as counsel for the defence of a young businessman named Frank Armstrong, Chairman and Managing Director of Sun-Sand Holidays Ltd, an organization which supplies mobile homes to holidaymakers in allegedly desirable sites in the West Country, the Lake District and other places which have every known inconvenience, including being much too far away from Pommeroy's Wine Bar. The case itself may have some points of interest, including the mysterious mobility of Sun-Sand Mobile Homes, and the period about which I am writing contains another minor mystery, that is to say, the disappearance of a Mr Perivale Blythe, solicitor of the Supreme Court, a fellow who, so far as I am concerned, is fully entitled to disappear off the face of the earth, were it not for the fact that he has, for longer than I care to remember, owed me money.

One of the many drawbacks of life at the Bar is the length of time it takes to get paid for services rendered. As a loyal punter may not appreciate, he pays the solicitor for the hire of a barrister and, in theory at any rate, the solicitor passes the loot on to the member of the Bar, the front-line warrior in the courtroom battle, with the greatest possible despatch. In many cases, unhappily, the money lingers along the line and months, even years, may pass before it percolates into the barrister's bank account. There is really nothing much the average advocate can do about this. In the old days, when barristering was regarded as a gentlemanly pursuit for persons of private means, rather like fox-hunting or collecting rare seaweed, the rule grew up that barristers couldn't sue for their fees, on the basis that to be seen suing a solicitor would be as unthinkable as to be found dancing with your cook.

So it was not only a decline in the number of briefs bearing the Rumpole name, but a considerable slowing down in the paying process, which caused my account at the Temple branch of the United Metropolitan Bank to blush an embarrassing red. One day I called in to cash a fifty-pound cheque, mainly to defray the costs of those luxuries Hilda indulges in, matters such as bread and soap powder, and I stood at the counter breathing a silent prayer that the cashier might see fit to pay me out. Having presented my cheque, I heard the man behind the grille say, to my considerable relief, 'How would you like the money, sir?'

'Oh, preferably in enormous quantities.' Of course it was a stupid thing to say. As soon as the words had passed my lips, I thought he'd take my cheque off to the back of the shop and discover the extent of the Rumpole debt. Why was he reading the thing so attentively? The art of cheque-cashing is to appear totally unconcerned.

'How would I like the money?' I said rapidly.

'Oh, I'll take it as it comes. Nothing fancy, thank you. Not doubloons. Or pieces of eight. Just pour me out a moderate measure of pounds sterling.'

To my relief the notes came out on a little wheel under the glass window. I scooped up the boodle and told myself that the great thing was not to run. Break into any sort of jog trot on the way to the door and they check up on the overdraft at once. The secret is to walk casually and even whistle in a carefree manner.

I was doing exactly that when I was stopped with a far from cheery good morning by Mr Medway, the Assistant Manager. I should have made a dash for it.

'Paying in or drawing out today, are we?' Medway looked at the money in my hand. 'Oh. Drawing out, I see. Could you step into my office, sir?'

'Not now. Got to get to Court. A money brief, of course.' I was hastily stuffing the notes into my pocket.

'Just a moment of your time, Mr Rumpole.' Medway was not to be put off. Within a trice I found myself closeted with him as I was grilled as to my financial position.

'Gone right over the limit of our overdraft, haven't we, Mr Rumpole?' The man smiled unpleasantly.

'My overdraft? A flea bite, compared with what you chaps are lending the Poles.'

I searched for a packet of cigars, feeling that I rather had him there.

'I don't think the Poles are making out quite so many cheques in favour of Jack Pommeroy of Pommeroy's Wine Bar.'

'Those are for the bare necessities of life. Look here, Medway. A fellow's got to live!'

'There's bound to come a time, Mr Rumpole, when that may not be necessary at the expense of the United Metropolitan Bank.' A peculiarly heartless financier, this Medway.

'"The Bank with the Friendly Ear".' I quoted his commercial, lit the cigar and blew out smoke.

'There comes a time, Mr Rumpole, when the United Metropolitan goes deaf.'

'That little overdraft of mine. Peanuts! Quite laughable compared to my outstanding fees.' It was my time to bring out the defence. 'My fees'll come in. Of course they will. You know how long solicitors keep owing us money? Why, there's one firm who still hasn't paid me for a private indecency I did for them ten years ago. No names, of course, but . . .'

'Is that Mr Perivale Blythe?' Medway was consulting my criminal record. 'Of Blythe, Winterbottom and Paisley?'

'Yes. I believe that's the fellow. Slow payer, but the money's there, of course.'

'Is it, Mr Rumpole?' Medway was a banker of little faith. 'Every time we've had one of these little chats, you've told me that you're owed a considerable amount in fees by Mr Perivale Blythe.'

'Can't remember how much, of course. But enough to pay off my overdraft and make a large contribution to the National Debt.' I stood up, anxious to bring this embarrassing interview to a conclusion. 'Must be scooting along,' I said. 'Got to earn both of us some money. Engaged in Court, you know.'

'My advice to you, Mr Rumpole,' Medway said

285

darkly, 'is to take steps to make this Mr Perivale Blythe pay up. And without delay.'

'Of course. Get my clerk on to it at once. Now don't you worry, Medway.' I opened the door on my way to freedom. 'Having the Poles in next, are you? Hope you give them a good talking to.'

*   *   *

When I had told Medway that I had an engagement in Court it was a pardonable exaggeration. In fact I had nothing much to do but settle into my room at 3 Equity Court and write these memoirs. I had found the *tête-à-tête* in the bank somewhat depressing and I was in a low mood as I turned into the Temple and approached the entrance of our Chambers. There I met our demure Head, Sam Ballard, Q.C., who was standing on the step in conversation with a young man with dark hair, soft eyes and an expression of somewhat unjustified self-confidence which reminded me of someone. Ballard greeted me with 'Hullo there, Rumpole. How are you?'

'"Tir'd with all these, for restful death I cry,"' I told him candidly.

'As to behold desert a beggar born,
And needy nothing trimm'd in jollity,
And purest faith unhappily forsworn,
And gilded honour shamefully misplac'd...'

'What's this talk of death, Rumpole?' Ballard was brisk and disapproving. 'You know young Archie Featherstone, don't you? Mr Justice Featherstone's nephew.' He introduced the young man, who smiled vaguely.

'My God. More Featherstones!' I was amazed. '"What! will the line stretch out to the crack of doom?"'

'I'm sure he'd like your advice about starting out at the Bar.'

'My advice is, "Don't",' I told the young man.

'Don't?' he repeated, pained.

'Don't slog your heart out. Don't tramp for years round some pretty unsympathetic Courts. What'll you have to show at the end of it? You're up to your eyes in debt to the United Metropolitan Bank and they'll grudge you such basic nourishment as a couple of dozen non-vintage Château Thames Embankment.'

'Young Featherstone would love to get a seat in our Chambers, Rumpole.' Ballard had clearly not followed a word I'd said. 'I've told him that at the moment there's just not the accommodation available.'

'At the moment?' Was the man expecting a sudden departure from our little band of barristers?

'Well, I don't suppose you'll be in your room for ever.' Ballard didn't sound too regretful. 'The time must come when you take things a little more easily. Henry was saying how tired he thought you looked.'

'"Tir'd with all these, for restful death I cry..."' I repeated, and I looked at Ballard, remembering, '"And gilded honour shamefully misplac'd". Oh yes, Ballard. The time's got to come. Cheer up, young Featherstone,' I told him. 'You'll soon be able to take over my overdraft.'

I left them there and went to report to the clerk's room. When I got there I found Henry in position at his desk and Dianne rattling her typewriter in a corner.

'Henry, how much does Perivale Blythe owe me in fees?' I asked at once.

'Two thousand, seven hundred and sixty-five pounds, ninety-three pence, Mr Rumpole,' Henry said, as if he knew it all by heart.

'You tell me of wealth undreamed of by the United Metropolitan Bank. It's a debt stretching back over a considerable time, eh, Henry?'

'Stretching back, Mr Rumpole, to the indecency at Swansea in April, 1973.' Henry confirmed my suspicions.

'You have, I suppose, been on to him about it, Henry?'

'Almost daily, Mr Rumpole.'

'And what has this blighter Blythe to say for himself?'

'The last time his secretary told us a cheque was in the post.'

'Not true?' I guessed.

'Not unless it evaporated mysteriously between here and Cheapside.'

'Get after him, Henry, like a terrier. Get your teeth into the man Blythe, and don't let him go until he disgorges the loot.'

I looked at Henry's desk and my eyes were greeted with the unusual and welcome sight of a brief bearing the Rumpole name. 'Is that a set of papers for me you're fingering?' I asked with assumed indifference.

'Mr Myers brought it in, sir. It's a case at the Bailey.' Henry confirmed the good news.

'God bless old Myersy. A man who pays up from time to time.' I looked at the brief. 'What is it,

Henry? Murder? Robbery? Sudden death?'

'Sorry, Mr Rumpole.' Henry realized that I would be disappointed. 'It seems to be about Sun-Sand Mobile Homes.'

* * *

When I went up to my room to familiarize myself with the brief Henry had given me, I threw my hat, as usual, on to the hatstand; but, the hatstand not being there, the Rumpole headgear thudded to the ground. Of course, I knew what had happened. Erskine-Brown had always coveted the old hatstand that had stood in my room for years and, when he had a big conference, he put it in his room to impress the clientele. Before I started work I crept along the passage, found Erskine-Brown's room empty and purloined the old article of furniture back again. Then I sat down, lit a small cigar, and studied the facts in the case of R. *v.* Armstrong.

The trouble had started at a Sun-Sand holiday site in Cornwall. A family returned from a cold, wet day on the beach and had their mobile holiday home towed away before they could get at their high tea. Other punters were apparently sold holidays in mobile homes which were said to have existed only in the fertile imagination of my client, Frank Armstrong.

In due course police officers—Detective Inspector Limmeridge and Detective Sergeant Banks—called on Sun-Sand Holidays in North London. The premises were small and unimposing but the officers noticed that they were elaborately equipped with all the latest gadgets of computer technology. The young chairman of the company was there, busily pressing buttons and anxiously watching figures flash and hearing the bleeps and hiccoughs of such machines at work. When arrested, Mr Armstrong was given permission to telephone his solicitor, but when he did so he found that the gentleman in question had just slipped out of the office.

Eventually Frank Armstrong was allowed bail and turned up in my room at Chambers with old Myers, the solicitor's clerk (or legal executive, as such gentlemen are now called), whom I would rather have with me on a bad day at the Bailey than most of the learned friends I can think of. I had asked Miss Fiona Allways to join us and generally help with the sums.

'My brother Fred and I, we was born into the modern world, Mr Rumpole,' said Frank. 'And what is the name of the game, in the world today?'

'Space Invaders?' I hazarded a guess. My client looked at me seriously. In spite of a sharp business suit, his Gaucho moustache, longish hair, gold watch and bracelet, Playboy Club tie and the manner of a tough young businessman, Frank Armstrong looked younger than I had expected, and both pained and puzzled by the turn of events.

'The name of the game is leisure interests and computer technology,' he told me seriously. 'You won't believe this, Mr Rumpole. You will not believe it.'

'Try me.'

'Our old dad kept a fruit barrow in the Shepherd's Bush Market.'

'Not incredible,' I assured him.

'Yes, indeed. Well, he made a few bob in his time and when he died my brother and I divided the capital. Fred went into hardware, right?'

'Ironmongery?'

'You're joking,' Frank said. 'Fred joined the microchip revolution. Looking round your office now, Mr Rumpole, I doubt it's fully automated. There are delays in sending your bills out, right?'

'Sometimes I think my bills are sent out by a carrier pigeon with a poor sense of direction,' I admitted.

'Trust in the computer, Mr Rumpole, and you'd have so much more time, leisure-wise. That's the...'

'Name of the game?' I hazarded.

'Yes, indeed. That's why I saw my future definitely in the leisure industry.'

'"Leisure industry". Sounds like a contradiction in terms.'

Frank didn't hear my murmur. He was clearly off on a favourite subject. 'Who wants hotel expenses these days? Who needs porters, tips, waiter service? All the hassle. The future, as I see it, is in self-catering mobile homes set in A3 and B1 popularity, mass appeal holiday areas. That's the vision, Mr Rumpole, and it's got me where I am today.'

'On bail, facing charges of fraud and fraudulent conversion,' I reminded him.

'Mr Rumpole. I want you to believe this...'

'Try me again.'

'I just don't understand it. I want to tell you that very frankly. I was doing my best to run a go-ahead service industry geared to the needs of the eighties. What went wrong exactly?' Frank asked plaintively. I got up, stretched the legs and lit a small cigar.

'I imagine a close study of the accounts might tell

291

us that,' I said. 'By the way, that's one of the reasons I've asked you to give Miss Allways a little brief. She's got a remarkable head for figures.'

'And quite a figure for heads, I should think.' Frank gave our lady barrister one of his 'Playboy Club' leers and laughed. Fiona froze him with a look.

'Pardon me, Miss Allways. Probably out of place, right?' Our client apologized and Miss Allways ignored him and rattled out some businesslike instructions to old Myers. 'I'd like the accounts sent down to Chambers as soon as possible,' she said. 'There's a great deal of spadework to be done.'

'This is where we're in a certain amount of difficulty.' Myers coughed apologetically.

'Surely not?'

'You see, the accounts were all given to Mr Armstrong's previous solicitor. That was the firm that acted for his father back in the fruit barrow days and went on acting till after our client's arrest.'

'It's perfectly simple.' Fiona was impatient. 'You've only got to get in touch with the former solicitors.'

'Well, not quite as simple as all that, Miss Allways. We've tried writing but we never get an answer to our letters and when we telephone, well, the gentleman dealing with the matter always seems to have just slipped out of the office.'

'Really? What's the name of the firm?' Miss Allways asked, but I was ahead of her. 'Don't tell me, let me guess,' I said. 'What about Blythe, Winterbottom and Paisley?'

'Well,' our client admitted dolefully. 'This is it.'

*   *   *

At the end of the day I called into Pommeroy's Wine Bar and the first person I met was Claude Erskine-Brown on his way out. Of course I went straight into the attack.

'Erskine-Brown,' I said accusingly. 'Hatstand-pincher!'

'Rumpole. That's a most serious allegation.'

'Hatstand-pinching is a most serious crime,' I assured him.

'You don't need a hatstand in your room, Rumpole. Criminals hardly ever wear hats. I happened to have a conference yesterday with three solicitors all with bowlers.'

'That hatstand is a family heirloom, Erskine-Brown. It belonged to my old father-in-law. I value it highly,' I told him.

'Oh, very well, Rumpole. If that's the attitude.' He was leaving me.

'Goodnight, Erskine-Brown. And keep your hands off my furniture.'

As I penetrated the interior, I saw our clerk Henry, who is, far more effectively than the egregious Bollard, the true Head of our Chambers and ruler of our lives, in the company of the ever-faithful Dianne. I asked him to name his poison, which he did, in an unattractive manner, as Cinzano Bianco and lemonade.

'Dianne?' I included her in the invitation.

'I'll have the same.' She looked somewhat meltingly at Henry. 'It's what we used to have in Lanzarotte.'

'Did you really? Well, I won't inquire too deeply into that. And a large cooking claret, Jack, and no doubt you'd be happy to cash a small cheque?' I asked the host as he came past pushing a cloth along the counter.

'Well, not exactly happy, Mr Rumpole.' Pommeroy was not in one of his sunnier moods.

'Come on, you've got nothing to worry about. You haven't lent a penny to Poland, have you? This is a much safer bank than the United Metropolitan. Oh, give yourself one while you're about it,' I said, as Jack moved reluctantly to get the drinks and the money. Then I turned to my clerk in a businesslike manner. 'Now then, Henry, about this abominable Blythe. Not surfaced, by any stretch of the imagination?'

'No, Mr Rumpole. Not as yet, sir.'

'Not as yet. Lying in his hammock in some South Sea island, is he, fondling an almond-eyed beauty and drinking up our brief fees and refreshers?'

'I've made inquiries around the Temple. Mr Brushwood in Queen Elizabeth's Buildings had the same problem, his clerk was telling me. Blythe owed well into four figures, and they couldn't find hide nor hair of him, sir.'

'But poor old Tommy Brushwood is...' The claret had come and I resorted to it.

'No longer with us. I know that, sir. And as soon as he'd gone, Blythe called on Mr Brushwood's widow and got her to give him some sort of release for a small percentage. She signed as executor, not quite knowing the form, I would imagine. Cheers, Mr Rumpole.'

'Oh, yes. Cheers everso.' Dianne smiled at me over the fizzy concoction.

'But Henry, why has this Blythe not been reported to the Law Society? Why hasn't he been clapped in irons,' I asked him, 'and transported to the colonies?'

'All the clerks have thought of reporting him, of course. But if we did that we'd never get paid, now would we?'

'Despite that drink you indulge in, which has every appearance of chilled Lucozade, I believe you still have your head screwed on, Henry. I have another solution.'

'Honestly, Mr Rumpole? I'd be glad to hear it.'

'We need Blythe as a witness in the Sun-Sand Mobile Homes case.'

'R. *v.* Armstrong?'

'Your memory serves you admirably. We'll get Newton the Private Dick to find Blythe so he can slap a subpoena on him. If "Fig" Newton can't find the little horror, no one can. Isn't that all we need?'

'I hope so, Mr Rumpole,' Henry said doubtfully. 'I really hope so.'

*   *   *

Ferdinand Ian Gilmour Newton, widely known in the legal profession as 'Fig' Newton, was a tall, gloomy man who always seemed to be suffering from a heavy cold. No doubt his work, forever watching back doors, peering into windows, following errant husbands in all weathers, was responsible for his pink nostrils and the frequent application of a crumpled handkerchief. I have known 'Fig' Newton throughout my legal career. He appeared daily in the old-style divorce cases, when his evidence was invariably accepted. Since the bonds of matrimony can now be severed without old 'Fig' having to inspect the sheets or observe male and female clothing scattered in a hotel bedroom, his work has diminished; but he can still be relied upon to serve a writ or unearth an alibi witness. He seems to have no interest outside his calling. His home life, if it exists at all, is a mystery. I believe he snatches what sleep he can while sitting in his battered Cortina watching the lights go on and off in the bedroom of a semi-detached, and he dines off a paper of fish and chips as he guards the door of a debtor who has gone to earth.

'Fig' Newton called at the offices of Blythe, Winterbottom and Paisley early one morning and asked to see Mr Perivale Blythe. He was greeted by a severe-looking secretary, a lady named Miss Claymore, with spectacles, a tweed skirt and cardigan, and a Scots accent. Despite her assuring him that Perivale Blythe was out of the office and not expected back that day, the leech-like 'Fig' sat down and waited. He learned nothing of importance, except that round about noon Miss Claymore went into an inner office to make a telephone call. The detective was able to hear little of the conversation, but she did say something about the times of trains to Penzance.

When Miss Claymore left her office, 'Fig' Newton followed her home. He sat in his Cortina in Kilburn outside the Victorian building, divided into flats, to which Miss Claymore had driven her small Renault. He waited for almost two hours, and when Miss Claymore finally emerged she had undergone a considerable change. She was wearing tight trousers of some satin-like material and a pink fluffy sweater. Her feet were crammed into high-heeled gold sandals and she was without her spectacles. She got into the Renault and drove to Soho, where she parked with considerable daring halfway up a pavement, and went into an Italian restaurant where she met a young man. 'Fig' Newton kept observation from the street and was thus unable to share in the lasagne and the bottle of Valpolicella, which he carefully noted down. Later the couple crossed Frith Street and entered a Club known as the 'Pussy Cat A-Go-Go', where particularly loud music was being played. 'Fig' Newton was later able to peer down into the basement of this Club, where, lit by sporadic, coloured lights, Miss Claymore was dancing with the same young man, whom he described as having the appearance of a young business executive with features very similar to those of our client.

★   ★   ★

On the evening that Mr Perivale Blythe's secretary went dancing, I was reading on the sofa at 25B Froxbury Court, smoking a small cigar and recovering from a hard day of writing this account in my Chambers. Suddenly, and without warning, my wife, She Who Must Be Obeyed, dropped a heavy load of correspondence on to my stomach.

'Hilda,' I protested. 'What are these?'

'Bills, Rumpole. Can't you recognize them?'

'Electricity. Gas. Rates. Water rates.' I gave them a glance. 'We really must cut down on these frivolities.'

'All gone red,' Hilda told me.

'It's only last month's telephone bill.' I looked at a specimen. 'We should lay that down for maturing. You don't have to rush into paying these things, you know. Mr Blythe hasn't paid me much of anything since 1972.'

'Well, you'd better tell Mr Perivale Blythe that the London Electricity Board aren't as patient as you are, Rumpole,' She said severely.

'Hilda. You know we can't sue anyone for our fees.'

'I can't think why ever not.' My wife has only a limited understanding of the niceties of legal etiquette.

'It wouldn't be the gentlemanly thing to do,' I explained. 'Against the finest traditions of the bar.'

'Perhaps it's a gentlemanly thing to sit here in the dark with the gas cut off and no telephone and nasty looks every time you go into the butcher's. All I can say is, you can sit there and be gentlemanly on your own. I'm going away, Rumpole.'

I looked at Hilda with a wild surmise. Was I, at an advanced age, about to become the product of a broken home? 'Is that a threat or a promise.' I asked her.

'What did you say?'

'I said, "Of course, you'll be missed,"' I assured her.

'Dodo's been asked to stay with a friend in the Lake District, Pansy Rawlins, whom we were both at school with, if you remember.'

'Well, I don't think I was there at the time.'

'And Pansy's lost her husband recently.'

'Careless of her,' I muttered, moving the weight of the bills off me.

'So it'll be a bachelor party. Of course, when Dodo first asked me I said I couldn't possibly leave *you*, Rumpole.'

'I am prepared to make the supreme sacrifice and let you go. Don't worry about me,' I managed to say bravely.

'I don't suppose I shall, unduly. But you'd better worry about yourself. My advice to you is, find this Colindale Blythe.'

'*Perivale*, Hilda.'

'Well, he sounds a bit of a twister, wherever he lives. Find him and get him to pay you. Make that your task.' She looked down at me severely. 'Oh, and while I'm away, Rumpole, try not to put your feet on the sofa.'

*   *   *

Today I arrived in good time at the Old Bailey. I like to give myself time to drink in the well-known atmosphere of floor polish and uniforms, to put on the fancy dress at leisure and then go down to the public canteen for a cup of coffee and a go at the crossword. I needed to build up my strength particularly this morning, as Henry had let me know the name of our Judge the evening before. I therefore ordered a particularly limp sausage roll with the coffee, and I had just finished this and was lighting a small cigar, when Myers appeared carrying Newton's latest report, accompanied by Miss Fiona Allways, wigged and gowned and ready for the fray. Since the curious sighting of Blythe's secretary tripping the light fantastic at the Pussy Cat A-Go-Go, 'Fig' had kept up a patient and thorough search for the elusive Perivale Blythe, with no result whatsoever.

'I still think Blythe's an essential witness.' Fiona was sticking to her guns.

'Of course he is,' I agreed.

'We just need more time for Newton to make

299

inquiries. Can't we ask for an adjournment?' Myers suggested hopefully.

'We can ask.' I'm afraid my tone was not particularly encouraging.

'Surely, Mr Rumpole, any reasonable judge would grant it.'

Perhaps Myers was right; but it was then that I had to remind him that we'd been landed with his Honour Judge Roger Bullingham. I stood up in front of him, with the jury out of Court and Ward-Webster, our young and eager prosecutor, relaxing in his seat, and asked for an adjournment in no less than five distinct and well-considered ways. It was like trying to shift a mountain with a teaspoon. Finally his Honour said, in a distinctly testy tone of voice,

'Mr Rumpole! For the fifth time, I'm not adjourning this case. So far as I can see the defence has had all the time in the world.'

'Your Lordship may know how long it takes to find a solicitor.' I tried the approach jovial. 'If your Lordship remembers his time at the Bar.' The joke, if it can be dignified with such a title, went down like a lead balloon.

'Mr Rumpole, neither your so-called eloquence nor your alleged pleasantry are going to change my mind.' Bullingham was beginning to irritate me. I raised the Rumpole voice a couple of decibels. 'Then let me tell you an indisputable fact. For years my client's business life was in the hands of Mr Perivale Blythe.'

'Your client's business life, such as it was, was in his own hands, Mr Rumpole.' The Judge was unimpressed. 'And it's about time he faced up to his responsibilities. This case will proceed without

300

any further delay. That is my final decision,.'

There is a way of saying 'If your Lordship pleases' so that it sounds like dumb insolence. I said it like that and sat down.

'You did your best, sir,' Myers turned and whispered to me. Good old Myersy. That's what he always says when I fail dismally.

For the rest of the day I sat listening to prosecution evidence. From time to time my eyes wandered around the courtroom and, on one such occasion, I saw a severe-looking female in spectacles sitting in the front of the Public Gallery, taking notes.

It was a long day in Court. When I got back to the so-called mansion flat, I noticed something unusual. She Who Must Be Obeyed was conspicuous by her absence. I called, 'Hilda!' in various empty rooms and then I remembered that she had gone off, in none too friendly a mood, to stay with her old school chums, Dodo and Pansy, in the Lake District. So I poached a couple of eggs, buttered myself a slice of toast and sat down to a bottle of Pommeroy's plonk and this account. Now I am up to date with my life and with events in the Sun-Sand Mobile Holiday Home affair. Tomorrow, I suppose, will bring new developments on all fronts. The only thing that can be said with any certainty about tomorrow is that I shan't become any younger, nor will Judge Bullingham prove any easier to handle. Now the bottle's empty and I've smoked the last of my small cigars. The washing up can take care of itself. I'm going to bed.

THE NARRATIVE OF MISS FIONA ALLWAYS

301

I should never have taken this on. From the first day I met him in Chambers, after I had received a severe ticking-off from Mrs Erskine-Brown, Q.C., Rumpole was extremely decent to me. I'm still not absolutely sure how he managed to persuade the men at 3 Equity Court to take me on, but I have a feeling that he did something pretty devious for my sake. I took a note from him in quite a few of his cases and he was able to winkle a junior brief in R. v. Armstrong for me out of his instructing solicitor. So you see, although a lot of people found him absolutely impossible, and he could say the most appalling things quite unexpectedly, Rumpole was always extremely kind to me and, above all, he saved my sister Jennifer from doing a life sentence for murder.

So you can imagine my feelings about what happened to Rumpole in the middle of the Armstrong trial. Well, you'll have to imagine them, I'm afraid to say, because although I never got less than B+ for an essay at school, and although I can get a set of facts in order and open a case fairly clearly at Thames Mags Court now, I'm never going to have Rumpole's talent for emotional speeches. All I can say is that the day R. v. Armstrong was interrupted, as it was, was a day I hope I never have to live through again. What I'm trying to say is, my feelings of gratitude to old Rumpole made that a pretty shattering experience.

All the same, I do realize that the records of one of Rumpole's more notable cases should be complete, and that's why I've agreed to give my own account of the closing stages of the Armstrong trial. I suppose my taking this on is the least I can do for him now. So, anyway, here goes.

I have to say that I never particularly liked our client, Frank Armstrong. He had doggy eyes and a good deal of aftershave and I got the feeling that he was trying to make some sort of a pass at me at our first conference; and that sort of thing, so far as I am concerned, is definitely not on. When he came to give evidence I think Rumpole soon realized that Armstrong wasn't going to be a particularly impressive witness, and he looked fairly gloomy as we sat listening to our client being cross-examined by Ward-Webster, who was doing a pretty competent job for the prosecution. I took a full note and, looking at it now, I see that the moment came when the witness was shown the photograph of the Sun-Sand Mobile Home site in Cornwall, and Judge Bullingham, who didn't seem to like Rumpole, turned to the jury and said, 'Hardly looks like the Côte d'Azur, does it, members of the jury? It looks more like an industrial tip.'

'Looking in the other direction, there's a view of the sea, my Lord.' I remember our client sounding distinctly pained.

'What, between the crane and the second lorry?' Bullingham was still smiling at the jury.

'A great deal of our patrons' time is spent on the beach,' Armstrong protested.

'Perhaps they want a quiet night!' the Judge suggested, and the jury laughed.

'Mr Armstrong. Do you agree that on no less than fifty occasions holidays on the site in Cornwall turned out to have been booked in non-existent mobile homes?' Ward-Webster went on with his cross-examination.

'Yes indeed, but ...' the witness was sounding

303

particularly hopeless.

'And that your firm was paid large deposits for such holidays?' Ward-Webster went on.

'Well, this is it, but...'

'And on one occasion at least a mobile home was actually removed from an unhappy mother just as she was about to enter it?'

'It was one of those things...'

'Instead of mother running away from home, the home ran away from mother?'

I remember that the Judge made his joke at that point, and Rumpole muttered to me, 'Oh well done, Bull. Quite the stand-up comic.'

'And that letters of protest from the losers and their legal advisers remained unanswered?' Ward-Webster went on when the laughter died down.

'If there were complaints, the information should have been fed into the office computer.'

'Perhaps the people in question would rather have had their money back than have their complaints consumed by your computer.'

'Quite frankly, Mr Ward-Webster, our office at Sun-Sand Holidays is equipped with the latest technology.' Our client sounded deeply offended. At this the Judge told him that it was a pity it wasn't also equipped with a little old-fashioned plain dealing.

Of course, Rumpole objected furiously and said that was the point the jury had to decide. My note reminds me that the Judge then smiled at the jury and said, 'Very well, members of the jury, you will have heard Mr Rumpole's objection. Now, shall we get on with the trial?'

'Mr Armstrong, are you telling us that these

events are due to the inefficiency of your office?'
Ward-Webster was only too glad to get on with it.

'My office is not in the least inefficient. My
brother's business is computer hardware and...'

It was at about this point in the evidence that I
saw Rumpole closely studying the report of Mr
Newton, the inquiry agent.

'What's the relevance of that, Mr Armstrong?'
Ward-Webster was asking.

'My brother supplies our office equipment,' our
client told him proudly.

'Mr Ward-Webster,' said the Judge. 'This family
story is no doubt extremely fascinating, but has it
really anything to do with the case?'

'I agree, my Lord. And I will pass to another
matter...'

While this was happening, Rumpole asked me in
a whisper if I thought that our client had ever
danced with Blythe's secretary. I told him that I
had no idea. In fact, I couldn't see the point of the
question. But Rumpole leaned forward and asked
Mr Myers, of our instructing solicitor's office, to
get Mr Newton down to the Old Bailey during the
lunch adjournment.

Mr Newton came and we met him with our client
in the public canteen. He took a look at Frank
Armstrong and said that Blythe's secretary's
dancing partner did look like our client but he was
sure that he wasn't the same man. Rumpole, who
seemed to have a great deal of confidence in this
detective whom he always called 'Fig' Newton,
seemed to accept this and asked Frank Armstrong if
he had a photograph of his brother.

'Yes, indeed.' Frank Armstrong got out his
wallet. 'Taken in Marbella. The summer before

305

last.' He handed a photograph to Newton.

'That's the gentleman,' Mr Newton said. 'No doubt about it.'

'Fred's been dancing!' Rumpole laughed. 'Where is he now?'

'In the Gulf. Dubai. So far as I know. He's been asked to develop a computer centre,' Frank Armstrong answered vaguely.

'How long did you think he'd been away?'

'Six months. All of six months.'

'Since before you were arrested?' Rumpole was puzzled. 'You see, Newton saw him a couple of weeks ago in London.'

'Mr Rumpole, I don't know what you're getting at. I'm sure Fred would help me if he possibly could,' Mr Armstrong said.

'You've never quarrelled?'

'Only one little falling out, perhaps. When he wanted to buy the land in Cornwall.'

'Did he offer you much money?' That seemed to interest Rumpole.

'Enormous! Stupid sort of price, I called it. But I wasn't selling. Bit unbrotherly of me perhaps, but I wanted to build up my empire.'

'Perhaps Fred wanted to build up his,' Rumpole said, and then he turned to us and gave orders. He seemed, at that moment, quite determined and in charge of the case.

'There's a lot to be done,' he said. 'Newton's got to find brother Fred.'

'In Dubai?' Mr Newton protested.

'Keep a watch on the office of Sun-Sand Holidays after hours, late at night, early in the morning. Blythe, too. We *have* to get hold of Blythe. You may have to go to Cornwall,' he told Newton.

'I suppose you want all that before two o'clock?' Mr Myers was used to Rumpole's moments of decision.

'No. No, Myersy. Come on, Fiona. This time I've got to get the Mad Bull to give us an adjournment, or die in the attempt!'

So much of what Rumpole said that day sticks in my memory—that last sentence is one I shall never forget, as long as I live.

Of course, when Rumpole got to his feet after lunch Judge Bullingham was as unreceptive as ever.

'So what is the basis of this application, which you are now making for the fifth time since the start of this case?' the Judge asked, and when Mr Mason, the Clerk of the Court, rose to remind him of something, he was delighted to correct himself. 'Is it? Oh, thank you, Mason. For the *sixth* time, Mr Rumpole!'

'The basis should be clear, even to your Lordship,' Rumpole said; it was pretty typical of him, actually. 'It is vital that justice should be done to the gentleman I have the honour to represent.'

'Mr Rumpole. This case has been committed for six months. If Mr Blythe could have helped you he'd have come forward long ago.'

'That's an entirely unwarranted assumption! Perivale Blythe may have other reasons for his absence.'

'It seems you know very little about Mr Blythe. May I ask, have you a proof of his evidence?'

'No.'

'No?' The Judge raised his voice angrily.

'No, I haven't.' I remember Rumpole spoke casually and I remember he sounded quieter than usual.

307

'So you have no idea what this Mr Blythe is going to say?'

'No, but I know what I'm going to ask him. If he answers truthfully, I have no doubt that my client will be acquitted.'

'A pious hope, Mr Rumpole!' The Judge was smiling at the jury now.

'Of course, if your Lordship wishes to exclude this vital evidence, if you have no interest in doing justice in this case, then I have little more to say...' His voice was really tired and quiet by then, and I wondered if he was going to give up and sit down, but he was still on his feet.

'Well, I have a lot more to say. As you should know perfectly well, Mr Rumpole, getting through the work at the Old Bailey is a matter of considerable public importance...'

'Oh, of course. Far more important than justice!' Rumpole's voice was still faint and I thought he looked pale.

'In my view these constant applications by the defence are merely an attempt to put off the evil hour when the jury have to bring in a verdict,' the Judge went on, quite unnecessarily I thought. 'It's my duty to see that justice is done speedily. Mr Rumpole, I believe you have a taste for poetry. You will no doubt remember the quotation about the "law's delays".'

'Oh yes, my Lord. It comes in the same passage which deals with "the insolence of office". My Lord, if I might say...'

'Mr Rumpole!' the Judge barked at him. 'This application for an adjournment is refused. There is absolutely nothing you could say which would persuade me to grant it.'

Then Rumpole seemed to be swaying slightly. He raised a finger to loosen his collar. His voice was now hoarse and almost inaudible.

'Nothing, my Lord?'

'No, Mr Rumpole. Absolutely nothing!' The Judge had reached his decision. But Rumpole was swaying more dangerously. Judge Bullingham watched, astonished, and the whole Court was staring as Rumpole collapsed, apparently unconscious. The Judge spoke loudly over the gasps of amazement.

'I shall adjourn this case.' Judge Bullingham rose, and then bent to speak to Mr Mason, the Clerk of the Court. 'Send for Matron!' he said.

*   *   *

In a while, when the Court had cleared, Mr Myers, the usher and I managed to get Rumpole, who seemed to have recovered a certain degree of consciousness, out into the corridor and sit him down. He was still looking terribly grey and ill and the Usher went off to hurry up Matron.

'Always thought I'd die with my wig on,' Rumpole just managed to murmur.

'Did he say die?' A woman in glasses, whom I had noticed in Court, asked the Usher and, when he nodded at her, walked quietly away. I took his wig off then and stood holding it. 'Nonsense, Rumpole.' I tried to sound brisk. 'You're not going to die.'

'Fiona.' His voice was now a sort of low croak. I had to bend down to hear what came out like a last request. 'Air... Miss Allways... Must have air. Take me... Take me out...'

309

He was pulling feebly at his winged collar and bands. I managed to get them undone and then he rose to his feet and stood swaying. He looked absolutely ghastly. Mr Myers was supporting him under one arm. 'Just a breath of air... Want to smell Ludgate Circus... Your little runabout, Fiona... Is it outside? Can't spend my last moments outside Bullingham's Court.'

I suppose I shouldn't have done it, but he looked so pathetic. He whispered to me about not being taken to some hospital full of bedpans and piped Capital Radio, and promised that his wife would send for their own doctor—he could at least die with dignity. Myers and I helped him out to my battered Deux Chevaux and I drove Rumpole to his home.

It took a long time to help him up the stairs and into his flat, but he seemed happy to be home and managed a sort of fleeting smile. His wife wasn't there but he muttered something about her having only just slipped out—said that she'd be back in a moment from the shops and that Dr MacClintock would look after him—for so long, he murmured, as anything could be done. At least, I told him, I'd help him into bed. So we moved towards the bedroom, but at the door he seemed to have second thoughts.

'Perhaps... Better not. She Who Must Be Obeyed... Bound to stalk in... Just when I've lowered the garments... Gets some ... funny ideas ... does She.'

All the same, I helped him as he staggered into the bedroom and I hung his wig and gown, which I was carrying, over the bedrail as he lay down, still dressed. It was very cold in the mansion flat and I thought that the old couple must be extremely hardy. I covered Rumpole with the eiderdown and he was babbling, apparently delirious.

'Ever thought about ... the hereafter, Fiona?' I heard him say. 'Hereafter's all right. Until Bollard gets there... He's bound to make it... Have to spend all eternity listening to Bollard ... on the subject of "Lawyers for the Faith" ... Difficult to make an excuse ... and slip away. He'll have me buttonholed ... in the hereafter. Go along now...'

'Are you sure?' I hated to leave him but I knew that our wretched client had been taken down to the cells when the trial was interrupted.

Someone would have to go and get him released until he was needed again.

'And bail,' Rumpole was muttering very faintly, echoing my thoughts. 'Ask bail ... from the dotty Bull. For Frank. Suppose Bullingham'll be turning up there too ... in the hereafter. Apply for bail ... Fiona.'

'I'll ring you later,' I promised as I moved to the door.

'Later... Not too late...' Rumpole closed his eyes as I went out of the door; he was quite motionless, apparently asleep.

★ ★ ★

Judge Bullingham was looking at me, smiling, apparently deeply sympathetic, when I applied for bail. Mr Mason, the Court Clerk, later told me that the Judge had taken something of a 'shine' to me and was considering sending me a box of chocolates. Life at the Bar can be absolute hell for a girl sometimes.

'Bail? Yes, of course, Miss Allways. By all means,' said the Judge. 'On the same terms. And what is the latest news of Mr Rumpole?'

'He is resting peacefully, my Lord,' I told him truthfully.

'Peacefully.' The Judge sounded very solemn. 'Yes, of course. Well, that comes to all of us in time. Nothing else for this afternoon, is there, Mason?'

The Judge went home early. But in the Old Bailey, round the other London Courts and in the Temple the news spread like wildfire. Rumpole had collapsed, the stories went, it was all over and the old boy had gone home at last. I heard that in the cells villains, with their trials due to come up, cursed because they wouldn't have Rumpole to defend them.

Some said he'd died with his wig on, others told how he'd been suddenly taken away before the Matron could get at him. Quite a lot of people, from Detective Inspectors to safe-blowers, said that, if he had to go, Rumpole would have wanted it to come as it did, when he was on his feet and in the middle of a legal argument.

When I got back to Chambers I found a crowd gathered in our clerk's room. Henry had been trying the phone in Rumpole's flat over and over again and getting no reply.

'No reply from Rumpole's flat!' said Hoskins, a rather dreary sort of barrister who's always talking about his daughters.

'Probably no one at home,' Uncle Tom, our oldest inhabitant, hazarded a guess.

'That would appear to be the natural assumption, Uncle Tom.' Erskine-Brown was as sarcastic as

312

usual.

'Surely, we've got absolutely no reason to think ...' Hoskins said.

'I agree. All we know is that Rumpole suffered some sort of a stroke or a seizure,' Ballard told them.

'Rumpole often said Judge Bullingham had that effect on him,' Uncle Tom said.

'And that he's clearly been taken somewhere,' Erskine-Brown added.

'"Taken somewhere" expresses it rather well.' Uncle Tom shook his head. '"Taken somewhere" is about the long and short of it.'

Then I told them I'd taken Rumpole home where his wife would be able to get their own doctor to look after him. In the pause that followed Henry gave me the good news that he had got me a porn job in Manchester and I'd have to travel up overnight.

'A porn job!' Our Head of Chambers looked shocked. 'I'd've thought this was hardly the moment for that sort of thing.'

'Mr Rumpole would want Chambers to carry on, sir, I'm sure. As usual,' Henry said solemnly.

'Poor old fellow. Yes,' Uncle Tom agreed. 'Well. One thing to be said for him. He went in harness.'

'I don't really think it's the sort of subject we should be discussing in the clerk's room,' Ballard decided. 'No doubt I shall be calling a Chambers meeting, when we have rather more detailed information.'

As they went, I lingered long enough to hear Dianne, our rather hit-and-miss typist, give a little sob as she pounded her machine.

'Oh, please, Dianne,' Henry protested. 'Didn't

313

you hear what I said to Mr Ballard? Chambers must go on. That would have been *his* wishes.'

*   *   *

So I went to Manchester and read a lot of jolly embarrassing magazines in a dark corner of the railway carriage. Meanwhile Mr Newton, the inquiry agent, was still keeping a watch on the offices of Sun-Sand Holidays every night. Of course, I saw his reports eventually and it seemed that the office was visited, late at night and in a highly suspicious manner, by our client's brother Fred, who spent a long time working on the computers.

And there were other developments. Archie Featherstone, the Judge's nephew, was still very anxious to get into our Chambers and, when there was no news of Rumpole's recovery, I suppose the poor chap felt a bit encouraged in a horrible sort of way.

Perhaps I can understand how he felt because, although I never liked Archie Featherstone much (he'd danced with me at some pretty gruesome ball and his way of dancing was to close his eyes, suck in his teeth, and bob up and down in the hope that he looked like Mick Jagger, which he didn't), I knew jolly well what it was like to be desperate to get a seat in Number 3 Equity Court.

It was while I was still in Manchester that Henry received a telemessage about Rumpole and immediately took it up to our Head of Chambers. Sometime later, when I bought him his usual Cinzano Bianco in Pommeroy's Wine Bar, Henry gave me a full account of how his meeting with

314

Ballard went. First of all our Head read the message out aloud very carefully and slowly, Henry told me.

'"Please let firm of Blythe, Winterbottom and Paisley know sad news. Deeply regret Rumpole gone up to a Higher Tribunal. Signed Rumpole."' Ballard apparently looked puzzled. 'What *is* it, Henry?'

'It's a telemessage, sir. Telegrams having been abolished, *per se*,' Henry explained.

'Yes, I know it's a telemessage. But the wording. Doesn't it strike you as somewhat strange?'

'Mr Rumpole was always one for his joke. It caused us a good deal of embarrassment at times.'

'But presumably this can't be signed by Rumpole. Not in the circumstances.' Ballard was working on the problem. 'On any reasonable interpretation, the word "Rumpole", being silent so far as sex is concerned, must surely be construed as referring to *Mrs* Rumpole?' He was being very legal, Henry told me, and behaving like a Chancery barrister.

'That's what I assumed, sir,' said Henry. 'Unfortunately I can't get through to the Gloucester Road flat on the telephone. It seems there's a "fault on the line".'

'Have you tried calling round?'

'I have, sir. No answer to my ring.'

'Well, of course, it's a busy time in any family. A busy and distressing time.' But Ballard was clearly worried. 'Does it strike you as rather odd, Henry?'

'Well, just a bit, sir.'

'As Head of Chambers I surely should be the first to be informed of any decease among members. Am I not entitled to that?'

'In the normal course of events, yes.' Henry told

315

me he agreed to save any argument.

'In the normal course. But this message doesn't refer to me, or to his fellow members, or even to the Court where he was appearing when he was stricken down. This Blythe, Sidebottom and ...'

'Winterbottom, sir. And Paisley.'

'Was it a firm to which old Rumpole was particularly attached?'

'I don't think so, Mr Ballard. They owed him money,' Henry said he told him frankly.

'They owed him money! Strange. Very strange.' Ballard was thoughtful, it seems. 'From the way he was talking the other day, I think the old fellow had a queer sort of premonition that the end was pretty close.' And then our Head of Chambers went back to the document Henry had given him. 'All the same, Henry. There is something hopeful in this telemessage.'

'Is there, sir?'

'I mean the reference to a "Higher Tribunal". You know, I'm afraid I'd always found Rumpole a bit of a scoffer. I couldn't get him interested in "Lawyers As Churchgoers". He wouldn't even come along to one meeting of LAC! But his wife's message says he was thinking in terms of a "Higher Tribunal". It suggests he found faith in the end, Henry. It must have been a great comfort to him.'

As I say, Henry told me this after I got back from Manchester, when I was buying him a drink in Pommeroy's Wine bar. As we were talking I noticed that the funny sort of woman in glasses, the one who'd been listening to the Armstrong trial, was doing her best to overhear our conversation. She carried on listening when Jack Pommeroy slid his counter cloth up to us and said to Henry,

316

'I say. Has old Rumpole really had it? I've got about twenty-three of his cheques!'

'My clerk's fees aren't exactly up to date either,' Henry said. 'You'll miss him round here, won't you, Jack?'

'Well, he did use to pass some pretty insulting remarks about our claret. Called it Château Thames Embankment!' Jack Pommeroy looked pained. 'Didn't exactly help our business. And when he wasn't paying cash . . .'

I wasn't really listening to him then. I was watching the woman in glasses. She was talking into the telephone on the wall and I distinctly heard her say, 'True? Yes, of course it's true.'

Mr Newton, the inquiry agent, later pointed her out to me as Blythe's secretary, whom he had once seen dancing in Soho wearing, incredibly enough, pink satin trousers.

★   ★   ★

Oddly enough I won my case in Manchester. My solicitor told me that an elderly man on the jury had been heard to say that if a nice girl like me read those sort of magazines there couldn't be much harm in them. It seems I'm to get a lot more dirty books from Manchester! Anyway, I was back in time for the Chambers meeting and all of us, except for Mrs Erskine-Brown who was apparently doing something extremely important in Wales, assembled in Ballard's room. I was taking the minutes so I can tell you more or less exactly what happened. It started when Ballard read out the telemessage again in a very sad and solemn sort of way.

317

'Bit rum, isn't it? What's he mean exactly, "Higher Tribunal"?' Uncle Tom said.

'I have no doubt he means that Great Court of Appeal before which we shall all have to appear eventually, Uncle Tom,' Ballard explained.

'I never got to the Court of Appeal. Never had a brief to go there, as a matter of fact. Probably just as well. I wouldn't've been up to it.' Uncle Tom smiled round at us all.

'Knowing Rumpole,' said Erskine-Brown, 'there must be a joke there somewhere.'

'It must have been sent by Mrs Rumpole. Poor Rumpole is clearly not in a position to send "telemessages",' our Head of Chambers told us.

'Not in a position? Oh. See what you mean. Quite so. Exactly.' Uncle Tom got the point.

'Now, of course, this sad event will mean consequent changes in Chambers.' Ballard moved the discussion on.

'So far as the furniture is concerned. Yes.' Erskine-Brown opened a favourite subject. 'I don't suppose anyone will have any particular use for the old hatstand which stood in Rumpole's room.'

'His *hatstand*, Erskine-Brown?' Ballard was surprised.

'I happen to have conferences, from time to time, with a number of solicitors. Naturally they have hats. Well, if no one else wants it...'

'I don't think there'll be a stampede for Rumpole's old hatstand,' Uncle Tom assured him.

'I was thinking that there ought to be a bit more work about,' Hoskins said. 'I mean, I suppose Henry can hang on to some of Rumpole's solicitors. Myers and people like that. Now the work may get spread around a bit.'

'I'm not sure I agree with Hoskins.' Erskine-Brown was doubtful. 'There's some part of Rumpole's work which we might be glad to lose. I mean the sort of thing you were doing in Manchester, Allways.'

'You mean porn?' I asked him brightly.

'Obscenity! That's exactly what I do mean. Or rape. Or indecent assault. Or possessing house-breaking instruments by night. I mean, this may be our opportunity, sad as the occasion is, of course, to improve the image of Chambers. I mean, do we *want* dirty-book merchants hanging about the clerk's room?'

'Speaking for myself,' Ballard agreed, 'I think there's a great deal in what Erskine-Brown says. If you're not *for* these moral degenerates, in my view, you should be *against* them. I'd like to see a great deal more prosecution work in Chambers.'

'Well, you are certain of the money, with prosecutions.' Hoskins was with him. 'Speaking as a man with daughters.'

'There is a young fellow who's a certainty for the Yard's list of prosecutors,' Ballard said. 'I think I've mentioned young Archie Featherstone to you, Erskine-Brown?'

'Of course. The Judge's nephew.'

'It may be, in the changed circumstances, we shall have a room to offer young Archie Featherstone.'

'He won't be taking work from us?' Hoskins was more than a bit nervous at the prospect.

'In my opinion he'll be bringing it in,' Ballard reassured him, 'in the shape of prosecutions. Now, there are a few arrangements to be discussed.'

'I hope "arrangements" doesn't mean a

crematorium,' Uncle Tom said mournfully. 'I always think there's something terribly depressing about those little railway lines, passing out through the velvet curtain.'

'Of course, it is something of an event. I wonder if we'd get the Temple Church?' Hoskins seemed almost excited.

'Oh, I imagine not.' Erskine-Brown was discouraging. 'And, of course, we've seen nothing in the *Times* Obituaries. I'm afraid Rumpole never got the cases which made legal history.'

'I suppose they might hold some sort of memorial service in Pommeroy's Wine Bar,' Uncle Tom said thoughtfully. Our Head of Chambers looked a bit disapproving at that, as it didn't seem to be quite the right thing to say on a solemn occasion.

'I think we should send a modest floral tribute,' he suggested. 'Henry can arrange for that, out of Chambers expenses. Everyone agreed?' They all did, and Ballard went on, 'In view of the fact that at the eleventh hour he appeared to be reconciled to the deeper realities of our brief life on earth, you might all care to stand for a few minutes' silence, in memory of Horace Rumpole.'

So we all stood up, just a bit sheepishly, and bowed our heads. The silence seemed to last a long time, like it used to in Poppy Day services at school.

* * *

As I have been writing up this account for the completion of Rumpole's papers, I have got to know Mrs Rumpole and, in the course of a few teas, come to get on with her jolly well. As we all knew in

320

Chambers, Rumpole used to call her She Who Must Be Obeyed and always seemed to be in tremendous awe of her, but I didn't find her all that alarming. In fact she always seemed grateful for someone to talk to. She told me a lot about the old days, when her father, C. H. Wystan, was Head of Chambers, and of how Rumpole always criticized him for not knowing enough about bloodstains; and she described how Rumpole proposed to her at a ball in the Temple, when he'd had, as she described it, 'quite enough claret cup to be going on with'. During one of our teas (she took me, which was very decent of her, to Fortnum's) she described the visit she had received at her flat in the Gloucester Road shortly before Mr Myers restored R. *v.* Armstrong for a further hearing before Judge Bullingham.

One afternoon there came a ring, so it seemed, at the door bell of the Rumpole mansion flat. Mrs Rumpole—I'll call her 'Hilda' from now on since we've really become quite friendly, opened the door to see a small, fat, elderly man (Hilda described him to me as toad-like), who had a bald head, gold-rimmed spectacles and the cheek to put on a crêpe armband and a black tie. As he sort of oozed past her into her living room, he looked, Hilda told me, like a commercial traveller for a firm of undertakers. She wasn't entirely unprepared for this visit, however. The man had rung her earlier and explained that he was Mr Perivale Blythe, a solicitor of the Supreme Court and anxious to pay his respects to the Widow Rumpole.

When he had penetrated the living room, Mr Blythe sat on a sofa with his briefcase on his knee and began to talk in hushed, respectful tones, Hilda

321

told me.

'I felt I had to intrude,' he said softly. 'Even at this sad, sad moment, Mrs Rumpole. I do not come as myself, not even as Blythe, Winterbottom and Paisley, but I come as a representative, if I may say so, of the entire legal profession. Your husband was a great gentleman, Mrs Rumpole. And a fine lawyer.'

'A fine lawyer?' Hilda was puzzled. 'He never told me.'

'And, of course, a most persuasive advocate.'

'Oh, yes. He told me *that*,' Hilda agreed.

'We all join you in your grief, Mrs Rumpole. And I have to tell you this! There are no smiling faces today in the firm of Blythe, Winterbottom and Paisley!'

'Thank you.' Hilda did her best to sound grateful.

'Nor anywhere, I suppose, from Inner London to Acton Magistrates. He will be sorely missed.'

'I have to tell you what will be sorely missed, Mr Blythe,' Hilda said then, and said it in a meaningful kind of way.

'What, Mrs Rumpole?'

I think she said she stood up then and looked down on her visitor's large, pale, bald head, 'All those fees you owe him. Since the indecency case, I believe, in 1973.'

Blythe was clearly taken aback. He cleared his throat and began to fiddle nervously with the catch on his briefcase. 'You have heard a little about that?'

'I've heard a lot about it!'

'Well, of course, a great deal of that money hasn't been completely recovered from the clients. Not in full. But I'm here to settle up,' he assured her. 'I imagine you're the late Mr Rumpole's executor?'

He opened his briefcase; Hilda looked into it and noticed a cheque book. Blythe got out a document and shut the briefcase quickly.

'Of course I'm his executor,' Hilda told him.

'Then no doubt you're fully empowered to enter into what I think you'll agree is a perfectly fair compromise. Now, the sum involved is...'

'Two thousand, seven hundred and sixty-five pounds, ninety-three pence,' Hilda said quickly. She has a jolly good memory.

'Quite the businesswoman, Mrs Rumpole.' The beastly Blythe smiled in a patronizing manner. 'Now, would an immediate payment of ... let's say ten per cent, be a nice little arrangement? Then it'll be over and done with.'

'Mr Blythe. I have to face the butcher!' Hilda told him.

'Yes, of course, but...' Blythe didn't seem to understand.

'And the water rates. And the London Electricity Board. And the telephone has actually been cut off during my visit to the Lake District. I can't offer them a nice little arrangement, can I?'

'Well. Possibly not,' Blythe admitted.

'But I will offer *you* one, Mr Perivale Blythe,' Hilda said firmly.

'Well, that's extremely obliging of you...' Blythe took out his fountain pen.

And then Hilda spoke to him along the following lines. It was undoubtedly her finest hour. 'I will offer you this,' she said. 'I won't repeat this conversation to the Law Society, although this year's President's father was a close personal friend

323

of *my* father, C. H. Wystan. I will not take immediate steps to have you struck off, Mr Blythe, just provided you sit down and write out a cheque for two thousand, seven hundred and sixty-five pounds, ninety-three pence, in favour of Hilda Rumpole.'

The effect of this on the little creep on the sofa was apparently astonishing. For a moment his mouth sagged open. Then, in desperation, he patted his pockets. 'Unfortunately forgot my cheque book,' he lied. 'I'll slip one in the post.'

'Look in your briefcase, Mr Blythe. I think you'll find your cheque book there.' Hilda's words of command were interrupted by the sound of a ring at the door. As she went to open it she said, 'Excuse me. And don't try the window, Mr Blythe. It's really a great deal too far for you to jump.'

No doubt about it, she was a woman born to command. When she was out of the room, Blythe, with moist and trembling fingers, wrote out a cheque for the full amount. She returned with a tall, lugubrious figure who was scrubbing the end of his nose with a crushed pocket handkerchief.

'Thank you, Mr Blythe,' Hilda said politely as she took the cheque. 'And now there's a gentleman to see you.'

At which the new arrival whisked a paper out of his pocket and put it into the hand of the demoralized Perival Blythe.

'"Fig" Newton!' he said. 'Whatever's this?'

'It's a subpoena, Mr Blythe,' Mr Newton explained patiently. 'They want you to give evidence in a case down the Old Bailey.'

*   *   *

The case was, of course, R. *v.* Armstrong. On the morning when it started again I sat in Rumpole's place, the only defending barrister. When the jury was reassembled the Usher called for silence and his Honour Judge Bullingham came into Court, looked towards me, noticed the gap that used to be Rumpole, and clearly decided that it would be in order to say a few words of tribute to the departed. They took the form of a speech to the jury in which his Lordship sounded confidential and really jolly sincere. 'Members of the jury,' he said, and they all turned their faces solemnly towards him. 'Before we start this case, there is something I have to say. In our Courts, warm friendships spring up between judges and counsel, between Bench and Bar. We're not superior beings as judges; we don't put on "side". We are the barristers' friends. And one of my oldest friends, over the years, was Horace Rumpole.' Both Ward-Webster for the prosecution and I looked piously up to the ceiling. We carefully hid our feelings of amazement.

'During the time he appeared before me, in many cases, I can truthfully say that there was never a cross word between us, although we may have had trivial disagreements over points of law,' Bullingham went on. 'We are all part of that great happy family, members of the jury, which is the Criminal Court.'

It was at that moment that I heard a sound beside me and smelt the familiar shaving soap and small cigar. The Judge and the jury were too busy with each other to notice, but Ward-Webster and almost everyone else in Court were looking towards us in silent stupefaction. Rumpole was, I must say, looking in astonishingly fine condition, pinker than usual and well rested. He was obviously enjoying the Judge's speech.

'Mr Horace Rumpole was one of the old brigade.' By now Judge Bullingham was clearly deeply moved. 'Not a leader, perhaps, not a general, but a reliable, hard-working and great-hearted old soldier of the line.'

Of course, Rumpole could resist it no longer. He got slowly to his feet and bowed deeply, saying, 'My Lord.' The jury's faces swivelled towards him. Bullingham looked away from the jury-box and into the Court. If people who see ghosts go dark purple, well, that's how Bullingham looked.

'My Lord,' Rumpole repeated, 'I am deeply touched by your Lordship's remarks.'

'Mr Rumpole . . . Mr Rumpole . . . ?' The Judge's voice rose incredulously. 'I heard . . .'

'Greatly exaggerated, my Lord, I do assure you.' Of course, Rumpole had to say it. 'May I say what a pleasure it is to be continuing this case before your Lordship.'

'Mason. What's this mean?' Bullingham leant forward and whispered hoarsely to the Clerk of the Court. We heard Mr Mason whisper back, 'Quite honestly, Judge, I haven't a clue.'

'Mr Rumpole. Have you some application?' The Judge was looking at Rumpole with something like fear. Perhaps he thought he was about to call someone from the spirit world.

'No application.' Rumpole smiled charmingly. 'Your Lordship kindly adjourned this case, if you remember. It's now been restored to your list. Our inquiries are complete and I will call Mr Perivale Blythe.'

326

After the sensation of Rumpole's return from the tomb, where Bullingham quite obviously thought he'd been, I'm afraid to say that the rest of R. *v.* Armstrong was a bit of an anti-climax. Perivale Blythe padded into the witness-box, took the oath in a plummy sort of voice, and I have the notes of Rumpole's examination-in-chief.

'Mr Blythe,' the resurrected old barrister asked, 'After their father's death, did you act for the two Armstrong brothers, my client Frank and his brother Frederick?'

'Yes, I did,' Blythe agreed.

'And did Fred supply the computers set up in the offices of Sun-Sand Holidays, my client Frank Armstrong's firm?'

'I believe he did.' Blythe sounded uninterested.

'Mr Blythe, would you take the photograph of the Cornish holiday site?'

As the usher took the photograph to the witness-box, Bullingham staged a bit of a comeback and said, 'The industrial area, Mr Rumpole?'

'Exactly, my Lord.' Rumpole bowed politely. 'Do you know what that industry is Mr Blythe?'

'Tin mines, my Lord. I rather think.' Once again, Blythe sounded deliberately unconcerned.

'You *know*, don't you? Didn't you visit that site on behalf of your client Mr *Frederick* Armstrong?'

'I did. He was anxious to buy his brother Frank's site.'

'Because he knew tin would also be discovered there.'

'Yes, of course.' And then Blythe forgot his lack

of interest. 'I don't believe he told his brother that.'

'I don't believe he did.' Rumpole was after him now. 'And when his brother refused, didn't Fred take every possible step to ruin his brother Frank's business, no doubt by interfering with the computers that he'd installed so that they constantly gave misleading information, booked non-existent holiday homes and gave false instructions for caravans to be towed away?'

'I never approved of that, my Lord. I am an officer of the Court. I wouldn't have any part of it.' Perivale Blythe was sweating. He patted his bald head with a handkerchief and protested his innocence. I'd say he made a pretty unattractive figure in the witness-box.

'Although you knew about it. Come, Mr Blythe. You must have known about it to disapprove.' Rumpole pressed his advantage but the Judge, back to his old form, was getting restless. 'Mr Rumpole! I take the gravest objection to this in examination-in-chief. It is quite outrageous!'

'A trivial objection, surely?' Rumpole gave a sweet smile. 'Your Lordship has told the jury we only have trivial disagreements.'

'You are putting an entirely new case to this witness, so far as I can see, on no evidence.'

'Oh, there will be evidence, my Lord.'

'I hope my learned friend doesn't intend to *give* that evidence?' Ward-Webster rose to his feet to object for the prosecution.

'I hope that my learned friend doesn't wish to conceal from the jury the fact that Detective Inspector Limmeridge arrested Frederick Armstrong when he had entered his brother's office by night and was reprogramming the computers.

There has been a charge of Perverting the Course of Justice,' Rumpole said, looking hard at the jury. 'In fact, Mr Newton has given the results of all his observations to the officer in charge of the case.'

'Is that right, Mr Ward-Webster?' Bullingham asked incredulously.

'So I understand, my Lord.' Ward-Webster subsided.

'I shall be recalling the Detective Inspector, my Lord,' Rumpole said triumphantly, 'as a witness for the defence.'

Well in the end, of course, the jury saw the point. Brother Fred had set out to ruin brother Frank's business by interfering with the computers so that they sold non-existent holidays, or removed existing caravans. With Frank in prison Fred could have got hold of the Cornish mobile home site and a great deal of tin. It wasn't one of Rumpole's greatest cases, but a jolly satisfying win. Horace Rumpole has taught me a lot about criminal procedure, but I don't think I'd ever dare try his way of getting an adjournment.

Well, I've written my bit. I hope it's all right and that someone will check it through for grammar. It tells what happened so far as I knew it at the time, or almost as far as I knew it.

(Signed) Fiona Patience Allways, barrister-at-law.

3 Equity Court
Temple
London, E.C.4

*   *   *

I'm extremely grateful to my learned friend, Miss

329

Fiona Allways, for dealing with that part of the story. It had been necessary, as I expect you have guessed, to take her into my confidence (a little earlier than she divulges in her account) when I decided to lie doggo, to feign death and lure the wretched Perivale Blythe out of hiding. Of course I saw Hilda as soon as she got back from her 'bachelor holiday' in the Lake District and I had to let her in on the scheme. But I must say, She was something of a sport about the whole business and the way she dealt with the appalling Blythe, much of which I heard from a point of vantage near our bedroom door, seemed to me masterly. When She Who Must Be Obeyed is on form, no lawyer can possibly stand up to her.

On the whole the incident gave me enormous pleasure. One of the many drawbacks of actually snuffing it will be that you can't hear the things people say about you when they think you're safe in your box. I enormously enjoyed Fiona's account of the Chambers meeting and the silent prayer which marked my passing—just as I will never let Judge Bullingham forget his funeral oration.

Oh, and one other marvellous moment: Hilda and I were sitting at tea one afternoon when I was out of circulation and a ring came at the door bell. Some boy was delivering Hilda a socking great wreath from Chambers, compliments of Sam Ballard and all the learned friends. The deeply respectful note to Hilda explained that the tribute was sent to her home as they didn't quite know when the interment was due to take place.

After I had won Frank Armstrong's case I walked up to Chambers and called on our learned Head. For some reason my appearance in the flesh seemed

330

to irritate the man almost beyond endurance.

'Rumpole,' he said, 'I think you've behaved disgracefully.'

'I don't know why you should say that,' I told him. 'Isn't there a Biblical precedent for this sort of thing?'

'I suppose you're very proud of yourself,' Ballard boomed on.

'Well, it wasn't a bad win.' I lit a small cigar. 'Got the Sun-Sand Mobile Homes owner away and clear. Made the world safe for a few more ghastly holidays.'

'I am not referring to your case, Rumpole. You caused us all... You caused me personally ... a great deal of unnecessary grief!'

'Oh, come off it, Bollard. I understand you couldn't wait to relet my room to young Archie Featherstone.

A little month; or ere those shoes were old
With which you follow'd poor old Rumpole's
      body,
Like Niobe, all tears...'

I gave him a slice of *Hamlet* which he didn't appreciate.

'We had to plan for the future, Rumpole. Deeply distressed as we all were...'

'Deeply distressed indeed! I hear that Uncle Tom suggested a memorial service in Pommeroy's Wine Bar.'

Ballard had the decency to look a little embarrassed. 'I never approved of that,' he said.

'Well, it's not a bad idea. And I happen to be in funds at the moment. Why don't I invite you all to

331

a piss-up at Pommeroy's?'

Ballard looked at me sadly. 'And I thought you had finally found faith!' he said. 'That's what I can never forgive.'

In due course the learned friends assembled in Pommeroy's at the end of a working day. I had invited Hilda to join us. We were on friendly terms at the time and, as a result of Blythe's cheque, her bank balance was in a considerably more healthy state than mine. So I got Jack Pommeroy to dispense the plonk with a liberal hand and during the celebrations I heard She Who Must Be Obeyed talking to our Head of Chambers.

'It was very naughty of Rumpole, of course,' She said, 'but there was just no other way of getting his fees from that appalling man, Perivale Blythe.'

'Mrs Rumpole. Can I get this clear? You were a knowing party to this extraordinary conspiracy?'

'Oh yes.' And Hilda sounded proud of it.

'I'll have you after my job, Mrs Rumpole,' Henry said. 'I couldn't get Mr Blythe to pay up. Not till we got this idea.'

'Henry! You're not saying *you* knew?'

'I'm not saying anything, Mr Ballard,' Henry answered with a true clerk's diplomacy. 'But perhaps I had an inkling.'

'Allways! You took Rumpole home. You must have thought...' Ballard clearly guessed that he was on to an appalling conspiracy.

'That he'd died?' Fiona smiled at him. 'Oh, I can't see how anyone could think that. He'd never die in the middle of a case, would he?'

'It was exactly the same when we believed he'd retired,' Uncle Tom told the world in general. 'Rumpole kept popping back, like a bloody opera singer!'

At which point I felt moved to address them and banged a glass on the bar for silence.

'Well, my learned friends!' I said in my final speech. 'Since no one else seems inclined to, it falls on me to say a few words. After the distressing news you have heard, it comes as a great pleasure to welcome Horace Rumpole back to the land of the living. When he was deceased he was constantly in your thoughts. Some of you wanted his room. Some of you wanted his work. Some, I know, couldn't wait to get their fingers on the old boy's hatstand. You are all nonetheless welcome to drink to his long life and continued success in a glass of Château Thames Embankment!'

I must say that they all raised their glasses and drank with every appearance of enjoyment. Then I went over to Jack Pommeroy and asked him to bring out, from behind the bar, the tribute from Ballard which I had concealed there before the party began.

'Bollard,' I said as I handed it to him, 'this came to my home address. I'm afraid you went to some expense over the thing. Never mind. As I shan't be needing it now, keep it for one of your friends.'

So, at the end of the day, Sam Ballard was left holding the wreath.